The Ne

GLOWING AURAS AND 'BLACK MONEY'
THE PENTAGON'S MYSTERIOUS U.F.O. PROGRAM

Los Angeles Examiner

AIR BATTLE RAGES OVER LOS ANGELES

USA TODAY

Arizonans Say the Truth About UFO Is Out There

ROSWELL JOHNSON SAVES THE WORLD!

ALSO BY CHRIS COLFER

The Land of Stories

The Wishing Spell
The Enchantress Returns
A Grimm Warning
Beyond the Kingdoms
An Author's Odyssey
Worlds Collide

A Tale of Magic . . .

A Tale of Magic...
A Tale of Witchcraft...
A Tale of Sorcery...

CHRIS COLFER

LITTLE, BROWN AND COMPANY
New York Boston

Text copyright © 2024 by Christopher Colfer
Illustrations copyright © 2024 by Godwin Akpan

Cover art copyright © 2024 by Godwin Akpan. Cover design by Sasha Illingworth.
Cover copyright © 2024 by Hachette Book Group, Inc.
Endpaper images copyright © various contributors at Shutterstock.com
Interior design by Michelle Gengaro.

Little, Brown and Company
Hachette Book Group
1290 Avenue of the Americas, New York, NY 10104
Visit us at LBYR.com

First Edition: June 2024

Little, Brown and Company is a division of Hachette Book Group, Inc.
The Little, Brown name and logo are trademarks of Hachette Book Group, Inc.

The publisher is not responsible for websites (or their content)
that are not owned by the publisher.

Little, Brown and Company books may be purchased in bulk for business, educational, or promotional use. For information, please contact your local bookseller or the Hachette Book Group Special Markets Department at special.markets@hbgusa.com.

Library of Congress Cataloging-in-Publication Data
Names: Colfer, Chris, 1990– author.
Title: Roswell Johnson saves the world! / Chris Colfer.
Description: First edition. | New York : Little, Brown and Company, 2024. |
Audience: Ages 8–12 | Summary: "A boy must team up with a group of quirky aliens to save Earth." —Provided by publisher.
Identifiers: LCCN 2023034485 | ISBN 9780316515047 (hardcover) |
ISBN 9780316515313 (ebook)
Subjects: CYAC: Science fiction. | Human-alien encounters—Fiction. |
LCGFT: Science fiction.
Classification: LCC PZ7.C677474 Ro 2024 | DDC [Fic]—dc23
LC record available at https://lccn.loc.gov/2023034485

ISBNs: 978-0-316-51504-7 (hardcover), 978-0-316-51531-3 (ebook),
978-0-316-57894-3 (Barnes & Noble), 978-0-316-57895-0 (Barnes & Noble signed),
978-0-316-57945-2 (int'l)

Printed in Indiana, USA

LSC-C

Printing 1, 2024

To my dad,
for helping me pave a path
to the stars.
And for an endless galaxy
of dad jokes.

AUTHOR'S NOTE

While some elements in this book are exaggerated for dramatic effect, all the science described in the story is based on actual astronomy, astrophysics, biology, botany, chemistry, ecology, genealogy, geology, microbiology, physics, psychology, technology, and zoology.

Also, the headlines mentioned in chapter 1 are from real publications, and the experiences described in chapter 2 are from real eyewitnesses. I strongly encourage every reader to research them further.

After all, the truth is out there....

Toilet Billionaire to Weaponize Space! (No, Seriously!)

By Shelly Simcox

RUMP ISLAND, SOUTHEAST FLORIDA—When the *Ostentatious Observer* broke the news last week, most of our readers thought the story was a practical joke. And how could we blame them? After all, the idea would be laughable if it were the plot of a science fiction novel or Hollywood blockbuster. So, consequently, the *Observer*'s mail room clerks worked overtime as they sorted through a tsunami of complaints about our publication's "terrible sense of humor" and "blatant unprofessionalism."

However, the *Observer* can now confirm the report is true—and the truth is so outrageous it could only exist in the clown show we call *reality*.

Last week I had the rare opportunity to interview billionaire Eli Rump on the top deck of his 652-foot superyacht, the *Hades*. The tycoon was in a trance as he gazed across the ocean and admired the launchpad towering over his private island.

"Beautiful, isn't it? It took me three decades and seven billion dollars to get here, but it's been worth every second and every penny."

As we spoke, Mr. Rump relaxed on a tufted lounge chair. Despite the sweltering Florida heat, he was dressed in a thick designer suit. Two members of the *Hades'* ninety-person crew continually refilled his glass of champagne and a dish of caviar. A third crew member fanned the billionaire with a giant palm leaf, while a fourth gave him a manicure. Meanwhile, I sat on the floor and asked for a glass of water that never came.

"What I'm doing may seem excessive, but it's all for the greater good. People only criticize me because I'm rich. But when was the last time *the poor* did something to help the planet?"

For those of you living under a rock, Mr. Rump is currently ranked as the richest man in the world. His estimated net worth is north of $300 billion, and (as the billionaire reminded me multiple times) his wealth grows significantly each day.

Mr. Rump credits his success to his "humble beginnings"—although I have no idea what he's talking about. After all, Mr. Rump is the twelfth son of an oil industry juggernaut. He was raised in an eighty-thousand-square-foot home in Upstate New York, he attended the finest private schools in Manhattan, and he never lived a day of his life without servants or chauffeurs.

"Sure, it was a nice house, *but* it was a very competitive household. My brothers and I were constantly pitted against one another. Father made us show our report cards at the dinner table. Whoever had the lowest GPA was banished to the guesthouse for a whole week. That sort of destitution builds character. It creates drive. And money can't buy *drive*."

After his father's passing in 1985, Mr. Rump used his inheritance to start Rump Dump Inc. and began manufacturing his infamous line of luxury toilets.

"I strongly believe everything in life should be enjoyed—and I mean *everything*."

The product and its memorable slogan—"You haven't taken a dump until you've taken a Rump Dump!"—were a hit with the American public. His late-night infomercials turned him into an instant celebrity among insomniacs. The extravagant toilets earned Mr. Rump an impressive fortune virtually overnight.

"Part of being a good businessman is recognizing a void and having the guts to fill it. No one had the courage to make *defecation* a lavish experience before me. But no risk, no reward. Gandhi said that. I think."

After his rampant toilet success, Mr. Rump wasted no time expanding his empire. In 1990 the billionaire opened Rump World, a theme park where families ride questionably shaped log flumes across swirling porcelain pools. In 1995 Mr. Rump created the film studio Rump Pictures and produced such hits as *The Godflusher, Interstinker*, and *Larry Plunger and the Septic Tank of Secrets*. In 2001 he bought a California football team and renamed them the San Diego Cloggers. Understandably, Mr. Rump's companies have received harsh criticism over the years from the squeamish.

"I have a brand. So what?"

His lucrative endeavors would surely quench any normal corporate thirst, but Mr. Rump wasn't finished yet. In 2009 the billionaire founded his most ambitious (and surprising) enterprise yet, Rump Rockets, a private space tourism company. For a small six-figure fee, Rump Rockets launches multimillionaire customers beyond Earth's atmosphere for the extraordinary experience of vomiting and losing consciousness in zero gravity.

"It wasn't until Rump Rockets' maiden voyage that I realized, *Wow. I'm a lucky man.* How many people own twelve homes, three superyachts, a theme park, a film studio, a football team, a fleet of rocket ships, and more wealth than ninety-nine percent of the global economy? Three? Four? Maybe *five* people at the most? Hashtag blessed."

Besides being the owner and CEO of Rump Rockets, Mr. Rump was also the first civilian his company hurled into space at twenty thousand miles an hour.

"Once I regained consciousness and cleaned the inside of my helmet, I gazed down at the breathtaking view of Earth and had the greatest epiphany of my life: *I wanted more.*"

The comment made me drop my pen.

"I mean, I wanted to *do* more—to protect Earth, that is. I love this planet so much. I want to do everything in my power to save it. So I decided to turn my affection into action."

Mr. Rump lovingly stroked the SAVE THE EARTH T-shirt he wore beneath his blazer. Meanwhile, his superyacht's CO^2 emissions turned the sky a dark shade of gray.

"Now, there are plenty of groups protecting the seas, the rainforests, endangered species, blah, blah, blah. We've got those covered. I'm concerned about the threats we *don't* see coming. It's a big universe out there—who knows what's lurking in the shadows of space? We need to be prepared for *anything*! So I called a meeting with my Rump Rockets board of directors and tossed around a few ideas. Eventually we came up with the revolutionary ERASE program."

The Eli Rump Apparatus for Space Emergencies is a system of twelve satellites that Mr. Rump plans to position around the globe. Each satellite will be equipped with a laser powerful enough to destroy any asteroid, comet, or debris that gets too close for comfort. Although Mr. Rump was extremely eager to start ERASE and prepared to fund the project himself, the program needed permission from the US government to proceed. But that was merely a speed bump for the impatient businessman.

"I just called my good friends in Congress and scheduled a meeting on Capitol Hill."

By "good friends" the billionaire is referring to the 252 congresspeople and 57 senators, both Democrat and Republican, whose campaigns received very generous donations from Mr. Rump's controversial super PAC: Rump, White, and Blue.

"We had a wonderful chat, and I pitched them my vision for the program. Congress couldn't have been more supportive. They said the Eli Rump Apparatus for Space Emergencies was the best proposal they had ever heard and a wonderful way to protect the planet. Then we all hopped on my private plane and went out for oysters in Monte Carlo."

Those must have been exceptional oysters. Just last week a vote to approve the program was presented before Congress. It passed the House and the Senate with flying colors and was sent to the White House the very same day. Many people—at least the *rational-minded* ones—hoped the president would stop Mr. Rump's project. But our commander in chief signed the bill without hesitation.

"The president's a good friend too. Horrible golfer, but a good friend."

Unfortunately, that's only where the controversy begins. Mr. Rump was not only given permission by the US government to *start* ERASE, but also given *full operational control* of the program. (Yes, you read that correctly—*full operational control*.) The greatest defense system ever assembled will *not* be controlled by military or government officials. Instead, the safety of our planet will be placed in the manicured hands of a glorified toilet salesman. God bless America.

"It's my technology. I should be the one running it. Plain and simple."

However, reaction to the news has been anything but plain and simple. When word spread about the agreement (and it was finally taken seriously), the United States was condemned by allies and adversaries alike. The British prime minister called the decision "dangerous and idiotic." The Chinese president referred to ERASE as "a reckless act of capitalism." The German chancellor warned it would lead to "devastating, worldwide consequences." The Supreme Leader of North Korea deemed it "proof the Western world has lost its stinkin' mind."

Concerns at home only echoed those abroad. The directors of the FBI, the CIA, and Homeland Security signed a joint statement urging the president and Congress to repeal the decision. The head of NASA released her own statement too, assuring the worried public that they have "never discovered anything to warrant an absurd project like the Eli Rump Apparatus for Space Emergencies."

Mr. Rump is not fazed by the world's concern.

"I understand the alarm. What's stopping me from turning the satellites around and pointing them at Earth? What's stopping me from using the lasers against my enemies and critics? What's stopping me from holding the whole world hostage?"

I held my breath as I waited for Mr. Rump to answer his own question.

"Come on, I'm rich! Why would I want to destroy the planet? Why would I want to start a war? No, no, no. Destruction takes too much *planning*. Wars take too many *meetings*. I just want to protect the planet so I can enjoy my wealth for as long as possible."

Following the government's green light, Mr. Rump immediately put ERASE into production. The first of twelve satellites is scheduled to launch on April 1 (yes, *this* April 1). Although Mr. Rump swears the program is not a colossal April Fools' prank. Rump Rocket's team of engineers are working around the clock to meet their boss's demands.

Across the ocean on Rump Island, I could see the team constructing the rocket that will carry the first of twelve armed satellites into space. I couldn't help but notice the vessel looks remarkably like the Rump Dump Sucker 400, the electric plunger Mr. Rump sells with his luxury toilets. I asked him if the resemblance is intentional.

"There's no sin in synergy."

The billionaire snapped his fingers, and a fifth crew member jumped forward—seemingly out of thin air—to slather his bald head with sunscreen.

"I know what people whisper about me behind my back. Everyone thinks I'm a *joke*. But I'm no stranger to mockery. My father and brothers laughed at me when I was a child. People laughed at me when I started Rump Dump Inc. And now they're laughing at the Eli Rump Apparatus for Space Emergencies. But we'll see who's laughing when *the world needs me*."

At this remark Mr. Rump's confident smirk sank into a rather vengeful scowl. It was out of character for the cocky billionaire, like an entirely different man was sitting before me. I asked the tycoon if he could describe a scenario when the world would need him. After all, why was Mr. Rump spending billions of dollars on a space project that NASA said was useless?

"Just because NASA hasn't seen them doesn't mean they aren't coming."

The loaded comment gave me pause. I asked Mr. Rump if he believed there were asteroids or comets headed for Earth that hadn't been discovered yet.

"Or something else."

The billionaire refused to elaborate. However, there was an unmistakable twinkle in his eye as he left me hanging. His coyness gave me chills, and it was abundantly clear our interview was over. I departed the *Hades* with more questions than answers, but one question in particular has haunted me since our discussion:

Is Mr. Rump just a privileged man who's excited about a new toy? Or does the billionaire know something about the universe that he isn't telling us?

Time will tell.

CHAPTER ONE

A NOT-SO-FAIR SCIENCE FAIR

The Cherokee Springs Intermediate School gymnasium hadn't seen so much panic since it was used as a tornado shelter in 1986. Dozens of anxious middle school students rushed through a labyrinth of folding tables as they frantically applied the final touches to their science fair projects. The sounds of clipping staplers, snapping hole punchers, and ripping duct tape echoed off the concrete walls like a chaotic symphony. The air was filled with the dizzying fumes of hot glue, permanent markers, and preteen body odor. It was a miracle no one fainted.

"Excuse me? May I have your attention, please?"

Principal Dunkin—more mustache than man—tapped the microphone at the front of the gymnasium to get everyone's attention. He was shorter than half the student body and had to stand on a stack of textbooks to reach the mic.

"This is your five-minute warning. I repeat, this is your five-minute warning," he said. "When the alarm goes off, all work must come to a complete stop. I repeat, a complete stop. Anyone who disobeys will automatically be disqualified from the competition. *Yes, even YOU, Mr. Zyskowski!*"

As if a bright light had been switched on in a room full of cockroaches, the five-minute warning sent the gymnasium into a frenzy. An eighth grader screamed as he accidentally set his miniature hot-air balloon on fire. A sixth grader burst into tears when their Popsicle-stick catapult flung itself across the room. Two seventh graders played tug-of-war with an extension cord until it snapped in half. Teachers patrolled the nervous preteens like linebackers, with first aid kits ready to go.

"Has anyone seen a gerbil in a parachute?" asked a sixth-grade boy.

"Who took a bite of my potato battery?" shouted a seventh-grade girl.

"That carpet is for static electricity, not your shoes!" yelled an eighth grader.

"Who put a snake in Bella's ecosystem?" asked a teacher.

In all the middle school madness, one student in the very back row managed to stay relatively calm and collected.

Eleven-year-old Roswell Johnson was unlike all the other students at Cherokee Springs Intermediate School for many reasons. He was one of the only Black students in his class, he was the only seventh grader who had skipped the sixth grade, and judging from the panicked faces around him, he was the only student *prepared* for the science fair. Roswell was also the only student who'd dressed to impress the judges. His blue sports coat and red bow tie stood out in a sea of flip-flops and Marvel T-shirts.

"How much mercury is considered poisonous?" asked a seventh-grade girl.

"I'll pay someone twenty bucks to use their hot spot!" yelled an eighth-grade boy.

"Get your petri dishes off my periodic table!" shouted a sixth-grade girl.

"Is anyone missing a gerbil in a parachute?" asked a teacher.

Roswell fiddled with his bow tie as he watched his flustered peers. He couldn't have been more prepared—he had his whole presentation memorized and was genuinely excited to share his research—but still, the chaotic atmosphere was contagious. Roswell had to take a couple of deep breaths to keep his nerves from getting the best of him.

"You've got this, Roz," he whispered to himself. "You know this stuff like the back of your hand. Just relax, make eye contact, keep the dad jokes to a minimum, and don't sniff your pits in front of the judges."

An enormous three-paneled poster board stood on the table beside Roswell. Big blue letters across the top spelled out ARE EXTRATERRESTRIALS REAL? THE PROOF IS OUT THERE! The poster board was decorated with photos of alleged UFO sightings, colorful illustrations of alien species, and a collage of celebrity eyewitnesses. There were also newspaper headlines, magazine articles, maps, police reports, and pictures of historical structures pinned along an expansive time line. Roswell had even run a string of green Christmas lights along the border and hung a few tinfoil flying saucers to give the presentation a little *paranormal pizzazz*.

"Remember what Gram and Pop said," Roswell whispered to himself. "Whatever happens, don't forget to have fun. If I'm enjoying the presentation, the judges will enjoy it too. But don't enjoy yourself *too much*. Nobody likes a cocky conspiracist."

The opening chords of Elton John's song "Tiny Dancer" played from Principal Dunkin's cell phone, and the gymnasium went dead silent.

"That's the alarm," the principal announced. "Tools down. I repeat, tools down. *That means YOU, Mr. Zyskowski!*"

All the students groaned and reluctantly stepped away from their projects.

"Before we begin, I would like to welcome everyone

to the Forty-Sixth Annual Cherokee Springs Intermediate School Science Fair," Principal Dunkin said. "Our school therapist, Dr. Gordon, asked me to remind you that 'everyone here is a winner.' And 'it's impossible to lose when you have an interest in science.' However, only one of you will receive the grand prize, an all-expenses-paid two-day stay at the Rump World Family Resort on Rump Island, Florida!"

The whole gymnasium cheered. Although no one was more excited than Roswell. He had never left the state of Oklahoma in his whole life. A trip to a bustling theme park with countless thrill rides, endless fried food, and overpriced merchandise was the adventure he had always dreamed of.

"Cherokee Springs Intermediate School would like to give a big thank-you to Mendez Mechanics for donating the grand prize. 'From smog checks to oil changes, the Mendez Mechanics are here for all your parents' mechanical needs,'" Principal Dunkin read from a card. "And now it is my pleasure to introduce our very special guest judge. You've seen him on the news and in local parades, please give a warm welcome to former NFL quarterback and owner of Monster Truck Steak House, the man who has served Cherokee Springs since 1992, *Mayor Sam Shallows*!"

Suddenly the gymnasium's front doors burst open. A strong gust of warm wind blew inside and knocked many of the science fair presentations to the floor. The blinding Oklahoma sun shined through the doorway and was eclipsed by an enormous silhouette.

"Howdy-ho, future constituents!"

Mayor Shallows was a beast of a man and barely fit through the entrance. He was an older gentleman with a thick white beard. He wore a white cowboy hat, a white suit, a white bolo tie, and a pair of white cowboy boots with spurs that jingled with every step. If it weren't for the red blotches covering his face, Roswell would have thought the mayor was an abominable snowman.

"We would also like to welcome Mayor Shallows's chief of staff, Ms. Crabtree, and his personal photographer, Mr. Ace," Principal Dunkin said.

Until now none of the students had noticed the staff members trailing the giant mayor. They were both very frail and trembled in their boss's presence, as if Mayor Shallows might turn around and eat one of them.

"I'd like to thank Mayor Shallows and his staff for generously taking time out of their busy schedule at city hall to be with—"

Mayor Shallows yanked the microphone from Principal Dunkin.

"It's always an honor to serve our community," the mayor said. "I know being near a *very* famous and *very* powerful man like myself can be intimidating—but I promise I don't bite. *Unless you're running against me, that is.* HEEHAA!"

Mayor Shallows roared with laughter at his own joke. No one joined him except for Ms. Crabtree and Mr. Ace. The staff members chuckled like they were being given invisible Heimlich maneuvers. It looked painful.

"In all seriousness, my staff and I can't wait to see what the brilliant young minds of tomorrow have in store for us today. It is a profound privilege to champion a generation that will undoubtedly make the world a better place. *You are the future.* Now let's make this quick. I've got a ribbon cutting at a slaughterhouse in thirty minutes."

Mayor Shallows tossed the microphone back to Principal Dunkin, and the Forty-Sixth Annual Cherokee Springs Intermediate School Science Fair officially began. The petite principal escorted the massive mayor through the rows of folding tables, and one by one the students presented their projects.

The first contestant was a sixth-grade girl in pigtails. She held a glass case with a small frog that sat in an inch of water.

"My project answers the daring question, Can you train a frog?" she said. "After spending a week bribing my pet frog—*Harry Styles the Second*—with treats and belly rubs in exchange for physical acts, I came to a stunning conclusion. Please observe.... *Sit! Stay! Roll over! Fetch!* As you can see from Harry's lack of interest, and the dirty look in his eyes, my experiment proves frogs cannot be trained, *but* they are easily annoyed."

"Sounds like the city council. HEEHAA!" Mayor Shallows laughed. "Nice work."

"Next!" Principal Dunkin said, and guided the mayor to the next contender.

"My project proves the laws of physics can be broken," said an eighth-grade boy in a football jersey. "You see these magnets? When I place them four inches apart, it takes exactly zero point five seconds for them to connect. But when I put one in a miniature Kansas City Chiefs uniform and the other in a miniature Denver Broncos uniform, the magnets *do not move*! Physics may be strong, but nothing is more powerful than a sports rivalry. *Go Chiefs!*"

"Are you sure the uniforms aren't weighing the magnets down?" Principal Dunkin asked.

"Actually, I think the little fella makes a solid point," Mayor Shallows said. "Some opposites aren't meant to attract—*and they should stay where they belong.*"

"Next!" Principal Dunkin called.

"I discovered rodents have preferences just like humans," said a gangly seventh-grade girl. "When I put cheese at the center of this cardboard maze, it takes the mouse a minute to find the food. But when I put a spoonful of peanut butter in the center, the mouse finishes the same maze in thirty seconds. Next, I conducted the same experiment with music.

When I played Taylor Swift, it took the mouse twenty-five seconds to find the peanut butter. But when I played Nickelback, the mouse chewed a hole through the maze and ran out of the room."

"Someone remind me to send peanut butter and Taylor Swift to the polls this election. HEEHAA!" Mayor Shallows laughed. "Great work."

"Next!"

"For my project I wanted to see if screen time was as bad as my mom says it is," said a sixth-grade boy with bulging eyes. "Over the past month I have spent two hundred and fifty hours on my iPad. I watched twenty seasons of TV shows and played fifteen games from start to finish. I am happy to report my vision is in the exact condition it was four weeks ago and my mom is wrong."

"Ummm...son?" Mayor Shallows asked. "You're talking to a trash can."

"We're standing over here, Mr. Lewis," Principal Dunkin said.

"Oh," the boy said, and faced the right direction. "In that case, I should probably reevaluate my findings."

"Next!"

"My project proves mosquitoes are attracted to certain blood types more than others," said an itchy eighth-grade girl covered in red bumps. "My blood type is B negative, and my little brother's is O positive. Last night we slept in a room with a dozen loose mosquitoes. This morning I woke up with eleven mosquito bites and my brother woke up with over two hundred! By the way, my brother was supposed to be here, but he's in the hospital."

"Fantastic work, little lady," Mayor Shallows said. "Put some cream on those."

"Next!"

"I made a volcano with baking soda and vinegar!" said a sixth-grade boy with braces.

Principal Dunkin and Mayor Shallows waited for the boy to elaborate, but he had nothing else to say.

"Care to explain why?" the principal asked.

The boy shrugged. "Because my parents told me that's what you're supposed to make for a science fair."

"Well, I appreciate a young man who keeps traditions alive," Mayor Shallows said.

"Also, my parents voted for you," the boy said. "They told me to mention it."

"You're clearly from a family of exceptional taste," the mayor said. "Terrific work."

Mayor Shallows winked at the boy and gave him a pat on the back. Roswell wondered if he should tell the mayor that Gram and Pop voted for him too, even though he knew for a fact they didn't.

"Next!"

The mayor and the principal snaked through the rows of folding tables as they inspected each and every science fair project. It was a forest of papier-mâché creations, battery-operated gadgets, and poster boards with headlines like SAVE THE BEES! USE A LANDLINE!, and YOU STINK: WHAT YOUR BODY ODOR IS TELLING YOU, and CRICKET FLOUR AND LENTILS: THE MENU OF THE FUTURE, and FAX MACHINES, RECORD PLAYERS, VCRS, AND OTHER ANCIENT MACHINERY, and GLOBAL WARMING ISN'T COOL, BRO!

In the back row Roswell became more and more excited as he watched his peers give their presentations. He thought the topics were predictable, the research was minimal, and the conclusions were obvious—they offered nothing that a quick Google search couldn't provide—but Roswell thought *his* project was exciting, informative, and unique. He might have a better shot at winning the trip to Rump World than he'd realized.

"Next!"

Finally, after what seemed like an eternity, Mayor Shallows and Principal Dunkin reached the back row. It was Roswell's turn to present his project, and a rush of adrenaline surged through his body.

Strangely, as soon as Mayor Shallows laid eyes on Roswell, his cheerful grin turned into a disapproving scowl. Mayor Shallows's scowl only stretched deeper as he read ARE EXTRATERRESTRIALS REAL? THE PROOF IS OUT THERE! across Roswell's poster board.

"Oh boy," the mayor muttered under his breath. "*This* should be interesting."

"Good afternoon, Mayor Shallows," Roswell said.

"Before I begin, I've got a question for you. Why don't scientists trust atoms? Because they make up everything! Get it? Get it?"

The mayor glared at him with less enthusiasm than a statue. Roswell instantly regretted opening with a joke and quickly moved on.

"My name is Roswell Johnson, and it's a pleasure to present my project to you today."

"Your name is *Roswell*? Like the city?" Mayor Shallows scoffed.

"Actually, my name is Roswell like *the greatest government cover-up of all time*!" he said with big theatrical hands. "But I'll tell you more about that in a moment. I don't want to put the flying saucer in front of the nuclear generator. Get it? Get it? That's like putting the cart in front of the horse."

Mayor Shallows checked his gold Rolex.

"I'm running out of time," he said. "Better get on with it."

"Um...certainly," Roswell said, and cleared his throat. "For my project I asked the most profound question in human history: Are we alone in the universe? Ever since human beings could lift their heads toward the night sky, we've wondered if there was anyone else out there. And, Mr. Mayor, by the time I'm finished with my presentation, I guarantee you'll believe we are *abso-UFO-lutely not alone*!"

Mayor Shallows raised a single eyebrow at him. "How is this a *science* project?"

"Well, science is about collecting data and forming a theory—and that's exactly what I've done," Roswell said. "I've collected just as much evidence to support my theory as my classmates have—if not more."

Mayor Shallows snorted. "We'll see. Go on."

Roswell was taken aback by the mayor's rudeness, especially since he had shown the other students nothing but kindness. Roswell knew his presentation was a challenging concept to sell—he knew it would take a lot of convincing to get the judges on board—but he had no idea his audience would be *this* tough. But Roswell didn't let the mayor discourage him. He took a deep breath and presented his project exactly as he had rehearsed.

"*The universe,*" Roswell said with another theatrical gesture. "Astronomers estimate there are over one hundred billion planets in our galaxy and over one hundred billion galaxies in the known universe. With numbers that high, even if there was a one-in-a-billion chance that alien life existed, that would still be a trillion chances! So it begs the question, Why is it so difficult for people to believe in extraterrestrial life?"

"Good judgment?" Mayor Shallows asked.

"No—because of *fear*! For the most part, extraterrestrials have been portrayed as hostile creatures in films, television shows, and books. The general public has been brainwashed into fearing them. The concept is so terrifying most people choose to *ignore* it. But if aliens wanted to destroy us, they surely would have done it by now! On the contrary, evidence suggests they've been *helping* mankind for thousands of years, not harming us."

"Young man, people don't believe in aliens because there *is* no evidence."

"Not with *that* attitude, Mr. Mayor," Roswell teased. "The proof is in the pudding—but you have to *acknowledge* the pudding first! So I hope you're hungry, Mr. Mayor, because the world is neck-deep in pudding."

Roswell excitedly turned to his poster board. He pointed to an illustration of a disk-shaped spaceship that had crashed in the middle of a desert. The illustration was pinned next to an old newspaper clipping:

ROSWELL DAILY RECORD

Tuesday, July 8, 1947

RAAF Captures Flying Saucer on Ranch in Roswell Region

"I'd like to start my presentation with the most famous encounter of all time—I'm talking about the jackpot, the Holy Grail, the *Beyoncé* of all conspiracies: *Roswell, New Mexico*!" he said. "On a mid-June morning in 1947, an unsuspecting rancher made a very strange discovery on his desert property. He woke up to find his ranch was covered in debris—some type of aircraft had crashed on his land! But the metallic wreckage was unlike any material the rancher had seen before. It was shiny like glass, it was thin like tin-foil, it was flexible like rubber, and it was tough as stone.

"The rancher took a sample of the debris to the local sheriff, who, upon inspection, was equally confused. The bewildered men contacted the Roswell Army Air Field to see if they knew what the wreckage was from. After examining the samples, the air force went to the ranch and conducted a thorough inspection of the rancher's property. They collected all the wreckage and took it to a secret location for further examination. The following day an army official, Major Jesse Marcel, gave an interview that changed the world forever! Major Marcel told the local press that the United States military had uncovered the wreckage of a *flying saucer*!

"The story spread like wildfire and caused a national frenzy! The American public began to panic and feared an alien invasion was on the horizon! The United States military knew they had to do something fast to put the public at ease. So they retracted Major Marcel's statement and said the whole thing was a big misunderstanding. The military claimed the wreckage wasn't from a flying saucer, but from a simple *weather balloon* instead."

"Sounds like a reasonable explanation," Mayor Shallows said.

"Perhaps," Roswell said. "*But* many employees who worked at the Roswell Army Air Field in 1947 have come forward to dispute the army's claim. They say a flying saucer was *most definitely* discovered on the ranch—and it wasn't the only thing discovered that day either. According to the employees, the dead bodies of *four humanoid beings* were uncovered too! The beings were described as about three feet tall, with thin bodies, gray skin, large black eyes, and only four fingers on each hand."

Mayor Shallows rolled his eyes. "Of course they were."

"Just for a moment let's pretend the United States military was telling the truth and they *did* discover a weather balloon on the ranch. Why would a highly respected official like Major Marcel tell such an outlandish lie to the press? And why would the airfield employees put their careers and reputations in jeopardy to back up Major Marcel's original claims?"

"Many small towns come up with tall tales to generate tourism," Mayor Shallows said. "Like the Loch Ness Monster and Bigfoot."

"Maybe," Roswell said. "If the Roswell incident was the *only* incident of its kind, I might believe it was a hoax too. But the Roswell incident is just one of *many* that have happened all over the world! And as we all know, where there's smoke, there's fire! You might want to take a step back, Mr. Mayor, because I'm about to blow a *lot* of smoke your way!"

Roswell pointed to a photograph of a married couple from the 1960s. The husband was Black, the wife was white, and they posed with their pet dachshund. The photograph was pinned next to a news article:

BOSTON TRAVELER

Monday, October 25, 1965
A UFO Chiller:
Did THEY Seize Couple?

"It happened on a late evening in the fall of 1961," Roswell said. "Betty and Barney Hill were driving home from a vacation at Niagara Falls with their dog, Delsey. While they were on the road, they noticed an odd light in the sky. Strangely, the light seemed to be following them— it slowed down when they slowed down, it sped up when they sped up, and it paused whenever they paused. The couple pulled over and stepped out of their car to inspect the light. They quickly realized the object wasn't a plane, a helicopter, or a satellite, but a *flying saucer*! Just like the one described in the Roswell incident!

"The last thing the Hills remembered from their encounter was the saucer landing on the road in front of them. They woke up two hours later inside their car—and to their amazement, they were over thirty-five miles down the road from where they had parked!

"In the following years the couple underwent hypnosis to recall the lost time. During their sessions they uncovered memories of being abducted and experimented on by strange *humanoid beings* with—I'm sure you've guessed it, Mr. Mayor—thin frames, gray skin, large black eyes, and only four digits on each hand. Just like the bodies discovered in—say it with me, Mr. Mayor—*the incident in Roswell, New Mexico!* Since the Hills' story went public in 1965, over two million people have come forward and reported similar abduction experiences."

"People will say anything for attention," Mayor Shallows said.

"*Some* people, perhaps," Roswell said. "But the only people who knew about Betty and Barney's abduction were their therapists and close friends. The Hills only became famous because the *Boston Traveler* published a story about them. And remember, this happened in the early sixties. Betty and Barney were an interracial couple in the middle of the civil rights movement! Their marriage was illegal in thirty-one states! National attention was probably the last thing they wanted."

Roswell noticed Mayor Shallows cringed at the words *interracial couple*.

"Perhaps the stress of their *alternative lifestyle* caused them to hallucinate," he said.

"Um…I suppose that's possible," Roswell said. "Although hallucinations tend to be individual experiences. And I doubt a hallucination can be shared by *thousands* of people at once—which brings me to my next story!"

"Mr. Johnson? How much longer is this presentation going to last?" the mayor asked.

"Oh, I'm just getting to the good stuff!" Roswell said.

Obviously, Mayor Shallows was growing restless and eager for the presentation to end, but Roswell was still confident he could win him over. Besides, *Roswell was on a roll*—he couldn't stop now even if he wanted to.

Roswell pointed to a photograph of the US Capitol building. A cluster of seven disk-shaped objects hovered over the Capitol's enormous dome. The photograph was pinned beside a news article:

DAILY NEWS

Monday, July 28, 1952

Jets Chase D.C. Sky Ghosts

"It was 1952 in Washington, DC," Roswell said. "A group of UFOs were detected on radar at Andrews Air Force Base. The objects were moving toward DC at over a hundred miles an hour! When fighter jets arrived on the scene, the UFOs disappeared! As soon as the jets returned to the base, the objects reappeared again, flying over the White House and the Capitol building! Later the UFOs vanished without a trace. At a press conference, General

John A. Samford confirmed the objects did not belong to the United States Air Force. To this day, no one knows what they were!"

"It was very easy to be *mistaken* back then," Mayor Shallows said. "Thankfully we have better technology now. People are less likely to get *confused*."

"That's the perfect segue to my next point, Mr. Mayor!" Roswell said, and pointed to another newspaper clipping on his board:

THE NEW YORK TIMES

Saturday, December 16, 2017

Glowing Auras and 'Black Money': The Pentagon's Mysterious U.F.O. Program

"Even though the most notorious encounters happened several decades ago, UFO sightings are still happening to this day," Roswell said. "In 2017, the *New York Times* published a story about a secret US military program that studied unidentified flying objects! The *Times* even posted videos from the United States Air Force that showed UFOs caught on camera! And recently, in the summer of 2023, retired military officials David Grusch, Ryan Graves, and David Fravor testified before Congress about UFOs and the nonhuman biologics discovered at crash sites!"

"*Alleged* crash sites," the mayor said.

"Riiiiight. *Alleged* crash sites."

Roswell winked at the mayor, but he didn't wink back.

"Thank you, Mr. Johnson. I've heard enough."

"I'm almost done, Mr. Mayor! I swear!"

Roswell pointed to a collage on his poster board with photographs of historical structures and ancient artwork.

"If these modern events haven't convinced you, then just take a look at history! In almost every culture and religion, there are tales of ancient messengers who gifted mankind with knowledge and tools to survive. In most of those stories the messengers *descended from the sky*! Could the angels and prophets described in the Bible, the Tanakh, and the Koran actually have been *extraterrestrials*?"

"Mr. Johnson?"

"There are also hieroglyphs in Egypt, petroglyphs throughout North America, and paintings from ancient China that depict *aircraft* and *humanoid beings* that look eerily similar to the saucers and beings described in the Roswell incident. From the Holy Ghost group in Canyonlands National Park in Utah to the Kimberley rock art in the caves of Western Australia to the Nazca Lines in the Peruvian desert—it's abundantly clear that indigenous people around the globe were exposed to something extraordinary!"

"MR. JOHNSON!"

"SO IN *CONCLUSION*, MR. MAYOR!" Roswell said, and gestured to everything on his poster board at once. "If we set aside our egos and our fears, if we focus on *what* is being said instead of *who* is saying it, if we agree *there's no such thing as a frequent coincidence*, then we'd be on the verge of the greatest discovery in human history! And what could unite the world more than that? *Okay, now I'm finished.*"

Roswell didn't know how to pose at the end of his presentation, so he just smiled and awkwardly put his hands on his hips like a superhero. Mayor Shallows was so relieved the presentation was finished his posture sank a foot.

"Young man, I can tell you're passionate about these... *stories*," Mayor Shallows said. "Unfortunately, you haven't provided a single piece of *actual* evidence. If you expect me to believe such an eccentric theory, you'll need much more than *eyewitnesses*."

Roswell heard his classmates starting to laugh at him. It seemed Mayor Shallows had made up his mind, but Roswell had worked too hard to quit now.

"With all due respect, Mr. Mayor, witness testimonies are considered evidence in the court of law," Roswell said. "And if every scientist gave up because their ideas seemed *eccentric*, we wouldn't have science at all."

Roswell had never debated anyone before—let alone an elected official. He hoped standing up for himself would earn the mayor's respect. However, according to the heated glare aimed in Roswell's direction, Mayor Shallows was not a man who enjoyed a debate.

"Mr. Johnson, in the court of law witnesses are brought to the stand," the mayor said. "Did you bring one of these witnesses with you today? *No.* Did you collect any of these accounts yourself? *No.* You based your entire theory on tabloids and total strangers."

"Actually, my dad saw a UFO," Roswell said. "That's the reason he named me Roswell—he hoped it would inspire me to ask questions and think outside the box."

"And where is your father? Why didn't you bring him with you?"

A lump came to Roswell's throat.

"Because...because...because he's dead, sir."

A quiet hush swept through the gymnasium. Everyone's eyes were glued to the mayor, curious how he'd respond. Surprisingly, Mayor Shallows looked even more annoyed than he did before, like Roswell had mentioned his late father only to make the mayor look bad.

"I'm sorry for your loss—truly I am—but I'm afraid your presentation did not have the results you were hoping for," Mayor Shallows said. "Now if you'll please excuse me, I am a very busy man with a very tight schedule. I can't waste any more time listening to fairy tales about aliens or spaceships or government conspiracies. Especially from someone of *your* background."

"My background?" Roswell asked. "What's that supposed to mean?"

"Good day, Mr. Johnson."

The mayor tried to walk away, but his chief of staff stopped him.

"Sir? May I have a quick word?" Ms. Crabtree whispered. "The next election is four months away. It might be good to have a photo with, you know...*a minority*."

"Oh. Good idea."

Before Roswell knew what was happening, Mayor Shallows threw his arm over Roswell's shoulder and Mr. Ace snapped a picture of them together. Next, the mayor pushed Roswell away and headed to the microphone at the front of the gymnasium.

Roswell felt like his heart had broken and the pieces had sunk into the pit of his stomach. He wasn't upset because he had obviously lost—he was upset because *he'd never had a chance to begin with*. There was nothing Roswell could have said or done to win over a man like Mayor Shallows.

"Before I announce the winner, I'd like to congratulate all of today's participants," the mayor said. "I am blown away by your innovation, your creativity, and your dedication to science. However, there was one project that went above and beyond my expectations. I award the Forty-Sixth Annual Cherokee Springs Intermediate School Science Fair first-place prize to...*the young fella with the baking soda volcano!*"

The bitter losers gave the winner a weak round of

applause. The champion triumphantly collected his first-place trophy and tickets to Rump World.

Roswell suddenly realized why aliens had lived in secrecy for so long. If given the choice, he wouldn't want to be part of his world either. Roswell imagined himself climbing into one of the spaceships on his poster board and leaving Earth, the science fair, his classmates, and Mayor Shallows far behind him.

And although it was impossible for him to know it then, in just a few hours that's *exactly* what would happen....

CHAPTER TWO

THE JOHNSON FAMILY CHICKEN FARM

As soon as the science fair was over, Roswell went straight to the dumpster behind the school and tossed his poster board into the trash. The day he'd hoped would end in a grand celebration had become one of the worst days of his life. He flung off his blue sports coat, yanked off his red bow tie, and had a seat on the curb while he waited for his ride home. Roswell was so distraught he barely noticed the warm Oklahoma sun on the back of his neck. All he could think about was what an epic failure his science fair project had been and how foolish he was for getting his hopes up.

His spiral of despair was briefly interrupted when his

cell phone buzzed in his pocket. Roswell saw a text message from his grandmother.

> Hi exclamation point I'm driving and will bee-tee-eye-five-em smiley face emoji send

Roswell scrunched his forehead. Decoding his grandmother's voice-to-text messages was like translating another language.

> Gram what does BTI5M mean?

> Be there in five minutes period thumbs up emoji send

> Gram that's not a thing.

> What do you mean question mark confused emoji send

> I think you mean OMW. On my way.

> Fine I'm OMW then eyeroll emoji period for the love of God how the heck are we supposed to keep up with

these kids and their dang phones Siri
play the Fugees oh crap I forgot to say
send send send

Four minutes later Roswell heard the rattling engine
of Gram's 1970 Volkswagen Beetle in the distance. The
beat-up burgundy car pulled up to the school, and Roswell
hopped into the passenger seat. Gram was a short and
plump woman in her sixties, but Roswell thought she
had the moxie of a WWE wrestler. Her curly dark hair
sprouted like a firework behind a pink bandanna that
matched her heart-shaped sunglasses. Gram was a care-
taker at the Cherokee Springs Assisted Living Home and
was dressed in her purple polka-dot scrubs.

"Sorry I'm late, Roz—Mrs. Felderman escaped," Gram
said. "We found her down the street at the casino—*again*.
She was up seven hundred bucks on the Wheel of Fortune
machine. I told them to check the casino first, but no one
ever listens to me. I've worked there for twenty-six years,
but what do I know? Anyway, how did the science fair go?
Did the judges love it? Tell me everything!"

Roswell folded his arms and didn't look away from the
road ahead.

"It was fine," he mumbled.

Gram side-eyed Roswell as she drove. He was convinced she had X-ray vision, because she could always see
right through him.

"Just *fine*, huh?" she asked. "I'm guessing that means you didn't win the tickets?"

Roswell shook his head.

"I'm sorry, Rozzy," Gram said. "I know you had your heart set on going to Rump World. I wish Pop and I could afford to take you, but money has been tight lately. Even with all my extra shifts at the home, we're barely getting by."

"It's okay, Gram," Roswell said. "It's just a dumb theme park anyway."

"You worked so hard on that project—I thought you had it in the bag," she said. "Someone must have split the atom to beat you. What ended up winning?"

"A baking soda volcano."

"A what?"

"And he didn't even use it!"

"Who was judging this dog and pony show?"

"Mayor Shallows."

Gram went quiet, and Roswell knew they were thinking the exact same thing.

"I see," she said. "Well, Mayor Shallows has a *reputation*."

"That's putting it nicely," Roswell said.

"On the bright side, this was your very first middle school science fair. Next year there'll be a different judge—hopefully one with half a brain—and if you keep working on your project, there'll be nothing standing in your way."

"Gram, you've said the same thing a million times! On

History Day the judges loathed my report on the Apollo 11 mission because I *implied* the Space Race was a hoax to bankrupt the Soviet Union. At Career Day people laughed at me when I said I wanted to be an astrophysicist for the SETI Institute—and then they laughed even harder when I told them what the SETI Institute was. At the seventh-grade talent show the audience yawned when I recited the hundred closest exoplanets and their exact distances to Earth from memory. And today at the science fair Mayor Shallows hated my project before I even said a word. Don't you get it? It doesn't matter how hard I work on something! People don't like me, they don't like my ideas, or they don't like the color of my skin. How can I win in a world like this? Why even bother trying? I give up."

Gram suddenly slammed on the brakes. The cars behind them honked and swerved around the Volkswagen.

"What are you doing? You're gonna cause a crash!" Roswell cried.

His grandmother whipped off her sunglasses, stopped her music, and grabbed Roswell by the chin, forcing him to look her directly in the eyes.

"Roswell Johnson, you may live in a stupid world but that does not give you permission to *be* stupid!" she said. "You are allowed to be upset, you are allowed to be angry, but you are not allowed to *give up* because bigots like Mayor Shallows are too dense to recognize a good thing when they see one."

"You didn't see the way he looked at me," he said. "It was like he hated me without even knowing me."

"Trust me, I've seen that look many times myself. And unfortunately, it may not be the last time you see it either. But we can't let someone else's stupidity stop us from living our best lives. If we did, we'd be just as dumb as they are."

Roswell let out a long, defeated sigh.

"It's so unfair," he said.

"Life isn't always fair or easy—you of all people know that—but life has also blessed you with a brilliant mind. That's a gift that can take you anywhere you want to go. And as long as you're living under my roof, I will *not* let you waste it."

"But no one listens to me, Gram," Roswell said. "What's the point of having a gift if no one recognizes it?"

"*You* recognize it—and that's all that matters," Gram said. "Brilliance is like art, Roz. Not everyone is going to like or appreciate you—and their reasons may be maddening and as dumb as a box of rocks—but that doesn't mean you *quit*. It means you work harder and search wider until you find the people who *will* believe in you. For every Mayor Shallows there's a Gram and a Pop. You are too smart to believe anything else. Do you understand me?"

Roswell didn't agree, but he knew she wouldn't drive the car unless he pretended.

"Yes, ma'am," he mumbled.

"Good," she said, and released his chin from her grip.

"Remember, you're a *Johnson*. We don't give up. Not now, not ever."

His grandmother put on her sunglasses, turned up her music, and drove.

"Siri, play Whitney Houston," Gram told her phone. "Roswell needs her."

Roswell sat in silence and stared out the window for the rest of the drive. Gram tried to get him to sing along with her, but he refused. Roswell appreciated her attempt to cheer him up, but in that moment nothing in the world could encourage him.

At least, nothing in *his* world.

Gram drove her Volkswagen through the small city of Cherokee Springs and headed into the flat countryside on the north side of town. After a few miles of nothing but power lines and grass on either side of the road, Gram made a right turn at a large wooden sign:

THE JOHNSON FAMILY CHICKEN FARM
Est. 1918
"Where everything is fowl!"

The Johnson Family Chicken Farm was like a living postcard—at least, it had been forty years ago. The farmhouse needed a new coat of paint, the barn needed a new door, the chicken shed needed a new roof, and the fences needed to be replaced altogether. However, what the farm lacked in ambience, it made up for with its unique history. It was the first free-range farm in Cherokee Springs County and one of the first Black-owned farms in the state of Oklahoma. The farm had been in the Johnson family for five generations, and ever since Roswell's grandfather inherited the property from Roswell's great-grandfather, Pop had single-handedly run the farm.

Gram parked her Volkswagen next to Pop's bright turquoise Chevrolet pickup truck. Roswell desperately wanted to lock himself in his bedroom and forget about the day, so he tried to sneak into the farmhouse without being noticed. Before Roswell reached the front porch, Pop poked his head out of the chicken shed. He was smiling from ear to ear.

"Hey, you two! Come check this out!" Pop said.

Pop was a very tall and broad man, and his skin was rough and weathered from a lifetime of working outdoors, but Roswell thought he had the gentleness of a giant teddy bear. For as long as Roswell could remember, he'd never seen his grandfather dressed in anything but his denim overalls and his Kansas City Royals baseball hat.

"Uh-oh. What are you up to now?" Gram asked.

"I taught Persephone a new trick!" Pop declared. "You won't believe it!"

"Oh Lord," Gram said under her breath. "Here we go again."

Roswell didn't want to be rude, so he followed Gram into the shed. He stayed close to the door, though, hoping to make a quick escape before Pop asked him about the science fair.

The shed was home to thousands of clucking chickens. Roswell and Gram found Pop standing over one chicken in particular—but *this* was no ordinary chicken. Persephone was a bearded black silkie and, as Gram often joked, was the true love of Pop's life. Her black feathers were perfectly groomed and so fluffy she looked like an aristocrat in a fur coat—and she had the attitude to match. Persephone held her beak high and walked around the other chickens with a bouncy strut, like a queen among peasants. Pop had even built her a private coop that resembled a miniature castle.

"Watch this," Pop said. "Persephone, *dance.*"

On his command the silkie stretched out her dark wings and ran in place, as if she were performing the flashdance. Pop cheered and rewarded her with handfuls of cracked corn. He bestowed the grains like he was showering an opera singer with roses.

"Bravo, Persephone! Bravo!" Pop praised. "Isn't she incredible?"

"Nice one, Pop," Roswell said.

Gram rolled her eyes and folded her arms.

"A true revelation," she said. "Has *America's Got Talent* called yet?"

"Make fun of us all you want," Pop said. "The Oklahoma State Poultry Show is next week. We'll see who's laughing when Persephone wins the five-thousand-dollar grand prize! We'll finally afford a new fence!"

"You think *that* deserves five thousand dollars?" Gram asked.

Persephone squawked and nipped in Gram's direction, clearly offended by the remark.

"Yes!" Pop said. "Persephone is a twelfth-generation, purebred bearded black silkie. Do you know how rare that is? She's guaranteed to win Best in Breed! And if I can teach her a full dance routine and how to locate Brazil on a map, she'll be a shoo-in for the talent portion too. *Won't you, Persephone? Who's my little star? Who's my little dancing queen?*"

Pop scooped Persephone off the ground and rubbed her fluffy belly. The chicken blissfully cooed and nuzzled his big arms.

"Teach her the Macarena and then I'll be impressed," Gram said. "In the meantime, I'm going to scrounge up something for dinner."

Roswell tried to sneak out with Gram, but Pop stopped him.

"How was the science fair, Roz? Are we going to Rump World?"

Roswell went tense. The last thing he wanted to do was explain it all over again.

"Um...no," he said. "I lost."

"Really?" Pop said. "Gosh, that's a shame. I thought your project was terrific. It made me so paranoid I've been eyeing the sky suspiciously all week. I saw a crop duster this morning and nearly had a heart attack."

"I guess the judge didn't dig it as much as you and Gram did," Roswell said.

"Don't beat yourself up about it," Pop said. "Remember, life isn't about the finish line, it's about the race."

Roswell nodded along. "Apparently, it's *all* about race."

"Well, I'm proud of you regardless. And I know *he* would be too."

Pop nodded toward the front of the shed. On the wall above his workbench was a framed photo of a handsome man who looked just like Roswell. The man stood in front of an American flag and was dressed in a dark blue suit with several military metals pinned to it. Roswell gazed up at the photo of his father, but his eyes quickly dropped to the floor. He had had enough grief for one day.

"How was your day, Pop?" Roswell asked to change the subject.

"Not too shabby," he said. "I fixed the sprinklers and delivered eggs to the bakery. The hens in the north coop still haven't laid anything since last Friday—I think they're on strike. But in good news, the Royals game is about to start. Do you want to watch it with me?"

"No thanks," Roswell said. "I've got homework."

"Suit yourself," Pop said. "I'll be here if you change your mind."

Pop went to his workbench and clicked on a small television. As he flipped through the channels, he passed several news programs that were reporting the same story. Roswell saw footage of a bald man in a sleek suit. There were headlines like CONTROVERSIAL BILLIONAIRE TO WEAPONIZE SPACE, RUMP SAYS HE IS "ECSTATIC" FOR DEFENSE PROGRAM TO START, FIRST OF TWELVE ROCKETS WILL LIFT OFF ON APRIL 1, and A-LIST CELEBRITIES AND MEMBERS OF CONGRESS TO ATTEND ERASE LAUNCH.

Pop grunted and shook his head at the news.

"These billionaires and their pathetic spaceships," he scoffed. "They act like they're doing everybody a favor. If they actually cared about the planet, they wouldn't be trying so hard to leave it."

"What's happening with Eli Rump?" Roswell asked.

"That knucklehead just spent seven billion dollars on satellites we don't need," Pop said. "Do you know what else he could have done with that money? Do you know how many homeless people he could have housed or how many hungry people he could have fed? Let this be a lesson to you, Roz. You'll be in his shoes one day—I'm certain of it. And when you are, don't forget what's really important. When you have an opportunity to help people, don't miss it."

Roswell gave his grandfather a fake smile. After such a

disappointing day, he sincerely doubted he'd ever reach the success of someone like Eli Rump.

"I should get started on my homework," he said. "See you later, Pop."

Roswell left the shed and went inside the farmhouse. Just like the outside, the inside of the farmhouse was in dire need of repairs. The floral wallpaper was peeling, the floorboards were loose, the ceiling was cracked, and the furniture hadn't been upgraded since the early 1980s. Despite all the flaws, the house still had a lot of homey charm. The walls were decorated with framed family photos, and all the surfaces were covered in Gram's collection of porcelain chickens. Every piece of furniture was draped with a colorful afghan that Pop had knit himself.

"I know it's not Tuesday, but I've got the stuff for tacos," Gram called from the kitchen.

"I'm not hungry," Roswell said.

Gram peered around the corner. "Are you sure?"

"Yeah. I'm gonna do some homework and go to bed early."

"Okay then. I'll leave you a plate in the fridge in case you get hungry."

"Thanks."

Roswell hurried up two flights of stairs to his attic bedroom. He promptly shut the door behind him and exhaled, grateful to *finally* be alone. Unfortunately, his bedroom didn't provide the serenity he was hoping for. Absolutely everything in it reminded him of his science fair project.

The slanted walls were decorated with posters of movies such as *Guardians of the Galaxy*, *Men in Black*, and *Close Encounters of the Third Kind*, and television shows like *Star Trek*, *The X-Files*, and *Ancient Aliens*. The ceiling was covered in glow-in-the-dark stars, the rug in the center of the floor was shaped like Saturn, and the lamp on Roswell's desk was a little green alien that lit up when you turned the knob on its belly button. His bookshelf was overflowing with titles like *2001: A Space Odyssey*, by Arthur C. Clarke; *Cosmos*, by Carl Sagan; *Dawn*, by Octavia E. Butler; *The War of the Worlds*, by H. G. Wells; *Out on a Limb*, by Shirley MacLaine; *I Was a Sixth Grade Alien*, by Bruce Coville; and *A Wrinkle in Time*, by Madeleine L'Engle. He had a large telescope stationed at his window, a rocket ship alarm clock, and a life-size cardboard cutout of astrophysicist Neil deGrasse Tyson.

Roswell crawled into bed and pulled his Star Wars sheets over his head to block everything out. He desperately wanted the day to be over—he wanted to wake up tomorrow and pretend it all had been a bad dream—so Roswell got comfortable and let his hopelessness rock him into a deep, deep sleep....

Five years earlier, in that very same room, First Sergeant Curtis Johnson was reading a bedtime story to a six-year-old Roswell. Their eyes were wide with excitement as they looked over the pages of their favorite book, *Saucers, Spacemen, and Secrets: Extraterrestrial Sightings Through the Ages*, by Professor Walter Prescott. The soft guitar of a David Bowie song played from Roswell's radio as his father read aloud.

"'On September sixteenth, 1994, a sighting occurred outside Ruwa, Zimbabwe,'" Curtis read. "'During recess over sixty pupils at the Ariel School saw several silver craft descend from the sky. The students claimed the craft were piloted by strange beings with large heads and big eyes. A psychologist evaluated the children and confirmed they were being honest. The school's headmaster conducted an experiment to make sure the students weren't playing a practical joke. He called each of the children into his office and, one at a time, asked them to draw what they had seen. All of the drawings depicted the same spaceships and humanoid beings. To this day, the students swear they witnessed an authentic extraterrestrial phenomenon.'"

"Whoa," Roswell said. "They must have been telling the truth!"

"It's very convincing," Curtis said.

"Will you read one more?"

"Okay, but this is the last one," his father said, and flipped through the book. "Here's a good one. 'It happened an hour north of New York City, in a sleepy area known as the Hudson Valley. From 1983 to 1986 over a thousand residents reported a strange cluster of colorful lights floating over their homes. Many said the lights came from a V-shaped aircraft that was two hundred to three hundred yards in length. The residents said the object flew much slower than any plane or helicopter they had ever seen. Since the Hudson Valley phenomenon, the same type of sighting has occurred in multiple places all over the United States.'"

"That's wild!" Roswell said. "Could that have been the UFO you saw, Daddy?"

"It sounds pretty similar, doesn't it?"

"Will you tell me the story again?"

Curtis chuckled. "Roz, you've heard it a hundred times!"

Roswell pouted. "Pretty please?"

"Okay, okay, okay," Curtis said. "Let's see....I was twelve years old, George W. Bush was president, *Signs* was the biggest movie of the summer, and Ja Rule was on every hit song."

"Who?"

"It doesn't matter—I'm just adding color. Anyway, it was the night of my twelfth birthday. I was in the living room playing video games when your gram told me to take out the trash. I went outside, dropped the trash into the bin, and headed back inside—all perfectly normal. But as

I walked back to the house, I suddenly had a strange feeling that *someone was watching me*. I looked all around the farm but didn't see a soul. That's when I looked up and saw it! *A huge spacecraft was floating above me!*"

Roswell clutched his bedsheets a little tighter.

"What did it look like?" he asked.

"It was shaped like a giant boomerang!" Curtis said. "It was about a hundred feet long and had six bright lights on its base. And strangest of all, the spacecraft didn't make a sound! It was as quiet as a cloud!"

"Wow," Roswell said with a wide grin. "What did you do?"

"Absolutely nothing—I was terrified!" Curtis said. "I was frozen and couldn't take my eyes off it! One of the lights shined over me, and I could feel my body slowly start to *levitate off the ground*! I was almost a foot in the air when I panicked. I wiggled free from whatever force was lifting me up and ran back to the house. I immediately found Gram and Pop and told them what I saw. They could tell from the fear in my eyes that I wasn't making it up. Pop grabbed his baseball bat, and Gram grabbed her shotgun, and we all raced outside. But when we got there, *the spacecraft had vanished*!"

"Did you call the police?" Roswell asked.

"The police didn't take me seriously," Curtis said. "I called Vance Air Force Base up in Enid, too. They said their radars hadn't detected anything in the area that night. I even wrote a letter to NASA. They wrote me back and said it must have been a satellite or a weather balloon."

"It's always weather balloons with those people!" Roswell said.

"And we know what *NASA* really stands for, don't we?" Curtis said.

"*Never A Straight Answer.*" They laughed together.

"I saw the same UFO on the day I graduated high school, on the day I married your mom, and then again on my first day in the military. They've been following me my entire life. It used to scare me, but now I consider them an old friend. It's like I have a guardian alien."

An idea came to Roswell that made the excitement fade from his face.

"Daddy? Could Mommy have been abducted by aliens? Could she still be out there somewhere?" he asked.

Curtis gave his son a bittersweet smile and gently rubbed his head.

"No, Roz, Mommy wasn't abducted by aliens," he said softly. "She got very sick and passed away—you were just too young to remember. But wherever Mommy is, I bet *she* has the answers to all of life's greatest mysteries."

"Really?"

"Yup! In fact, she's probably watching us right now and having a good laugh! That's what I believe happens when we die—our spirits leave our bodies and we learn about everything in the universe!"

"*Everything?*"

"Oh, you name it! We get to see all the stars and planets, we learn about the laws of space and time, and we finally get to know where everything came from! The universe is so much bigger and better than any of us realize. Our human brains could never grasp how magnificent it is!"

Roswell was giddy as he thought about how wonderous the universe was.

"I wish I could see it all," he said.

"Me too," his dad said. "Even though we don't have all the answers, it's important to stay curious. That's the greatest trait a person can have, Roz! Curiosity will fuel your imagination and take you places the fastest spaceship could never reach. Promise me you won't forget that."

"I promise," Roswell said.

Curtis pulled back the sleeve of his camouflage uniform and checked his watch.

"Oh, look at the time," he said. "My plane leaves in three hours, and Pop has to drive me to the airport. I should get going."

Roswell frowned. "Daddy, do you *have* to go back to Afghanistan?"

"I'm afraid so, champ," Curtis said. "There's still a war going on over there, and a lot of people need my help. But don't worry, I'll be back in six months. Gram and Pop will take great care of you while I'm gone."

"Will you read me one more story before you leave?"

"I don't know—it's already past your bedtime."

Roswell pouted again. "Pretty please?"

"Okay, fine—*one* more story, but that's it."

Curtis flipped through *Saucers, Spacemen, and Secrets: Extraterrestrial Sightings Through the Ages.*

"Here's one of my favorite stories—it's called 'The Battle for Los Angeles'! 'In 1942 a strange object was reported hovering over Southern California. The United States Army fired antiaircraft guns at the object for over an hour. Five civilians were killed from the falling shrapnel. However, nothing brought the mysterious aircraft down. The object eventually drifted over the ocean and was never seen again....'"

Roswell's eyes became heavier and heavier as he listened to his father's voice, and eventually he drifted off to sleep. It was a special night that Roswell would never forget, not because of the stories they shared or because of the promise he made, but because it was the last time Roswell ever saw his father.

Roswell awoke with a jolt and sat up in bed. It was late and his bedroom was pitch-black. The rocket ship alarm clock on the nightstand showed it was half past midnight. His eyes felt puffy and his cheeks were wet. Roswell wasn't surprised, though—he always cried in his sleep when he had *that dream* of his father.

He hopped out of bed and opened his bedroom window. Roswell stared up at the stars with the same questions he had been asking for years. But tonight more desperation beamed from his swollen eyes than ever before.

"Is anybody out there?" he asked. "Are we alone in the universe?"

Roswell waited for a response, but the stars didn't answer him.

"Has my entire life been a total waste of time? Is Earth just a big cosmic accident? Were *any* of my dad's stories real? Or..."

He was afraid to ask his next question. Saying it out loud might make it true.

"Or am I as alone and insignificant as I feel?"

Once again the twinkling stars held on to their secrets. Roswell was used to the universe's silence, but this time it was soul crushing. He turned back to his colorful bedroom and felt a sharp pain in his gut. His decorations were reminders of everything he had lost—his father, the science fair, his self-confidence, even his faith in the world—and he never wanted to see *any* of it again.

Roswell plucked the glow-in-the-dark stars off his ceiling, he ripped the posters off his wall, he pulled the books off his shelves, and he tossed it all into the trash. He placed his rocket ship alarm clock, his alien lamp, his telescope, and his cardboard cutout of Neil deGrasse Tyson on the floor and then rolled everything up in his Saturn-shaped rug. Roswell sighed with relief at the sight of his bare bedroom, as if he had just stripped his brain of all his painful memories too. *Out of sight, out of mind.* Or so he hoped.

Next, Roswell changed into a pair of jeans, a green T-shirt, sneakers, and his favorite red hoodie. He held the trash can under one arm, the rug under the other, and quietly carried his belongings down the stairs and out of the house. He walked across the farm and dumped the belongings into the trash bins on the side of the chicken shed.

The night air was cool and crisp, the full moon shined down on the farm like a giant floodlight, and the property was dead silent except for a few chirping crickets. But when Roswell headed back to the house, he heard a strange noise behind him.

Tap, tap … Tap, tap … Tap, tap …

Roswell turned toward the sound but didn't see what it was coming from. Everything on the farm was perfectly still.

Tap, tap … Tap, tap … Tap, tap …

Roswell followed the noise across the farm. It got louder and louder the closer he walked to the fence at the edge of the property.

Tap, tap … Tap, tap … Tap, tap …

To his surprise, Roswell saw a fluffy, dark blob at the bottom of the fence. It was *Persephone*! She had gotten out of the shed somehow. The chicken was pecking at the metal mesh between the fence's wooden panels.

"Persephone? How did you get out here?" Roswell asked.

The chicken wasn't fazed by Roswell's voice and kept pecking.

Tap, tap…Tap, tap…Tap, tap…

"What the heck are you doing?" Roswell asked.

Slowly but surely the metal mesh came loose and formed an opening. Persephone crawled through the fence and waddled down the country road.

"Persephone! Get back here!" Roswell called. "A coyote is going to get you!"

He hurried across the farm and hopped over the fence. Roswell chased the chicken down the road, but Persephone was walking fast—he had never seen a chicken move so quickly before. Every time he got close to her, she either sped up or dodged him completely. Soon they were almost half a mile away from the farm. Roswell was winded, and sweat was dripping down his face. If his grandfather weren't so fond of her, he would have given up.

"I can't believe this!" he griped. "It's midnight and I'm chasing a chicken down the road! Could this day get any worse?"

Strangely, Persephone didn't seem like herself at all. Her strut was missing its usual bounce, her eyes were twice their normal size, and she moved with the determination of a marathon runner. If Roswell hadn't known any better, he might have thought the chicken was possessed.

Persephone followed the road to the top of a small hill and came to a dead stop. Roswell was grateful for the chance to catch his breath.

"What's wrong with you?" he panted. "Where do you think you're—"

BOOM! Suddenly the chicken was illuminated by a blinding white light. It shined down on her like a massive spotlight. Roswell screamed and had to shield his eyes.

"What the heck?!"

When his vision adjusted to the brightness, he saw the light was coming from something round and dark hovering in the sky. Roswell's brain knew exactly what the object was from the second he laid eyes on it, but he couldn't believe he was actually seeing it.

"No," he gasped. "It can't be!"

There was no denying it. *Roswell Johnson was staring at a real-life flying saucer!*

CHAPTER THREE

THE ACCIDENTAL ABDUCTION

Roswell couldn't move. He couldn't breathe. He couldn't think. He couldn't even *blink*. All he could do was stare up into the night sky. After a lifetime of speculating and questioning the unknown, confirmation of the world's most controversial theory was floating directly above his head.

"This can't be real," he said to himself. "I want this too much."

The flying saucer was a hundred feet long and fifty feet tall. It was perfectly symmetrical and made from a perfectly smooth silver material. A shallow dome poked out from the roof, giving the spacecraft the shape of a long-brimmed hat. The base of the saucer looked like a neon dartboard. Several multicolored lights spun around the spotlight shining over Persephone. Strangest of all, the saucer was completely silent. Roswell couldn't hear any engines or propellers keeping it afloat.

"I must be dreaming," he said. "Any moment now I'm going to wake up in my room.... Yup, any moment now... *aaaaany moment now...*"

Roswell pinched himself to speed up the process, but nothing changed. Once he realized he *wasn't* dreaming, Roswell convinced himself it was a hallucination.

"Obviously, the stressful day has pushed me over the edge, and I'm experiencing a psychotic break," he said. "The hallucination will eventually fade away.... Yup, any second now...*aaaaany second now...*"

However, the flying saucer never vanished. Roswell checked his head for injuries but didn't find any wounds. He tried to come up with another reasonable explanation, but he was out of excuses. The longer Roswell watched the spacecraft, the more reality sank in. His eyes grew wide, and a bewildered smile stretched across his face.

"Holy Steven Spielberg!" Roswell said. "This *is* real! I'm looking at a *FLYING SAUCER!*"

PURBADA-PURBADA-PURBADA-PURBADA! The silence was broken by a low humming noise. The blinding spotlight over Persephone began to flicker. To Roswell's horror, his grandfather's beloved chicken slowly rose off the ground and floated toward the spaceship! *Persephone was being abducted!*

"Persephone, snap out of it!" Roswell yelled. "You're being kidnapped by aliens! They've got you in a tractor beam!"

The chicken wasn't frightened at all. Persephone remained completely still and continued staring off with blank, bulging eyes. Roswell regained his senses and ran to her rescue. He leaped into the air and grabbed the chicken. However, instead of pulling her back to the ground, Roswell got caught in the tractor beam himself! He wiggled and jerked his limbs, desperate to escape, but he only rose higher and higher.

"You stupid chicken!" Roswell said. "Now they've got *both* of us!"

Roswell and Persephone were pulled through a small opening in the saucer's base. Once they were inside, the opening twisted shut beneath them. The country road, the Johnson Family Chicken Farm, and all of Cherokee Springs disappeared from sight.

The tractor beam was deactivated, and Roswell and Persephone landed on a shiny floor. He found himself in a circular chamber in the core of the spacecraft. It was a very bright space, and the whole ceiling was lit up like one giant light. Just like the outside of the saucer, the floor and walls were made from perfectly smooth silver material. The chamber was also wrapped with round windows like portholes on a cruise ship.

"*Oh my God! Oh my God! Oh my God!*" Roswell

panted. *"We've been abducted! We've been abducted! We've been abducted!"*

Still the chicken didn't seem bothered. Roswell's heart was pounding like a jackhammer. This was an experience he'd always wondered about, but now that it was happening to him, his body was pulsing with terror. Roswell searched the chamber for an exit, but there were no doors along the smooth silver walls. He tried to open a window, but they didn't budge, and the glass was too thick to crack. *He and Persephone were trapped!*

SHOOOOOSHEEEEEK! A rectangular table rose from the floor and lifted Persephone three feet into the air. *PSSSSSPOP!* Next, a spiral staircase descended from the ceiling like a turning corkscrew. Roswell heard voices and footsteps coming from above them. He quickly dived behind the table and hid.

"Follow me downstairs, Bleep, and I'll show you how we conduct an examination," said a voice. "After you've deactivated the tractor beam, you'll find the subject in the examination room. It's important to keep the hypnophaser on until the subject is returned—especially if the subject is a human."

"Beep-beep boop-boop?" asked a second voice.

"Because humans don't know we exist yet. If they wake up and see us, they might have a seizure or a heart attack. Or worse, they could poop themselves. Believe me, you don't want to travel across the galaxy with *that* smell lingering."

"Boop-boop."

The voices didn't sound masculine or feminine, but somewhere in between. Roswell peeked over the table and saw two pairs of gray feet climbing down the steps. To his utter amazement, *two extraterrestrials entered the chamber*!

"Holy Sigourney Weaver!" Roswell whispered. *"ALIENS!"*

The aliens looked exactly like he always thought they would. They had pale gray skin, huge egg-shaped heads, big black eyes, tiny mouths, and rail-thin torsos. They didn't have noses or ears, they were completely hairless, and they had only four digits on their hands. The aliens wore glossy black jumpsuits that covered their whole bodies. The only difference between the two was their height. The first alien was just under six feet, while the other was just over three feet tall.

"Once a subject is collected, we take a body scan and collect a DNA sample," the tall alien told the shorter one. "The scan will give us a health report and show any evolutionary changes. If we find anything useful in their DNA, we take the sample to the laboratories at home."

The tall alien pulled a lever on the wall, and a keypad popped out. They entered a code using the keypad's glowing green buttons. Suddenly a long silver cord slithered down from the ceiling like a metallic snake. The tip of the cord had a blue bulb that looked like a large eyeball. It emitted a blue laser and scanned Persephone up and down. Once the scan was finished, the cord retracted into the ceiling.

A moment later, a detailed hologram of Persephone was projected in front of the aliens. It revealed all the muscles, bones, and organs in her body. The aliens walked around the hologram and studied the chicken's anatomy. The tall alien took a close look at Persephone's brain.

"Good news! The scan found an evolutionary development. The bearded black silkie is developing an *attitude*. It's four generations away from being a complete jerk."

"Peep-peep poop-poop peep?"

"It's actually quite common on this planet. The same thing happened with cats and cuckoo birds."

"Boop-boop beep-beep boop-boop?"

"Yes, I *do* think it's ironic that chickens are direct descendants of the *Tyrannosaurus rex*. Earth's ultimate predator is now the ultimate entrée. Evolution has a sick sense of humor."

Roswell watched as the tall alien typed in a different code. Another cord snaked down from the ceiling with a very thin needle. The needle poked Persephone's wing and extracted a drop of blood. A moment later a second hologram appeared and showed a strand of the chicken's DNA. A small particle was highlighted with a yellow glow.

"Score! This chicken was born with a mutation that strengthens her immune system. The lab Grays will be thrilled!"

"Peep-peep poop-poop peep."

"I agree—Earth *is* a disgusting place. But what doesn't kill Earthlings makes them stronger. And what makes them stronger makes *us* stronger."

The tall alien entered another code. The opening in the floor twisted back open. Roswell saw the country road several yards below the spacecraft. With one quick somersault he could easily escape, but the fall might break every bone in his body.

PURBADA-PURBADA-PURBADA-PURBADA! The tractor beam was restarted. Persephone floated off the table and was lowered back to the road.

"After we complete the scan and collect the DNA, we return the subject to its habitat," the tall alien said. "You *must* return the subject to the exact spot they came from. It's against intergalactic law to 'disturb, disrupt, or displace' a stage-two life-form. Any 'interaction, interference, or indoctrination' must be approved by the Milky Way Galactic Alliance ahead of time. Once the subject returns home, the hypno-phaser will dissipate, and they won't remember a thing."

"Beep-beep boop-boop?"

"Yes, *occasionally* we'll get a subject with a strong subconscious. They'll remember bits and pieces of the examination. Luckily, the subjects usually think it was a dream, and their friends will think they're crazy if they mention it."

A third hologram appeared of a list written in a strange alien language. Each letter reminded Roswell of a tiny crop circle. The tall alien skimmed the list and added holographic check marks.

"Okay, let's take inventory. Albino rhinoceros? Check. Spotted giant squid? Check. Red panda? Check. Island forest frog? Check. Sea llama? Check. *Fun fact! Humans won't discover those for another fifty years.* And finally, bearded black silkie? Check. Well, we're finished with Earth. Time to collect DNA on the next planet."

The small alien put their hands on their hips.

"Peep-peep poop-poop peep!"

"I *know* you wanted to see Disneyland, but you spent too much time at Mardi Gras."

"Beep-beep boop-boop!"

"Don't swear at me! You should have listened when I said it was time to go. We can wear disguises and ride Big Thunder Mountain next time. Now come on. I'd like to get home before the galactic week ends."

The tall alien entered a final code into the keypad. *SHOOOOOSHEEEEEK!* The table sank back into the floor. *PSSSSSH!* The opening in the floor twisted shut. Roswell had nowhere to go and nowhere to hide!

Luckily, the aliens returned to the upper level before they noticed him.

"Don't panic. Don't panic. Don't panic," Roswell whispered to himself. "Deep breath, Roz...Everything is going to be okay....You've always said aliens are *peaceful* beings....You've always said they're here to *help* people....If you explain what happened, I'm sure they'll let you go....*What am I saying?! They might harvest my organs, for all I know!*"

"So long, Earth!" the tall alien called from the level above.

"Beep-beep boop!" the small alien said.

Roswell looked through a window and gasped—*the spacecraft was moving!* It was a complete surprise because the saucer felt perfectly still. The craft flew down the country road, moving faster and faster with every passing second.

"Oh gosh! Oh gosh! Oh gosh!" Roswell panted. *"This is NOT good!"*

The spacecraft soared above Cherokee Springs, flying at speeds Roswell didn't think were physically possible. It zoomed into the night sky, rising higher and higher. Soon all the light pollution faded outside the window. Roswell saw thousands of sparkling stars and the clearest view of the Milky Way he had ever seen.

"We've left Earth's atmosphere!" he said in disbelief. "I'm in *SPACE!*"

Before he could process what was happening, the spacecraft rocketed past the moon. Roswell was close enough to see the details of each crater on the ashy surface. They reminded him of pepperonis on a slice of pizza. A moment later Earth and the moon disappeared far behind them.

Roswell was in complete shock. If his eyes were telling him the truth, that meant he—*Roswell Johnson, an eleven-year-old from Cherokee Springs, Oklahoma*—had traveled farther from Earth than any human in recorded history!

"We're approaching Mars," the tall alien announced.

"Beep-beep boop-boop beep?"

"Nothing lives there now, but humans are planning to colonize it."

"Peep-peep poop peep?"

"I bet it takes them a century to build the first Martian base but only a week to build the first Martian Starbucks."

"Beeeepbeepbeepbeep!" The small alien laughed.

Sure enough, Mars whizzed by Roswell's window. The spacecraft passed the red planet so quickly it was gone in the blink of an eye. A few moments later the saucer zigzagged through the rocky field of the asteroid belt. Roswell was terrified the craft would collide with one of the enormous rocks, but the saucer glided through the asteroid field with ease.

After they left the asteroid belt, it took only a minute for the spacecraft to reach the *next* spectacular sight. A gargantuan planet appeared in the distance with dozens of tiny moons. Several stripes of brown, beige, and orange gases circled the surface like flavors of a multilayered cake. Roswell instantly recognized the planet thanks to the massive red spot in its southern hemisphere.

"Beep-beep! Beep-beep!"

"We are *not* taking a joy ride through Jupiter's Great Red Spot!" the tall alien said.

"Peep-peep poop-poop-poop peep."

"I don't care if the other trainees did it—we're on a tight schedule."

"Beep-beep boop beep-beep."

"I don't need a best friend."

"Peeeeeeeeeeeeeep?"

"Ugh! We'll go in for five minutes. But that's it!"

"Beep-beep!"

"You're welcome. Now fasten your seat belt. It's more fun when the gravity is off."

POOOOOVE! A gentle vibration rumbled through the spacecraft. Roswell felt his stomach rise toward his chest. Soon his entire body floated off the floor and hovered in the air. He waved his arms and kicked his legs, trying to grab hold of something, but everything was out of reach.

"They can't be serious!" Roswell said. "Jupiter's red spot is the most powerful cyclone in the solar system! It'll tear us apart!"

Before Roswell could voice his concerns to the aliens, the spacecraft dived toward Jupiter's colorful surface. The saucer plunged into the Great Red Spot and sank into a sea of scarlet clouds. The treacherous storm was unimaginably violent. The winds tossed the saucer back and forth, hurtling the spacecraft thousands of miles in every direction. The craft was rattling so hard Roswell worried it would get shaken apart.

"Woo-hoo!"

"Beep-beep!"

The aliens cheered and applauded like they were on a roller coaster. Meanwhile, Roswell was thrown across the examination chamber. He slammed into the silver walls and bright ceiling like he was in a pinball machine.

"*DEAR—GOD—PLEASE—MAKE—THIS— STOP!*" Roswell cried.

"We've had our fun. Let's get back to work."

"Boop-boop."

VOOOOOP! The artificial gravity returned and Roswell hit the shiny floor. The spacecraft left Jupiter's Great Red Spot, completely unscathed. Roswell, on the other hand, felt like he had been hit by a bus. He had had enough space travel for one lifetime—if Roswell didn't get off the craft soon, he might get killed!

Once he'd caught his breath and built up the courage, Roswell slowly crawled up the spiral staircase. He stuck his head through the ceiling and peeked into the level above.

From what he could tell, the dome at the top of the saucer was a cockpit. A long dashboard wrapped around the whole room with thousands of glowing gears and blinking controls. There were 3D maps of the solar system, and holograms of nearby planets and moons. Although the dome had looked completely solid on the outside, the inside of the cockpit was as clear as glass. The room offered a 360-degree view of the universe surrounding them.

The aliens were seated in oval chairs that hovered a foot off the floor. The tall alien was steering the spacecraft with a sphere built into the dashboard. The small alien pressed buttons and pulled gears beside them.

Roswell was so nervous he could barely speak.

"Excuse me? Sir? Ma'am? Alien?" he asked in a faint voice. "Pardon my interruption, but I don't think I'm supposed to be..."

Roswell suddenly went speechless—but this time from *wonder.* The spacecraft was approaching the planet Saturn, and it was the most beautiful sight Roswell had ever seen. Saturn looked like it was painted in gold, and its gigantic rings glowed like pure sunshine. Roswell knew the rings were made of rock and icy particles, but up close it was like the planet had been crowned with millions of angelic halos. Photographs could never capture the sheer magnificence Roswell was witnessing with his own eyes. It made him forget about absolutely everything else in the galaxy.

"I'm going to slingshot the ship around Saturn," the tall alien said. "It'll give us a boost and help us make up time."

"Beep-beep."

The tall alien rolled the steering sphere forward, and the spacecraft glided toward Saturn. The saucer circled the planet, following its rings like a car on a racetrack. The craft became locked in Saturn's orbit and was pulled faster and faster around it. Soon the saucer was spinning so fast everything outside became one golden blur.

"Departing in five...four...three...two...*ONE!*"

The tall alien hit a red button on the dashboard. The spacecraft rocketed straight forward and broke free from Saturn's gravitational pull. They were flung into the depths of space, and they soared beyond Uranus and Neptune in a matter of seconds. The giant planets passed the saucer as quickly as oncoming traffic on a freeway.

It was that moment when Roswell hit his mental limit. Knowing he was inside an alien spaceship...Knowing he was traveling faster than the speed of light...Knowing he was two billion miles away from home...it was all too much for his brain to handle.

Roswell's eyes rolled into the back of his head, he collapsed on the floor, and everything went dark....

CHAPTER FOUR

THE TRUTH IS OUT THERE

Roswell was having the *craziest* nightmare. He dreamed he had accidentally been abducted by aliens and taken across the solar system in a flying saucer. Roswell had dreamed similar scenarios in the past, but *this* dream was so vivid it almost felt real.

As he slowly stirred to life, Roswell felt something strange under his body. Instead of his cushy twin bed, he was lying on a very solid surface. His eyes fluttered open and he discovered he was not in his bedroom, but in an extremely bright chamber. Once his eyes adjusted to the light, he noticed a pair of familiar faces staring down at him. However, the enormous heads, the big black eyes, and the pale gray skin did *not* belong to Gram and Pop.

It wasn't a dream after all.

"AAAAAAAAAAH!" Roswell screamed.

"AAAAAAAAAAH!" the aliens screamed back.

Roswell jumped off the examination table and backed against the wall.

"Thank the Source! He's alive!" the tall alien said.

"Don't touch me!" Roswell yelled. "I'm warning you! *I know karate!*"

It was a complete lie, but he clenched his fists and swung his arms anyway.

"Beep-beep boop-boop?"

"It's a form of self-defense on Earth," the tall alien said.

"Peep-peep poop-poop?"

"I think he's trying to intimidate us."

"Beep-beep boop."

"I agree—not at all."

Roswell slid to the floor and shielded himself with his trembling arms.

"Please don't hurt me!" he pleaded. "I'm only a child!"

The tall alien rubbed their temples and frantically walked in circles.

"This is a complete disaster! *There is a conscious Earthling on our craft!* Do you know how many rules this violates? Do you know how much trouble we'll get into if anyone finds out about this? How did he even get on the ship?"

"You abducted me with the chicken!" Roswell said.

The tall alien crossed their arms and glared at the small alien.

"Bleep? Did you check the bio-radar before you turned on the tractor beam?"

The small alien shrugged innocently. "Boop-boop."

"What do you mean '*oopsie*'? I specifically told you *not* to abduct the chicken unless there were no other life-forms nearby!"

"Beep-beep boop-boop?"

"Yes, this is a big deal! We just broke intergalactic law!"

"Peep-peep peep-peep poop?"

"We can't drop him off on Pluto! What's the matter with you?"

"Beep-beep boop-boop beep?"

"I'm thinking! I'm thinking! I know there's a protocol for this." The tall alien paced in more circles while they thought. "Okay, I remember! The protocol is to erase the subject's memory, return them to their planet, and then report the incident when we get home."

"What?!" Roswell cried. "Don't erase my memory!"

"Bleep, you go upstairs and turn the ship around. I'll fire up the de-memorizer."

"Whoa, whoa, whoa!" Roswell said. "Time out! Can we talk about this first?"

"Beep-beep boop-boop beep?"

"Only *mild* brain damage—like drinking too much diet

soda," the tall alien said. "He'll wake up tomorrow and won't remember any of this."

"No!" Roswell said. "You don't have to do this! I promise your secret is safe with me!"

"Poor thing. His mind won't handle much more. We've got to zap him before he has a heart attack or a seizure."

"Peep-peep poop-poop!"

"I don't want him to poop his pants either! So hurry!"

"STOP TALKING ABOUT ME LIKE I'M NOT HERE!" Roswell shouted. "Listen to me! I'm *not* going to have a heart attack, I'm *not* going to have a seizure, and I'm definitely *not* going to poop my pants! In fact, for someone who's been abducted, propelled across space, assaulted by Jupiter, and spun around Saturn, I think I'm handling this quite well, *thank you very much*!"

"You mean, you're not terrified beyond belief?" the tall alien asked.

"That depends. Are you going to kill me?"

"No."

"Experiment on me?"

"No."

"Probe me?"

"That happened *one time* and it was an accident!"

"Are you going to harvest my organs and eat them?"

"Ewww! Kid, the only thing that's gonna hurt you is that sick imagination!"

Roswell was relieved to hear it. Now that he wasn't in

immediate danger, he smiled and looked around the examination room with a newfound excitement.

"In that case, this is the most amazing thing that's ever happened to me!"

The aliens tilted their heads like confused puppies.

"Come again?"

"This might sound crazy, but *I'm your biggest fan!*" Roswell confessed. "I've been studying extraterrestrials and UFOs my entire life! *And now here you are!* That's why you can't erase my memory! I can't go back now!"

"I'm sorry, kid, but we don't have a choice," the tall alien said. "There are things your planet isn't supposed to know yet. We could get into serious trouble with the Milky Way Galactic Alliance if we don't follow the rules."

"What's the Milky Way Galactic Alliance?" Roswell asked.

"It's like Earth's United Nations but much, *much* bigger."

"Beep-beep boop-boop."

"I agree—the gift shop is nicer too."

"Where is the alliance located?" Roswell asked. "Is it on a planet? A spaceship?"

"The Milky Way Galactic Alliance is in Star City," the tall alien explained. "It's a megastructure built around the biggest star in the center of our galaxy—*wait, what am I doing? I shouldn't be telling you any of this!*"

Roswell grunted. "Oh, come on! You're going to erase

my memory anyway, right? The least you could do is answer a few questions after kidnapping me!"

"What's the point in answering questions you'll only forget?" the tall alien asked.

A lump came to Roswell's throat. It was difficult for him to explain.

"Because…because…because I finally know what it feels like to be *right*," he said. "You don't understand, everyone thinks I'm crazy for believing in you. But now I know my life *hasn't* been a complete waste of time! So even if I don't remember it later, I've *got* to know more. Even if it only lasts a moment, I'd give anything for a moment of knowing the secrets of the universe. Please?"

Roswell could tell the aliens were surprised by how emotional he'd become. They looked to each other and shrugged.

"Beep-beep boop-boop beep-beep."

"No—I suppose a *couple* questions wouldn't hurt," the tall alien said. "You've got five minutes, kid. Ask away."

Roswell was so thrilled he became light-headed. His mind was racing with so many questions it took him a minute to choose one.

"Okay…um…where are we?" he asked.

"We're between Pluto and the Oort cloud," the tall alien said.

"The OORT CLOUD?!"

"It's a collection of icy particles at the very end of your solar system."

"I know what the Oort cloud is! I just can't believe—wow—*the Oort cloud*! Gosh, this is so cool! Okay, next question. Who are you guys?"

"I'm Commander Nerp, and this is my trainee, Bleep."

"Peep-peep *poop*!"

"I think *friends* is a strong word."

"And where are you from?" Roswell asked.

"We're Grays from the planet Grayton. We come in peace."

"Beep boop beep boop."

"I know that's a cliché saying! Old habits die hard!"

"Are you male? Female? Nonbinary?" Roswell asked.

"We're genderless, actually," Nerp said. "Our species has been genetically altered to eliminate all useless appendages and biological hassles. No hair, no sinuses, no ears, no nails, no genitalia, no pinkies—*no problems*."

"Then how do you reproduce?" Roswell asked.

"Grays are grown in laboratories. It's way less messy than the human approach. Think of all the time Earthlings waste with mating and dating and pairing off. That's why Grays travel the universe collecting DNA. Whenever we find something beneficial, we incorporate it into our own biology. We're the most genetically advanced species in the Milky Way."

"How old are you?" Roswell asked.

"Even on our planet, that's kind of a rude question."

"Sorry! Um...how long is a Gray's life span?"

"Since we genetically enhance our bodies, we don't age like human beings. We only perish if something goes wrong, like a crash or bad shellfish."

"Why is Bleep smaller than you?" Roswell asked.

"Small Grays are younger and shorter than Tall Grays."

"Why don't they speak?"

"What do you mean? Bleep doesn't shut up."

"Beep-beep."

"That *wasn't* a compliment."

"I mean, why can't I understand Bleep?" Roswell asked.

"It takes Small Grays several Earth centuries to grow and develop their frontal lobes. Once Bleep reaches my height, they'll speak every language in the galaxy."

"So there are *more* aliens out there? It's not just Grays and Earthlings?"

Nerp and Bleep chuckled like he was making a joke.

"Peep poop peep-peep?"

"Oh—he *is* being serious," Nerp said.

"Well? How many alien species are there?" Roswell asked.

Apparently, the Tall Gray needed help answering *this* question. Instead of giving him a verbal answer, Nerp entered a code into the glowing keypad, and the bright examination chamber went dark. A hologram of Roswell's solar system appeared. Earth was the only planet high-lighted in a yellow glow.

"This is Earth—the only inhabited planet in your solar system," Nerp said. "And *these* are all the inhabited planets in the Milky Way galaxy."

The hologram expanded to show the entire Milky Way. The spiral galaxy filled every inch of the examination chamber. To Roswell's amazement, he was surrounded by thousands and thousands of glowing yellow specks.

"There must be a million of them!" Roswell said in disbelief.

"Millions, actually. And *these* are all the inhabited planets in the known universe."

The hologram expanded even more and showed all the galaxies in the universe. The Milky Way shrank smaller and smaller, eventually becoming microscopic. There was so much life in the known universe that the hologram turned into one enormous yellow glow. Roswell was speechless as he gazed around the chamber.

"There are over ten million intelligent species in the Milky Way galaxy and over one hundred trillion intelligent species in the known universe," Nerp said. "And since the universe is constantly growing, new species are discovered every day."

"Unbelievable!" Roswell said. "Why doesn't Earth know about this?"

"That's by design," Nerp explained. "Every planet in the

known universe is categorized into one of three stages. A stage-one planet hosts nonintelligent life-forms, like bacteria and small insects. A stage-two planet hosts semi-intelligent life-forms, like animals and human beings. *No offense, I don't make up the terms.* And a stage-three planet hosts ultra-intelligent life-forms, like me and Bleep. *Well, like me at least.* Once a stage-two planet evolves into a stage-three planet, it's invited to join its local galactic alliance. Every galaxy has its own alliance, and all the galactic alliances in the known universe are part of the Great Universal Alliance."

"How does a stage-two planet become a stage-three planet?"

"There are two qualifications. First, a stage-two planet must be peaceful and self-sustainable. Second, its life-forms must develop their own technology to discover and travel to their local galactic alliance. Until those requirements are met, every stage-two planet will stay in the dark."

"Peep-peep poop-poop peep-peep."

"I agree, Bleep—good hygiene isn't required, but it should be."

"Do stage-three planets help stage-two planets evolve?" Roswell asked.

"It's against intergalactic law for a stage-three planet to 'disturb, disrupt, or displace' the life-forms or ecosystems of a stage-one or stage-two planet. Any 'interaction, interference, or indoctrination' must be approved by the local galactic alliance ahead of time. Sometimes, if a planet shows potential, a galactic alliance will share resources to speed up the planet's evolution. Or if a planet is in danger, a galactic alliance will save it. Otherwise, each planet must be left alone to evolve or suffer the consequences of its actions."

"Has the Milky Way Galactic Alliance ever shared resources with Earth?"

"Many times! We taught the Neanderthals how to hunt and garden. We taught native and indigenous people how to build and govern. We've also secretly tipped off philosophers and scientists over the years. We convinced Socrates to give his first speech, we made Thomas Edison afraid of the dark, and we put the mold on Alexander Fleming's petri dish."

"Beep-beep boop-boop beep-beep."

"That's right, Bleep—we *also* helped the Boston Red Sox win the 2004 World Series. Someone had to."

"Has the Milky Way Galactic Alliance ever saved Earth?" Roswell asked.

"Oh, please! Earth is like a child running with scissors. We've stopped more asteroids than you could count, we stopped a second ice age from occurring, we stopped the bubonic plague from spreading worldwide, and we stopped the hole in the ozone layer from growing."

"Peep-peep poop-poop peep poop peep."

"That's right, Bleep—we *also* stopped the actor Matt Damon from going into American politics. Again, someone had to."

"Was there anything the Milky Way Galactic Alliance *didn't* save Earth from?" Roswell asked.

"Unfortunately, there were a number of times we voted *not* to intervene. We didn't stop the asteroid that killed the dinosaurs, we didn't stop Atlantis from sinking, and we didn't stop the development of nuclear weapons. *Fingers crossed that one pans out.* Galactic alliances don't intervene when a stage-two planet becomes hostile or poses a threat to other planets. Sometimes, learning lessons the hard way is the only way a planet evolves."

"Why do the galactic alliances help stage-one and stage-two planets at all? What do you guys get out of it?"

"Beep-boop beep-boop boop-boop."

"I agree—that's *such* an Earthling question," Nerp said.

"What's that supposed to mean?" Roswell asked.

"Earth hasn't figured this out yet, but the more potential you give, the more potential you get. Who knows how many great discoveries are still waiting to be discovered? Who knows how many great creations are still waiting to be created? And who knows where they'll come from or who will make them? The more planets with intelligence and resources, the faster we'll *all* benefit. Earth should be in the Milky Way Galactic Alliance by now, but sadly,

Earthlings are more focused on tearing one another apart than advancing themselves. Source only knows if that'll change."

"Who's Source? Are they an alien?"

The Tall Gray gasped. "Did this kid just ask who the *Source* is?"

"Beep-beep boop-boop."

"Yes—bless his human heart."

"Could you enlighten his human brain first?" Roswell asked.

"The Source is everything and anything around you. It's the past, the present, and the future. It's the force that created our universe and all the universes beyond it. It wrote the laws of space, time, and physics. The Source was the spark that started the big bang, it was the seed that sprouted life, it was the cradle of consciousness, and it was the energy that initiated intelligence. Even with all the knowledge and technology in the universe today, no one knows the source of the Source. It's the greatest mystery of all time."

Roswell was practically euphoric as he listened to Nerp. Most exciting of all, his theories about extraterrestrials were true! Aliens *were* peaceful beings, and they *had* helped mankind throughout history. However, the more he learned, the more bittersweet it became. The validation coursing through his veins was only temporary. By this time tomorrow he wouldn't remember a thing.

"Well, that's the universe in a nutshell," Nerp said. "Now we *really* need to take you back to Earth. We've got a lot of mileage to make up."

Roswell let out a deep, disappointed sigh.

"I understand," he said softly. "Let's get it over with."

"Don't worry, you won't feel a thing."

The alien typed another code into the keypad. A long cord descended from the ceiling and placed a silver bowl on top of Roswell's head.

"Pay attention to this next part, Bleep," the Tall Gray said. "Before you erase a subject's memory, you have to check their status in the Galactic Registry."

"Beep-beep boop-boop beep-beep-beep?"

"The Galactic Registry is a list of stage-two life-forms with stage-three clearance. It's against intergalactic law to erase their memories. Earthlings rarely make the Galactic Registry—just a few military officials, Shirley MacLaine, and David Bowie so far—but it's still mandatory to check."

"You know who David Bowie is?" Roswell asked.

"Everyone in the galaxy knows who David Bowie is," Nerp said. "Extraterrestrials are obsessed with Earthling culture. Despite your aggressive ways, Earth has some of the best music, stories, artwork, and cuisine in the galaxy."

"Beep-beep boop-boop beep-beep-beep!"

"You're right—the *Kentacohut* is a remarkable culinary achievement."

The Tall Gray entered a code to get the de-memorizer ready.

"What's your name, age, and place of birth, kid?" they asked.

"Roswell Johnson. Eleven years old. Cherokee Springs, Oklahoma."

Nerp did a double take. "Your name is *Roswell*? Like the tragedy?"

"No, it's Roswell like the greatest government conspiracy of all—oh, wait. I suppose it was a tragedy to you guys. I never thought about it that way."

"Peep-peep poop peep-peep."

"Yes, Bleep—we *did* lose a lot of good Grays in that crash," Nerp said.

The Grays lowered their heads for a quick moment to pay their respects. Afterward, Nerp typed Roswell's information into the keypad. A moment later a life-size hologram of Roswell was projected. To the aliens' surprise, a large green check mark appeared beside him.

"That *can't* be right," Nerp said.

The Tall Gray reentered Roswell's information into the keypad. Once again Roswell's hologram appeared with the green check mark beside it.

"Beep-beep boop-boop beep?"

"Don't look at me—I'm just as confused as you are!"

"Is something wrong?" Roswell asked.

"*You're* in the Galactic Registry!"

"*What?!*" Roswell asked in disbelief. "But...but... *how*?!"

"There's only one way to find out."

Nerp entered another code. *BUUUUUBEEEEEP!* A silver pole rose from the center of the floor. The pole held a white orb that was made from an alien crystal. The examination chamber went dim, and the de-memorizer started to vibrate on Roswell's head. The crystal orb shined like a disco ball and projected thousands of tiny squares onto the circular wall.

Roswell looked closely at one of the squares—each of them was a different moving image! It was like the orb was playing thousands of small movies at once. As Roswell watched the strange videos, the images became more and more familiar.

"Wait a second... *these are moments from my life!*" he exclaimed.

"The de-memorizer is scanning your hippocampus and projecting your memories," Nerp explained. "I'm going to search through them and find out why you're in the Galactic Registry."

Roswell recognized most of the memories instantly. He saw the *Star Trek*–themed cake from his fourth birthday....He saw his classmates and the zoo animals from a kindergarten field trip....He saw the baseball field and the crowd from his first T-ball game....He saw the day

Pop taught him how to drive a tractor....He saw the evening Gram sewed him into his Chewbacca Halloween costume....He saw the nights he and his father read about alien conspiracies....

There were also memories Roswell didn't remember at all: He was lying in a crib at the hospital and could see Gram and Pop waving at him through a window....His father was feeding him baby food and pretending the spoon was an airplane....He was sitting in Pop's lap while he read him a bedtime story....And he was splashing around in a bubble bath while Gram tried to wash him.

Then Roswell found a memory he didn't know existed until now: His mother was hugging him very tight.... Tears were spilling down her pretty face....She looked scared and very, very tired....She kept repeating the same message....

"Please don't forget me....Please don't forget me.... Please don't forget me...."

Unfortunately, there were bad memories too. Roswell saw the afternoon two men in military uniforms came to the farmhouse....They said his father had died while protecting a civilian family in Afghanistan....His grandparents held him on the sofa until he cried himself to sleep.... Gram wouldn't accept her son was gone....She didn't want his photo in the house and told Pop to hang it in the chicken shed....

"I just don't believe it....I just don't believe it," she cried.

"This doesn't make any sense," Nerp said. "None of these memories explain why you're in the registry. Bleep and I are the only stage-three beings you've ever been in contact with!"

"Beep-beep boop-boop."

"I agree—it must be a glitch."

"Peep-peep poop-poop?"

"We'll take him to Grayton and figure this out."

Roswell gasped. "I get to see your home planet?!"

BWAAAAAMP! BWAAAAAMP! BWAAAAAMP! Before Roswell could get too excited, a deafening siren blared from the cockpit. Nerp and Bleep hurried up the spiral stairs, and Roswell followed them. When they arrived, the cockpit was covered in strobing red lights.

"Are we sinking or something?" Roswell asked.

"The radar has detected an aggressive species nearby," Nerp said.

"Aggressive? Like a *bad* alien?"

"Exactly."

"I thought you said stage-three planets can't be hostile!"

"Yes, to *join* a galactic alliance—that doesn't mean they all *want* to."

Roswell peered into the starry space ahead. The Oort cloud sat at the edge of his solar system like a snowy mist. As the saucer flew closer, Roswell could make out the individual particles of ice. Some were as small as the spacecraft, while others were the size of mountains. However, something *else* was among the icy field that didn't belong.

A fleet of spaceships lurked between the particles like predators in a thick forest. There were hundreds of them—maybe thousands! They were the same size as the flying saucer, but unlike the Grays' smooth and symmetrical craft, these spaceships were jagged and dark green. They reminded Roswell of giant tortoise shells—he half expected monstrous amphibians to emerge from the spacecraft, but luckily, no such creature appeared.

"Shellcrafts!" Nerp declared. "What are the Reptoids doing here?!"

"Who?" Roswell asked.

"Beep-beep boop!"

"I agree—a *despicable* species! The Reptoids were kicked out of the Milky Way Galactic Alliance because of their vile and violent behavior. They destroyed their home planet, Reptoidia, several millennia ago thanks to their greedy and wasteful ways. Now the Reptoids travel the galaxy like nomads and strip other planets of their resources to survive."

"What are they doing in the Oort cloud?" Roswell asked.

Before he got an answer, the whole saucer suddenly jerked forward. It was like the craft had been hit by an invisible baseball bat. *BWAAAAAMP! BWAAAAAMP! BWAAAAAMP!* The blaring alarms quadrupled, and the Grays looked around in terror. *BWAAAAAMP! BWAAAAAMP! BWAAAAAMP!* Nerp tried to spin the steering sphere, but the saucer only moved closer and closer to the Reptoids' shellcrafts.

"The Reptoids have us in a tractor beam! They're taking our ship by force!"

"By *force*?! What the heck does that mean?" Roswell asked.

"It means buckle up! We're all getting abducted now!"

CHAPTER FIVE

THE MOST DESPICABLE SPECIES IN THE GALAXY

BWAAAAAMP! BWAAAAAMP! BWAAAAAMP! Roswell had never heard so many alarms go off at once. *BWAAAAAMP! BWAAAAAMP! BWAAAAAMP!* The cockpit was covered in more flashing lights than a nightclub. *BWAAAAAMP! BWAAAAAMP! BWAAAAAMP!* The sirens were so loud Roswell could barely hear himself think. *BWAAAAAMP! BWAAAAAMP! BWAAAAAMP!* The strobing lights were so bright he could hardly see.

"Come on, you stupid saucer! It's a tractor beam, not a black hole!" Nerp yelled.

The alien used all their strength to spin the steering sphere, but the saucer didn't budge.

"What do they want with us?!" Roswell asked.

"I doubt it's to ask for directions!" Nerp said.

"Are we in danger? Are they going to *hurt* us?!"

"I don't know—but the Reptoids aren't known for their hospitality!"

BWAAAAAMP! BWAAAAAMP! BWAAAAAMP! Nerp pressed a button on the dashboard, and a third oval chair rose from the floor. *BWAAAAAMP! BWAAAAAMP! BWAAAAAMP!* The alien pushed Roswell into the seat, and the buckles fastened across his chest and waist.

"Hold on, kid! It might get bumpy!" Nerp warned. "Bleep, prepare the hyperbooster!"

BWAAAAAMP! BWAAAAAMP! BWAAAAAMP! Roswell clutched the chair so tight his knuckles went numb. *BWAAAAAMP! BWAAAAAMP! BWAAAAAMP!* Bleep pressed the buttons on the dashboard like they were playing a piano. *BWAAAAAMP! BWAAAAAMP! BWAAAAAMP!* The small alien gave Nerp a thumbs-up when the engines were ready.

"Beep-beep!"

"We launch in five...four...three...two...*ONE!*

Nerp slammed a big red button on the dashboard. *VOOOOOSH!* For the first time since boarding the craft, Roswell felt the engines roar beneath him. The saucer thrust backward, but the extra boost wasn't powerful enough to escape the Reptoids' tractor beam.

"Now what?!" Roswell asked.

"Bleep, send out a distress signal!" Nerp instructed. "Say we're on the edge of the Earthling solar system and the Reptoids are taking us captive!"

"*Captive?*" Roswell asked. "You mean they're taking us *prisoner*?!"

"What would you call this?! An invitation to brunch?!"

BAAAAAM! The saucer was struck by something that looked like a bolt of lightning. All the alarms went dead silent and the warning lights shut off. The 3D maps, holograms, and glowing buttons on the dashboard flickered and faded. The saucer drifted toward the Reptoids in complete darkness.

"They fried our engines!" Nerp yelled.

"What are we going to do?" Roswell cried.

"Peep-peep poop peep-peep!"

"Don't tell him to kiss *that* goodbye! Watch your mouth in front of children!"

"Seriously though!" Roswell said. *"I'm freaking out over here!"*

Nerp turned a paler shade of gray. "Does your family practice any religions on Earth?"

"I think my great-uncle was a Christian pastor!"

"Then start praying someone gets our distress signal!"

The tractor beam pulled the saucer deeper and deeper

into the Oort cloud. They passed hundreds of Reptoidian shellcrafts, but Roswell couldn't tell where their saucer was being taken. A moment later he had the answer. A Reptoidian spacecraft the size of a football stadium appeared in the distance. Just like the rest of the fleet, the gigantic spaceship looked like a massive tortoise shell.

"They're taking us to their *mother ship*!" Nerp exclaimed.

"Beep-beep boop-boop beep-beep?!"

"Yes, that's where the Reptiliz lives!"

"What's a Reptiliz?!" Roswell asked.

"The Reptoids are ruled by the Reptiliz Supreme! Reptiliz Reek VII is currently on the throne. He's the most ruthless and vengeful tyrant in the galaxy!"

"Peep-peep poop-poop peep-peep!"

"I agree—General Xelic is even worse!"

"Who?!" Roswell asked.

"General Xelic is the commander of the Reptoidian Army. He does all of Reptiliz Reek's dirty work. The Milky Way Galactic Alliance has tried to put the general behind bars for eons, but Xelic is very clever with his crimes. Although he's broken every law in the known universe, the alliance has never found any evidence to properly charge him."

Roswell gulped. "I'm sorry I asked."

The front of the mother ship opened like an enormous set of teeth. Roswell felt like a guppy being swallowed by a giant shark. The saucer was pulled inside the mother ship's massive hangar, which resembled the stomach of a gigantic creature more than a chamber in a spaceship. The floor was covered in dark green scales, and the walls were rugged like the skin of an avocado. The hangar was also covered in strange vines that grew across the floor and up the walls. Roswell couldn't tell if they were plants, wires, or—most concerning of all—*veins*. Several rows of shellcrafts were parked inside the hangar, ready to go at a moment's notice.

CRAAAAANK! The entrance slammed shut behind the saucer. *BAAAAAM!* Artificial gravity made the saucer hit the floor. *SHOOOOOSH!* The hangar filled with oxygen. The Reptoidian air had a greenish haze and the stench of rotting eggs.

WHAAAAAM! A wide door opened like a drawbridge, and twelve Reptoidian soldiers marched in. Each soldier was over seven feet tall and had a very broad body. They wore heavy scaled armor and masks with spikes at the ears and mouth. They carried sharp spears that buzzed with bright green electricity. The soldiers surrounded the saucer and aimed their weapons at the craft.

"Come out with your hands, claws, paws, fins, or synthetic appendages up!"

Roswell and the Grays looked to one another in terror.

"Let me do all the talking," Nerp said.

"Beep-beep boop?"

"Especially *you*! This is no time for sarcasm!"

"We're not seriously going out there, are we?" Roswell asked.

"We don't have a choice. Resisting will only make things worse."

Nerp climbed down to the examination chamber, and Roswell and Bleep reluctantly followed them. The Tall Gray pulled a lever on the wall, and the silver floor lowered like a ramp. Nerp took a deep breath and then charged out of the saucer.

"This is outrageous!" they shouted. "Who do you Reptoids think you are? Just wait until the Milky Way Galactic Alliance finds out you attacked my ship and forced us aboard your—"

ZAAAAASH! A soldier zapped Nerp with their electric spear. The Tall Gray collapsed and convulsed on the floor. Before Roswell and Bleep could help Nerp, the soldiers threw them onto the floor beside their quivering friend.

"The alliance *won't* find out."

The gruff voice came out of nowhere and echoed through the hangar. All the soldiers immediately stood at attention, and they crossed their arms over their chests in a Reptoidian salute. Another Reptoid stepped out from the shadows and lurched toward Roswell and the Grays. The sight was so chilling Roswell thought he had been electrocuted too.

"Ge-Ge-General Xelic!" Nerp sputtered on the ground.

The Reptoidian general was over nine feet tall and much broader than the other Reptoids. From the top of his head to the tips of his pointed fingers, Xelic was covered in scaly pea-green skin. He had piercing yellow eyes with narrow black pupils, two slits for nostrils, and a wide purple mouth. A fin stuck out from his skull like a razor-sharp mohawk, and a thick tail swung behind his legs. Just like his soldiers, the general wore scaled armor, but his uniform was much more decorated. He had spiked shoulder pads, a flowing black cape, and a collection of badges across his chest, and two sets of claws pierced through his tall boots. Xelic's long, muscular arms were exposed, showing off two biceps on each limb.

General Xelic glared at Roswell and the Grays like a hungry snake.

"Well, well, well—who do we have here?"

The Reptoid flicked his forked tongue and tasted the air.

"Smells like we've caught two Grays and…is that an *Earthling* I see? You'd think we were playing *inferior-species bingo*."

The Reptoidian soldiers hissed with laughter.

"What is the meaning of this?" Nerp said. "What are you doing in this solar system?!"

"I'm afraid that question has a need-to-know answer," the general said. "If we told you, we'd have to kill you. Oh, who am I kidding? We'll probably kill you anyway. But I hate ruining a good surprise."

"You can't do this! You're breaking intergalactic law!"

General Xelic leaned over Nerp with a menacing smile, exposing his sharp yellow teeth.

"I make my own laws," he whispered.

The comment sent shivers down Roswell's spine. He had never encountered anyone so terrifying. Even Mayor Shallows seemed like a kitten compared to the Reptoidian general.

"The Milky Way Galactic Alliance will never let you get away with this!" Nerp warned.

"And who's going to tell them?" the general scoffed. "By the time the alliance catches wind of our little *operation*, it'll be too late. And sadly, the three of you will be long gone."

"You'll pay for this, Xelic!"

"Take them away!" the general ordered.

The soldiers seized Roswell and the Grays by the collars. The Reptoids dragged the prisoners across the hangar to a large hole in the wall. The opening puckered, then opened wider as they approached, like the mouth of a hungry fish. The soldiers threw Roswell and the Grays into the hole, and they slid down a long, slimy tube on the other side. They screamed as they slipped deeper and deeper into the mother ship with no end in sight.

Finally the prisoners came to an abrupt stop. Roswell and the Grays were dropped into a dark and muddy chamber. They landed in a pile, and the tube sealed shut above them. They groaned from the rough landing and rubbed their injured limbs. Roswell helped the Grays to their feet, but Nerp could barely stand after being electrocuted.

"Are you okay, Nerp?" Roswell asked.

"I can't feel my toes or my fingers, but I'll live," they said.

"Beep-beep boop beep-beep beep-boop!"

"For once, I agree with your profanity—the Reptoids *are* a bunch of those."

Roswell looked around the dark chamber. They were surrounded by crisscross bars that buzzed with the same green electricity in the Reptoids' spears. A row of moldy boulders was the only place to sit or lie down. The muddy floor was covered in alien bones—at least, Roswell assumed they were bones; the remains weren't shaped like human parts.

"This must be a prison cell," he said.

"It's definitely not the Four Seasons," Nerp said.

"Peep-peep poop peep-peep poop."

"I agree—it does remind me of that hostel in Amsterdam."

"Are the Reptoids going to kill us?! Are we going to *die* here?" Roswell asked.

"No one's ever been captured by the Reptoids and lived to tell the tale. Like I said, the general knows how to cover his tracks."

Roswell was so frightened he began hyperventilating. He searched for an exit, but there were no doors and only one thin window. They could see a sliver of the Oort cloud outside, but even Bleep was too big to fit through the opening.

"Beep-beep boop beep-beep boop-boop!"

"This isn't how I thought I'd die either!" Nerp said.

"Stop talking like that!" Roswell said. "Listen, I've seen enough prison break movies to know there's always a way out! We've got to search the cell for any loose stones, hollow walls, or anything we can use as a—*AHHHHH!*"

To Roswell's horror, he and the Grays weren't alone.

"My sincerest apologies. I did not mean to frighten you."

At first glance Roswell thought he saw a human body-builder standing in the corner of the cell. The man was about six feet tall, with bulging muscles and a small waist. As Roswell took a closer look, he realized the man's entire body was made from white and silver pieces of metal. Instead of joints, he had hinges and bolts. And instead of a normal head, the man had a blue plasma screen that displayed a *digital* face.

"My monitors show your heart rate has increased to one hundred thirteen beats per minute. Do you require medical attention?"

The metal man's calm voice was projected through a speaker built into his neck.

"What the heck is that?" Roswell yelled.

"Relax, kid—he's just a Cyborg," Nerp said.

"How is that supposed to *relax* me?" Roswell asked.

"Cyborgs are harmless. They're programmed to help and assist living beings."

The Cyborg walked closer, and Roswell could hear his mechanisms turning and compressing with every step. His digital face displayed a friendly smile.

"Hello, I am R08-36119 of the Cyborg Station," he said. "For convenience, you may also call me Rob."

"I'm Commander Nerp, and this is my trainee, Bleep," the Tall Gray said. "The kid's a stowaway from Earth. It's a long story."

"My name's Roswell," he said. "I've never met a Cyborg before. It's a pleasure."

The Cyborg blinked curiously, and the word *processing* flashed on his digital forehead.

"What is a pleasure?" he asked.

"Um...meeting you," Roswell said.

"Even though I frightened you?"

"Well...I guess *that* part wasn't a pleasure."

"Then why would you say it was?"

"Oh...I was just being nice."

"What is nice about saying something you do not mean?"

The Cyborg didn't sound upset or confrontational, just naturally curious. Roswell was very confused and turned to Nerp for help.

"Did I offend him?" he asked.

"No, it's his artificial intelligence," Nerp said. "Cyborgs are programmed to interpret everything literally. It takes them a while to understand slang from beings they haven't encountered before."

"Beep-beep boop-boop beep-beep."

"That's right, Bleep—there's no such thing as an artificial sense of humor."

"I'm sorry we got off on the wrong foot, Rob," Roswell said, and offered the Cyborg a handshake. "Let's try that again."

"These are the only feet I have," Rob said.

"Oh—that's just a figure of speech. Forget I said it."

"What are you doing with your hand?"

"I'm offering it to you."

"To keep?"

"No! Just to shake it."

"Why would I shake your hand?"

"It's just something we do on Earth to be friendly."

Once again the Cyborg blinked curiously and the word *processing* flashed on his forehead. Rob studied Roswell's hand and then shook it awkwardly from side to side.

"Are you CRAZY? Don't TOUCH him!"

The unexpected voice made Roswell and the Grays jump. They saw that *another* prisoner was standing in the opposite corner. At first Roswell thought his eyes were playing tricks on him, because the prisoner was *a human-size praying mantis*! The giant bug had bright green skin and wore an emerald jumpsuit with yellow gloves and boots. Two antennae grew out of its wide head, and transparent wings rested on its back like a cape. A pair of thick glasses floated in front of its face and magnified its already enormous eyes.

"Who's that?!" Roswell asked.

"That is Mank," Rob said. "He is a Mantis from the Insectia Moon. My monitors show his heart rate has increased to two hundred fifty beats per minute."

"That's because there's an EARTHLING in here, Rob!" Mank shouted. "Do you know how many GERMS he might be carrying?! Or how many DISEASES he might be infected with?!"

"Hey, I don't have any diseases!" Roswell said defensively. "In fact, I just got a COVID booster last week."

"Oh, like *THAT'S* gonna save you!" Mank exclaimed. "With all of Earth's EARTHQUAKES and TORNADOES and TSUNAMIS and BLIZZARDS and FIRES and HURRICANES and VOLCANOES and FLOODS and MUDSLIDES and QUICKSAND and PLAGUES and PARASITES and PREDATORS and POLLUTION and WARS and COUNTY FAIRS, it's a miracle any Earthlings are alive at all!"

Roswell rolled his eyes. "I see you got Earth's brochure."

"Don't take it personally," Nerp said. "Mantises are extremely anxious beings. They're born paranoid."

"It's a survival tactic that's supposed to help us avoid

SITUATIONS LIKE THIS!" Mank moaned. "I can't believe this is happening to me! First, I get captured by REP-TOIDS, and now I'm forced to bunk with an INFEC-TIOUS PRIMATE! I am one stubbed toe away from a COMPLETE BREAKDOWN!"

The Cyborg played a soothing lullaby from his speakers and rubbed the Mantis's back.

"Deep breaths, Mank," Rob said. "Try counting to ten."

"One...two...three...," Mank whispered to himself. "Four...five...six..."

The Mantis manically rubbed his claws together as he counted. The numbers and the lullaby seemed to soothe him.

"I'm guessing you guys have been down here for a while," Roswell said.

"I have been in this cell for approximately three hundred sixty-six hours, forty-two minutes, and fifteen galactic seconds," Rob said. "Sixteen seconds...seventeen seconds... eighteen seconds...nineteen seconds—"

"That's NOTHING!" Mank declared. "I've been here for SIX GALACTIC MONTHS!"

"How long is a galactic month?" Roswell asked.

"Galactic time is about twice as long as Earth time—give or take a few nanoseconds," Nerp explained.

"Do you know how UNSANITARY it is to be trapped

in a small space for that long?" Mank asked. "We're basically standing in a PORT-A-POTTY!"

"Mank and I have suffered a grave misfortune," Rob said. "Although Cassi has been here longer than both of us combined."

"Cassi?" Roswell asked.

A loud yawn came from the other side of the cell. For the first time Roswell and the Grays saw a large dog curled up on the floor behind the moldy boulders. The dog was covered in shaggy brown fur, and a snaggletooth stuck out of her very pronounced underbite. Roswell assumed the dog was female because she wore a pink bow on top of her head. However, as he watched the dog stretch out and stand on her hind legs, Roswell realized she wasn't an ordinary canine.

"Ah man, I was right in the middle of a Chris Hemsworth dream." The dog yawned. "Did someone say my name?"

"Cassi, these are our new cellmates," Rob said. "Meet Nerp, Bleep, and Roswell."

The dog's green eyes lit up as soon as she spotted Roswell. She completely ignored the Grays and strutted toward him like a fashion model on a runway. She licked both of her paws and used the saliva to slick back her bushy eyebrows.

"Well, *hellooooo*, sweetcheeks!" the dog said. "The

name's Cassiopeia Furbottom, but all my suitors call me Cassi. Spoiler alert—*everyone calls me Cassi.*"

"Um...hi?" Roswell said awkwardly.

"Gosh, it's nice to finally get some eye candy around here! I've always thought Earthling boys were the cutest boys in the galaxy. I've been so deprived Mank was starting to look like Timothée Chalamet. What are the chances a hunk like you and a gorgeous gal like me would end up in the same prison cell? The universe works in mysterious ways, am I right?"

Cassi winked at Roswell and tickled his chin. He quickly backed away from her.

"Ma'am, I appreciate the compliments, but I'm eleven," Roswell said.

"What a coincidence!" Cassi said. "I'm a pup on my home planet too!"

"What kind of alien is she?" Roswell whispered to Nerp.

"She's a Furgarian," Nerp explained. "They're known for their *confidence.*"

"I mean, look at me," Cassi said, and slapped her plump belly. "Wouldn't you be confident if you looked this good?"

"How long have you been a prisoner, Cassi?" Roswell asked.

"A couple galactic years? A decade? A century maybe?

Who knows? I've been trapped in worse places. Luckily, I've been asleep for most of it."

"You've been asleep for a *century*?!" he asked. "I thought you said you were a pup."

"Furgarians are very heavy sleepers," she said. "We age only when we're conscious. I was born a hundred galactic years ago, but I've been awake for only about nine of them—nine very *eventful* years. Live fast, die fun—that's my motto!"

Roswell searched the cell, but there were no other prisoners hiding in the shadows.

"Does anyone know why the Reptoids captured us?" he asked the room.

"I do not understand whatsoever," Rob said.

"NEITHER do I!" Mank said.

"Obviously, I'm here because General Xelic is madly in love with me," Cassi said. "The poor guy is still working up the courage to make a move. Too bad I don't swing Reptoid. Learned that lesson the fifth time. Guess I'll have to break another heart."

"There's got to be a reason," Roswell said. "What were you guys doing when the Reptoids captured you?"

"I had just left the Cyborg Station and was en route to Star City," Rob said. "My ship alerted me of the Reptoidian fleet in the distance, but they were moving so fast I assumed they were a meteor shower. I did not believe I was in any danger, so I continued my journey. We crossed paths, and the Reptoids attacked my ship. I have been here ever since."

"I had just traveled to the planet Sterilith to pick up a shipment of my favorite DISINFECTANT," Mank said. "I was less than a light-year away from the Insectia Moon when the Reptoids INTERCEPTED my craft and forced me into this PATHOGEN PIT! By the way, Sterilith has the BEST sterilizers in the galaxy. Tell them Mank sent you for a DISCOUNT."

"Well, this is embarrassing, but I was on my way to meet a pen pal in the Andromeda Galaxy," Cassi said. "Don't worry, Roswell—it's platonic. No competition there. Anyway, I was at the edge of the Milky Way when the Reptoids showed up on my radar. There were so many spaceships that I assumed it was a music festival. Cassiopeia Furbottom *never* misses a party—so I did a U-turn and headed toward the action. Would you believe I was in this cell for a galactic week before I realized I *wasn't* at a music festival? I thought the tractor beam was a complimentary valet and the Reptoids were just really big heavy metal fans."

If Roswell were a Cyborg, the word *processing* would be flashing on his forehead. He paced across the cell as he thought about the abductions.

"There's only one thing we all have in common," he said.

"Carbon?" Rob asked.

"Beauty?" Cassi asked.

"SUSCEPTIBILITY?" Mank asked.

"Each of us was in the wrong place at the wrong time," Roswell said. "I don't think the Reptoids abducted us for any particular reason. I think they're capturing anyone who crosses their path. They don't want *anyone* to know what they're doing or where they're headed. Whatever they're planning, it must be *super* illegal."

Roswell went to the thin window and gestured to the Oort cloud outside.

"And another thing," he continued. "The Reptoids were *on the move* when they abducted Cassi, Mank, and Rob. But look outside—they aren't moving anymore! They've stationed themselves in the Oort cloud. Whatever they're after, it must be in *my* solar system!"

The evidence pointed to a theory that was so terrifying Roswell was afraid to say it out loud. Judging from his cellmates' timid faces, they were all thinking the same thing.

"Let's address the elephant in the room," Roswell said.

The Cyborg blinked curiously. "What elephant?"

"Not a real elephant—I mean, let's address the obvious," he clarified. "The Reptoids steal resources from other planets to survive, right? Well, my planet is the only planet in the solar system with everything they need! *The Reptoids are here for Earth!*"

"But Earth is still a stage-two planet," Nerp said. "It's

under the Milky Way Galactic Alliance's full protection. The moment a Reptoidian ship enters Earth's atmosphere, the alliance will send the Galactic Guard to arrest them."

"The Reptoids are RUTHLESS, but they aren't STUPID!" Mank said.

"You said General Xelic is very clever with his crimes," Roswell said. "Maybe the general's found a loophole? Maybe he knows a way to make it legal?"

Nerp rubbed their bald head as they thought it over.

"I wouldn't put anything past General Xelic—but I can't imagine a loophole that would allow Reptoids to legally steal from a stage-two planet."

Roswell's imagination spun like a cyclone as he tried to think of an answer. Even if he figured out General Xelic's plan, he was still the Reptoids' prisoner. How was he going to escape the mother ship, let alone save the world? And even if he did get out, what could he possibly do to stop an alien army?

"Have you guys tried escaping?" Roswell asked.

"WOW! The idea NEVER crossed our minds!" Mank said.

"Really?"

"ARE YOU KIDDING? OF COURSE WE'VE TRIED ESCAPING!"

"None of our efforts have been successful," Rob said. "The floors and walls are made from pure Reptoidian stone. And the bars are coursing with over two hundred thousand volts of electricity. The odds of escaping are four million seven hundred thousand three hundred eighty-eight to one."

Roswell became dizzy with despair and had a seat on the floor. Cassi curled up beside him and placed her head in his lap.

"There's a silver lining to all this," the Furgarian said.

"What's that?" he asked.

"If we're stuck, at least you're stuck with someone as attractive as me."

Cassi smiled so wide her snaggletooth almost touched her forehead.

"You wanna scratch my belly? I'll do a trick for ya!"

Roswell burst into tears. It was hard to believe what a tragic turn the day had taken. The ultimate adventure had become the worst nightmare imaginable. Unless there was a miracle, it was very unlikely Roswell would ever see Gram and Pop again.

Luckily for Roswell and his cellmates, help was on her way.

A PLEIADEAN TO THE RESCUE

Roswell couldn't sleep. Besides worrying about a likely apocalypse, his cellmates' eccentric sleeping habits made it impossible to rest. Both Nerp and Bleep were ferocious snorers. The Grays loudly inhaled and exhaled in perfect unison as if it were choreographed. To no one's surprise, Mank suffered from severe night terrors. Every fifteen minutes the Mantis sat straight up and screamed at the top of his lungs. Once the horror was out of his system, he quickly fell back to sleep as if nothing had happened.

Worst of all, Cassi kept snuggling with Roswell in her sleep. No matter how many times Roswell pushed her away, the Furgarian rolled back and wrapped herself around his body like a furry pretzel. Cassi also had wild dreams that made her run and kick Roswell while she slept. Her restless, hairy legs built up static electricity and zapped him every time she moved.

The Cyborg was the only prisoner having the same trouble as Roswell. Rob sat on a moldy boulder and stared off into space while the others slept.

"You can't sleep either?" Roswell whispered.

"Cyborgs do not sleep," Rob said.

"At all?"

"Once every galactic year, Cyborgs power down for an annual recharging. It is considered a holiday at the Cyborg Station. We call it Chargemas."

"Do you dream when you're powered down?"

"Not in a subconscious sense like Earthlings, but Cyborgs are programmed to experience individualized wants and longings while conscious."

Roswell noticed the word *processing* flashing on Rob's digital forehead. He untangled himself from Cassi's limbs and sat on a boulder beside the Cyborg.

"Penny for your thoughts?" Roswell asked.

The Cyborg blinked curiously. "How does someone purchase a thought?"

"Sorry, that's another figure of speech from Earth."

"Why are thoughts so inexpensive on your planet?"

"It's just a way of asking someone what's on their mind."

"Synthetic fibers."

"Huh?"

"Synthetic fibers hold my artificial mind in place."

"No—I meant, what are you *thinking*?"

The Cyborg looked somberly at the floor. "I am afraid I am not in an optimistic state."

"That's okay," Roswell said. "I'll take any distraction from my own worries."

Rob shrugged. "I was thinking about my journey to Star City. Before the Reptoids captured me, I was on a very important mission. I am scheduled to speak with the Milky Way Galactic Alliance about Cyborg rights."

"What are Cyborg rights?" Roswell asked.

"It is one of the most controversial topics in the galaxy. Although it has been proved that artificial intelligence is equivalent to biological intelligence, Cyborgs are still considered *objects*. That means we cannot be members of the Milky Way Galactic Alliance or have a say in galactic matters until we're recognized as living beings."

"That's horrible," Roswell said. "What's stopping them from changing it?"

"Many want to keep us as property. Right now millions of Cyborgs are treated like slaves across our galaxy. However, by bringing the matter to a vote, the alliance could grant freedom to the entire Cyborg population. I've made it my life cycle's mission to turn that dream into a reality."

"That's wonderful! When are you supposed to speak to them?"

The Cyborg's digital mouth curled into a frown. "Unfortunately, my audience is in three galactic days. Now that I am a prisoner, the odds of attending are five million three thousand five hundred seventy-two to one."

"Those are pretty steep."

"Indeed."

"Could you reschedule the audience?"

"It is a very complicated process. To receive an audience with the alliance, your matter must be sponsored by five stage-three planets. I traveled the galaxy for many galactic years and petitioned the leaders of many systems to gain the support. Once your petition has five signatures, there is a lengthy waiting list to speak with the alliance. It took over a galactic decade to get an appointment. Therefore, it would take a very long time to reschedule. It is unlikely the Cyborgs will be freed in the foreseeable future. I feel as though I have failed my mission and let down all the Cyborgs in the galaxy."

Digital tears ran down the Cyborg's digital face. The words *grievance mode* flashed across his forehead. Roswell didn't know how to comfort a Cyborg, but he put his arm around Rob's metal shoulder as if he were a human.

"I'm so sorry, Rob. It sounds like you've got a lot on your plate."

"What plate?"

"It's a metaphor—it means you have a lot of responsibility. If it makes you feel any better, I can relate. There's a lot of prejudice on my planet too. It's infuriating and makes you lose all hope. But you said the odds of attending your audience are five million to one. That's still better than impossible, right?"

The word *processing* flashed across the Cyborg's head.

"Technically, that is correct," Rob admitted. "Why is there prejudice on your planet?"

Roswell sighed. "I've been asking the same question my whole life. I guess it's because we look different, we speak different, and we have different beliefs. And Earthlings have always been afraid of what they don't understand."

"Would learning about one another not ease those fears?"

"I think they're afraid of *what* they'd learn."

"What lesson is that?"

"That *we're all equal*," Roswell said. "Some people have a ridiculous need to feel superior to everyone else—they act like life is a contest. But the fact is, no one is better or worse than anyone else! And we aren't nearly as different as we think we are! We're all just trying to do our best and make the most out of what we've been given."

"I cannot think of a more unifying concept."

"Me either," Roswell said. "Between me and you, sometimes I wonder if my world is even worth saving. If the Reptoids don't destroy us, we'll probably destroy one another. Maybe General Xelic is doing us a favor?"

"Do you truly believe that? Or is that an exaggeration brought on by physical and emotional exhaustion?"

Roswell went quiet as he thought about the question.

"Honestly, I wish I knew," he confessed. "I used to think the existence of alien life would bring Earthlings together. But now I know the universe is just as complicated as Earth. So I'm not sure what to believe anymore."

WHAAAAAM! The prison door flew open. The commotion woke the sleeping cellmates, and all six prisoners jumped to their feet. They instantly filled with dread as General Xelic marched inside the prison with two of his Reptoidian soldiers. He glared at the prisoners through the buzzing crisscross bars.

"Good morning, captives," he said with a wicked grin. "How'd you sleep?"

Bleep angrily shook their fist at the general.

"Beep-beep boop-boop beep-beep-beep boop-boop-boop beep!"

"Bleep says 'Fine, thanks,'" Nerp lied.

"I hope you're here to FINALLY put us out of our MISERY!" Mank pleaded.

"I'm here for an ego boost," General Xelic scoffed. "The sight of inferior life-forms always puts me in a good mood."

"Nice try, but reverse psychology doesn't work on me!" Cassi said. "You'll need chocolate and Adele tickets to win *my* heart!"

The general ignored the Furgarian and pressed a button

on his cuff. The crisscross bars separated, retracting into the floor and the ceiling.

"Actually, I've come to collect the Earthling," he said. "The boy and I are going upstairs for a little chat. *Get him.*"

"No!" Roswell gasped. "Don't touch me!"

The soldiers charged into the cell and seized Roswell by both arms. His cellmates watched helplessly as the Reptoids dragged Roswell out of the prison. General Xelic pressed the button on his cuff again, and the crisscross bars sealed shut. He gave the prisoners a menacing wave and then slammed the prison door behind him.

"Xelic, if you sour my sweetcheeks, it's *over* between us!" Cassi yelled.

Roswell was taken into a small chamber next to the prison. The room was so tall he couldn't see where the ceiling ended. The soldiers forced him onto a stone platform that looked like it was wrapped in a large rib cage. General Xelic pressed another button on his cuff, and the platform began to rise.

Roswell and the Reptoids traveled up a skeletal elevator shaft. Several levels of dark corridors rushed past them as they rose higher and higher. Roswell's terror grew with each passing floor. What did General Xelic want with him? Why was he being separated from the other prisoners? Was the general going to hurt him? Would he survive whatever was next?

The bony elevator traveled to the very top of the mother ship. A pair of stone doors opened, and the Reptoids dragged Roswell into their spacious command center. The center looked like an enormous empty skull. The floor and the walls were as pale and solid as bone. Two giant windows were shaped like a pair of empty eye sockets and showed the Oort cloud ahead. The command center was covered in the same mysterious vines as the hangar.

Roswell got an eerie feeling that all the Reptoidian spacecraft had been living creatures at one point, and the Reptoids had converted the carcasses into space vessels.

There were over a hundred Reptoidian pilots and operators sitting and standing behind controls. Unlike the controls in the Grays' flying saucer, the Reptoids' controls looked like reptilian body parts. The crew pulled tails, poked eyes, and twisted claws to keep the mother ship running.

"Put him in the Outliar," General Xelic ordered.

The soldiers took Roswell to an object that reminded him of a giant gingerbread-man cookie cutter. The soldiers placed Roswell inside the Outliar, and it shrank to fit the outline of his body. The Reptoids also fastened his hands and feet in metal clamps so he couldn't move.

"I'm going to ask you a few questions," General Xelic said. "The longer it takes to get the truth, the more painful this will be."

"I'll tell you anything you want to know!" Roswell said. "My life's an open book!"

General Xelic turned a dial on the Outliar. The contraption began to vibrate around Roswell's body.

"Let's start with an easy one," the general said. "Who are you?"

"My name is Roswell Johnson! I'm eleven years old! I'm in the seventh grade! I live in Cherokee Springs, Oklahoma! My birthday is August fourteenth! I'm a Leo with a Pisces moon! My favorite movie is *The Empire Strikes Back*! My favorite singer is David Bowie! My favorite band is OutKast! My favorite Avenger is the Scarlet Witch, but I've never admitted that to—"

The general raised a hand to silence Roswell's nervous ramble.

"This is an interrogation, not a dating profile," he said.

"Sorry! I've literally never been this scared before!"

"What is an Earthling doing so far from home?"

"I was accidentally abducted by the Grays!"

"Why didn't the Grays erase your memory and take you back to Earth?"

"Because my name was in the Galactic Registry!"

"LIAR!"

The general turned up the dial. The Outliar vibrated even stronger, and a sharp prickling sensation moved through Roswell's body. It made the hairs on the backs of his arms stand up.

"Who do you work for?" the general asked.

"No one! I'm not even old enough for a work permit!"

"You expect me to believe a *regular* Earthling is in the Galactic Registry?"

"I don't understand it either!"

General Xelic turned up the dial again. The Outliar sent an electric current through Roswell's body. It felt like he was being poked by hundreds of needles at once.

"OOOOOUCH!" he screamed.

"You're making this more difficult than it needs to be," General Xelic said.

"I'm telling you the truth!"

"Who sent you to spy on us?"

"I'm not a spy!"

"An Earthling wasn't in the Oort cloud by coincidence."

"I was! I swear!"

"LIAR!"

General Xelic turned the dial once more. Roswell was electrocuted so hard every muscle in his body contracted. It was the most painful sensation he had ever experienced in his life. It lasted for five seconds but felt like an eternity.

"AHHHHHH!" Roswell shrieked.

"Your resilience is impressive," General Xelic said.

"S-s-stop this! I'm not what you think I am!"

"Clearly, you've been trained to resist torture."

"I—I—I haven't been trained to do anything! I'm just a kid!"

"Perhaps feeling the Outliar's *full* capability will loosen your lips!"

"N-N-NO! I'M BEGGING YOU!"

SKWAAAAAMP-SKWAAAAAMP-SKWAAAAAMP!
Before General Xelic could electrocute Roswell again, an alarm echoed through the command center. *SKWAAAAAMP-SKWAAAAAMP-SKWAAAAAMP!* The alarm came from a beak that was built into an operator's dashboard. *SKWAAAAAMP-SKWAAAAAMP-SKWAAAAAMP!*

"What now?!" the general yelled.

"A spacecraft is approaching our fleet, sir," the operator said.

"What's the origin of the craft?"

The operator gulped anxiously—afraid to give the news.

"It's *Pleiadean*, sir."

The entire command center filled with tension. Roswell could tell the approaching ship made the whole crew very *nervous*. General Xelic's nostrils flared and he growled angrily.

"Pleiadeans," he mumbled with undeniable hatred.

"Should we strike, sir?" the operator asked.

"No! Pleiadean technology is more advanced than ours. If we show them an ounce of hostility, the whole Pleiades system will show up!"

A spaceship appeared in the Oort cloud outside the windows. The craft was shaped like a majestic bird, and the entire ship was made from a pure alien diamond. The material reflected all the light from the stars and the mother ship, giving the craft an angelic glow. It was the most beautiful vessel Roswell had ever seen. He could have sworn he heard a chorus singing as the ship flew closer, but it was just in his imagination.

"How many passengers are aboard the ship?" the general asked.

"Our bio-radar shows one life-form, sir," the operator said.

An orange tail started to wiggle on the operator's dashboard.

"Sir, the Pleiadean is trying to make contact!"

General Xelic glared at the Pleiadean ship while he contemplated his next move.

"Gag the Earthling and patch the Pleiadean through!" he ordered.

The soldiers shoved a severed reptilian foot into Roswell's mouth. The operator pulled the wiggling tail on the dashboard. A screech blared through the command center as a series of speakers were switched on.

"This is General Xelic of the Reptoidian Army," he said with a friendly tone of voice. "Whom do I have the pleasure of speaking with?"

"Greetings, General," said a voice through the speakers. "This is Stella Stargaze of the Pleiadean system. I'm a junior council member of the Seven Sisters Council."

The Pleiadean sounded like a cheerful young woman.

"How may we help you, Miss Stargaze?" General Xelic asked.

"I received a distress signal from a Grayton spacecraft with these coordinates," she said. "I suspect their engines failed before the full message was sent, because I received only a location. Have you seen any ships in the area that require emergency assistance?"

Roswell's weak posture and low spirits suddenly lifted. *The Pleiadean got the Grays' distress signal!* Did this mean they were saved? Could the Pleiadean rescue the prisoners and stop the Reptoids from destroying Earth?

General Xelic cracked his green knuckles while he thought of a response.

"As a matter of fact, we received the same distress signal," he said. "My fleet headed here as soon as the message arrived. I am happy to report the Grays are resting comfortably and their craft is being repaired."

"Oh, shnigglebotts!" the Pleiadean said. "That's a shame."

The general scrunched his forehead. "Excuse me?"

"Forgive my strong language, General. I was hoping to rescue the Grays myself. You see, I'm trying to earn points for my Pleiadean Public Service Portfolio. I've been searching the Milky Way for beings in distress and haven't had any luck. Saving the Grays would have been a slam dunk."

"Better luck next time! Goodbye, Miss—"

"While I'm here, is there anything I could help *you* with, General? Do you have any machinery that needs to be repaired? Any wounded passengers that require medical attention? Any toilets that need to be unclogged?"

"Thank you for the offer, Miss Stargaze, but we're perfectly content. I'm sure there are plenty of beings who need assistance elsewhere. Good luck finding the unlucky."

"Of course, I will still need to board your ship."

The general did a double take. "What? *Why?*"

"To make sure the Grays are all right."

"That isn't necessary, Miss Stargaze. Like I said, the Grays are resting comfortably."

"I'm afraid I don't have a choice. It's Pleiadean policy to personally check on the source of a distress call. I can't leave until I see the Grays are safe and sound. You wouldn't believe how many species take advantage of the vulnerable out here."

General Xelic clenched his jaw and his face turned dark green.

"Policy is policy," he said through his yellow teeth. "I'll send my finest soldiers to greet you in the hangar."

"Thank you for your cooperation, General."

Another screech blared through the command center as the speakers switched off. The Pleiadean's diamond ship sank below the windows and flew toward the mother ship's hangar. Clearly, having a Pleiadean come aboard was the worst thing that could have happened. General Xelic was breathing so furiously he sounded like a steam engine. He picked up the nearest crew member and threw them across the command center.

"Your orders, sir?" a soldier asked.

The general paced back and forth, huffing and puffing, as he orchestrated a plan.

"If she wants to see the Grays, I'll show her the Grays," he said. "Remove the Earthling from the Outliar and bring the Pleiadean here! We'll lock her in the prison before she has a chance to contact the Pleiadean system!"

The soldiers removed Roswell from the Outliar and then hurried to retrieve the Pleiadean. General Xelic yanked the foot out of Roswell's mouth and loomed over him.

"Say one word and I'll kill you on the spot!" he warned.

Roswell nodded fearfully and silently panicked. How would the Pleiadean know he was a prisoner if he couldn't speak? How could he make her understand they were both in danger? And what if the Pleiadean was captured herself? Was this his only chance of being saved?

A few minutes later the stone doors opened, and the soldiers escorted the Pleiadean inside. Roswell thought he was seeing a ghost because Stella Stargaze was the palest person he had ever laid eyes on. Her skin was the shade of an eggshell, and she had long platinum-blond hair. Stella wore a bright blue jumpsuit with a white belt, white gloves, and white boots. A shiny badge was pinned over her heart with the seven stars of the Pleiades cluster. The Pleiadean was also the most human-looking extraterrestrial Roswell had encountered so far. She could easily have been mistaken for an Earthling if her blue eyes hadn't been three times bigger than an average human's.

"Salutations, everyone!" Stella said, and greeted the Reptoids with a perky wave. "Would you believe this is my first time on a Reptoidian spaceship? And what a ship it is! You know, very few beings would create a fleet of spacecraft from the remains of an animal species they sent into extinction after single-handedly destroying their home planet, *but not the Reptoids*! The galaxy doesn't give you enough credit for being so resourceful!"

The general forced a smile. "Welcome aboard, Miss Stargaze."

Stella looked around the command center in awe. Her big eyes eventually landed on Roswell. General Xelic sent him a scathing look, reminding him to stay quiet.

"Oh, my neutron stars!" Stella gasped. "Are you an *Earthling*?"

"That's correct," the general answered for him. "The boy is so stunned to be in space he's forgotten how to speak."

"What's he doing so far from Earth?"

"He was accidentally abducted by the Grays. We offered to erase his memory and take him back to Earth on their behalf. The poor Grays endured such a ghastly ordeal with their ship, it's the least we could do."

"That is so kind of you, General! I don't care what the rest of the galaxy says about Reptoids. You are not the destructive, heartless, ruthless, selfish, tyrannical, vile, and violent species everyone thinks you are."

The general forced another smile. "Thank you, Miss Stargaze."

The Pleiadean gave Roswell a warm smile, but he didn't smile back. He hoped the fear in his eyes would tell her everything he wasn't allowed to say. Roswell's whole face flushed as he desperately tried to send the silent message. Sadly, it was obvious Stella wasn't getting the memo. Her perky and positive demeanor never changed.

"Would you like to see the Grays now?" General Xelic asked.

"Actually, if it isn't an imposition, would you give me a tour of your ship?"

"A tour?"

"Like I said, I've never been on a craft that was once a living creature. I'm so curious about your operational and navigational systems."

The general grunted and forced his most painful smile yet. "Right this way."

The Reptoid led the bewildered Pleiadean to the nearest dashboard.

"Before our home planet, Reptoidia, was *indisposed*,

our ancestors built a mighty fleet of ships to ensure our survival in space," the general explained. "They constructed the vessels from the remains of megashelled stratosauruses. The creatures were peaceful herbivores who lived in Reptoidia's atmosphere. Their massive bodies were able to float thanks to the significant amount of hot gas their bowels produced. The megashelled stratosauruses were quite magnificent once you got used to their smell...."

Suddenly Roswell was distracted by a high-pitched noise. It sounded like both his ears were ringing, but he couldn't tell where the sound was coming from. He was also the only person in the command center who seemed to notice it. Strangely, as soon as it started, a light tingling sensation began tickling the center of his forehead.

You're a prisoner, aren't you?

The voice came out of nowhere and made Roswell jump. However, no one was standing close enough to speak so clearly.

Don't be alarmed. You aren't going crazy, and I'm not going to hurt you.

"Who's there?" Roswell whispered.

Don't say anything! Think it!

Um...okay, Roswell thought. *What's happening? Who is this?*

This is Stella Stargaze. I'm inside your mind.

The Pleiadean quickly looked over her shoulder and winked at him when the general wasn't looking.

How are you doing this?! Roswell thought.

Pleiadeans are telepathic. But I didn't have to read your mind to know you're in trouble and the general is lying.

I was accidentally abducted by the Grays back on Earth—that part is true. We discovered the Reptoids at the edge of my solar system. They attacked our craft and took us prisoner! Now we're trapped with a Cyborg, a Mantis, and a Furgarian!

Why did the Reptoids capture you?

I think they're planning to steal resources from Earth! They're capturing anyone who catches them in the act!

But Earth is a stage-two planet and under full protection from the Milky Way—

I know, I know—but we're pretty sure the Reptoids have found a loophole!

Wow! This is FANTASTIC!

Huh?

Oh, my apologies! Imprisoning innocent beings and stealing from Earth is terrible. But I could earn a million Pleiadean Public Service Points if I stop them!

Does that mean you can rescue us?

Not alone, but I can return to my ship and call for help.

Hurry! The general is going to capture you next!

What's your name?

Roswell Johnson.

Hang in there, Roswell Johnson! Help is on the way!

The high-pitched noise and the tingling on Roswell's forehead disappeared. Stella continued her tour of the command center as if nothing had happened. Roswell grew paranoid he had imagined the whole conversation. He prayed it had been a real telepathic connection and not just a side effect of being electrocuted by the Outliar.

"Our controls are made from the appendages of other extinct species," General Xelic explained. "By connecting their nerves to the ship's nervous system, we're able to monitor and control different areas of the ship."

"What extraordinary ingenuity!" Stella said.

"This vessel is constructed from the remains of a mother megashelled stratosaurus—hence the term *mother ship*, which Reptoids were first to coin—and our fleet was built from the remains of the mother's hatchlings. Her stomach was converted into our hangar, her skull into our command center, her arteries and intestines into corridors and passageways, her lungs into our oxygen supply, and her heart into the chambers of the Reptiliz Supreme."

"Who knew corpses could be so homey?" Stella said, and backed toward the exit. "*Weeeeell*, this has been such an educational visit. Thank you so much for hosting me, General. I'm sure you have a very busy schedule, so I'll return to my ship now. Keep up the good work!"

The Pleiadean turned on her heel and headed for the exit. General Xelic raised a suspicious eyebrow at her.

"Miss Stargaze? Aren't you forgetting something?" he asked.

Stella innocently looked around the floor. "Did I drop something?"

"You haven't seen the Grays yet."

"On second thought, it may be better to let them rest."

"I thought it was Pleiadean policy to check the source of a distress call."

"Um...it is! But one of the Pleiadean system's core principles is *politeness*. It would be rude and very *un-Pleiadean* of me to disturb the Grays. *Golly, look at the time!* I better get back to my ship so I don't miss another distress call!"

Stella hurried to the doors. On her way she passed Roswell and gave him a confident nod. Roswell was so relieved he made the mistake of smiling and nodding back. General Xelic noticed the exchange, and all the fake pleasantry faded from his face. He pressed a button on his cuff, and the doors slammed shut just before Stella reached them.

"Is there a problem, General?" she asked.

"I should have known better than to let a telepath board my ship!" General Xelic roared. "Guards, throw that Pleiadean in the prison!"

The soldiers seized Stella and carried her across the command center.

"Unhand me at once!" Stella shouted. "I am a junior

council member of the Seven Sisters Council! I have diplomatic immunity! You can't arrest me without a warrant from the Milky Way Galactic Alliance!"

The soldiers took the Pleiadean to a large hole in the wall. Just like the hole in the hangar, the opening puckered, then spread wider as they approached it. The soldiers tossed the Pleiadean through the hole, and she slid down a slimy tube on the other side. Stella's screams faded as she sank deeper and deeper into the mother ship.

General Xelic threw Roswell on the floor. "I TOLD YOU NOT TO SAY A WORD!"

"I didn't *say* anything!" Roswell cried.

"YOU'LL DIE FOR THIS!"

General Xelic yanked a spear from a soldier and raised it over Roswell's head. Roswell shielded himself with his arms, expecting a deadly blow at any second.

"XEEEEEEEEEELIC!"

Luckily, Roswell's execution was interrupted. A raspy voice boomed through the chamber and caused the entire command center to rattle. As the sound traveled, a strong ripple moved through the mysterious vines covering the floor and walls. The plants rose off the floor and formed a hand with five fingers. The hand wrapped itself around General Xelic's body and pulled him toward the exit.

"COME TO MY CHAMBERS AT ONCE!"

If the Pleiadean had made the Reptoids *nervous* before, the raspy voice *terrified* the crew. They trembled and hid under their dashboards. General Xelic dropped the spear and followed the vines out of the command center.

"Put the Earthling back in the cell while I speak with the Reptiliz!" he ordered. "As soon as I return, *the boy dies*!"

CHAPTER SEVEN

THE ESCAPE PLAN

The Reptoidian soldiers threw Roswell into the hole, and he slid down the slimy tube on the other side. He felt like he was trapped in the galaxy's longest water slide. The mother ship was so enormous it took him twenty minutes to reach the prison at the bottom level. Roswell landed in the center of the cell with a painful thud.

"Roswell!" the Cyborg exclaimed.

"Beep-beep boop-boop beep!"

"Thank the Source you're all right!" Nerp said.

"I thought you were a GONER!" Mank said.

"When the blond girl dropped in, I was afraid the Reptoids had given you an *extreme* makeover!" Cassi said.

The Pleiadean was still on the ground, rubbing her injured limbs from the rough landing. The other prisoners were huddled in a corner as they cautiously watched their new cellmate.

"Who are you?" Rob asked her.

"Where are you from?" Nerp asked.

"When was the last time you WASHED YOUR HANDS?" Mank asked.

Roswell brushed himself off and helped the Pleiadean to her feet.

"Don't worry, she's on our side," he said.

"Greetings, fellow captives!" Stella said with an energetic wave. "I'm Stella Stargaze of the Pleiadean system. I'm a junior council member of the Seven Sisters Council."

The prisoners surrounded Stella like she was a celebrity.

"A Pleiadean!" Nerp cheered.

"Peep-peep poop peep-peep poop-poop peep!"

"That's right—Pleiadeans *are* the most advanced species in the Milky Way!" Nerp said.

"Pleiadeans are known for their CLEANLINESS too!" Mank added.

"That's for sure," Cassi mumbled. "Worst foam parties I've ever been to."

"Miss Stargaze, have you contacted the other Pleiadeans?" Rob asked. "Are they on their way to rescue us?"

The prisoners stood on the tips of their toes as they anticipated good news.

"Unfortunately, I was captured before I had the chance to call for help," Stella said. "But fear not, my fellow detainees! I graduated from the Pleiadean Academy with high honors. I was trained to handle any predicament by following the five Pleiadean *P*s: patience, perspective, politeness, positivity, and perseverance!"

"Oh great, now I'm sad *and* I have to pee," Cassi grumbled.

Despite the Pleiadean's optimistic smile, the cellmates moaned with despair. Their postures sank so deep their chins almost touched the ground. Roswell sat on a moldy boulder and rested his head in his hands.

"Roswell, my monitors indicate your cortisol hormones have risen to unhealthy levels," Rob said. "Do you require medical attention?"

"There's no point—I'm a dead man!" he cried.

"What are you talking about, kid?" Nerp asked.

"General Xelic thinks I'm a spy! He took me to the command center and tried *torturing* information out of me! The general is speaking to the Reptiliz right now, but as soon as he's finished, he's going to kill me!"

The cellmates were shocked, horrified, and outraged all at once.

"I can't TAKE THIS ANYMORE!" Mank shouted, and tugged on his antennae. "It's an emotional roller coaster that only goes DOWN!"

"Beep-beep boop-boop beep boop-boop."

"I agree—it's exactly like being a Raiders fan," Nerp said.

"This is all my fault," Cassi confessed. "None of this would be happening if I weren't so gorgeous. Xelic is going to kill Roswell to eliminate his competition. Gosh, why do I always find myself in the same love triangle?"

"I am so sorry, Roswell," Rob said. "My vernacular drive is not equipped with the necessary words to comfort you in this moment."

"I'VE HIT THE JACKPOT!" Stella cheered.

The Cyborg blinked curiously at the Pleiadean. "Apparently, neither is *hers*."

To everyone's complete surprise, Stella started dancing around the prison cell. She clapped her hands and dragged her feet like she was performing the electric slide. The celebration was so unexpected Roswell forgot why he was upset.

"Stella, are you feeling okay?" he asked.

"Okay? I've never been shnigglebotting better!" she declared. "This is the greatest thing that's ever happened to me!"

The prisoners were baffled by the Pleiadean's positivity.

"This chick is in a different story than the rest of us," Cassi said.

"She clearly has REPTOIDIAN RABIES!" Mank yelled. "Quick! Someone euthanize her before it SPREADS!"

"Please forgive my celebratory outburst," Stella said. "You see, my biggest dream is to be a senior member of the Seven Sisters Council. Whenever a sitting council member retires, she's replaced by the junior council member with the most Pleiadean Public Service Points. When they find out I helped six innocent prisoners escape, saved an Earthling from an unjust execution, *and* stopped the Reptoids from destroying a stage-two planet—I'll have more Pleiadean Public Service Points than any junior council member in history!"

"You *still* think we can escape?" Roswell asked.

"Absolutely!" she said. "At the Pleiadean Academy, I earned my certificate in geological problem-solving! That's like having a doctorate in escape rooms on your planet, Roswell. The key to escaping any situation is *knowing your surroundings*. So what have you learned about this prison cell so far?"

"Beep-beep boop-boop!"

"Yes, Bleep—we *know* what it smells like!" Nerp said.

"The floor and walls are made from REPTOIDIAN STONE!" Mank said.

"The bars are coursing with over two hundred thousand volts of electricity," Rob said.

"The lighting is horrible, but I still look fantastic," Cassi said.

The Pleiadean rubbed her chin as she took all the facts into consideration. She walked around the prison cell and thoroughly inspected every corner.

"Our first step is getting through these bars," Stella said. "Reptoids are great builders, but they are lousy electricians. In fact, their aversion to renewable energy is the main reason Reptoidia was destroyed! Their stone may be impenetrable, but I doubt these bars can handle more voltage than they're designed to hold. If we were to add *more* power, I bet we could fry the breakers and stop the electric current!"

"Where can we get extra electricity?" Roswell asked.

As soon as he asked the question, the answer came to all the prisoners at once. Everyone slowly turned to the only cellmate who was running on actual electricity. The Cyborg slowly backed away, and the word *concern* flashed across his digital forehead.

"Oh dear," he said.

"Rob, how much power is in your battery?" Stella asked.

The Cyborg checked a monitor built into his forearm. "My battery is at eighty-two percent, which means I have fifty-six thousand volts stored," he said.

"That *might* fry the breakers, but it's not enough to be certain," Stella said. "If we got your battery to sixty or seventy thousand volts, our chances would be much higher."

"We would need a MINI POWER PLANT to generate that kind of energy!" Mank said.

"Not necessarily," Stella said. "All we need is something to make a *spark*."

Everyone went quiet as they thought. Roswell remembered the Cherokee Springs Intermediate School Science Fair and thought about all the random objects his classmates had used to create electricity. Unfortunately, there weren't any solar panels, potatoes, or carpets in the prison cell. *Or were there?*

Suddenly Roswell was struck with an idea that made him jump to his feet. He excitedly turned to the Furgarian with a huge smile.

"Cassi!" Roswell exclaimed. "It's *you*! You're the *spark*!"

The Furgarian batted her eyes and stroked his face.

"I know, sweetcheeks. I felt it the moment I laid eyes on you too."

"No—I mean *you* could produce the energy we need!" he explained. "Earlier when you were sleeping next to me on the floor—"

"When we were *cuddling*, yes."

"Your legs rubbed together and—*wait, what? We were not cuddling!* Never mind—your fur was making static electricity that kept shocking me. I bet we could use your fur to produce extra energy to fry the breakers!"

"So you want to use the energy between us to power another man?" Cassi asked. "Wow, I didn't see that coming. This is a first for me."

Roswell ignored the comment and turned to Stella for approval. He could see mutual hope growing in the Pleiadean's big blue eyes.

"Rob, could you power your battery with static electricity?" she asked.

The word *processing* flashed across Rob's digital forehead.

"It is unconventional but possible," he said. "However, there is one factor you are not taking into consideration. After I transfer my energy, I will become powerless. I weigh four hundred twenty pounds in the current gravitational conditions. Carrying me through the mother ship will be very inconvenient. How will I escape?"

The Cyborg was right—no one had thought that far ahead.

"What if we separated you?" Roswell suggested. "Could we divide you into parts and each carry a piece?"

"Aw! Like a big friendship necklace!" Cassi said.

Rob's digital eyes went wide, and the word *concern* returned to his forehead.

"Once again, it is unconventional but possible," he said. "There is a lever beneath my left pectoral shield. If you pull it, my head and limbs will separate from my core."

"Beep-beep boop-boop beep-beep!"

"No, Bleep—you don't get to call *dibs* on anything!" Nerp said.

"Great, we've got step one figured out!" Stella said. "Now, moving on to step two. How are we going to get *through* the bars once they're deactivated? Any ideas?"

"Bleep could squeeze through the bars!" Nerp said.

"Beep! Boop-boop?"

"Because you're the smallest."

"Peep-peep poop-poop peep!"

"Grays don't have any bones to break!"

"Beep-beep boop-boop-boop beep!"

"I didn't say it would be comfortable!"

"Peep-peep poop-poop peep-peep-peep poop-poop?"

"There's got to be a button somewhere that opens the bars," Nerp said. "Stop making excuses and make yourself useful! You'll never be a Tall Gray with such a small mind!"

"Fantastic, we've got a step two!" Stella said. "Now for step three: After we get through the bars, how are we going to get out the prison door? Anyone have an idea?"

Roswell searched the cell. "I wish we had something to use as a battering ram," he said. "Does anyone see a loose boulder or a heavy piece of metal?"

Once again the answer came to everyone at the same time. All the prisoners slowly turned to the Cyborg. The word *concern* flashed across his digital forehead for a third time.

"I am starting to feel used," Rob said.

"Used but *appreciated*, my man," Cassi said, and patted him on the back.

"Aaaaand we've got ourselves a step three!" Stella said, and gave the group a mini round of applause. "This is becoming fun, isn't it? It's like we're playing a game! Now, moving on to step four. Once we break out of the prison, we'll need to find a way to the spaceships in the mother ship's hangar."

157

"How are we supposed to find the HANGAR?" Mank asked. "It's several levels ABOVE us! And we don't know our way AROUND!"

"Actually, I might know this ship better than you think," Stella said.

The Pleiadean kneeled in front of the biggest boulder. She used her finger to draw an illustration in the mold. All the prisoners gathered around her, and soon they could see Stella was drawing an animal with a massive shell. She included the creature's organs and bones as if the image were an X-ray.

"General Xelic said the mother ship was constructed from the remains of a megashelled stratosaurus," she explained. "Luckily for us, I have my Pleiadean certificate in extraterrestrial anatomy. That's like a doctorate of zoology on your planet, Roswell."

"How are you so young and so educated?" he asked.

"Pleiadean brains develop much faster than Earthling brains," Stella said. "We leave the womb with the equivalent of a high school education. Now, does anyone know what's on the other side of the prison door?"

"It's some kind of bony elevator," Roswell said.

Stella went quiet as she studied her illustration.

"Perfect! I know exactly where we are!" she said. "The Reptoids must be using the megashelled stratosaurus's hollow spine as an elevator! If the megashelled stratosaurus's anatomy is similar to other reptilian giants', that means we'd be *here*—inside the creature's colon!"

Mank turned pale green. "We've been in a COLON this whole time?!"

"Hey, Mank? Buddy? Perhaps you should sit this part out," Roswell said.

The Mantis took his advice and turned the other way. He used his hands to cover his ears and his antennae to cover his eyes.

"If the bottom of the spine is outside that door, that means we're directly beneath the creature's *aorta*," Stella continued.

"So it's a *boy* megashelled stratosaurus!" Cassi said.

"No—an aorta is a creature's main artery. It carries blood through the whole body. Theoretically, if we found the entrance to the aorta, we could follow it into any part of the ship! We would just need to take the elevator one level up!"

"I don't think the elevator will work for us," Roswell said. "Xelic used a control on his wrist to operate it."

"Did the Reptoids convert anything into a flight of stairs?" Nerp asked.

Stella looked over the illustration and shook her head.

"Nothing we could get to from here," she said. "If only we had a jet pack or a hover board or wings!"

For the third time all the prisoners had the same idea at

once. They turned to Mank with matching grins. Roswell pulled the Mantis's hands away from his ears and brushed his antennae away from his eyes.

"Hey, Mank? Buddy? We've got a job for you!" he said.

"PASS," Mank said.

"You don't even know what it is yet!"

"Does it involve PHYSICAL CONTACT?"

"Yes!"

"DOUBLE PASS."

Stella stretched out Mank's wings like she was measuring a roll of fabric.

"How strong are these? Can you actually fly?" she asked.

"Stop THAT! And of course I can FLY!" Mank said.

"If you took us one at a time—and maybe a couple trips for Rob—could you transport us up the spine?" Stella asked.

"TRIPLE PASS!"

"Come on, Mank! Would you rather carry some friends up a hollow spine? Or spend the rest of your life trapped in a dead creature's bowels?" Roswell asked.

The options only made the Mantis even more squeamish.

"WHEN do you need an answer by?" he asked.

"MANK!" everyone said together.

"Okay, okay, okay—I'll DO IT!" Mank said. "But I better not pull a MUSCLE!"

With their fourth step finalized, the prisoners' spirits

were starting to rise. Stella couldn't stop herself from dancing in place as they formed their plan. However, the dancing stopped when she looked at her drawing and discovered a problem.

"Uh-oh," she said.

"What's wrong?" Roswell asked.

"I just remembered the aorta travels directly through the *heart* on the way to the *stomach*! That means we've got to pass through the Reptiliz's chambers before the hangar! It'll be the most highly guarded room of the ship!"

Everyone went silent as they considered the dilemma. Several minutes passed and they still didn't have a solution. Roswell was first to have any idea whatsoever. He eagerly opened his mouth to share it but then realized how ridiculous the idea was.

"Well?" Nerp asked.

"Forget it," Roswell said. "It'll never work."

"Kid, we're using a hairy girl as a generator and a giant bug as an elevator," Nerp reminded him. "Now is not the time to be self-conscious!"

"Well, in *Star Wars*, Luke Skywalker and Han Solo sneak through the Death Star and rescue Princess Leia by dressing in the stormtroopers' uniforms," Roswell explained.

"What is a star war?" Rob asked.

"It's a religion on Earth," Nerp said.

"If we take some soldiers by surprise and steal their

uniforms, maybe we could dress up and sneak through the Reptiliz's chambers?" Roswell said.

"Aren't we a little short to be Reptoidian soldiers?" Stella asked.

"Ha! Princess Leia says the same thing to—*never mind, that's not important.* We could distribute our height to fit the uniforms. Bleep could sit on Nerp's shoulders, Stella could sit on Mank's, and Cassi could sit on mine."

The prisoners eyed one another with equal amounts of fear and excitement. They had a plan—an outrageous plan—but it was better than *no plan.*

"Okay, let's recap," Stella said. "Step one, we're going to use Cassi to charge Rob's battery, and then use his battery to fry the electric bars. Step two, Bleep will squeeze through the bars and open them from the other side. Step three, we're going to use Rob's powerless body to break down the door and then separate him into parts. Step four, Mank will carry us up the elevator shaft and we'll find the entrance of the aorta. Step five, we're going to steal some Reptoidian uniforms and sneak through the Reptiliz's chambers. And finally, step six, we'll go to the hangar, get into a craft, and leave this horrible place!"

Mank gulped nervously. "What could POSSIBLY go wrong?"

CHAPTER EIGHT

THE GALACTIC LOOPHOLE

"Alllllrighty, fellow prison breakers, Operation *Reptoidian Escape* has officially begun!" Stella said, and did a high kick like a cheerleader. "Remember, once we deactivate the electric bars, we'll have only a few minutes before the Reptoids detect it. So we've got to move through the rest of the plan as quickly as possible. Shall we proceed with step one?"

The prisoners anxiously nodded, but no one was more nervous than Roswell. Their outrageous plan *had* to work—his life depended on it.

"Are you ready, Rob?" Stella asked.

Two prongs stuck out from the Cyborg's left palm like an electric plug.

"Affirmative," he said.

"Are you ready, Cassi?" Stella asked.

The Furgarian cracked her knuckles and neck.

"My litter was born ready," she said.

"Fantastic!" Stella said. "Let's take position!"

Cassi placed her paw on Rob's charging prongs and the other prisoners started petting her. Roswell rubbed the Furgarian's arms, Stella rubbed her belly, the Grays rubbed her legs, and Mank begrudgingly rubbed her back. They petted Cassi for five whole minutes, but nothing happened.

"Rob, are you absorbing any power yet?" Stella asked.

The Cyborg checked the screen on his forearm.

"My battery is still at eighty-two percent," he said.

"We need to create more friction," Stella said. "Everyone rub harder!"

"And a little to the left, Nerp," Cassi said. "Give that hip a good dig. Don't be shy."

The prisoners increased their efforts, using all their strength to summon the static electricity they needed. Soon their arms grew achy and tired. Meanwhile, Cassi closed her eyes and blissfully panted, enjoying every second of the process.

"Any update, Rob?" Stella asked.

"Still nothing," Rob said.

"Speak for yourself," Cassi said. "This is the best moment of my life!"

The Furgarian's left leg started to kick and she growled euphorically. The sound made all her cellmates uncomfortable.

"Ooooooh yeah! Someone found my spot!" she said.

"Rob, *please* tell me this is working," Roswell pleaded.

"Unfortunately, my battery is not responding to the..."

The Cyborg rechecked his screen and smiled.

"Wait a moment! My battery just went up to eighty-three percent!"

Slowly but surely the team felt a tingling sensation beneath their hands. Cassi's fur started to rise as static electricity covered her body.

"Now I am at eighty-four percent!" Rob announced. "It is working!"

Small electric waves flashed across Cassi's fur like she was a miniature storm. Soon she became one large hair ball, and her face and limbs disappeared under all the fluff. The progress encouraged the prisoners, and they rubbed the Furgarian harder and harder.

"Ninety-two percent!" Rob said.

"Hallelujah!" Cassi happily sang.

"Ninety-four percent!"

"Hallelujah!"

"Ninety-six percent!"

"Hallelujah! Hallelujah!"

"Ninety-eight percent!"

"This is amazing!" Roswell said.

"This is a miracle!" Stella said.

"This is ABSOLUTELY INSANE!" Mank yelled.

"Haaaaallelujaaaaah!" Cassi belted out.

"ONE HUNDRED PERCENT!" Rob announced. "My battery is at full capacity!"

The Cyborg's battery absorbed the final bit of Cassi's static electricity, and the fluffy Furgarian deflated like a balloon. The words *battery full* flashed across Rob's digital forehead. His eyes went wide like a child who had eaten too much candy.

"Whoa! What a rush!" Rob said. "I cannot remember the last time I absorbed so much energy in such a short period of time."

The other prisoners collapsed on the floor and held their exhausted arms.

"Beep-beep boop-boop beep-beep!"

"How would *you* know what a spin class feels like?" Nerp asked.

The Pleiadean helped everyone to their feet and checked the Cyborg's screen.

"How many volts does your battery have now, Rob?" Stella asked.

"Over sixty-nine thousand," he said.

"That's got to be enough to fry the breakers, right?" Roswell asked.

"Let us find out," Rob said. "Everyone stand back!"

The prisoners huddled in the far corner, and the Cyborg moved to the front of the cell. A metal rod stuck out of Rob's right palm, and he aimed it at the electric bars. He looked over his shoulder, and the word *concern* flashed across his digital forehead.

"Good night and good luck," Rob said. "I hope to see you on the other side."

BAAAAAM! A blinding flash erupted from the Cyborg's rod like a bolt of lightning. *SPAAAAAZ!* The electric bars sparked! *FIZZZZZH!* The electric bars smoked! *BWAAAAASH-BWAAAAASH-BWAAAAASH!* The electric bars strobed!

The prisoners shielded their eyes and covered their ears. Eventually the noise and the flashing came to a stop. The cellmates looked up and saw the bars were no longer glowing with electricity. The Cyborg was lying on the floor and his digital face was blank. The words *sleep mode* briefly flashed across his forehead and then disappeared.

"He did it!" Roswell cheered.

"Way to go, Rob!" Nerp said.

"I wish we had some Furgarian champagne to toast him!" Cassi said.

"We don't have time to celebrate," Stella reminded them. "The Reptoids are probably getting notified as we speak! Bleep, it's time for step two. You've got to squeeze through the bars and find the button that opens them."

The Small Gray moped to the front of the cell. They

inspected the openings in the crisscross bars, holding their head up to each one within reach.

"This isn't a fedora shop! Just pick one!" Nerp said.

"Beep-beep-beep boop beep-beep-beep!"

"I'm *not* being bossy!"

"Peep-peep peep!"

"No, *you're* a jerk! Hurry up!"

Bleep pushed their large head through the bars. To Roswell's amazement, the Small Gray moved through the barrier like their body was made of rubber. Once their head was through the bars, gravity pulled Bleep the rest of the way, and they somersaulted to the other side.

"Great job, Bleep!" Roswell said. "Way to use your head!"

"Now find the button to open the bars," Stella said. "Everything on this ship is made from the body parts of extinct species, so it won't look like regular controls."

The Small Gray searched the walls and found a panel with four reptilian eyeballs.

"Beep-beep?"

"Yes—just like that!" Nerp said. "Poke one of the eyes and see what happens."

Bleep pressed a yellow eyeball first. *SWOOOOOSH!* The prison's thin window opened to space! Everything and everyone were instantly sucked toward it! Nerp quickly grabbed on to the bars, Roswell grabbed on to Nerp, Cassi grabbed on to Roswell, Stella grabbed on to Cassi, Mank grabbed on to Stella, and the prisoners were suspended in the air like a living chain!

Mank tried to grab hold of Rob as he flew by, but the Cyborg was too heavy. Rob hit the wall but didn't fit through the window. Instead he clogged the window and temporarily stopped the suction. The prisoners hit the ground, and Bleep poked the remaining red, green, and blue eyeballs on the panel. *SHOOOOOSH!* The thin window sealed shut. *CLAAAAANK!* Rob slid to the floor. *SWOOOOOT!* The crisscross bars opened.

"Well, that couldn't have gone better," Nerp grumbled sarcastically.

"Peep-peep poop-poop peep-peep?"

"I *didn't* say you did that on purpose."

"Beep-beep boop beep-beep boop!"

"There's *nothing* wrong with my tone!"

"Can you guys get couples counseling later? We need to stay focused," Roswell said.

"He's right—it's time for step three," Stella said. "Now we're going to pick Rob up and use him as a battering ram. On my count of three, we'll charge toward the prison door. It may take a couple tries, so don't lose your grip."

"Remember to lift with your LEGS and not your BACK!" Mank said.

The cellmates stood around Rob and scooped him up. Even with them working together, the Cyborg was difficult to lift.

"Ready? One...two...*three!*"

"Hold up!" Roswell said. "Maybe we should turn Rob around so his *feet* are facing the door? It seems rude to go headfirst."

"Solid point," Stella said. "About-face!"

The prisoners rotated until the Cyborg's feet were facing the door.

"Ready? One...two...*three!*"

The team raced toward the prison door as fast as they could. *BAAAAAM!* The Cyborg's feet slammed against the stone door with very little effect. The team quickly backed up and repeated the maneuver. *BAAAAAM! BAAAAAM!* After the third time the stone door started to quiver. *It was becoming loose!* The prisoners backed up as far as possible and charged toward the door again. *BAAAAAM! BAAAAAM! BAAAAAM!* The sixth time was the charm! The prisoners knocked the door open and fell into a pile.

"Nice work, team!" Stella said. "Now we're going to distribute Rob's body."

The Pleiadean opened Rob's left pectoral shield and pulled the lever underneath. *POP-POP-POP-POP-POP!* The Cyborg's head and limbs ejected from his torso. Stella took the Cyborg's right arm and gave his left arm to Roswell, his right leg to Cassi, his left leg to Nerp, and his head to Bleep. When she turned to give Mank the Cyborg's torso, the Mantis was still lying on the ground.

"Can we take a BREAK?" Mank wheezed.

"Mank, it's time for step four!" Stella said. "You've got to fly us up the elevator shaft!"

"I don't have the energy to STAND, let alone FLY!"

"Come on, Mank! Are you a Mant*is* or a Mant*isn't?*" Roswell asked. "Get it? Get it?"

"Beep-beep boop."

"Yeah—we got it," Nerp said.

"I CAN'T DO THIS!" Mank yelled. "I'm not meant for so much PHYSICAL EXERTION!"

Roswell and Stella shared a glance of concern. They had only another minute—seconds maybe—before the Reptoidian guards arrived. How could they possibly get up the elevator shaft without Mank? Roswell knew they didn't have time to be polite—*his life was at stake!*

"I'm sorry about this, Mank," he said. "You've left me no choice."

Roswell licked his finger and gave Mank a wet willy below his antenna. The Mantis screamed and jumped to his feet with a sudden burst of energy.

"AAAAAH!" Mank shouted. "WHAT'S WRONG WITH YOU?!"

Roswell started coughing without covering his mouth.

"YOU'RE DISGUSTING! STOP THAT!"

Roswell spit in his hands and wiped them on Mank's green jumpsuit.

"ROSWELL! CONTROL YOURSELF! KEEP YOUR EARTHLING GERMS OFF OF ME!"

The other prisoners realized what Roswell was doing and joined in. Together they chased the Mantis in circles, coughing and spitting on him. Eventually Mank was so disgusted he worked up the energy to flutter above them.

"HAVE YOU ALL LOST YOUR MINDS?!" Mank cried.

"Great! Now that you can fly, we can begin step four!" Roswell said.

Mank gave Roswell the dirtiest look he had ever seen. "You're BARBARIC!"

One by one, Mank transported his cellmates up the elevator shaft to the level above the prison. The Mantis started with the six pieces of Rob, and then, eleven trips later, he finished with Cassi.

"How are you the HEAVIEST of all?" Mank asked her.

"It's a gift," Cassi said with a proud smile.

The level above the prison was a very dark and damp space. It was roughly the size of Roswell's school gymnasium, and it had an awful stench of salt and sulfur. The walls were runny with condensation, and the floor was soaked with puddles.

"Beep-beep boop beep-beep-beep."

"I agree—it *does* smell like rotten asparagus in here," Nerp said.

"Outstanding! We've reached the bladder!" Stella announced.

174

"OUTSTANDING?" Mank asked, and then immediately dry heaved.

"The entrance to the aorta will definitely be in here," Stella said. "Everyone keep an eye out for a round doorway. When megashelled stratosauruses are alive, they have green blood that glows in the dark. Look for a lustrous residue."

"A LUSTROUS RESIDUE?" Mank asked. "Do you have to say EVERYTHING with a smile?"

"Sorry, it's a Pleiadean thing," Stella said.

The cellmates split up and searched the moist chamber. They held their noses and carefully watched their step to avoid the puddles. Roswell found a round doorway in the back of the room that led to a long hallway. Just as Stella had predicted, the corridor was coated with neon-green clumps of dried alien blood.

"Hey, guys!" Roswell said, and whistled to the others. "I think I found it!"

CLUUUUUM-BUUUUUNG! A strong and screechy rumble echoed down the elevator shaft. The prisoners looked at one another in terror.

"The Reptoids are coming!" Stella said. "Quick! Everyone into the aorta!"

"There's a sentence I NEVER want to hear again!" Mank moaned.

Roswell led the others into the round hallway. The

corridor curved and wound upward, traveling higher and higher into the mother ship. Every few hundred feet the prisoners found the entrance to another chamber. They took turns peering around each corner and quickly dashed past the doorways.

"We just passed the kidneys," the Pleiadean informed the group. "We're getting close to the megashelled stratosaurus's heart. I don't think it's safe to go any farther until we get Reptoidian uniforms."

"Let's find someplace to hide," Roswell said. "As soon as some soldiers walk by, we'll jump out, take them by surprise, and steal their clothes."

"Beep-beep boop-boop beep boop-boop?"

"Yeah—what does 'take them by surprise' mean?" Nerp asked.

Roswell shrugged. "I'm not sure—that's just what they say in the movies. Maybe we can knock them unconscious with Rob's limbs?"

"Wow, Rob is the gift that keeps on giving," Cassi noted.

"But will that work in REAL LIFE?" Mank asked.

"HEEEEEY!"

The prisoners turned around and saw five Reptoidian soldiers standing directly behind them. The soldiers raised their electric spears and lurched toward the frightened cellmates.

"What are you doing up here?" a soldier yelled.

"How did you get out of the prison?" yelled another.

"Beep-beep boop beep-beep?"

"No, Bleep—honesty is *not* the best policy here," Nerp said.

"NOW WHAT?!" Mank cried.

"Don't worry, I've got this," Cassi assured the others. "Time to whip out the old Furgarian charm."

"Cassi, wait!" Roswell said. "I don't think that's a good idea!"

Before anyone could stop her, the Furgarian confidently strutted up to the soldiers. Cassi batted her eyelashes and gave the Reptoids a wide, snaggletoothed grin.

"Well, hellooooo, handsomes!" she said. "There's nothing I love more than men in uniform. You're tall glasses of water for a pair of thirsty eyes. The name's Cassiopeia Furbottom. What's yours?"

No one said a word. The soldiers and the prisoners were equally confused about what the Furgarian was doing.

"I know, I know—my beauty has left you speechless," Cassi said. "Let's cut to the chase, fellas. Obviously, you've caught us in the middle of an escape. Naturally, you'll want to throw us back in the slammer and alert the general. But what if I told you there was *another* option? What if I told you there was a way to make *everyone* happy?"

"Beep boop beep boop-boop?"

"I don't know where she's going with this!" Nerp said.

"Listen up, gentlemen, because I'm about to make you

an offer you can't refuse," Cassi said. "Instead of imprisoning us, *come with us*! Why stay in this *turtle shell* when you could travel the galaxy with a *bombshell* like me? And if you boys help us, I'll take you out for a wild night on Furgaria that you'll never forget! I'm talking the best restaurants, the best nightclubs, and the best Frisbee golf courses you've ever seen! So what do you say? Do we have a deal?"

A soldier zapped Cassi with his spear, and the Furgarian fell to the floor.

"We choose option one, you ugly mutt!" the Reptoid shouted.

At first Cassi didn't move a muscle, and Roswell worried she was dead. The soldiers lunged forward to seize the Furgarian, when suddenly a ferocious growl erupted from deep within her. Cassi jumped onto her hands and knees, she arched her back, and she bared her sharp underbite. Her claws stuck out, the hair on the back of her neck stood straight up, and foam dripped from her mouth. Cassi glared at the soldiers with so much anger her cellmates didn't recognize her. The friendly Furgarian had turned into a dangerous animal right before their eyes.

"*That's it!*" Cassi growled. "*No more Miss Nice Furbottom!*"

It all happened so fast Roswell could barely process what he was watching. Cassi crawled in circles around the Reptoids like a bear, but with the speed of a race car. The soldiers tried to strike and zap her with their weapons, but they became dizzy and hit one another instead. Cassi leaped onto their helmets and clawed at their faces like a cat. Next, the Furgarian climbed up the wall and slammed her whole body into the Reptoids like a professional wrestler. The soldiers fell backward and hit the ground like dominoes. Once they were on the floor, the Furgarian grabbed a Reptoid's spear and electrocuted them until all five soldiers were unconscious.

The cellmates' jaws dropped open like broken mailboxes.

"What just happened?" Stella asked.

"Cassi took the soldiers *by surprise*," Roswell said.

"She took us ALL by surprise!" Mank said.

The Furgarian dropped the weapon and took a deep breath. Her claws retracted, her mouth dried, and the hair on the back of her neck went flat. Her friendly demeanor returned, and she smiled at her cellmates like everything was perfectly normal.

"Sorry about that," Cassi said. "It's been a while since I went *beast mode*."

"Are you kidding?" Roswell said. "That was unbelievable!"

"Remind me to NEVER upset you!" Mank said.

Cassi bashfully shrugged. "I'm just glad I didn't lose my temper. That would have been *really* embarrassing."

The prisoners shuddered at the thought of what *else* Cassi might be capable of. Stella clapped her hands to get the group's attention.

"Don't lose steam—we're nearly there," the Pleiadean said. "Let's get dressed in the soldiers' uniforms and sneak through the Reptiliz's chambers. Go, team, go!"

The cellmates quickly undressed the unconscious Reptoids. The soldiers had the same green skin, yellow eyes, wide mouths, and slit nostrils as General Xelic. Even though they were shorter than the general, the Reptoids were still much taller than the prisoners. As planned, the cellmates doubled up to fill out the uniforms. Bleep sat on Nerp's shoulders, Stella sat on Mank's shoulders, and Cassi climbed on top of Roswell. Mank was right—the Furgarian was much heavier than she looked, but there wasn't time to switch partners now.

The duos carefully dressed themselves in the Reptoids' spiky helmets and scaled armor. They each left a button unfastened so Roswell, Mank, and Nerp could see where they were walking. Thankfully, the uniforms were roomy enough to conceal the pieces of Rob too.

The prisoners continued up the winding corridor and traveled to the center of the mother ship. They found the entrance to the Reptiliz's chambers at the end of the aorta. *POOOOOSH! POOOOOSH!* Two enormous doors opened like a pair of living valves. A platoon of soldiers exited the chamber through the right door, while a second platoon entered through the left.

"They must be changing the guard," Roswell whispered.

"Quick! Let's join the soldiers headed inside!" Stella whispered back.

The prisoners followed the soldiers on the left. They marched into the mother ship's heart, and the valve shut tightly behind them. *There was no turning back now.*

The Reptiliz's chamber was the eeriest room Roswell had ever set foot in. The megashelled stratosaurus's heart had been converted into a shadowy chamber with massive stone pillars. Every inch of the floor and walls was covered with the same mysterious vines from the hangar and the command center, which made it difficult for the prisoners to walk.

Roswell discovered that all the vines grew from a single spot in the heart of the mother ship. However, the vines didn't grow from a seed or a set of roots; they grew from a *person.* Seated on a tall throne in the center of the chamber was the most grotesque being Roswell had ever seen.

Reptiliz Reek VII looked like he was a million years old. His green face was as wrinkled as a tree stump, his back was hunched like a camel's, his black fingernails were over a foot long, and he wore a dark robe with tattered ends. To Roswell's surprise, all the vines were growing out of the Reptiliz's skull! They stretched high toward the ceiling, then snaked down the walls and grew out the doors. Reptiliz Reek covered the mother ship like a weedy monster.

The Reptoidian ruler was asleep when Roswell and his

cellmates arrived, but the marching soldiers stirred him awake. The platoon stood in a circle around the chamber and bowed to their leader. The prisoners mimicked the movements—although they were a couple of seconds delayed. Their bows where also very shallow so that Stella, Cassi, and Bleep didn't fall off Mank's, Roswell's, and Nerp's shoulders.

After the first ten minutes in the chamber, Roswell's whole body started to ache from the Furgarian's weight. He could hear Mank and Nerp getting restless too. For all they knew, it might be *hours* before they got to leave.

COOOOOF! Another valve opened and General Xelic entered the heart. The general approached the Reptiliz and kneeled.

"Well?" Reek grumbled.

The Reptiliz's voice was so raspy it sounded like four voices were speaking at once.

"My lord, I have made contact with the Earthling," General Xelic said.

"Finally," Reek said. "Put him through."

The general pressed a button on his cuff. A hologram of a giant human ear appeared between the Reptoids.

"Hello? Is this thing on?"

Roswell grew more tense than he already was. *He recognized that voice!*

"We can hear you, but you aren't using the holophone correctly," General Xelic said. "Move it away from your ear!"

The giant ear was replaced with the top of a bald head.

"How about now? Can you see me?"

"All we see is your head!" the general said.

"Is this better?"

"No! Move it lower!"

"I still can't see either of you."

"For the love of the Source! Put the device on the ground and step back!"

The hologram became a middle-aged man in a sharp designer suit. Roswell had to cover his mouth to silence a gasp. *He knew exactly who it was!*

"We want an update, Mr. Rump," the Reptiliz said. "Is everything still on schedule?"

The hologram of Eli Rump straightened his jacket and gave the Reptoids a cocky grin.

"Perfectly," the billionaire said. "The equipment has passed the inspections, and the weather forecast is clear. The launch will happen at noon on April first, and the first satellite will enter Earth's orbit at precisely twelve ten PM."

"And you're confident it will stay that way?" the general asked.

"I don't foresee any hiccups whatsoever," Rump said. "Rump Rockets has never been more prepared. The only thing left to finalize is the guest list. As of today over thirty United States senators, two hundred congresspeople, and seven Real Housewives will be in attendance. I've booked the Rolling Stones to perform at the reception, and the actor Matthew McConaughey will be reading the count-down. Netflix is even producing a documentary about the—"

The Reptiliz raised a hand to silence the eager billion-aire.

"Don't get distracted by pageantry, Mr. Rump," Reek said. "I have explained how important this launch is. If your rocket fails, you will not survive my wrath."

The Reptoidian ruler gave the tycoon a threatening scowl, but Rump wasn't fazed by the warning. On the con-trary, the billionaire casually checked his fingernails.

"Nothing will go wrong on my end," he said. "In fact, everything is running so smoothly I'd like to revisit our *agreement*."

The remark outraged General Xelic. "You *what?*"

"This endeavor has required much more effort, money, and public scrutiny than I expected. I've been the joke of every late-night show and the punching bag of every blog. It's only fair to reward my endurance and *increase* my end of the bargain. After all, you need this project to work more than I do. And I'm the only man on Earth who can make it happen."

"You ungrateful parasite!" General Xelic roared. "We are six Earth days away from the launch! How dare you try to renegotiate!"

Unlike the general, the Reptiliz wasn't angered in the slightest.

"Spit it out, Mr. Rump," Reek said. "What else do you want?"

"In addition to North America, I've decided I deserve Europe too," Rump said. "That would still leave the Reptoids five continents and four oceans to reign over."

"This is ludicrous!" the general yelled.

"Very well," Reek said without missing a beat. "Once everything is complete, you can have North America *and* Europe. We'll even give you Australia as a token of our appreciation."

The billionaire was so excited he lost his breath.

"Wow! That's very generous of you, Reek!"

"*Reptiliz* Reek," General Xelic barked.

"Forgive me, *Reptiliz*."

"Do not mistake my generosity for anything but incentive," Reek said. "Moving forward, we want a briefing every day at this time. And should any issues present themselves, you are to notify us immediately. Is that clear?"

"Crystal," the billionaire said.

"Then goodbye, Mr. Rump," Reek said.

General Xelic pressed a button on his cuff and the hologram vanished.

"Who does that Neanderthal think he is?!" the general shouted.

"Calm down, Xelic," Reek said. "That man is a moron if he expects a square foot from us. Once we touch down, he'll be the first human we kill."

"I hope you'll allow me the honors," the general said.

"The same warning goes for *you*, Xelic," Reek said. "I cannot stress enough how significant this launch is. As soon as Mr. Rump's first rocket leaves the atmosphere, the Earthlings will have officially weaponized space. Earth will be considered hostile and dangerous to other systems, they will lose the Milky Way Galactic Alliance's protection, and our *invasion* will be completely legal. Once we colonize Earth, our resources will be boundless, our potential will be limitless, and the Reptoids will become the dominant species of the galaxy. However, none of that will happen without a successful launch. Make sure *nothing* sabotages it."

General Xelic kneeled before the throne again.

"Yes, my lord," he said. "You have my word."

SKWAAAAAMP-SKWAAAAAMP-SKWAAAAAMP! An alarm blared through the Reptiliz's chamber. *SKWAAAAAMP-SKWAAAAAMP-SKWAAAAAMP!* A valve opened and a soldier hurried inside. *SKWAAAAAMP-SKWAAAAAMP-SKWAAAAAMP!*

"This better be important," General Xelic shouted.

"Forgive the interruption, General," the soldier said. *"The prisoners have escaped!"*

"WHAT?!" the general yelled in disbelief.

The Reptiliz was so furious a ripple traveled through all the vines in the mother ship.

"XEEEEELIC!" Reek roared. "HOW COULD YOU LET THIS HAPPEN?"

A vine rose off the floor and struck General Xelic across the face. The blow was so powerful it knocked the general off his feet.

"FIND THOSE PRISONERS AT ONCE!" Reek demanded.

General Xelic quickly turned to the soldiers surrounding the chamber.

"You heard the Reptiliz! Search every corner of this ship!" he ordered.

SKWAAAAAMP-SKWAAAAAMP-SKWAAAAAMP! The Reptoids scattered and exited the heart in every direction. *SKWAAAAAMP-SKWAAAAAMP-SKWAAAAAMP!* As the soldiers left, Roswell heard a familiar high-pitched noise and felt a tingling sensation on his forehead.

Now's our chance! Everyone follow me and Mank to the hangar! Stay close!

Stella and Mank hurried out of the chamber, and Nerp and Bleep trailed behind. However, Roswell didn't move. The conversation he'd just witnessed was so shocking it paralyzed him. He didn't even feel the Furgarian's weight on his shoulders anymore.

So that's the loophole! Roswell thought. *The Reptoids figured out the perfect way to make their agenda legal! They're using Eli Rump to weaponize space! But they don't want our resources—they want our whole planet! The Reptoids are going to invade Earth and destroy everything and everyone on it!*

"Sweetcheeks, we've got to go!" Cassi whispered.

The Furgarian tugged on Roswell's hair like the reins of a horse. She steered Roswell across the chamber, and they followed their cellmates out of the heart. The chaotic breach was the perfect cover for the prisoners to move freely through the mother ship. Before Roswell knew it, they had reached the hangar.

The team ducked down behind a row of Reptoidian shellcrafts. Besides the Grays' flying saucer and the Pleiadean's diamond bird, Roswell saw three other impounded spaceships he hadn't noticed before. The first was a red craft that looked like a giant dragonfly, the second was a metal ship that resembled an enormous television remote, and the third looked like a big purple sea urchin. Roswell assumed the spacecraft belonged to Mank, Rob, and Cassi.

"Beep boop beep boop-boop!"

"We can't take our ship! They fried our engines, remember?!" Nerp said.

"I think we should take my Priscilla," Cassi said. "She doesn't have engines to fry."

"Your ship is *ALIVE?*" Mank asked.

"Of course Priscilla's alive—she's a space urchin!" Cassi said. "They're the easiest way to get around the galaxy! Just tell Priscilla where you want to go, and she does all the work. And her passenger pouch is quite comfortable once you get used to her smell."

"I'm not getting in that thing for all the SANITIZER in the galaxy!" Mank said.

"We can't take any of our ships!" Stella told the group. "We've got to take a Reptoidian shellcraft to blend in! Does anyone know how to pilot one?"

The Tall Gray gulped. "Bleep and I can give it a try."

"Great," Stella said. "Everyone inside!"

"I'll come back for you one day, Priscilla!" Cassi whispered to the urchin. "I promise!"

The three duos boarded the closest Reptoidian shellcraft. As soon as they were inside, Bleep, Stella, and Cassi climbed off the others, who moaned with relief. They pulled off the soldiers' uniforms and placed the pieces of Rob in a pile.

Just like the mother ship, all the shellcraft's controls were made from body parts. Nerp and Bleep sat behind the dashboard and began pulling the tails, turning the claws, and poking the eyes to start the engines. *VROOOOOM!* The shellcraft roared to life and hovered above the hangar floor.

"Beep-beep boop!"

"Bleep's right—I think we figured this thing out!" Nerp said.

"WE'VE GOT COMPANY!" Mank yelled.

The Mantis frantically pointed outside. A platoon of

soldiers had noticed the rumbling shellcraft. The Reptoids could see the fleeing prisoners behind the shellcraft's windshield. They charged toward the ship and fired lasers at the craft. The shellcraft rocked back and forth as it was pelted.

"We need a way out of the hangar!" Nerp said.

"Peep-peep poop!"

"We *can't* open the doors! Only the command center can!"

"Beep boop beep-beep!"

"What? That's madness!"

"Beep boop beep-beep!"

"Everything will get sucked out!"

"BEEP BOOP BEEP-BEEP!"

"FINE!" Nerp shouted. "Everyone hold on! We're about to do something very stupid!"

The Tall Gray yanked a red tail on the dashboard three times. *BOOOOOSH! BOOOOOSH! BOOOOOSH!* The shellcraft fired three powerful lasers at the hangar's doors. *BAAAAAM!* The lasers blasted a huge hole through the exit! *SHOOOOOSH!* In a matter of seconds, all the spacecraft and soldiers in the hangar were sucked into space! Everything floated away from the mother ship and drifted into the Oort cloud.

"Nice work!" Stella said.

"That was GENIUS!" Mank cheered.

"Beep boop beep boop-boop!"

"Yes—we know it was your idea!" Nerp said.

"Quick! Shoot the tractor beam so they can't pull us back in!" Stella said.

The Tall Gray spun the shellcraft around to face the mother ship. *BOOOOOSH! BOOOOOSH! BOOOOOSH!* They fired another round at the Reptoids' tractor beam. *BAAAAAM!* The device exploded and the shellcraft was free to flee.

"You're free, Priscilla!" Cassi called to the space urchin floating past their craft. "Get out of here! Start a family! Open a boutique! Live your best life!"

"Where to next?" Nerp asked.

"It doesn't matter!" Stella said. "Just pick a direction and go!"

Nerp pulled a green tongue on the dashboard. The shellcraft rocketed through the Oort cloud and soared far away from the Reptoidian fleet. The mother ship disappeared in the distance behind them, and the passengers celebrated their escape with cheers, hugs, high fives, and high fours.

Unfortunately, Roswell couldn't muster any joy to join the aliens. It was impossible to be cheerful while knowing about the Reptoids' planned invasion.

"Roswell, are you okay?" Stella asked him.

His mind was racing so fast he couldn't form words to answer her question.

Are you okay?

The Reptoids don't want Earth's resources, they want

to invade us! And they figured out the perfect loophole to make it legal!

I know. I heard the Reptiliz too.

As soon as Eli Rump's rocket leaves Earth's atmosphere, that's it! Game over!

That's still six days away! We'll find a way to save Earth!

But how?

The Pleiadean didn't have an answer. Roswell and the aliens might be safe—for now—but Earth, his grandparents, and everyone he knew had never been in so much danger.

The nightmare was over, but the apocalypse had just begun.

CHAPTER NINE

ALLEN ASTRO'S ASTEROID BAR AND GRILL

The stolen shellcraft zoomed through space with no destination in mind. The escapees' only goal was to get as far away from the Reptoids as possible. After six hours of interspace travel, the passengers were confident they weren't being followed or tracked. They took their first collective deep breath since their departure. And according to the orchestra of empty stomachs that followed, they were all collectively *starving* too.

"Beep-beep boop beep-beep."

"I could use some food too," Nerp said. "I know a place nearby that's never busy. It's just a chain restaurant—but we should keep a low profile."

"I'll take anything!" Cassi said. "I'm so hungry I'm

starting to think Bleep would taste good with a side of ranch."

"Peep-peep-peep!"

"Relax, Bleep—she's kidding," Nerp said. "I think."

The Grays steered the shellcraft to a lone asteroid in the middle of space. The asteroid had a single structure built on its rocky surface. Allen Astro's Asteroid Bar and Grill looked exactly like a classic American diner. The neon sign and long tin building reminded Roswell of restaurants in Cherokee Springs, except Allen Astro's had a domed force field to prevent its patrons from getting sucked into space. The diner also had a statue of a chubby blue alien in a chef's hat. The mascot held a plate of extraterrestrial cuisine as it slowly rotated on the roof.

The shellcraft sank through the force field and landed in the diner's parking lot. The passengers exited the shellcraft with the pieces of Rob and entered the restaurant. The inside of the diner had cushy red booths, a long countertop, and even a jukebox. Elvis Presley's "Jailhouse Rock" was playing as they walked in, which Roswell thought was ironic given their situation.

"Weird," he said. "Is this *supposed* to look like the diners on Earth?"

"Or maybe the diners on Earth are supposed to look like *this*," Nerp said.

The group was greeted at the door by a robotic waitress. She had four metal arms, and a serving tray built around her waist, and the robot rolled around the diner on a single wheel.

"Welcome to Allen Astro's," the waitress said. "How many in your party?"

"Six, please," Nerp said. "And a chair for the Cyborg if you don't mind."

"Would you like carbon, hydrogen, or helium menus?"

"CARBON!" Mank decided. "Helium makes me GASSY!"

The waitress escorted them to a booth in the middle of the diner. Roswell and his friends were the only customers except for an alien sitting at the counter. The guest had two arms and two legs and wore a dark blue space suit. Their round helmet was tinted so dark the alien's face wasn't visible. The stranger watched Roswell and the others closely as they walked by. Even as they took their seats in the booth, the curious alien never looked away.

"What kind of alien is that?" Roswell whispered.

"A NOSY one!" Mank said.

"*Hey buddy!*" Cassi yelled. "*Take a hologram! It lasts longer!*"

Despite her remark, the alien never looked away. Their unwavering interest made Roswell feel uneasy. The Furgarian, on the other hand, was flattered by the attention.

"This happens to me every time I visit a new place," Cassi said. "Poor thing has never seen someone as good-looking as me."

The robotic waitress placed an empty chair next to their booth. Nerp and Bleep propped Rob's torso on the seat and popped his head and limbs back into their sockets. The powerless Cyborg slouched in the chair like a metal scarecrow. Once Rob was reconfigured, the waitress handed each of them a thin menu that showed videos of the diner's food options. The waitress rolled away to give them a minute and then rolled back to take their order.

"What can I get for you?" she asked.

"Beep-beep boop beep-beep-beep."

"Two moondust puddings," Nerp said.

"The proton protein bowl," Stella said.

"The crispy Cyclorrhapha salad—*HOLD* the thoraxes," Mank said.

"I'll take Allen Astro's famous aluminum meat strips, the nebula nuked nuggets, two Condor Galaxy steaks well done, the white dwarf pasta Andromeda style, and a comet ice cream shake," Cassi said.

"Oh, and a battery on the side for the Cyborg," Stella added.

Roswell was overwhelmed by the menu. It was written in an alien language, and he didn't recognize the food in any of the videos.

"Can you do a burger and fries?" Roswell asked.

"Would you like that gamma fried, solar flared, or radiated?" the waitress asked.

"Um...medium rare?"

"Coming right up!"

A narrow funnel descended from the ceiling and began 3D-printing the orders on the table. The waitress rolled into the back room and returned with an enormous battery. She plugged Rob's left hand into the battery, and the word *charging* blinked on his digital forehead. Once the food was done printing, everyone dug in like they were in an eating contest.

Roswell hadn't eaten in over a day, but he barely touched his food. All he could think about was the Reptoids' pending invasion of Earth. Stella knew exactly what he was thinking without having to read his mind—in fact, everyone at the table did. No one knew how to comfort him, so they sat in silence as they finished their meals.

"AAAAAH!" Rob screamed.

The Cyborg powered back on and abruptly sat up in his chair. The motion caused the others to jump in their seats as well. Rob's digital features returned to his face, and the word *rebooting* flashed across his forehead. The Cyborg looked around the diner in bewilderment.

"We are out of the mother ship!" he noted. "Did we escape? Are we free?"

"Free as a Furgarian divorce," Cassi said.

"The plan worked perfectly," Stella said.

"I wouldn't say PERFECTLY, but we managed," Mank added.

The Cyborg was exhilarated by the good news. However,

it was obvious the others didn't share his enthusiasm. The word *confusion* flashed across his forehead.

"Why does everyone look so distraught?" Rob asked.

"We found out the Reptoids are going to invade Earth," Stella said. "They weren't in the Earthling solar system to steal resources—they want the *whole* planet!"

"An *invasion?*" the Cyborg asked. "But Earth is a stage-two planet."

"The Reptoids found a loophole to make it legal," Stella explained. "A billionaire named Eli Rump is going to weaponize space. Once his rocket leaves the atmosphere, Earth will officially lose the Milky Way Galactic Alliance's protection. And their invasion will be perfectly legal."

It was the first time Roswell had heard someone besides the Reptiliz say the horrible plot out loud. Hearing it from Stella's mouth made the situation seem real, and Roswell couldn't hold back his devastation anymore. He folded his arms and rested his head on the table to hide the tears spilling down his cheeks.

"There, there, sweetcheeks," Cassi said, and gently stroked his hair. "Did you know *stressed* is just *desserts* spelled backward?"

"Is that supposed to make him feel BETTER?" Mank asked.

"No, but I'm hoping someone will split the cosmic cream pie with me," she said.

"Don't give up, Roswell," Stella said. "I have my Pleiadean certificate in intergalactic diplomacy, and if there's one thing I know for sure, it's that nothing is over until it's over. We still have six Earth days before the launch—that gives us three galactic days to stop the Reptoids! Now that we all have some food in our bellies, we should discuss our next steps."

Mank almost spit out his Cyclorrhapha salad.

"NEXT steps?" the Mantis exclaimed. "We just escaped a REPTOIDIAN PRISON! My next step is going HOME!"

"Mank, don't be selfish!" Stella said. "Billions of innocent Earthlings will perish if we don't do something! We need to put our heads together and come up with a solution!"

"How will touching heads help?" Rob asked.

"It means 'brainstorm,'" Stella said. "Any ideas?"

"Beep-beep boop-boop beep-beep-beep!"

"No, Bleep—we don't have time to produce a true-crime series," Nerp said.

"Loophole or no loophole, the Reptoids have broken every INTERGALACTIC LAW in the book!" Mank said. "They KIDNAPPED us! They DAMAGED our ships! They tortured ROSWELL! And they CONSPIRED with Eli Rump to weaponize space! That's blatant stage-two planetary INTERFERENCE!"

"The Reptoids *will* be brought to justice—but justice takes time," Stella said. "Even if we reported them to the

Milky Way Galactic Alliance today, the alliance would need to conduct their own investigation. It could take them a galactic week to gather evidence and charge the Reptoids. We need something *fast*."

The table went quiet as they tried to think of *anything* to save Earth. Unfortunately, the solution didn't come as easily as Stella had hoped.

"I suppose there's only one option," the Pleiadean said. "We have to convince the alliance to keep Earth under their protection *despite* the launch. Once they hear about the Reptoids' collusion with Eli Rump, I'm sure they'll make an exception."

"Speaking with the alliance could take galactic YEARS!" Mank said. "Some beings wait DECADES for an appointment!"

Everyone sank into their seats and silently stared down at their plates. However, just as the group was about to accept defeat, the word *processing* flashed across Rob's forehead. The Cyborg had an idea and beamed with artificial hope.

"Wait a moment," Rob said. "We could use *my* appointment."

"Appointment for what, babe? Oil change?" Cassi asked.

"I am scheduled to speak to the Milky Way Galactic Alliance in two and a half galactic days," Rob said. "I am speaking on behalf of Cyborg rights, but the subject can be anything I choose. We could use my appointment to save Earth!"

The idea made everyone sit straight up in their seats. Even Roswell looked up and dried his tears with the sleeve of his hoodie.

"You're telling us you RANDOMLY have an appointment with the MILKY WAY GALACTIC ALLIANCE?" Mank asked.

"My appointment has been several galactic years in the making," Rob said. "Although I never imagined I would escape in time to attend it."

"Shnigglebotts! Rob, that would be perfect!" Stella exclaimed.

"Beep-beep boop-boop beep-beep-beep."

"Yeah—it *does* seem too good to be true," Nerp said.

Mank groaned. "That's because it IS too good to be true!" he said. "You're all forgetting one NOT-SO-SMALL detail! Even if we used Rob's appointment, the topic would still need SPONSORSHIP from the leaders of FIVE STAGE-THREE SYSTEMS! That's a lot of space to cover in THREE GALACTIC DAYS!"

"You know what else is challenging? *Escaping a Reptoidian prison!* But we did it!" Stella reminded the group. "Maybe fate put us together for a reason? Maybe we were imprisoned at the same time because we were meant to save Earth?"

"Still thinking about those Pleiadean Public Service Points, huh?" Cassi asked.

"Of course I am—but this is so much bigger than that!" Stella said. "A whole planet is going to be destroyed, and millions of stage-two species will be exterminated! Nerp and Bleep, if Earth is destroyed, think of all the priceless *DNA* that will be lost! Mank, think of all the new germs that will evolve from the unsanitary war zones! And Cassi, think of all the boy bands that will perish!"

"Even the *K-pop* bands?!" Cassi asked.

The Pleiadean nodded. "Even the K-pop bands!" she said. "Whether we succeed or not, we have to try!"

"Peep-peep poop-poop peep-peep?"

"Good question—who could we get sponsorship from in such a hurry?" Nerp asked.

"We need five signatures, and there are five alien species at this table," Stella said. "I know every member of the Seven Sisters Council, so the Pleiades system will be a breeze. And I'm sure the rest of you have connections on your home planets too."

"The Cyborg Station does not have a leader," Rob said. "Every political issue is voted on virtually by all the Cyborg citizens. I will simply go to Data City and submit a public ballot."

"Terrific!" Stella said. "Nerp? Bleep? Could you get us a meeting with your leader?"

"Beep-beep boop-boop beep boop-boop-boop."

"Bleep's right—there's a *possibility* we'll know the president," Nerp said. "On Grayton, all roles of leadership are assigned weekly. It's designed to prevent corruption. You'd be amazed at how efficient politics can be when there are no politicians."

"Fantastic!" Stella said. "Cassi? What about Furgaria?"

"Are you kidding?" she said. "My uncle Clancy is the Fuzzfurr."

"What's a Fuzzfurr?" Roswell asked.

"The Fuzzfurr is Furgaria's version of an emperor," Cassi explained.

"Does that mean you're *Furgarian royalty?*" Roswell asked.

Cassi shrugged like it was obvious. "You couldn't tell?"

"Wonderful—that's four out of five," Stella continued. "How about you, Mank? Do you know anyone with clout on the Insectia Moon?"

Mank quivered at the thought. "I would have to speak with MOTHER."

"Your *mom* is the leader of the Insectia Moon?" Roswell asked.

"She's EVERYONE'S mother!" Mank said. "She lays over a THOUSAND EGGS a day!"

"Dang," Cassi said. "Holiday shopping must be impossible."

"Could you find a way to speak with her?" Stella asked.

"I share a hatchday with her current HEAD OF

SECURITY," Mank said. "I might be able to pull some strings with HIM."

"Outstanding—that's five out of five!" Stella said. "So it's settled! We'll travel to each of our home systems and get the sponsorship to speak with the Milky Way Galactic Alliance!"

The Pleiadean gave the table a cheerful round of applause. It was planned so quickly Roswell had a difficult time wrapping his head around it.

"Guys, I appreciate the offer, but I can't let you do this," Roswell said. "Especially you, Rob. The Cyborgs have waited too long for Cyborg rights. You can't give up your appointment!"

"But the Cyborgs *can* wait—Earth cannot," Rob said. "Besides, I would still be in the Reptoids' prison cell if it were not for you. I owe you, Roswell. We all do."

The rest of the group nodded along with the Cyborg's statement—even Mank couldn't argue. Roswell's eyes welled with tears as he looked around at his alien friends, but this time they were tears of happiness.

"I can't believe you'd do this for Earth," he said. "I can't believe you'd do this for *me*."

"I'd give you a kidney, sweetcheeks," Cassi said. "And I only have four left!"

The Pleiadean's pleasant smile faded into a serious frown.

"It's *not* just for you," she said. "This invasion will affect the whole galaxy. If the Reptoids had their own planet, they'd become more powerful than ever! Who knows what planet they'll destroy after Earth? Who knows which of our homes will be attacked next? The Reptoids' invasion of Earth isn't their endgame, it's only the beginning."

The chilling notion sent shivers down everyone's spines. If the team wasn't motivated enough already, they certainly were now. Cassi put her paw in the center of the table.

"For the galaxy!" she told the others.

One at a time the others placed their hands on top of her paw.

"For the galaxy!" Roswell said.

"For the galaxy!" Stella said.

"For the galaxy," Rob said.

"Beep-beep boop-boop-boop!"

"Agreed—for the galaxy," Nerp said.

"Come on, Mank—we're just waiting on you!" Cassi said.

The Mantis rolled his big eyes. "Okay, okay, okay—FOR THE GALAXY! But I already know I'm going to REGRET this!"

"Beep boop-boop beep boop-boop."

"You're right—we better get going if we're going to pull this off," Nerp said.

"Check, please!" Stella called to the waitress.

"And seven cosmic cream pies to go!" Cassi said.

Strangely, as soon as they requested their bill, the alien

at the counter abruptly left the diner. Roswell had a hunch they had been eavesdropping on their entire conversation. A few moments later the alien flew by the diner, and Roswell caught a glimpse of their spacecraft. The sight made his stomach drop.

The alien's ship was pitch-black, about a hundred feet long, and had six bright lights on its base. To Roswell's disbelief, the craft was shaped like a giant *boomerang*. Roswell felt like he was seeing a ghost—but a ghost he had never personally laid eyes on. The ship looked exactly like the UFO from his father's stories.

"Roswell, are you feeling ill?" Rob asked. "My monitors have detected a sudden spike in your blood pressure."

"What kind of craft is that?" he asked.

Stella squinted as she studied the ship.

"I'm not sure," she said. "I've never seen one like that before. Why do you ask?"

"Never mind," Roswell said. "It's probably just a coincidence."

Roswell couldn't take his eyes off the spaceship. The craft eventually disappeared from sight, but not from his mind. Roswell couldn't shake the eerie feeling that he and the mysterious boomerang would cross paths again.

COOOOOF! A valve opened and General Xelic entered the Reptiliz's chamber. He walked with his head held low and his green tail between his legs. The general kneeled before his superior with more depth than usual.

"Well?" Reek grumbled. "Did you find them?"

General Xelic was hesitant to share the bad news.

"My lord, the prisoners have escaped the mother ship," he said.

"WHAAAAAT?"

"They stole a shellcraft from the hangar and fled into space."

Reptiliz Reek roared with more anger than the general had ever seen before. The entire mother ship rattled from the sound of his furious voice. His vines rose off the floor and wrapped around General Xelic's neck. The Reptiliz lifted the general into the air and choked him.

"HOW COULD YOU LET THIS HAPPEN?" the Reptiliz shouted.

"*We…will…find them!*" General Xelic wheezed. "*I've… already…organized…a search party! They…will… depart…at once!*"

The vines squeezed General Xelic's throat even tighter.

"NO! THIS IS *YOUR* MESS! *YOU* FIND THEM!"

"*But…the…invasion! Shouldn't…I…stay…here?*"

"There won't be an invasion if the alliance finds out what we've done!"

"My lord...it is...very unlikely...they could...arrange an audience—"

"Escaping our prison was *unlikely* too, but it happened right under your nostrils! Find those prisoners before they humiliate us further!"

The Reptiliz released General Xelic and he collapsed on the floor.

"Yes, my lord," he said. "I will *not* fail you."

CHAPTER TEN

GRAYTON

The robotic waitress at Allen Astro's boxed up Cassi's cosmic cream pies and brought the check. The aliens paid the bill with a galactic currency called Milky Way galactic credits. Instead of using cash, credit cards, or apps, they settled up with a quick scan of their fingers, paw, claw, or metal digits.

"I gotta put lunch on my left paw," Cassi said. "I'm still paying off my right one from a shopping spree in the Bow Tie Nebula."

Once the bill was paid, Roswell and the aliens returned to the stolen shellcraft. Nerp and Bleep fired up the engines, and they soared into space. Stella pressed a button on her Pleiades pin, and a screen and keyboard were projected over her legs like a holographic laptop. She quickly typed up a document in her native language. The Pleiadean letters were shaped like stars, and some of the sentences had *shooting stars* instead of exclamation marks.

"Okey dokey, alien artichokey, I've written the sponsorship petition!" Stella said. "We just need the signatures of five stage-three leaders and then we'll be off to Star City!"

"Your positivity is EXHAUSTING," Mank said.

"A smile burns less calories than a frown," Stella said.

"Then Mank must be an athlete," Rob said without a hint of sarcasm.

Stella went to the dashboard and poked a blue eyeball. A holographic map of the Milky Way galaxy appeared before her. The Pleiadean studied the map for a few minutes. Roswell recognized some of the constellations she swiped through.

"We should start with the system farthest from Star City and work our way back," Stella suggested. "That means we'll travel to Grayton first, then to the Pleiades, Furgaria, the Cyborg Station, and finish on the Insectia Moon. Does everyone agree?"

None of the aliens objected. Roswell didn't know the first thing about interspace travel, but he trusted Stella knew what she was doing.

"Can I ask a LOGICAL question that may seem PESSIMISTIC?" Mank asked. "What happens if we DON'T get sponsorship from our home systems? Do we have a BACKUP plan?"

"I've already come up with a list of alternative systems," Stella said. "But for now let's try our hardest and hope for the best. Shall we proceed to Grayton?"

"Beep-beep boop-boop beep-beep!"

"Let's see what this shellcraft can do!" Nerp said.

The Tall Gray pulled the dashboard's green tongue as far as it would stretch. The shellcraft's engines roared and the ship launched forward, causing all the passengers to jolt backward. To Roswell's amazement, all the stars in the distance began to *move*. It wasn't as dramatic as space travel in movies and television, but it was still a phenomenal sight. The stars flew past the shellcraft like tiny bubbles floating by a submarine.

"How fast are we going?" Roswell asked.

"Beep-beep-beep boob beep-beep beep boop-boop."

"Three hundred thirty-three light-years per Earth hour," Nerp translated.

Roswell was so stunned he accidentally inhaled his saliva.

"I didn't think it was physically possible to travel that fast!" he said.

Nerp gazed at Roswell with pity, and Bleep patted his head like he was a puppy.

"Beep-beep."

"He *is* cute," Nerp said. "I bet he thinks pi is *limitless* too."

"It's not?" Roswell asked.

"Earthlings will catch up one day," Nerp said. "Now, everybody get comfy. We've got three galactic hours until we reach Grayton."

The passengers spread out across the shellcraft and made themselves comfortable. Roswell couldn't move away from the windshield. He stood behind the window for the entire journey and marveled at every star outside.

A couple of hours later the constellation Orion appeared in the starry distance ahead. Roswell discovered that the entire constellation was veiled in the crimson gases of an ancient supernova. It was as if the legendary Orion were draped in a long, flowing scarlet cape.

Soon the shellcraft soared past a humongous cloud that was shaped like the knight of a chessboard. Roswell realized he was looking at the famous Horsehead Nebula, and he excitedly pressed his whole body against the windshield. The formation couldn't be seen with the naked eye from Earth, but now Roswell had a front-row seat.

"That's the Horsehead Nebula," he said.

"We call it the Phony Little Pony on Furgaria," Cassi said.

Roswell was mesmerized by the nebula. "Gosh, my dad would have loved this."

Another hour passed, and the saucer headed for the center star in Orion's belt. It was bright blue and sent azure beams of light through space.

"That's Alnilam!" Roswell said. "It's a blue supergiant!

It's forty times the size of Earth's sun and nearly half a million times brighter!"

"I'm impressed—you know your astronomy," Nerp said.

"Is Grayton nearby?"

"It's the only planet in Alnilam's orbit."

As if on cue, a small gray dot appeared ahead.

"Beep boop beep!"

"Yup—home sweet home!" Nerp said.

All the passengers gathered around the dashboard, and the planet grew larger and larger outside the windshield. Grayton's atmosphere was cloaked with swirling gray clouds—the planet was covered in hundreds of hurricanes! The shellcraft descended through the chaotic storms, and Roswell discovered Grayton had no land whatsoever. The whole surface was covered in a gray ocean of thrashing tidal waves.

"Not exactly yacht friendly, is it?" Roswell asked.

"Grayton's ocean is made of nitric acid, and it rains sodium hyperoxide," Nerp explained. "The constant chemical reaction is what creates the choppy waters. Grayton is also four times the size of Earth and twice as hot."

"And you live here on purpose?" Roswell asked.

"Are you kidding? It's perfect for us!" Nerp said. "Absolutely nothing can survive the conditions outside. That means not a single virus, bacterium, or fungus can interfere with the Grays' experiments."

"It sounds perfect!" Mank said.

"If it's impossible to survive, how do the Grays live here?" Roswell asked.

"You'll see," Nerp said with a playful grin. "Now I just need to find a parking spot."

"Peep-peep poop-poop."

"I know—it's usually *packed* at this hour."

The shellcraft sank lower, and Roswell noticed something *else* on the planet's surface. Thousands and thousands of flying saucers were perched on round beams that stuck out from the ocean. It was like Grayton was covered in millions of Seattle Space Needles. The shellcraft hovered over the sea of flying saucers until the Grays found a vacant beam. *CLUUUUUNK!* The ship landed on the beam with a heavy thud.

"Beep-beep boop-boop beep-beep-beep?"

"Who cares whose spot it is? This is an emergency!" Nerp said.

"Peep-peep poop-poop."

"I *hope* it gets towed! We'll get a new saucer while we're here!"

Suddenly the whole shellcraft began to rattle. A round tube pierced through the center of the floor. The tube held a round elevator with transparent walls.

"Everybody hop in!" Nerp said. "The lift will take us to the Grayton base."

All the passengers stepped into the elevator, and they

descended through the beam. Roswell's anxiety rose as the elevator sank closer and closer to the ocean's surface. He had no idea what to expect beneath the violent acid waves.

The elevator dropped below the ocean's surface, and Roswell's eyes bulged with wonder. The seafloor was home to thousands of enormous silver domes. The structures spread out for miles in every direction, and they were all connected by round silver tunnels. Absolutely everything underwater was caked in a thick layer of sodium nitrate— another side effect from the constant chemical reaction above. If Roswell hadn't known any better, he would have mistaken the Grayton base for a winter wonderland.

The elevator entered a dome through the roof and then slid down its curved wall. Just like Nerp and Bleep's flying saucer, all the domes were made from a perfectly smooth silver metal, and the ceilings were beaming with bright white light. At first glance it looked as if they'd entered a massive ant colony. Hundreds and hundreds of Tall and Small Grays moved throughout the dome like it was a busy intersection. Dozens of hovering trams floated back and forth, transporting the Grayton citizens like a subway system. Huge holographic signs were projected over the tunnels like highway directions.

To everyone's alarm, all the Grays in Grayton looked exactly like Nerp and Bleep. It would be impossible to tell them apart if they got separated.

"Wow, we stick out like sore thumbs," Roswell said.

"Beautiful, manicured sore thumbs," Cassi said.

Before the elevator came to a complete stop, Nerp and Bleep hopped out and sprinted to a 3D monitor. The monitor showed a list of names written in the Grayton language.

"Yeeeees!" Nerp cheered. "Deek is president this week!"

"Are they a friend of yours?" Stella asked.

"A *great* friend!" Nerp said. "Deek and I have known each other since we were Small Grays! We did field training together!"

"Beep-beep boop-boop beep-beep."

"What are you talking about?"

"Peep poop peep *poop-poop*!"

The Tall Gray winced. "Oh yeah—that *did* slip my mind."

"Beep-beep boop-boop beep-beep!"

"It's not *that* big of a deal! I doubt Deek remembers."

Nerp tried to wave off the subject, but the others weren't convinced.

"Is something wrong?" Stella asked.

"Deek and I had a little *misunderstanding* a few galactic years back."

"Will they still *help* us?" Roswell asked.

Nerp anxiously bit their lip. "Just let me handle it," they said. "Follow me. The Grayton Administrative Office is this way."

Roswell and the aliens followed Nerp across the dome. They joined a queue of Grays and boarded a tram to the

Grayton Administrative Office. The tram's small carts were designed for the Grays' slender bodies, so the seats were a tight squeeze. Rob had to straddle two seats sideways, and his metal limbs *still* hung over the sides.

The tram sped through a tunnel and entered the dome next door. The second dome was lined with tall glass jars and test tubes full of colorful liquids, gases, and bubbles. Long cords swung from the ceiling with machinery that poked, stirred, and transported the substances. Everywhere Roswell looked, there were Tall Grays in white lab coats and oversize goggles. The Grays worked in pairs, trios, and quartets as they huddled over holograms of DNA strands.

"This is one of Grayton's famous laboratories," Nerp said, and gestured like a tour guide. "Whenever a commander returns from a DNA retrieval mission, they deliver their samples to our scientists. The scientists study the samples and extract genetic codes that can enhance our species. They apply the discoveries to genetically engineered embryos and create vaccines to upgrade the rest of us. The Grays are the closest thing to *genetic perfection* in the Milky Way galaxy!"

"Tell that to Michael B. Jordan," Cassi muttered.

The tram traveled down another tunnel and flew into a third dome. The inside was ringed with floor-to-ceiling stacks of cylinder tanks. They were filled with yellow liquid, and to Roswell's utter amazement, the tanks contained

Gray fetuses! The babies were at various growth stages, and they each had two curly umbilical cords. The dome also hosted a staff of Tall Gray nurses in scrubs and medical masks.

"This is one of Grayton's nurseries," Nerp said. "Once a batch of genetically engineered embryos is created, the embryos are placed inside artificial wombs. It takes a Gray fetus four galactic months to develop. If a fetus perishes while inside the artificial womb, their cells are recycled into the next batch of embryos. *Oh, look! One's being born right now!*"

Everyone turned in the direction Nerp pointed. Two Tall Gray nurses drained the yellow liquid from an artificial womb and lifted a newborn out of the tank. The Gray baby rubbed their big black eyes and giggled at their first glimpses of life. The nurses cut the baby's umbilical cords, washed their small body, and dressed them in an aluminum diaper.

"That's adorable!" Stella said.

"That's APPALLING!" Mank said.

The tram exited the nursery and entered a fourth dome. Hundreds of Small Grays sat behind hundreds of small silver desks. Tall Gray teachers stood beside holograms of mathematical equations, scientific formulas, geographical coordinates, chemical compounds, planetary alignments, biological strains, and historical figures from Grayton's past. The students passed notes and threw paper flying saucers when their teachers weren't looking.

"This is a Grayton academy," Nerp said. "When a Small Gray is five galactic years old, they come here for a basic education. After they graduate the academy, they move next door to choose a career."

The fifth dome was like a hectic mash-up of the previous three. Tall Grays watched over Small Grays while they practiced different skill sets. Teachers hovered over students as they mixed chemicals that accidentally blew up in their faces. The instructors shook their heads as pupils boiled Gray baby dolls in fake artificial wombs. The Tall Grays also chased after Small Grays with fire extinguishers as they crashed miniature flying saucers.

In the back of the academy, a holographic poster caught Roswell's attention. It showed a burning saucer in the middle of a desert on Earth. Although he couldn't read the Grayton language, he knew the poster said ROSWELL, NEW MEXICO. NEVER FORGET.

"This is a Grayton university," Nerp said. "Here the Small Grays have the opportunity to try out every profession. As you can see, most Grays become geneticists, caregivers, or flight commanders. Once they choose a job, the Small Grays receive six galactic years of intense training. Afterward they're assigned an instructor for four galactic years of field training."

"Why did you become a flight commander?" Roswell asked.

"I wanted to explore the galaxy!" Nerp said. "I wanted to go where no Gray had gone before and see what no Gray had ever seen. I wanted to help solve the mysteries of the universe and uncover the secrets of the Source that created it all!"

"That's inspiring," Roswell said. "What about you, Bleep?"

"Beep-beep-beep boop-boop beep-beep."

"Bleep says the performing arts department was full."

Eventually the tram arrived at the Grayton Administrative Office and the tour ended. Roswell and the aliens climbed off the tram and found themselves at a pair of impressively tall silver doors. The entrance had no doorknobs, markings, or security of any kind.

"This is your PRESIDENT'S office?" Mank asked. "Shouldn't they have more PROTECTION?"

"Oh please, no one wants to be here—*especially* the president," Nerp said. "That's what separates Grays from other species in the galaxy. None of us want *more* responsibility."

The Tall Gray pressed a button and spoke into a microphone on the door.

"Hello, I'm here to speak with the president!"

"Do you have an appointment?" a voice responded.

"No, but it's urgent!"

"I'm sorry, the president is very busy. You'll need to come back later."

"Deek, I know that's you! I recognize your voice!"

"*Nerp?*"

"Yes, I need to talk with you!"

"Too bad! I'm never speaking to *you* again!"

"This isn't personal—it's political! I need the president of Grayton!"

"Then come back when someone *else* is president!"

"I wouldn't be here unless it was an emergency! *Please!*"

There was a moment of silence while President Deek considered the request. Roswell and the aliens went stiff with anticipation. *BAAAAAMP!* A loud buzzer blared, and the silver doors slowly opened. Nerp hurried inside, and the others followed. The Grayton Administrative Office was a small dome in the center of the Grayton base. The round walls were filled with hundreds of 3D monitors that surveyed the whole planet. The office also had an impeccable view of the acid waves crashing high above the ocean floor.

The Grayton president was sitting behind a long silver desk when Roswell and the others arrived. Deek looked exactly like Nerp except for the presidential sash over their black jumpsuit. The president rose to their feet and gave Nerp a seething scowl.

"You've got some nerve barging in here!" Deek shouted.

"Deek, I know we have a rocky history, but I don't have time to dwell on the past!"

The president was outraged by Nerp's choice of words.

"*A rocky history?!* Is *that* what you call it?"

"We were young! I made a mistake!"

"You sabotaged my career and ruined my life!"

The tension between Nerp and Deek piqued everyone's curiosity.

"Okay, I have to ask, what happened between you guys?" Roswell asked.

"It's a long story," Nerp said.

"And worth every second!" Deek interjected. "Nerp and I had just finished our field training and were assigned our first solo missions. My test scores were higher than Nerp's, so I was given a better assignment. The Board of High Commanders instructed me to collect DNA from a string of stage-two planets—it was every commander's dream! Meanwhile, Nerp was instructed to collect organisms from a string of underdeveloped stage-one planets—it was every commander's nightmare! However, on the eve of our departure Nerp went to the board and *had our assignments switched*!"

Roswell and the aliens collectively gasped.

"No way!" Stella said.

"He did *WHAT*?!" Mank asked.

"I feel like I'm watching *Grays of Our Lives*!" Cassi said.

Nerp laughed anxiously and blushed a shade of dark gray.

"It was a miscommunication!"

"You said, 'Deek and I want to switch jobs'—they had you on tape!"

"That was ages ago! Are you still mad about it?"

"I spent two galactic decades with algae, Nerp! *Algae!* Do you know how dull that was?"

"Of course I do! Why do you think I switched our assignments?"

"GET OUT, NERP!"

"Listen to me, Deek! If I could change the past, I would do it in a Gray heartbeat. But I'm here for something much more important than us. The whole galaxy is in grave danger!"

For the first time the president's angry gaze drifted away from Nerp. Deek was very surprised to see so many different beings in their office. Their big black eyes doubled in size when they landed on Roswell.

"Nerp, what is an *Earthling* doing in my office?!" Deek asked.

"Bleep accidentally abducted him," Nerp said.

"Beep boop beep boop-boop beep!"

"I'm *not* throwing you under the bus! You *did* accidentally abduct him!"

"How could you two be so reckless?" the president asked. "You should have erased his memory and taken him home immediately!"

"He's in the Galactic Registry!" Nerp said.

"*What?* How is an Earthling child in the Galactic Registry?"

"We don't know! The Reptoids attacked us before we figured it out!"

"The Reptoids *attacked* you?!"

"That's why I'm here! The Reptoids damaged our ship and took us prisoner! We barely made it out alive! As we escaped, we found out Reptiliz Reek and General Xelic are planning an invasion of Earth!"

"That's impossible! Earth is a stage-two planet!" Deek said.

"Man, if I had a nickel," Roswell said.

The Cyborg blinked curiously. "How would a nickel help?"

"Forget about it," he said. "Back to you, Nerp."

"The Reptoids discovered a technicality to make their invasion legal," Nerp said. "We all know how ruthless and power hungry they are. If the Reptoids invade Earth, it'll only be a matter of time before they start attacking other systems too! We need to convince the Milky Way Galactic Alliance to stop the Reptoids! But first we need sponsorship from stage-three leaders like you. So will you help us? Or is a decades-old feud more important than saving the galaxy?"

The president was overwhelmed by all the information. Deek slid into the seat behind their desk and massaged their gray temples while they processed the news.

"I don't know," Deek said. "I have only four days left of being president. I shouldn't do anything drastic. The last thing I want is to be *remembered*."

Roswell's desperation skyrocketed while the group waited for an answer. He stepped forward to take matters into his own hands.

"President Deek, I know it's a lot to consider," Roswell said. "It would be easier to stay out of it—but think how the destruction of Earth would affect Grayton. There are over a million known species on Earth—and our scientists predict there are millions more just waiting to be discovered. If the Reptoids destroy Earth, think of all the DNA that would be wasted! Think of all those mutations and genetic codes that would be lost forever! And if you're the Grayton president who let all *that* go to waste, you'll definitely be remembered *forever!*"

The president glared at Roswell—making the situation *personal* had been a smart move. Right when Roswell thought his pitch had worked, Deek's big eyes lit up with excitement. Roswell could tell the president was too eager to be thinking about Earth—they were distracted by another matter entirely.

"What's your name?" the president asked.

"Roswell," he said.

"Like the *tragedy*?!"

"Sorry—it was my dad's idea."

"What part of Earth are you from?"

"Cherokee Springs, Oklahoma."

"And what's your race?"

Roswell raised an eyebrow. "It isn't obvious?"

"I mean, what's your heritage?" Deek said. "And please be specific."

"Um...according to the ancestry kit I got last Christmas, I have Nigerian and Comanche on my dad's side, and Cameroonian and French Creole on my mom's side."

"Is that all?"

"It also said I was one percent German. I'm guessing those are recessive genes."

"Would you mind if I took a sample of your blood?"

Roswell turned to his friends, but they were just as puzzled.

"Er...I suppose not?" he said.

The Grayton president hurried to one of the 3D monitors on the wall. They typed in a code, and a long cord descended from the ceiling with a needle. The needle was so thin Roswell didn't even feel it take a drop of blood from his arm. Once the sample was collected, a hologram of Roswell's body was projected over the president's desk. The hologram showcased all his organs, veins, and bones. Parts of his body were highlighted in yellow circles that flashed like warning signs.

"What are those?" Roswell asked.

"Those are deficiencies in your DNA," the president said. "According to your genes, you'll need a root canal in your thirties, your appendix will burst in your forties, you'll need a knee replacement in your fifties, and your hair will start to go gray in your sixties. But in good news, you have a very strong heart, you don't carry the Alzheimer's gene, and you'll live into your nineties with proper diet and exercise."

Roswell was flabbergasted. "You can tell all of that from a drop of blood?!"

The president looked at him like he was joking. "My boy, blood tells us *everything*! DNA is the blueprint, the road map, and the history book of every living being in the universe! In fact, DNA can store so much information that all the knowledge on Earth could be contained in a *coffee cup* of human blood. In Earth's future, data won't be saved on servers or hard drives, it'll come from microscopic strands that resemble living DNA."

"So what do you want with mine?" Roswell asked.

"The subtle differences in our genetic coding is what makes us who we are. DNA is the reason you are you, I am me, a tree is a tree, a fish is a fish, and a honeybee is a honeybee. However, with a quick swap of cellular proteins, we can alter the appearance, the intelligence, the life span, and the *purpose* of anything we want. We could create plants that grow meat, fish that walk, and humans that live forever. With DNA, the smaller you think, the bigger the possibilities!"

"And you think my DNA can help the Grays somehow?"

"The Grays pride themselves on being the best geneticists in the galaxy. However, recently we've noticed an unfortunate trend in the new generation of Small Grays. Every five hundredth infant is born with a dent in their head. It isn't a big issue—the Small Grays grow, learn, and live normally—they just look very *judgmental* while doing so. It makes people uncomfortable. *But* we could easily fix the problem if we found the right genetic code. And given your unique heritage, I think the answer may be floating in your veins."

A second hologram of an enlarged DNA strand appeared over the president's desk. A group of proteins was highlighted in yellow, and a green check mark flashed beside it.

"I was right!" the president cheered. "You have a Comanche great-great-great-great-great-grandfather on your father's side, and a German great-great-great-great-great-great-grandmother on your mother's side! That's the *exact* genetic combination we've been searching for! I'm going to send your DNA sample to the laboratory right now so they can start replicating it!"

Bleep jumped between Deek and Roswell. The Small Gray waved their hands dramatically like a traffic officer stopping a speeding car.

"Beep-beep boop-boop!"

"What do you mean *not so fast?*" Deek asked.

"Peep-peep poop-poop."

"Why not?"

"Beep-beep boop-boop-boop beep-beep!"

A wide smile stretched across Nerp's face. "Bleep's right—you can't replicate DNA from a member of the Galactic Registry. You need his written permission first. Even though Roswell is from a stage-two planet, he has stage-three rights. That genetic code is his biological property."

"Beep-beep boop-boop beep boop."

"I agree, Bleep—if only Deek had something they could *trade* him."

"Peep-peep poop-poop peep-peep."

"Yes—he would be *much* more inclined!"

Nerp and Bleep scratched their heads as they pretended to think.

The president's face flushed dark gray—Deek knew *exactly* what they were doing. "Fine, I'll sign your petition," they said.

"Beep-beep boop-boop beep-beep."

"We'll also need a new saucer," Nerp added.

"Peep-peep poop peep-peep-peep!"

"One with a Gray-ray player and an espresso maker."

"Don't push it, Nerp!" Deek said.

"Just an espresso maker, then."

The Grayton president let out a long, irritated sigh.

"You have a deal," Deek said.

Stella projected their holographic petition, and the president presented a holographic release form. Deek exchanged their signature for Roswell's thumbprint. Roswell and the aliens jumped for joy after the trade was complete.

"We got our first SIGNATURE!" Mank said in disbelief.

"Thank you, Deek!" Nerp said. "I'll return the favor someday!"

"I won't hold my breath," Deek said. "You can take the saucer on beam G478Q. But don't tell the next president who gave it to you."

"I won't," Nerp said. "And for what it's worth, I'm really sorry for sabotaging your career and ruining your life. Maybe we could grab dinner when I—"

"Get out, Nerp!"

Roswell and the aliens obeyed the president's wishes and hurried out of the office. They took a tram to the opposite side of the Grayton base—passing through an endless row of domed labs, nurseries, and schools—and finally arrived at beam G478Q. The team took an elevator up the beam and entered a brand-new flying saucer.

"Beep-beep boop beep-beep boop."

"You're right—it's got that new-saucer smell!" Nerp said.

The group went into the cockpit and were grateful to

234

see controls that *weren't* reptilian body parts. The Grays turned on the engines, and the saucer soared into Grayton's atmosphere. Stella pressed a button on the dashboard and skimmed through a holographic map of the Milky Way galaxy.

"It'll take us eight galactic hours to reach the Pleiades system," she said. "But if you swing by the Witch Head Nebula, I might know a shortcut."

"Everyone take a seat!" Nerp instructed. "I'm going straight to light speed!"

Everyone strapped themselves into the oval chairs. As the saucer rose through Grayton's turbulent clouds, Roswell had a strange feeling in the pit of his stomach. He might never visit Grayton again, but thanks to his genetic code, part of him would *always* be there.

"Thanks for convincing Deek to sponsor us!" Roswell told the Grays. "We couldn't have done it without you! Who would have thought my DNA would be so—"

Roswell went silent and his eyes grew wide. He spotted something in the sky outside the saucer's transparent walls. Roswell could barely see it through the stormy haze, but he knew exactly what he was looking at. A large black boomerang was hovering in the distance, watching the saucer like a hungry hawk.

"Aaaaand we're off in *three…two…one*!"

Before Roswell had the chance to tell the others, Nerp slammed a red button on the dashboard. The saucer rocketed out of the atmosphere at light speed. In less than a second Grayton's swirling gray clouds were replaced by the dark void of space.

"Roswell, my monitors indicate an unhealthy rise in your blood pressure," Rob said. "Do you require medical attention?"

"You are a little PALE," Mank said.

"What's the matter, sweetcheeks?" Cassi asked.

Roswell was so stunned he couldn't look away from Grayton. Even as the planet disappeared in the distance, his eyes were fixated on the space behind their craft.

"*We're being followed!*" he said.

CHAPTER ELEVEN

THE PLEIADES

"It was the alien from Allen Astro's!" Roswell told the others. "I'd recognize that ship anywhere! They followed us all the way to Grayton!"

Roswell could tell the aliens *wanted* to believe him, but they were hesitant because they hadn't seen the craft themselves.

"I swear I'm telling the truth," he said.

"According to my health monitors, your cortisol levels are stable," Rob said. "This generally indicates honesty."

"No one's calling him a LIAR," Mank said.

"Beep-beep boop."

"I agree—it just seems odd," Nerp said.

"Why would a complete stranger follow us halfway across the galaxy?" Stella asked.

"Obviously, they're stalking me," Cassi said. "Can you blame them?"

Roswell paced around the saucer's cockpit while he searched for an answer. It didn't make sense to him either.

"Maybe they *aren't* a complete stranger," he hypothesized. "Maybe they're working for the Reptoids! Maybe General Xelic hired a bounty hunter to find and kill us!"

"Reptoids don't usually work with other species," Stella said.

"Yeah, they aren't exactly TEAM PLAYERS," Mank said.

The word *processing* flashed across Rob's digital forehead. "Roswell, you said you could recognize their craft anywhere. Why is the ship so memorable? Have you encountered it before?"

"I've never seen it, but my dad did," Roswell said. "He saw a boomerang-shaped spacecraft on his twelfth birthday. He saw it again when he graduated high school, on the day he married my mom, and then again on his first day in the US military. They followed him around his entire life, and now they're following us!"

Despite Roswell's passionate narrative, the aliens were still uncertain.

"The alien eavesdropped on our entire conversation at the diner," he said. "Whoever they are, they heard our whole plan and know where to find us! You've gotta believe me! We could be in danger!"

"I'll *always* believe you, sweetcheeks," Cassi said. "If you saw a giant boomerang, then I saw *two* boomerangs! Heck, I saw a whole *swarm* of them!"

Roswell sighed with desperation. "Stella, what if you read my mind?" he asked. "Could you look into my memory and see it for yourself?"

Before the Pleiadean answered, Roswell heard the high-pitched noise and felt the familiar tingling sensation on his forehead. The tingling traveled through his brain while Stella skimmed his memories.

"Well?" Roswell asked. "Did you see it?"

"You definitely saw *something* on Grayton—but I'm not sure it was *real*," she said.

"You think I *hallucinated*?"

"Sometimes our brains trick us into seeing what we *want* to see instead of what's actually there. Perhaps you saw the craft because you *wanted* to see your father."

"Beep boop-boop."

"I agree—very deep," Nerp said.

The theory hit Roswell like a bag of bricks. He quietly sank into his oval chair and thought about the Pleiadean's analysis. There were more mental and emotional layers to peel back than he could count.

"My dad would have loved all of this," Roswell said softly. "Exploring the galaxy was something we used to dream about together. Part of me feels guilty for doing it without him."

"You just miss him and wish he were here—what son wouldn't?" Stella asked. "And consequently, the void of your father may be materializing in strange ways. Trust me, I have my Pleiadean certificate in intergalactic psychological studies."

"SHOCKING!" Mank said sarcastically.

Roswell slowly nodded as he came to terms with the idea.

"I think you're right," he said. "Forgive me."

Cassi sat on the arm of Roswell's oval chair and put her fuzzy arm around him.

"The Furgarians have an old belief about death," she said. "When someone dies, they give their heart to the person they loved the most. And then it's that person's job to *live* and *love* enough for both hearts. So there's nothing to feel guilty about. You're not exploring space *without* him, you're doing it *for* him."

Roswell was very touched—and *surprised*—by the Furgarian's moving words.

"Wow, that's beautiful," he said. "Thanks, Cassi."

"You're welcome, sweetcheeks," she said. "Although I wish Furgarians didn't take everything so literally. Those hearts start smelling after a while."

The flying saucer soared through space and entered the lower half of the Orion constellation. As they approached Rigel, a supergiant star in Orion's bottom corner, the Grays slowed the ship's engines so they wouldn't miss their next stop.

"Beep-beep boop-boop beep-beep!"

"We're approaching the Witch Head Nebula!" Nerp announced.

A muster of purple and indigo gases appeared in the distance ahead. True to its name, the Witch Head Nebula was shaped like the profile of a ghoulish face, complete with a sharp nose and protruding chin. The nebula reminded Roswell of decorations Gram put up during Halloween—all it was missing was a pointed hat.

"Isn't she magnificent?" Stella said in awe.

"She's MALIGNANT!" Mank moaned. "Why would you bring us HERE?"

"Unbeknownst to most galactic travelers, the witch nebula has a secret!"

"Is she really a warlock nebula?" Cassi asked.

"There's a hidden *wormhole* at the tip of the witch's chin!" Stella declared.

Rob blinked curiously. "That must be a very large worm."

"Wormholes are tunnels that connect one point of space to another," the Pleiadean explained. "They're the ultimate shortcuts, and if we enter the wormhole at the right angle, it'll take us directly to the Pleiades!"

"And if we DON'T enter it at the right angle?" Mank asked.

"We'll end up in the center of the star Aldebaran," Stella said.

Everyone glared at the Pleiadean like she was making a bad joke, but she was being serious.

"Well, *sun of a witch*," Roswell said with a nervous laugh. "Get it? Get it?"

"We got it," Nerp said.

"Beep boop beep."

"But not his *worst* either."

"Don't worry—I use wormholes all the time," Stella said. "This will trim seven galactic hours off our trip. Now aim for the witch's chin and swoop in low."

Nerp steered the flying saucer closer to the nebula. Just as the Pleiadean had described, a hidden wormhole sat at the tip of the witch's chin like a gigantic mole. The wormhole looked less like a hole and more like a sphere. It reminded Roswell of a crystal ball. The passengers could see through it, but the stars were warped and magnified on the other side. Stella hovered over Nerp and Bleep as they guided the saucer directly into the sphere.

"Move the ship to a negative forty-three-degree angle and head for the wormhole's southern hemisphere," the Pleiadean instructed. "That's it...nice and easy... steady...a little lower...keep going...*perfect*!"

Suddenly the whole spacecraft started to shake violently. The passengers quickly strapped into their oval seats. The sphere became an enormous tunnel, and the stars began to swirl around them. Roswell felt like they had entered a hall of mirrors in a fun house. All the stars shrank and stretched and whirled past the spacecraft. Parts of the galactic horizon rippled like a sheet blowing in the wind, while other sections remained perfectly still. The sight made the passengers nauseated.

"*I think I'm going to be sick!*" Roswell said.

"*My observation sensors are starting to short-circuit!*" Rob said.

"*Those cosmic cream pies are about to say hello!*" Cassi said.

"LET ME OUT! LET ME OUT! LET ME OUT!" Mank shouted between dry heaves.

"Hang in there, we're almost at the end!" Stella said. "Now move the ship to a positive sixty-two-degree angle, and when I say *go*, hit the engines! Great job…nice and slow…don't stop now…nearly there…a little higher…*GO!*"

Nerp slammed a big red button on the dashboard, and the saucer rocketed forward. All the warped stars shrank to their regular sizes, the horizon stopped rippling, and the shaking spacecraft became perfectly still. The Pleiadean started an energetic round of applause, but everyone else was too nauseated to join her.

"We did it!" Stella cheered. "Welcome to the Pleiades system!"

A bright cluster of stars appeared ahead, and Roswell recognized them immediately. Although there were more than a thousand stars in the Pleiades, the ten largest stars stood out. The whole cluster was veiled in blue gas, and the Pleiades shined like a collection of twinkling sapphires. Just like the first time Roswell saw Stella's spaceship, he could have sworn he heard an angelic chorus singing as their ship approached the stars, but it was only in his imagination.

"It's gorgeous!" Roswell said.

"Thank you," Stella said, and gazed lovingly at her home. "There are over a thousand stars and seven habitable planets in the Pleiades system. We'll be going to the capital, Prosperity City, where the Seven Sisters Council is located. It's on the planet orbiting the star Electra."

"Are the council members actual sisters?" Rob asked.

"The name is purely ceremonial," Stella explained. "It's based on the seven sisters who founded the Pleiades several millennia ago. There have been male council members before, but now the Pleiades system is run entirely by women. The current council adopted me after I was abandoned at birth. The Sisters trained me to be a junior council member and taught me everything I know. They're my heroes!"

The Pleiadean's tone was so cheerful the others thought they had misheard her.

"Wait, you were ABANDONED at birth?" Mank asked.

Stella shrugged like it wasn't a big deal. "True story."

"But that's horrible," Roswell said. "Doesn't that make you angry or sad? How are you so perky and positive all the time?"

"I wasn't always this way," she confessed. "When I was younger, I spent a lot of time feeling sorry for myself. Thankfully, the Seven Sisters taught me about the five Pleiadean *P*s. Nothing can change the past, but patience, perspective, politeness, positivity, and perseverance can change the future. I learned that anger and sadness may be warranted, but they aren't very productive qualities. So I converted all my sorrow into motivation, and now I put all my energy into making the universe a better place."

Roswell sighed—he was very envious of the Pleiadean's mindset.

"You're a bigger person than I am," he said.

The Cyborg blinked curiously. "I would say you are relatively the same size."

"Don't worry, Roswell," Stella said. "You'll get there one day. I know it."

The Grays flew the saucer toward Electra, and soon the spacecraft was approaching a blue planet with thirteen moons.

"There it is!" Stella said. *"Paradise!"*

"I wish I thought of my planet that way," Roswell said.

"No, that's the planet's actual name."

The saucer dived into Paradise's atmosphere, and

Roswell saw why it was called that. The skies were clean and filled with fluffy white clouds. The surface was home to sparkling blue oceans and luscious green continents. The landmasses shimmered like they were covered in glitter.

"It's like a photoshopped version of Earth," Roswell said. "Why is everything so shiny?"

"Paradise is covered in diamond like Earth is covered in rock," Stella explained. "It's our greatest natural resource. All our buildings and spaceships are constructed from it."

Roswell's jaw dropped. "Everything is made from *diamond*?"

"Oh, that's nothing!" Stella said. "Paradise's skies are pollution-free, the oceans are purified, and all the forests are perfectly preserved. Our planet doesn't spin on an axis, so we enjoy the same pleasant weather year-round. There's plenty of space and resources for everyone, so we don't have crime, poverty, or a class system. There are no infections or diseases thanks to our excellent health care systems. The Pleiadean Academies are open to everyone who wants an education. Pleiadeans are the most technologically advanced species in the Milky Way because of our early interest in renewable energy. We haven't been involved in a war in over thirty million years and have *never* been the cause of one."

"What a dump," Cassi whispered to Roswell.

The saucer followed a river as it snaked through a rolling

field of emerald grass and colorful flowers. To Roswell's amazement, the Pleiadean blooms were shaped like hearts, stars, and smiley faces. Throughout the fields Roswell also spotted herds and flocks of Pleiadean animals. The mammals were fluffy and plump, the reptiles seemed happy and harmless, and all the birds were as majestic as peacocks. Just like Stella, the Pleiadean animals had massive eyes.

"This place is like an anime toy store," Roswell noted.

"Every animal in the Pleiades is adorable, friendly, and housebroken," Stella said. "Also, all the citizens are vegetarians, so the animals get to live as peacefully as the people."

"That's a bummer," Cassi said. "They look delicious."

The river led to an enormous city with thousands of diamond towers. Each tower stood over a mile high and had a pointed roof. They were so sharp and narrow they reminded Roswell of Pop's knitting needles. A stunning waterfall flowed through the very center of Prosperity City, and the metropolis was surrounded by a breathtaking range of violet mountains. The skies were filled with rainbows and thirteen crescent moons. The city was illuminated, not just by Electra, but by all ten prominent stars of the Pleiades system.

"It's OBNOXIOUSLY perfect," Mank said, and scratched himself. "I might be ALLERGIC!"

Stella smiled. "Thanks—we're very proud."

The Pleiadean directed the Grays to a landing strip in the

heart of the city. They touched down, and the passengers exited the craft. Prosperity City was bustling with Pleiadean citizens. Everywhere Roswell looked, he saw people walking down diamond-paved streets, crossing over diamond bridges, and riding diamond spacecraft through the air. Roswell was pleasantly surprised to see that the Pleiadeans had just as many races as Earthlings—if not *more*. Roswell saw Pleiadeans who were far paler and far darker than the people of Earth. However, everyone had platinum-blond hair and enormous eyes, and they all wore the same blue uniform. Stella happily greeted each citizen they passed.

"Hello! Salutations! Good day! Warm greetings! Prosperity be with you!"

"Do you KNOW all these people?" Mank asked.

"'No One Is a Stranger on Paradise,'" Stella said. "At least, that's what it says on the T-shirt! Now, the Seven Sisters Council headquarters is just down this street."

Roswell and the aliens followed Stella through the sparkling capital. She took them to the tallest tower in the center of Prosperity City. It was so tall half of the tower rose above the clouds. Five words were engraved over the entrance. Even though Roswell couldn't read the Pleiadean language, he was pretty sure they were the five Pleiadean Ps: PATIENCE, PERSPECTIVE, POLITENESS, POSITIVITY, and PERSEVERANCE.

"Here we are!" Stella said. "I just need to sign in."

She placed her hand on the diamond door and it scanned her palm.

"Welcome, Junior Council Member," said a voice in the scanner.

The entrance opened, and Stella escorted her friends inside the tower. Instead of entering a lobby like Roswell expected, the group stepped directly into a diamond tube. A powerful gust of air blew them all the way up the building and spit them out on the top floor. Stella was the only one who landed on her feet. As Roswell stood, he found himself inside a large pyramid-shaped chamber. The triangular walls were made of a crystal-clear Pleiadean glass, and he could see the entire city below them.

"Junior Council Member Stargaze, this is a surprise."

Roswell and the aliens weren't alone. Seven Pleiadean women were seated at the tops of seven diamond pillars. The women's faces were very relaxed, they sat with their legs folded and palms open, and they each wore a diamond on the center of their forehead. They reminded Roswell of a yoga class. He wondered if the Seven Sisters Council lived in a constant state of meditation.

Stella bowed to each member of the Seven Sisters Council. "Hello, First Sister, Second Sister, Third Sister, Fourth Sister, Fifth Sister, Sixth Sister, and Seventh Sister. I hope you're having a prosperous day."

"You're back early," the First Sister said.

"We weren't expecting you for another galactic week," the Second Sister said.

"Have you finished your public service already?" the Third Sister asked.

The council members' voices were so soothing they almost put Roswell to sleep.

"Sisters, I'm here to share some very important news," Stella said. "A horrible tragedy is about to occur. We need your help to prevent it."

"Oh no!" the Fourth Sister said.

"What's the matter?" the Fifth Sister asked.

"Tell us everything!" the Sixth Sister said.

"It's a very long and complicated story," Stella said. "It would be much more convenient to *show* you."

"As you wish," the Seventh Sister said.

All the Pleiadeans closed their eyes and went silent. Roswell noticed that the diamonds on the council members' foreheads lit up like Christmas lights. He assumed Stella was telling the council about their escape telepathically, because the council gasped and flinched without hearing a word. When Stella was finished, the Pleiadeans opened their eyes and looked at one another with distress.

"That is outrageous!"

"Thank the Source you are alive!"

"We are so proud of you for escaping!"

"You will be generously rewarded with Pleiadean Public Service Points!"

Stella burst into a Pleiadean dance but quickly collected herself.

"I appreciate the points, Sisters, but my main concern is Earth," she said, and nudged Roswell forward. "This is an Earthling named Roswell Johnson. We wouldn't have escaped the Reptoids without his help. As a token of our gratitude, we're taking him to speak with the Milky Way Galactic Alliance. We're hoping they'll keep Earth under their protection and stop the Reptoids' invasion. If Reptiliz Reek and General Xelic succeed, there's no telling how powerful and dangerous the Reptoids will become. Will you sign our petition and sponsor our cause?"

"Absolutely!"

"Without hesitation!"

Roswell thought his ears were deceiving him. "Wait, just like that? There's no catch?"

"Of course not!"

"We wouldn't dream of delaying this mission!"

"It is far too important!"

Roswell grinned ecstatically from ear to ear.

"That's terrific!" he exclaimed. "Thank you so much!"

"However," the First Sister said, "this council cannot lend its support unless we know the Earthling has a noble character and a pure heart. Before we sign your petition, we must examine his aura."

"What's an aura?" Roswell asked.

"It's a belly button that sticks out," Cassi said confidently.

"The fuzzy girl is mistaken," the Second Sister said. "An aura is an energetic field our souls emit into the universe. It tells us the type of person someone *is*, and the type of person someone will *become*."

"How do you check an aura?" Roswell asked.

"We must examine you on the astral plane," the Third Sister said.

"Is that somewhere in Prosperity City?"

The Seven Sisters were amused by his question.

"Yes *and* no," the Fourth Sister said. "The astral plane is everywhere *and* nowhere at once. It's the energy that connects every living being in the universe."

"So...is it walking distance?"

"The astral plane is the highest level of consciousness," the Fifth Sister said. "Only the most enlightened minds can access it. It takes years of practice and discipline for someone to find it on their own."

"Luckily, we have something to speed up the process," the Sixth Sister said.

"Everything is SMILES and SHORTCUTS with these people," Mank grumbled.

"Junior Council Member Stargaze, will you please retrieve the astral projector?" the Seventh Sister said. "We will meet the boy there."

The Seven Sisters Council closed their eyes, and the diamonds on their foreheads lit up again. Stella eagerly went to the opposite side of the chamber. A diamond pyramid the size of a lampshade was displayed on a pillar like a vase at a museum. Stella cautiously picked it up and carried it toward Roswell.

"Don't worry," Stella told him. "The council does this with everyone they meet. Just close your eyes and clear your mind, and the astral projector will do the rest."

The Pleiadean placed the pyramid on top of Roswell's head. He closed his eyes and tried his best to relax, but it was difficult given the current circumstances.

"This isn't going to work," Roswell said. "All I can think about is the invasion and the KitKat theme song for some reason."

"Just focus on your breathing," Stella said. "Listen to my voice as I count backward. Five...four...three...two..."

Suddenly Roswell felt like his soul was being sucked through a hole at the top of his skull. He left his physical body and the Pleiades far behind him. Roswell was floating in an endless dimension of stars, planets, and galaxies. He felt weightless and limitless at the same time—there was no beginning and no end to him. Unlike the stars in space, all the stars here felt reachable. Roswell didn't need a spaceship to travel through this dimension; he could go anywhere he wanted simply by *thinking* about it.

Roswell looked down and discovered he was *shining*. Multicolored light radiated out of him like he was a star himself.

"Welcome to the astral plane, Mr. Johnson."

Roswell noticed that the Seven Sisters were floating in the space around him. The council members were also glowing, but their light was much brighter than Roswell's. Each Sister looked like a blinding rainbow.

"What is this stuff?" Roswell asked. "Why do we look like a Pride parade?"

"*This* is your aura."

"Every living being in the galaxy has one, and no auras are the same."

"Every emotion you feel gives your aura a color."

"And every aura has a unique blend of shades."

"Your colors reflect the energy you project into the universe."

"The brighter your aura, the more *positivity* you spread."

Roswell scrunched his forehead. "So an aura is like a big spiritual mood ring?"

"More or less."

"Then what does my aura say about me?" he asked. "What kind of energy am I projecting into the universe?"

The Seven Sisters flew around Roswell like ghosts and inspected his bright colors. Roswell became nervous as they examined him. He hoped there was nothing to dissuade them from signing the petition.

"I see pink in your aura," the First Sister said. "Pink is the color of love and compassion. You are very sympathetic and care a great deal for others."

"I see orange," the Second Sister said. "Orange is the color of knowledge and curiosity. You are a very intelligent child who loves to learn and ask questions."

"I see yellow," the Third Sister said. "Yellow is the color of drive and determination. Once you start a project, you'll do everything in your power to finish it."

"Those are all good qualities, right?" Roswell asked.

"Some colors are more telling than others," the Fourth Sister said. "For example, I see green in your aura. Green is the color of honesty and sensitivity, but when green becomes too faint, it indicates fear and helplessness."

"That's not a surprise," Roswell admitted. "I've never been so afraid in my entire life. I'm terrified of the Reptoids' invasion."

"I see blue," the Fifth Sister said. "Blue is the color of faith and humility, but your blue is much lighter than those shades. Your aura is heavy with sadness and despair."

"I suppose that makes sense too," he said. "I lost both of my parents when I was young, and now I'm on the verge of losing everything else."

"I see red in your aura," the Sixth Sister said. "Red can be the color of integrity and inner justice, but unfortunately, your red is the unmistakable shade of *anger*."

Roswell felt like he was on trial. Was anger a dealbreaker? Would the council still sign the petition? If he told the Sisters they were mistaken, would they know he was lying?

"I don't *want* to be angry, I just am," he admitted.

"What angers you so?" the Seventh Sister asked.

Roswell's aura faded slightly as he thought about it. "Living on Earth isn't like living on Paradise," he said. "There's inequality, injustice, and ignorance. There's starvation, suffering, and violence. People are hated and hurt because of their skin color, because of who they love, and because of what they believe. Who wouldn't be frustrated by a planet like that?"

Roswell could tell his confession concerned the council.

"Is it wrong to feel angry or sad or afraid?" he asked. "Does that make someone less noble? Or less capable of doing the right thing?"

"It's never wrong to *feel*."

"The more we feel, the more colorful our auras become."

"The more color, the more energy we project."

"The more energy we project, the more potential we have."

"But the weaker our aura, the less light we can spread."

"And without light, there is no potential."

Roswell went quiet as he let the message sink in. Before he could fully process their words, the Seventh Sister gasped. She pointed to a patch of *white light* in Roswell's aura. The other council members gathered around it and whispered among themselves.

"What's wrong?" Roswell asked.

"I've found *white* in your aura," the Seventh Sister said. "White is the color of *doubt*."

"And that's bad?" he asked.

"Doubt is a cancer of the soul!"

"Just like in a painting, one drop of white can dilute an entire aura!"

"It turns sensitivity into fear, humility into sadness, and integrity into anger!"

"Doubt will dim your light and deplete your energy!"

"You must destroy your doubt before doubt destroys you!"

"But how does someone destroy *doubt*?" Roswell asked.

"By eliminating the cause!"

"What makes you so doubtful, Mr. Johnson?"

Roswell knew exactly what the cause was, but he was afraid to admit it.

"If I'm honest, sometimes I have doubts about Earth," he confessed. "Even if we stop the Reptoids' invasion, I worry Earth will just destroy itself. Everyone is constantly fighting, people lie and spread misinformation, we pollute our skies and our oceans, and we go to war like it's a sport. I want to save my planet, but deep down part of me doubts Earth *can* be saved."

"Then the Reptoids have already won."

"If you want to save your planet, you must change the way you *see* your planet."

"You must focus on all the good your planet has to offer."

"And believe in Earth fullheartedly."

"Certainty is the only antidote to doubt."

Despite their good intentions, the Seven Sisters were starting to frustrate Roswell. The red light spread through his aura right before the council's eyes.

"Your anger is growing."

"Why are we upsetting you?"

"Because destroying doubt isn't that easy!" Roswell said. "Gosh, I'm so tired of people telling me to *think positively* and to *believe in myself*—as if those are the answers to everything! You all live in Paradise—you have no idea what it's like to be on Earth! Especially to be young and Black on Earth! Sometimes situations are complicated and can't be fixed! Sometimes people are bad and can't be changed! *Sometimes life is unfair and it doesn't get better!*"

Roswell was just as surprised by his outburst as the council was. He couldn't remember the last time he'd lost his temper like that. His aura was suddenly consumed in *gray light.* Roswell didn't need the Seven Sisters to tell him what gray meant—it was obviously the color of *shame.* In just a few seconds Roswell had blown the entire trip. There was no way the council would sign the petition now.

"I'm so sorry," he said. "I didn't mean that—at least, I don't *want* to mean it."

"I suggest you make up your mind."

"Not for our sake, but for your planet's."

"If *you* don't believe in Earth, the Milky Way Galactic Alliance won't either."

"You must convince the alliance that Earth is worth saving."

"But first you must convince yourself."

"No one can win a race when they doubt the track."

"We will sign your petition if you take our advice to heart."

The gray light in Roswell's aura was replaced with purple beams of *hope*.

"You mean, you're still going to sign our petition?" he asked. "Even after everything I've said and all the doubt I feel?"

"Doubt is not a character flaw, Mr. Johnson."

"Even the most noble have to battle it sooner or later."

"And no battles are alike."

"There is a star and a black hole within each of us."

"One gives light, the other takes light away."

"Only one can win."

"The choice is yours."

Roswell began to sink through the astral plane. He felt like a boulder plummeting to the bottom of the ocean. All the stars disappeared, his senses returned, and he felt heavier with every passing second.

"Beep-beep boop-boop beep-beep?"

"Roswell, can you hear us?" Nerp asked.

Roswell's eyes fluttered open. Strangely, instead of waking up in the Seven Sisters' headquarters, he was in the flying saucer's examination chamber. His alien friends were gathered around him, staring down with concerned faces.

"My monitors indicate an abnormal fluctuation in your brain waves," Rob said.

"Sweetcheeks, how many fingers am I holding up?" Cassi asked.

"You don't have fingers," Roswell mumbled.

"Good job, that was a trick question," the Furgarian said. "You're gonna be okay!"

The aliens helped Roswell sit up on the examination table. He felt loopy and weak, like he was waking up from anesthesia. Roswell looked outside and saw Paradise shrinking in the distance.

"What happened to me?" he asked.

"You PASSED OUT!" Mank said. "We had to CARRY you back to the ship!"

"Everyone's first trip to the astral plane is a little jarring," Stella said. "Did I mention you might lose consciousness?"

"No," Roswell groaned.

The Pleiadean shrugged and quickly changed the subject. "In good news, the Seven Sisters Council signed our petition!" she said. "We're on our way to Furgaria!"

"About time!" Cassi said. "Goodbye, hippies, hello, hunks!"

While the saucer traveled to Furgaria, the Seven Sisters' warning haunted Roswell like a bad memory. *He knew they were right.* Roswell would never save his planet if he thought Earth's destruction was inevitable. But how could he defeat a lifetime of doubt in just a few days? How could he convince himself *and* the alliance that Earth wasn't destined to fail? Defeating his doubt might be the most challenging part of the mission.

However, unbeknownst to Roswell and his friends, the real challenges were *only* getting started. And the most dangerous threat of all was right beneath their noses....

The flying saucer flew past a Pleiadean moon as they left Electra's orbit. Nestled in a dark crater, completely hidden from view, was a large Reptoidian shellcraft. Roswell and the aliens were completely oblivious as they soared by the ship.

Inside the shellcraft, General Xelic pulled an orange tail on his dashboard to contact the Reptoidian mother ship.

"Command center," said a voice through the speaker.

"This is General Xelic with a message for the Reptiliz."

"Copy that, General. What is your message?"

A menacing smirk stretched across General Xelic's scaly face.

"Tell the Reptiliz I have located the prisoners," he said. "They'll be terminated shortly."

CHAPTER TWELVE

FURGARIA

Roswell was standing in the chicken shed with Gram and Pop. They were joined by Elvis Presley, the Scarlet Witch from the Avengers, and a circus clown. There was something unusual about the situation, but Roswell couldn't put his finger on it.

"Thanks for coming, everybody," Pop said. "The girls and I have been working on a new routine. I wanted you to be the first ones to see it!"

"Here we go again," Gram said, and rolled her eyes. "I hope it's better than the 'Single Ladies' dance from last week."

Pop eagerly blew a whistle around his neck. All the chickens at the farm entered the shed and stood in a straight line. The farmer pressed play on his phone and the song "Y.M.C.A." blasted through a speaker. To everyone's amazement, the chickens performed the song's iconic choreography perfectly. Roswell didn't know chickens could bend their wings like that. Persephone led the dance and even lip-synched along to the lyrics.

"That's incredible, Pop!" Roswell said. "It's their best dance yet!"

"Oh Mama," Elvis said, and swiveled his hips. "Those are some seriously chic cluckers!"

"Holy Stan Lee!" the Scarlet Witch said. "What sort of chaos magic is this?"

"No magic needed," Pop said with a proud smile. "I taught them all on my own."

"That's the neatest trick I've ever seen, and I'm a circus clown," said the circus clown.

"Roswell, record this and put it on the YouTubes!" Gram said. "We're going to be rich!"

Roswell whipped out his phone to document the dancing chickens. However, before he had the chance to press the record button, he was distracted by a deep rumbling. The Johnsons and their guests left the shed to see what was causing the strange commotion. As they stepped outside, the whole farm was suddenly eclipsed by an enormous shadow. To Roswell's absolute horror, *the Reptoidian mother ship was hovering over the farm*!

"No!" Roswell gasped. "They've started the invasion!"

"How could you let this happen, Roz?" Gram asked.

"You were supposed to save us!" Pop said.

"I don't understand," Roswell thought aloud. "What am I doing back on Earth? I was just with the aliens on the flying saucer!"

"This isn't my battle," the Scarlet Witch said. "I'm going back to the Multiverse!"

"Count me in, Scarlet Mama," Elvis said. "Let's scram like grubs in a henhouse!"

"This is too much excitement for me, and I'm a circus clown," said the circus clown.

Without missing a beat, Elvis, the Scarlet Witch, and the circus clown transformed into black boomerangs and whirled out of sight.

"Wait! You can't just leave!" Roswell yelled.

A fleet of shellcrafts descended from the mother ship. General Xelic was standing on top of the first craft and gazed down at Roswell with hungry eyes.

"Your time is up, Roswell," the general said. "You *failed* and Earth is ours!"

Roswell skimmed the horizon and saw his worst nightmare happening all around him.

In the north, Reptoidian shellcrafts knocked down Big Ben, the Eiffel Tower, and the Leaning Tower of Pisa like bowling pins. In the east, the Reptoids pelted the Taj Mahal, the Great Wall of China, and the Kremlin with laser beams.

In the south, the shellcrafts demolished the Christ the Redeemer statue, the Sydney Opera House, and the Easter

Island statues like the ships were wrecking balls. In the west, the Reptoids zapped the Hollywood sign, the Golden Gate Bridge, and Mount Rushmore until they were nothing but piles of ash.

Herds of animals ran for their lives as the Reptoids torched the grasslands, jungles, and forests. Marine animals washed along the shores as the oceans and lakes were boiled and vaporized. With a bright green flash, all the chickens at the Johnson Family Chicken Farm were turned into steaming rotisserie dishes.

"This can't be happening!" Roswell screamed. "We were so close!"

"SAY GOODBYE TO YOUR PATHETIC PLANET!"

Roswell looked over his shoulder and saw Reptiliz Reek standing on his front porch. The whole farmhouse was consumed by the vines growing from the Reptiliz's skull. Reek squeezed the house tighter and tighter, and the home collapsed. Next, the Reptiliz wrapped his vines around Gram and Pop and dragged them toward the debris.

"Roswell! Help us!" Gram screamed.

"Do something!" Pop shouted.

"Let them go!" Roswell yelled.

He tried running toward them, but his feet were stuck. Roswell looked down and saw he was trapped in a big white spot. The more he struggled to free himself, the deeper and deeper he sank, like he was stuck in quicksand.

"YOU'LL NEVER SAVE ANYONE WITH ALL THAT DOUBT!" the Reptiliz roared.

BAAAAAM! Roswell looked over his shoulder and saw an enormous spacecraft hovering over Washington, DC. A blinding laser erupted from the craft and blew the White House into smithereens. The explosion traveled outward, destroying everything in its path, and headed straight toward the Johnson Family Chicken Farm.

"NOOOOO!" Roswell screamed. "MAKE IT STOP! MAKE IT STOP!"

"Roswell, wake up!"

Roswell opened his eyes and gasped for air. He looked around in terror and, thankfully, realized he was still aboard the flying saucer. He had dozed off in his oval chair in the cockpit.

"Sorry to wake you," Stella said. "You were talking in your sleep. I read your mind and saw you were having a horrible nightmare."

Roswell sat up and caught his breath. "I had a dream we failed the mission and the Reptoids invaded Earth," he said. "I watched them destroy my whole planet. It felt so *real.*"

"It was just a nightmare," Stella said. "Except for the last part about the White House. That was from the movie *Independence Day.* That's been in your subconscious for a while."

"Beep-beep boop."

"I agree—a classic film," Nerp said.

Roswell sighed with incredible relief. "I hope it all stays in my subconscious," he said. "How much time do we have left?"

A countdown appeared on the Cyborg's digital forehead. "Exactly two days, ten hours, twenty-six minutes, and nine galactic seconds until our audience with the Milky Way Galactic Alliance," Rob said. "Eight seconds...seven seconds...six seconds...five seconds..."

"Is that enough time?" Roswell asked.

"It'll be close, but we're doing well so far," Stella said.

"Beep-beep boop-boop beep-beep-beep!"

"We're approaching Zosma now!" Nerp announced.

Everyone gathered around the Grays' dashboard and peered into the distance. Zosma was one of nine stars that formed the constellation Leo back on Earth. The stars outlined the shape of a lion, and Zosma was at the base of the beast's tail. The saucer's engines decelerated as it reached a small planet in the star's orbit.

Roswell could tell Cassi was very excited to be home. She started wagging a tiny tail he hadn't noticed until now.

"Ladies and Gentlemen, Bugs and Bots, Small Thems and Tall Thems," Cassi announced. "Welcome to the greatest planet in the galaxy! It's the entertainment capital of the universe! It's where rock stars go to be among rock stars! It's where the rich go to become filthy rich! It's where the beautiful go to blend in! And it's the only planet in the Milky Way where the party never stops! *Give it up for Furgaria!*"

The Cyborg blinked curiously. "Give what up?"

"Your EXPECTATIONS!" Mank groaned.

Contrary to Cassi's high praise, Furgaria was a *mess*. It was a dry and rocky planet about the size of Earth's moon. The northwestern hemisphere had been blown off, and the missing chunks had created an asteroid field that floated through Furgaria's low orbit.

"*That's* Furgaria?" Roswell asked.

"Beep-beep boop-boop beep-beep?"

"No—we didn't make a wrong turn," Nerp said.

Even the Pleiadean had trouble faking a smile. "It certainly has character."

Cassi gave her a sympathetic pat on the shoulder. "I know what you're thinking, Stella. But please don't be intimidated by Furgaria. *Both* our planets can be paradise. It's not a competition." The Furgarian winked at the others behind the Pleiadean's back.

"Why is a huge chunk missing?" Roswell asked.

"It's a funny story," Cassi said. "Furgaria was hit by a comet two galactic decades ago. Luckily, it was during our hibernation season. We were all sleeping in a deep cave and didn't even notice the impact. We woke up and were like, 'Well, this is different.' The Furgarians were the only species on the planet that survived."

"How is that a FUNNY STORY?" Mank asked.

"I guess you had to be there," Cassi said. "But in good news, now all Furgarian real estate comes with a view!"

The Grays steered the saucer to the largest asteroid floating in Furgaria's low orbit. The asteroid had a massive cave with bright lights shining out of it. The saucer passed through a force field and then parked in a landing zone at the edge of the cave. The zone was full of space urchins that were tied to posts like horses outside a saloon in the Wild West.

At first glance Roswell thought he was looking at Las Vegas. A wide dirt road stretched through the middle of the cave, and it was lined with casinos, hotels, pubs, dance clubs, restaurants, and stores. The Furgarian language was a series of scratches and paw prints, but Roswell didn't need a translator to know what each establishment was. Every business had holograms of the services they offered.

"So Furgaria is just a cave full of casinos, clubs, and shops?" Roswell asked.

"Pretty great, huh?" Cassi said. "You can't spell *Furgarian* without *fun*! You can't spell it without *ragin'* either—but *fun* looks better on a bumper sticker."

Roswell and the aliens exited the saucer, and Cassi escorted them through the cave.

"This is the universe-famous *Furgarian Strip*!" she announced. "It's the only habitable part of Furgaria left.

Remember, what happens in Furgaria stays in Furgaria. Don't be afraid to let loose!"

"Let what loose?" Rob asked.

"Anything your artificial heart desires, my metal man!" Cassi said. "Although if someone offers you Furgarian fungi, *just say no*! You'll wake up in the Sombrero Galaxy missing a foot."

The Furgarian Strip was packed with short, stout, and fuzzy citizens. Their fur coats were different shades of brown, beige, and black, but everyone had the same mischievous, snaggletoothed grin. The Furgarians wore unique accessories on their heads—Roswell saw top hats, baseball caps, fedoras, bonnets, tiaras, and wraps—but no one had a stich of clothing on their hairy bodies.

While Roswell and the aliens walked the strip, the male Furgarians stopped and gawked at Cassi. They acted like she was the most attractive female they had ever seen. They foamed at the mouth and slapped their bellies as she passed. The attention gave Cassi an extra bounce in her step.

"WOOT! WOOT! WOOT! WOOT!" the Furgarians chanted at her.

"Oh my gosh, *staaaaawp* it!" Cassi said.

"WOOT! WOOT! WOOT! WOOT!"

"Guys, you're making me blush!"

"WOOT! WOOT! WOOT! WOOT!"

"I'd love to join you, but I'm taking these nerds to the Fuzzfurr."

"WOOT! WOOT! WOOT! WOOT!"

"Rain check, fellas!"

Roswell was shocked at how *honest* Cassi had been about her attractiveness in Furgaria. If anything, she had been *downplaying* it.

"This section of the strip is my old stomping ground," Cassi told the others. "Over there is my favorite casino, Belly Scratchers. One time I won a moon in a lucky hand of cards! Next door is my favorite pub, Fetch. They have the best slappy hour in the Furgarian Strip. Behind that is my favorite restaurant, Kibbles and Grits. Their snarf 'n' barf specials are worth the food poisoning. Across the road is my favorite dance club, Spay and Neuter. I'm not allowed back."

BOOOOOM! A Furgarian inside Fetch was shot out of a cannon. He soared across the strip, slammed into the side of the cave, and slid to the ground.

"What was that?" Roswell asked.

"He couldn't pay his tab," Cassi said.

BOOOOOSH! Two Furgarians crashed through the window of Belly Scratchers. They exchanged punches and wrestled each other to the ground.

"It's so VIOLENT here!" Mank said.

"What are you talking about? Those guys are best

friends!" Cassi said. "Wrestling is a Furgarian love language."

SMAAAAASH! Another pair of Furgarians burst through the door of Spay and Neuter. They rolled across the strip as they hit and kicked each other.

"That is a peculiar way to express affection," Rob said.

"Actually, those two are definitely fighting," Cassi said. "We should get out of here before the cops come. I'm pretty sure there's a warrant out on me."

Roswell and the aliens followed Cassi to the very end of the Furgarian Strip. The dirt road concluded at a spacious theme park. Over the gates Roswell could see the tops of a winding roller coaster, an enormous Ferris wheel, and a carousel of bizarre alien animals. It looked just like the amusement parks on the boardwalks of Earth.

"Here we are!" Cassi announced. "Welcome to the Furgarian Royal Residence!"

"Your uncle lives in a theme park?" Roswell asked.

Cassi shrugged. "Wouldn't you?"

She approached the entrance, where two Furgarian soldiers stood guard. The soldiers wore gladiator helmets and were armed with axes that looked like lollipops. The Furgarians greeted one another by bumping bellies and tickling each other's chins.

"Welcome home, Your Royal Hairiness," the guards said together.

"Good to see you, Scratch and Sniff," Cassi said. "How's it hanging?"

"Old dogs, old tricks," Scratch said. "We haven't seen you in a while."

"Were you put in the detention pound again?" Sniff asked.

"I wish!" Cassi said. "I've been traveling the galaxy with these dorks, trying to prevent an apocalypse! Is my uncle Clancy home? I need to speak with him."

"He's on the throne but doesn't want to be disturbed," Scratch said.

"Let me guess, *Baywatch*?" Cassi asked.

"It was *Murder, She Wrote* last time we checked," Sniff said.

"He'll need to put old Jessica on pause," she said. "This is a Furgarian furmergency!"

Cassi pushed past the soldiers and walked through the gate. Roswell and the others followed her to the center of the theme park. They found the Furgarian Fuzzfurr relaxing in a pit of bubbling, steaming mud. He wore a velvet crown and was served drinks with colorful umbrellas by fuzzy servants. Cassi and her uncle had a strong family resemblance. They could have been twins if it weren't for the gray in the Fuzzfurr's beard.

"Your uncle governs Furgaria from a muddy hot tub?" Roswell asked.

Cassi shrugged. "Wouldn't you?"

The Fuzzfurr didn't notice Roswell and the aliens. His eyes were glued to a wall of televisions from Earth. Some were brand-new with 4K screens, while others were boxy wooden sets from the 1960s and 1970s. Every television was showing a classic sitcom like *I Love Lucy*, *Bewitched*, *Leave It to Beaver*, *The Jeffersons*, *The Brady Bunch*, and *The Golden Girls*. The biggest screen was playing an episode of *Murder, She Wrote*.

"The Fuzzfurr watches old American television?" Roswell asked in disbelief.

"He's *obsessed*," Cassi said. "Uncle Clancy missed my cousins' birth because there was a *Munsters* marathon. And when *M*A*S*H* ended, he went to war to fill the void."

Cassi had to stand in front of the televisions to get her uncle's attention.

"Uncle Clancy! How's it going, you old hair ball?" she said. "Have you gained weight? Those pizza Pilates are paying off!"

"Who are you?" the Fuzzfurr grumbled.

"It's Cassiopeia. I'm your niece."

"I have four hundred and seventy-two nieces."

"I'm from your sister Plucky's fifth litter."

"Still not ringing a bell."

"I ate a brother in the womb."

"Oh, *that* Cassiopeia," the Fuzzfurr said. "Do you need another pardon?"

"Probably, but that's not why I'm here," Cassi said. "Me and these geeks are on a mission to save Earth. We need your help."

"Could this wait until a commercial?" he asked. "Jessica just found the murder weapon."

Cassi snatched a remote from her uncle's paw and put all the shows on pause. She pulled Roswell to the edge of the muddy pit.

"Uncle Clancy, this is my friend Roswell Johnson," she said. "Actually, we're a little *more* than friends. We're taking things slow."

"We are *absolutely* just friends!" Roswell said.

"We're taking things *really* slow. Anyway, the seven of us were recently captured by Reptoids! While we escaped, we discovered the Reptoids are planning to invade Earth! If we don't stop them, everything and everyone on Roswell's planet will die. We need you to sign our petition so we can speak to the Milky Way Garlic Allowance."

"The Milky Way *Galactic Alliance*!" Stella interjected.

"What do you say, Uncle Clancy? Will you help us help Roswell?"

"Cassi, you know Furgaria has a very strict diplomatic policy," the Fuzzfurr said.

"I know, I know," she groaned. *"You scratch our backs, we'll scratch yours."*

The Cyborg blinked curiously. "How is scratching a diplomatic policy?"

"It means the Furgarians don't give favors unless we get a favor first," Cassi said.

"Beep-beep-beep-beep."

"Yeah—*very* straightforward," Nerp said.

"Come on, Uncle Clancy!" Cassi pleaded. "Could you make an exception for your favorite niece? Or for the nephew she consumed?"

"I'm sorry, but rules are rules," the Fuzzfurr said. "Furgarians have been taken advantage of too many times to be charitable. We've loaned galactic credits that were never paid back. We've traded natural elements for unnatural elements that never arrived. Heck, we even invested in Bitcoin. I wouldn't be a good Fuzzfurr if I didn't learn from the past."

"But your favorite thing in the universe is American television!" Cassi said. "If Earth gets destroyed, you won't have any new shows to watch!"

"Earth hasn't made a decent television show in thirty years," the Fuzzfurr said. "Now if you'll excuse me— Jessica is about to prove the butler is innocent."

The Fuzzfurr snatched the remote back and restarted the televisions.

"Well, I tried," Cassi said. "Anyone wanna catch slappy hour at Fetch?"

Roswell wasn't ready to give up so easily. He dashed to the wall of televisions and unplugged the cord that powered them all.

"Hey!" the Fuzzfurr yelled. "Plug that back in!"

"Forgive me, Your Royal Hairiness, I just need another moment of your time," Roswell said. "I understand why Furgaria doesn't hand out favors—honestly, it's a solid policy. Mad respect. But what if we gave you a favor? Would you scratch our back if we scratched your back first?"

"For the record, I'm not touching ANYONE'S back!" Mank said.

The Fuzzfurr went silent and rubbed his belly as he considered.

"I suppose that would work—but it would have to be a *very* big favor," he said.

"I'd do anything to get your signature," Roswell said.

The Fuzzfurr's furry face lit up with an idea.

"As a matter of fact, there *is* something you could do for me!" he said.

"We're all ears!" Roswell said.

"We are much more than ears!" Rob said.

"I lost something very dear to my heart when Big Bertha hit Furgaria."

"Sorry, who's *Big Bertha*?" Roswell asked.

"Uncle Clancy named the comet after his ex-wife," Cassi explained.

"The impact reshaped our planet and separated us from our belongings," the Fuzzfurr said.

"Just like Aunt Bertha!"

"If you were to retrieve my most prized possession, I would happily sign your petition."

"Wonderful!" Roswell said. "What did you lose?"

"Come with me," the Fuzzfurr said. "I want to show you something first."

He climbed out of the hot tub and shook his body like a wet dog, splashing his guests with hot mud. Roswell and the aliens followed the Fuzzfurr to a Haunted Maze attraction. However, the maze wasn't the labyrinth of creepy puppets and jump scares Roswell expected. All the walls had been knocked down, and the inside had been turned into a shrine for a very familiar television show.

"No way!" Roswell gasped. "You're a *Trekker*?"

Roswell had never seen so much *Star Trek* merchandise and memorabilia in one room. A row of mannequins wore the costumes of the original cast. Glass display cases held laser guns, communicators, medical tricorders, and other props from the series. There was a whole wall of action figures, board games, lunch boxes, and bedsheets. A model of the USS *Enterprise* hung from the ceiling, and a rug on the floor featured the phrase SPACE: THE FINAL FRONTIER.

"I have the biggest *Star Trek* collection on this side of the Milky Way," the Fuzzfurr said.

"I've seen every episode a dozen times!" Roswell said. "I even had a *Star Trek* party for my fourth birthday. Gram dressed up like Lieutenant Uhura and Pop dressed up like a tribble to surprise me."

Roswell noticed a bust of the actor Leonard Nimoy. The sculpture was all marble except for a pair of pointy prosthetic ears.

"Are those Spock's *real ears*?" he asked in awe.

"The majority of my collection was used on the actual show," the Fuzzfurr boasted.

"This is amazing!" Roswell said. "I'm in the middle of actual space, standing in a room dedicated to a show set in the middle of space! *How meta is that?!*"

"Is not *everything* in the middle of space?" Rob asked.

"Where did you get all this stuff?" Roswell asked.

"At auctions mostly," the Fuzzfurr said. "My brother is an undercover bidder on Earth. Humans think he's a capybara in the Buenos Aires Zoo."

"Please tell Uncle Monty I said hello!" Cassi said.

Stella checked the time and stepped between Roswell and the Fuzzfurr.

"I hate to interrupt this wonderful moment of fanboy brotherhood, but what does *Star Trek* have to do with the favor you need?" she asked.

The Fuzzfurr let out a heavy sigh and gestured to an empty space on the wall.

"Unfortunately, my collection hasn't been complete since Big Bertha," he said. "I've recovered most of my treasures, but I'm still missing the greatest treasure of all: an autographed picture of the great William Shatner."

"William Shatner?" Roswell gasped.

"WHO?" Mank asked.

"William Shatner was the star of the show!" Roswell explained. "He played Captain James T. Kirk in all seventy-nine episodes of the original series, twenty-two episodes of the animated series, and seven of the motion pictures!"

"He's the greatest actor Earth has ever known!" the Fuzzfurr declared.

Roswell snorted. "Well, I wouldn't go *that* far."

The Fuzzfurr shot him a dirty look.

"Um...I'd say he's the greatest actor in the *universe*!" Roswell recovered. "And you want *us* to retrieve your photograph?"

The Fuzzfurr nodded. "William Shatner wrote me a deeply personal message on the picture. His meaningful words changed my life forever. Unfortunately, I've never met anyone brave enough to salvage it."

"Where's the photograph now?" Stella asked.

"It's inside a vault at my summer home," the Fuzzfurr said. "Before the comet hit, the property sat on the shore of the beautiful Furgarian Brown Sea. Today the property sits on the edge of a ferocious volcano."

"WHAT?" Mank exclaimed.

"I'm sure that's an exaggeration," Stella said.

"I wish I were exaggerating," the Fuzzfurr said. "Mount There-She-Blows is the most perilous location on the surface of Furgaria. Thousands of good Furgarians have perished at the volcano. Hundreds of bad ones too. No one has reached its fiery peak and lived to tell the tale."

"Uncle Clancy, you've got yourself a deal!" Cassi said.

Roswell quickly pulled Cassi to the side of the shrine.

"Are you nuts?" he whispered. "We can't go to the edge of a volcano! That's way too dangerous!"

"Are you kidding? That's the *least* dangerous favor he's going to ask!" Cassi whispered back. "My uncle also lost Adam West's original Batmobile in a black hole. At least the William Shatner photograph is local."

Before Roswell or the other aliens could object, Cassi bumped bellies with her uncle to cement the agreement. The Fuzzfurr happily turned to Roswell and raised his paw. Even though he didn't have fingers, Roswell could tell the Furgarian was trying to give him *Star Trek*'s classic Vulcan salute.

"Live long and prosper," the Fuzzfurr said.

Roswell spread his fingers and returned the salute.

"Live long and prosper," he groaned.

After striking a deal with the Fuzzfurr, Roswell and the aliens headed back to the flying saucer. They gathered in the craft's examination chamber to get ready for the mission ahead.

"I HATE you!" Mank moaned. "I hate you all SO MUCH!"

"Don't get cold wings now, Mank," Stella said. "We all knew saving Earth would be challenging. Let's turn that mandible into a mandi*smile*."

"I still don't understand why we ALL have to go!"

"Because we're a team, and teams stick together."

"So does MILDEW!"

Nerp entered a code into a keypad, and a rack of red space suits popped out of the wall. Everyone got dressed and helped one another screw in their gloves, boots, and helmets. Rob was the only one who didn't need a space suit—the Cyborg could survive the elements of space all on his own. Cassi squeezed into a suit that was meant for a Small Gray. Her big belly barely fit inside of it.

"Dang, I look good in anything," she said. "You guys ready or what?"

"Let me get this straight," Roswell said. "The only way to the Furgarian surface is to bounce from asteroid to asteroid *on foot*?"

"Pretty cool, huh?" Cassi said.

"Beep-beep boop-boop beep-beep?"

"Good question—why can't we take the saucer to the surface?" Nerp asked.

"The asteroid field is too thick for a spacecraft," Cassi

explained. "Just keep your bounce low, your momentum steady, and you'll be fine. I used to go asteroid bouncing all the time when I was a young pup. It's a lot of fun once you forget the fear of drifting off into the endless abyss of space."

"Your parents let you PLAY in an ASTEROID FIELD?!" Mank asked.

"They *encouraged* it!" she said.

Roswell and the aliens left the saucer and walked to the edge of the Furgarian cave. They toed up to the force field and waited for Cassi's instructions. The Furgarian charged forward with a running start. Cassi leaped through the force field and glided through space like a frog in slow motion. She landed on the nearest asteroid and then immediately hopped to the next.

"First one to the surface gets to eat a rotten egg!" Cassi said.

Roswell and the aliens took a collective deep breath and copied the Furgarian. They jumped through the force field with running starts, and the gravity disappeared. Roswell felt his stomach rise, and his spine grew two inches taller. He landed on the first asteroid and skidded across it like a rock skipping across water. It took him and the others a few jumps before they were bouncing as gracefully as Cassi. Once they got the hang of it, the group followed the Furgarian to Furgaria's surface.

Although no one wanted to admit it, Cassi was right— *asteroid bouncing was fun!* Roswell felt like he was connected to an invisible bungee cord. Everyone was enjoying the activity and laughing at the thrilling sensation—except for Mank. The Mantis slammed into each asteroid like a dodgeball and screamed bloody murder.

Bleep was also having issues along the journey. The Small Gray was so light they couldn't gain momentum to move among the asteroids. Roswell and the aliens had no choice but to pass Bleep back and forth like a football.

"I've got 'em!" Roswell said. "Hey, Rob, go long!"

"Where is long?" the Cyborg asked.

"Beep-beep boop beep-beep!"

"We are *not* disrespecting you—we're *helping* you!" Nerp said.

"Peep-peep poop peep-peep-peep!"

"The only thing *embarrassing* is your attitude!"

The asteroid field became thicker and thicker the closer they got to the planet. Some of the asteroids were so close together that Roswell and the aliens had to crawl between them. Eventually the group touched down on Furgaria's dry and rocky surface. The planet's gravity was only twenty percent of the gravity on Earth.

"There she is!" Cassi announced. "Mount There-She-Blows!"

The Furgarian pointed to a volcano on the horizon. It was twice the height and four times the width of Mount Everest. A powerful geyser of magma blasted from the volcano's peak and jetted straight into the sky. The magma cooled as it rose, filling the atmosphere with enormous black rocks. The rocks disintegrated as they fell back to the ground, and the sky rained tiny stones.

"Isn't she a beauty?" Cassi asked.

Roswell gulped. "She makes *Mount Doom* look like an anthill."

"Everyone stay positive!" Stella said. "We'll need all our energy to get up that volcano."

"And a touch of MENTAL ILLNESS!" Mank griped.

The group proceeded across Furgaria's rocky terrain. The low gravity made Roswell feel like he was walking across a bounce house. Once again the Small Gray was too light to gain any momentum. Nerp had to grab hold of Bleep before they floated off like a loose balloon.

"Beep-beep boop-boop beep-beep!"

"Obviously, you *can't* do it by yourself!" Nerp said.

"Bleep, try thinking heavy thoughts!" Cassi suggested. "Always works for me."

The Small Gray eventually gave up and accepted a piggyback ride from Nerp.

The group finally reached the base of Mount There-She-Blows and started their climb. Luckily, the low gravity made the ascent very easy. Roswell and the aliens hopped up the volcano with the speed and strength of kangaroos. They reached the peak within a few minutes. Seeing the volcano up close was a humbling experience for all of them. Roswell had never seen something that was so powerful, so terrifying, and yet so *beautiful* at once. Their space suits were designed to withstand extreme pressures and temperatures, but the volcano's heat still made him sweat.

"My uncle's summer home is on that slope!" Cassi said.

The Furgarian pointed to a structure of curly pipes, curvy slides, and winding tunnels. The property was hanging over the edge of Mount There-She-Blows's peak. The home looked like it might fall into the volcano at any moment.

"Is that a *water park*?" Roswell asked.

"It *was* until Big Bertha vaporized all of Furgaria's water," Cassi said.

"Your uncle lived in a *water park* during the summer?"

Cassi shrugged. "Wouldn't you?"

"Oh, give me a BREAK!" Mank cried. "That thing is one SNEEZE from toppling over!"

"For once, I agree with Mank," Stella said. "Even in this gravity I don't think the water park can hold all our weight without falling. Trust me, I have my Pleiadean certificate in architectural engineering."

"Well, I *have* to go inside," Cassi said. "I'm the only one who knows where my uncle's vault is."

"Someone should go with you in case you need help," Stella said.

"I nominate Bleep," Nerp said.

"Beep-beep boop-boop!"

"I am *not* trying to get you killed!"

"Peep-peep poop-poop-poop!"

"Because *you* don't weigh anything on this planet!"

"Beep-beep!"

"Watch your language!"

"Guys, we're here to save *my* planet—*I'll* go with Cassi," Roswell decided. "The rest of you stay here and give us a signal if you see anything fishy."

The Cyborg blinked curiously. "How could a fish survive these conditions?"

"He means dangerous," Stella said. "I wish we had a siren of some kind."

"I am equipped with an alarm system," Rob said. "Allow me to demonstrate."

The Cyborg's eyes lit up like headlights, and his head spun like a lighthouse beacon. *WAAAAAMP-WAAAAAMP-WAAAAAMP!* A piercing alarm erupted from the speaker in his neck. *WAAAAAMP-WAAAAAMP-WAAAAAMP!* The word *caution* flashed across Rob's digital forehead.

"Is that sufficient?" he asked.

"That'll do," Roswell said. "Wish us luck!"

Roswell and Cassi carefully walked along the edge of the volcano. They entered the water park through a green tube slide that stuck out like a drawbridge. As soon as they took their first step, the whole property creaked. The structure sank a foot deeper into the volcano as it adjusted to their weight. They waited a few moments, then proceeded when the water park remained still. Roswell followed Cassi up the green tube and through an obstacle course of tunnels and slides.

"How much farther until we reach the vault?" Roswell asked.

"We're getting close," Cassi said. "My uncle's chambers are at the top of this lazy river."

The Furgarian chuckled to herself and batted her eyes at him.

"What's so funny?" he asked.

"Us," she said. "This isn't how I pictured our first date, but it sure is memorable."

Roswell rolled his eyes. "Cassi, this is not a date!"

"We're in an abandoned water park hanging over the edge of a volcano. What's platonic about that?"

"Um...everything?"

Cassi winked at him. "It'll be a great story for our grandpups someday."

Roswell couldn't decide what was more dangerous—hanging over the edge of an active volcano or being alone with Cassiopeia Furbottom.

"We're here!" the Furgarian said. "Keep an eye out for a vault."

The Fuzzfurr's chambers were in a cabana at the top of the water park's tallest waterslide. Roswell felt like he was stepping into the bedroom of a 1970s teenager. Everything was singed from the volcano's heat but still recognizable. The walls had posters of the television shows *Charlie's Angels*, *Mork and Mindy*, and *Three's Company*. A large bookcase contained hundreds of old *TV Guides*. There was also a record player, a broken lava lamp, and an orange shag carpet. Roswell found an olive-green locker with a combination lock. It looked like the lockers at his middle school.

"Um...is *this* the vault?" he asked.

"You found it!" Cassi said.

"What's the combination?"

"Shoot! I forgot to ask Uncle Clancy!"

The Furgarian spun the lock and entered a dozen combinations, but none of them worked.

"Dang it!" she growled. "I'm usually so good at invading personal space."

"What have you entered so far?" Roswell asked.

"His coronation day, his birthday, all his children's birthdays, all his wedding anniversaries, and all his divorce dates."

"Try nine-eight-six-six."

"What's that?"

"The original *Star Trek* series premiered on September eighth, 1966. It's like Christmas for the Trekker community."

Cassi entered 9-8-6-6 into the lock. To her and Roswell's extreme relief, the locker popped open. The only object inside was a framed photograph. Roswell's heart fluttered when he saw William Shatner's smoldering face staring back at him. The deep and personal message that had changed the Fuzzfurr's life read, "To Clancy, Much love, William Shatner."

"We did it, sweetcheeks!" Cassi cheered.

"Great work, Cassi!" Roswell said.

The two jumped up and down and hugged. Unfortunately, the celebration was cut short. Roswell heard a creaking noise and felt a rumble beneath his feet.

"Cassi, do you feel that?" he asked.

"It's called *love*, sweetcheeks!" she said.

"No! We're moving!"

It was the same movement they had felt when they entered the water park, but this time it didn't stop! *WAAAAAMP-WAAAAAMP-WAAAAAMP!* The Cyborg's alarm echoed in the distance. *WAAAAAMP-WAAAAAMP-WAAAAAMP!* Roswell's hunch was confirmed—*the water park was sliding into the volcano!*

"We gotta get out of here!" he yelled.

Roswell and Cassi hurried through the water park as fast as they could—the Furgarian even ran on all fours. They watched in horror as sections of the water park broke off and fell into the volcano. Roswell held the photograph of William Shatner tightly against his chest. He felt the frame crunching in his arms.

Soon Roswell and Cassi reached the green tube they'd entered from. As they raced through it, the tube tilted back and teetered over the edge. Roswell and Cassi clutched each other as they slid toward the volcano.

"*I'm glad we get to die in each other's arms, sweetcheeks!*" Cassi said.

Suddenly Roswell felt something grab his arm. The entire water park plummeted into the volcano, but Roswell and Cassi remained in the air. He looked up and saw Rob, Mank, Stella, and Nerp above them! They had grabbed one another's ankles and created a living chain! And the aliens had saved Roswell and Cassi in the nick of time! The Cyborg was standing on the volcano's edge while he held on to the others.

"Rob, pull us up!" Stella said.

The Cyborg lost his balance and began rocking back and forth.

"Your weight is pulling me forward!" Rob said.

"Lean back as far as you can!" Nerp said.

"I am trying," the Cyborg said. "The low gravity is working against me!"

"QUICK, ROSWELL! DROP CASSI!" Mank demanded.

"Hey!" the Furgarian growled.

Despite all Rob's effort, he couldn't get his balance back. The Cyborg was pulled forward, and the others dropped deeper into the volcano.

"BEEP-BEEP-BEEEEEP!"

Bleep floated through the air and landed on Rob's shoulders. The Small Gray pulled on the Cyborg's neck with all their might. Bleep's limited weight was exactly what Rob needed to regain his footing. Slowly but surely, the Cyborg walked backward and pulled his friends to safety.

"Bleep! You're a hero!" Nerp exclaimed. "How did you do that?!"

The Small Gray shrugged. "Peep-peep poop-poop peep."

"You thought *heavy thoughts?*"

"Told you it would work!" Cassi said.

Stella patted Mank on the back with a sly smile. "And *that's* why teams stick together."

Roswell was so out of breath he could barely speak. Before he had the chance to thank his friends for saving him, he was distracted by something in the sky. A strange being was flying through the atmosphere above them. Roswell took a closer look and saw they were wearing a jet pack and shelled space suit. The stranger landed on the other side of the volcano, and Roswell gasped. He immediately recognized the scaly face inside the helmet.

"Roswell, my monitors indicate a severe spike in your heart rate," Rob said. "Do you require medical attention?"

"Ge...Ge...Ge...," he wheezed, but couldn't get the words out.

"Gemini?"

"George Lucas?"

"GERMS?!"

"Gen...Gen...Gen...," Roswell struggled to say.

"Genes?"

"Geena Davis?"

"GINGIVITIS?"

"*GENERAL XELIC!*" Roswell shouted.

He pointed across the volcano, and the aliens saw the Reptoid for themselves. General Xelic gave the group a sinister wave. He removed an object from the inside of his space suit. It was a black sphere with several small spikes and a long string. The Reptoid pulled the string, and the sphere started strobing in different colors. Roswell had no clue what he was looking at, but the aliens screamed.

"Peep-peep poop-poop!"

"He's got a shellnuke!" Nerp said.

"A what?" Roswell asked.

"It is the most powerful bomb in the Reptoidian arsenal!" Rob said.

"STELLA, WHAT DO WE DO?!" Mank asked.

The Pleiadean's big eyes grew twice in size, and her ghostly skin became paler.

"*Run,*" she said.

Roswell and the aliens dashed down the volcano as fast as their legs would carry them. They had to kick Bleep back and forth like a soccer ball so the Small Gray could keep up. As they ran for their lives, General Xelic dropped the shellnuke into the volcano. The Reptoid's jet pack roared, and he rocketed back into the sky, fleeing the scene.

BAAAAAAAAAAM! Just as the group reached the base of the volcano, Roswell heard the loudest noise he had ever heard in his life. The shellnuke's explosion was so powerful the sound alone knocked everyone off their feet. Mount There-She-Blows erupted ten times stronger, ten times higher, and ten times hotter than before. More geysers burst through the volcano's sides, spewing lava in every direction. Roswell and the aliens had to dodge and dive to avoid the magma.

The group hurried across the rocky surface and returned to the lowest asteroid in Furgaria's orbit. They climbed on top of the rock and started bouncing back to the Furgarian Strip. When Roswell and the aliens were halfway through the asteroid field, the entire planet began to quiver below them. So much pressure had built up inside Mount There-She-Blows, the whole volcano exploded! Magma spread across the planet's surface and through the asteroid field like a giant tsunami!

Roswell and the aliens looked to one another with the same thought behind their terrified eyes. The magma was moving too high and too fast to escape it. *They weren't going to survive.* They stopped bouncing and all held on to the same asteroid.

"Beep-beep boop-boop?!"

"Yes, Bleep—this is the end," Nerp said.

"GOODBYE, CRUEL UNIVERSE!" Mank cried.

"At least we get to die heroes," Stella said.

"Gorgeous heroes," Cassi said.

"Thank you for helping me," Roswell said. "Even though we didn't succeed, this has been the greatest adventure of my life."

Roswell and the aliens joined hands and waited for the wave of magma to consume them. *VOOOOOSH!* Just before the magma reached their asteroid, a boomerang-shaped craft suddenly swooped in. The boomerang spun in a quick circle, and its wing hit their asteroid like a baseball bat. The asteroid soared through the field, taking Roswell and the aliens with it. They flew high into Furgaria's orbit and avoided the tsunami—and *death*—by a split second.

"HOLY SOLAR FLARE!" Mank screamed. "WHAT WAS THAT?"

"The boomerang craft!" Roswell yelled. *"It's real!"*

Their asteroid slammed into a bigger asteroid in the field. The collision flung the group directly toward the Furgarian Strip. They passed through the force field, and their bodies rolled across the landing zone before coming to a stop. Roswell was relieved to see the photograph of William Shatner was still tight in his grip. The frame was ruined, but the picture was intact.

"Beep-beep boop-boop beep-beep!"

"Yeah—that was *very* unexpected!" Nerp said.

Roswell and the aliens hurried to the front of the landing zone and gazed down. The magma had consumed most of the planet and nearly half of the asteroid field. But there wasn't any sign of the mysterious boomerang ship that saved them.

"Roswell's mind wasn't playing tricks on him after all," Stella said in disbelief. "Someone *has* been following us!"

"Whoever they are, they really SAVED our necks back there!" Mank said.

"They saved the rest of us too!" Rob noted.

"Best stalker I've ever had," Cassi said.

"But *why* did they save us?" Roswell asked. "Who are they? And what do they want?"

CHAPTER THIRTEEN

THE CYBORG STATION

The Fuzzfurr was ecstatic to reunite with his prized photograph of William Shatner. Tears filled the Furgarian's eyes as he watched his servants reframe the picture and hang it on the wall of his *Star Trek* shrine. The ruler was so grateful he wanted to throw Roswell and the aliens a parade through the Furgarian Strip. To Cassi's dismay, they had to decline the offer because of their tight schedule.

Once the Fuzzfurr signed their petition, the group departed Furgaria and headed for the Cyborg Station. The mystery of the boomerang craft hung in the air like a bad scent, and no one knew where the smell was coming from. Stella sat at the flying saucer's dashboard and flipped through a thousand holograms of different spaceships.

Roswell was fascinated by all the unique and quirky models.

"What are you looking at?" he asked.

"The Milky Way Galactic Spacecraft Archive," Stella said.

"Beep-beep boop beep-beep-beep boop beep-beep."

"Bleep's right—it's like the galaxy's DMV," Nerp said.

"Peep-peep-peep poop-poop-poop."

"Yes—but *much* faster service."

"I've searched through the archive twice and can't find a single spacecraft that matches the one we saw on Furgaria," Stella said. "Whoever is following us, their transportation isn't registered. That explains why I didn't recognize them at Allen Astro's. They might be from another galaxy altogether."

Roswell was so puzzled it gave him a headache. "What does an alien from another galaxy want with us?" he thought aloud. "And why were they so interested in my dad?"

None of the aliens had an answer.

"Can I remind the room of ANOTHER dilemma?" Mank asked.

"Better than anyone I know," Rob said blankly.

"General Xelic tried to KILL US!" the Mantis exclaimed. "HE'S been following us too! What if he tries to kill us AGAIN?!"

"The general doesn't know we're alive," Stella said.

"Let's be honest, it was a miracle we survived the volcano. If I were him, I'd be headed back to the Reptoidian mother ship for a victory lap."

"I bet the general thinks *I* survived the magma," Cassi said.

"WHY?" Mank asked.

The Furgarian shrugged like it was obvious. "Because I'm already so hot," she said. "The poor guy is probably trying to dig me up as we speak. Gosh, I'm starting to respect his hustle. It's a shame I'm already in a relationship."

"We're *not* in a relationship," Roswell said.

"I agree, sweetcheeks—it's too early for labels," Cassi said, and blew him a kiss.

General Xelic rocketed high above the Furgarian atmosphere and returned to his shellcraft. The ship was stationed in the planet's outer orbit, so it took the general a while to reach it with his jet pack. Once he was back on board, he removed his helmet and stared down at Furgaria. The Reptoid grinned as he surveyed the damage his shellnuke had caused. The explosion had consumed the entire surface and half the asteroid field. There was no possible way Roswell and the aliens had survived—the general was *positive*.

The orange tail on the dashboard began to twirl.

General Xelic pulled the appendage to answer a call from the Reptoidian mother ship.

"This is General Xelic," he said.

"I have the Reptiliz for you, General."

"Please put him through."

A moment later Reptiliz Reek's raspy voice bellowed through the speaker.

"Well?" he asked.

"My lord, I'm pleased to inform you the prisoners have been eliminated," General Xelic said. "They will *not* interfere with our invasion. We can proceed as planned."

"Return to the mother ship at once, General. We must prepare the troops."

"Yes, my lord. I'll depart Furgaria immedia—"

General Xelic lost his train of thought. He was distracted by a flying saucer in the distance. The spacecraft flew out of the Furgarian Strip and then zoomed into another part of the galaxy at light speed. It happened so quickly the general almost missed it.

"No!" General Xelic yelled. "That's impossible!"

"What's impossible?" Reptiliz Reek asked.

The general was so enraged he could barely speak.

"ANSWER ME!"

"It…it…it appears I was mistaken," he said. "The prisoners have *not* been terminated."

"YOU'RE WASTING MY TIME *AND* TESTING MY PATIENCE, XELIC!" the Reptiliz roared.

"Don't be alarmed, my lord! I will fix this!"

"YOU HAVEN'T FIGURED OUT THE SEVERITY OF THIS SITUATION! THEY HAVE VISITED *THREE SYSTEMS* SINCE ESCAPING THE MOTHER SHIP! TWO MORE SIGNATURES AND THEY'LL HAVE ENOUGH SUPPORT TO SPEAK WITH THE MILKY WAY GALACTIC ALLIANCE!"

"My lord, it would take galactic years to schedule an audience with—"

"THE CYBORG WAS EN ROUTE TO STAR CITY WHEN WE ABDUCTED HIM! ACCORDING TO OUR SPIES IN THE GALACTIC CAPITAL, A CYBORG IS SCHEDULED TO SPEAK BEFORE THE ALLIANCE IN TWO GALACTIC DAYS!"

The Reptiliz was right—General Xelic *didn't* understand how serious it had become.

"FIND THEM! END THIS!"

"Yes, my lord. Consider it done."

The transmission ended, and General Xelic angrily hit the dashboard with a clenched fist. He glared into space as he contemplated his next move. Apparently, nuking a volcano wasn't enough—his next move had to be much more direct.

The flying saucer left Zosma far behind, and the Grays set a course for their fourth stop. The distance between

Furgaria and the Cyborg Station was the longest stretch of the mission. To pass the time, Cassi taught Stella, Mank, and Rob how to play Furgarian cards.

"Aha! Three Furgarian slugs!" she said. "I win again!"

Cassi happily collected the pile of holographic chips between them.

"This game doesn't make SENSE!" Mank objected. "I had slugs last round and LOST!"

"That's because I had a pair of Furgarian tubs—and tubs beat slugs."

"But ROB had a pair of tubs in the first round, and you STILL won!"

"Because I had the Furgarian blemish card. That's an automatic win."

The words *processing* and *suspicion* flashed across the Cyborg's digital forehead.

"It seems like the rules keep changing to your benefit," Rob said.

"Stella, read Cassi's MIND!" Mank said. "I wanna know if she's LYING!"

The Pleiadean fearfully shook her head. "Are you crazy? I'm not going in *there*!"

"Y'all are the sorest losers I've ever played with," Cassi said. "If this game isn't your style, how about a round of Furgarian charades? It's impossible to cheat without a bucket of grease."

Roswell wasn't in the mood for games. His anxiety

grew with every passing hour, and he was tormented by a galaxy of concerns. Would he and the aliens get the final two signatures in time? Would General Xelic attack them again? Who was the pilot of the boomerang craft? Where was the alien from? Why were they following them? Was it just to protect them, or did the alien have *another* motive?

The white spot of doubt in Roswell's aura felt like a thorn in his side. He tried to follow the Seven Sisters' advice and fight the uncertainty with hope, but summoning hope was like summoning rain in the middle of a drought. If he couldn't diminish his fears, Roswell figured it was wise to distract himself from them. He asked Nerp to teach him how to fly the saucer, and the Tall Gray was happy to oblige.

"The small red button is the accelerator," Nerp explained. "It's like a gas pedal for your finger. The harder you press it, the faster the ship will fly. The big red button controls the nuclear thrusting engine. Hit it once for a boost, hit it twice for light speed, and hold it down for hyper–light speed. And *don't* mix those commands up."

"Beep boop beep boop beep-beep."

"Yes, Bleep—you *did* learn that lesson the hard way. Moving on, the blue dial adjusts the ship's altitude, the orange switch is for landing, and the steering sphere controls the ship's navigation. Spin the sphere forward to fly forward, spin it backward to fly backward, et cetera, et cetera. It's like moving a cursor on an Earth computer. Want to give it a try?"

The Tall Gray let Roswell sit in the piloting seat. He cautiously placed his hands on the controls and followed Nerp's instructions. Roswell felt the engines' vibrations in his fingertips. It was exhilarating to know he could take the ship to any corner of the universe he wanted. His first attempt at steering was a little bumpy, but he eventually learned the correct movements and developed muscle memory. The saucer's dashboard was like a complicated video game controller.

"How's this?" Roswell asked.

"Nicely done!" Nerp said. "Try taking the ship around the Owl Nebula. A quick spin around those stars will propel us even faster."

"We call that one the Big Bowling Ball on Furgaria," Cassi said.

Roswell recognized the famous nebula as it appeared ahead. He understood why the Furgarians had named it after a bowling ball. The nebula was a massive emerald orb, and three bright stars shined in the very center. He gently turned the steering sphere, and the saucer glided around the orb. Next, Roswell hit the big red button for a boost, and the craft broke free from the nebula's gravitational pull. The maneuver launched the craft even faster into space.

"How'd I do?" Roswell asked.

"That was perfect!" Nerp said. "You're a natural."

Bleep rolled their big eyes. "Peep-peep *poop-poop*."

"Don't be jealous," Nerp said. "Green isn't your color."

The flying saucer sped toward the most famous constellation to Earthlings. The Big Dipper had seven stars that formed the shape of a giant ladle. The saucer entered the space in the very center of the spoon. The Cyborg Station appeared on the saucer's holographic radar. However, there were no stars or planets in the area.

"Where is it?" Roswell asked.

"The Cyborg Station is a mobile facility," Rob explained. "It is not locked in the orbit of a celestial body and is free to roam about the galaxy."

"So it's like a big motor home?" Roswell asked.

The word *processing* flashed across the Cyborg's forehead.

"I suppose that is an accurate description," he said.

A few moments later a square object came into view. The Cyborg Station looked like a giant motherboard floating in the middle of space. The facility was constructed from billions of microchips and circuit boards. Millions of bright electric dots traveled between sensors like cars in a busy city. The roof held a gigantic storage disk, and large fans cooled off thousands of servers surrounding it. The station's perimeter was lined with massive solar panels that soaked up all the energy from the distant stars.

"It looks like a big naked computer," Roswell noted.

The word *pride* flashed across Rob's digital forehead.

"The Cyborg Station has the most advanced processing

system in the galaxy, and it holds the largest digital storage unit in the universe," he said. "The central processor operates at a speed of sixteen million petaflops per galactic second, and the central disk holds ten billion googolplex terabytes."

"Bless you," Cassi said.

"How do we get inside?" Roswell asked.

"Through the visitor center," Rob said. "Once we enter the station, I will escort you to Data City. I will submit a public ballot at the town hall and asks the Cyborg citizens to support our mission. The Cyborgs will vote mentally, and the results will come back immediately."

"Do you think the Cyborgs will help us?" Roswell asked.

"Cyborgs are programmed to make practical and logical decisions. We are not designed to hold grudges or prejudices or biases that may influence us. Therefore, if supporting the petition makes sense, you will have the Cyborgs' approval. However, if supporting the petition does not make sense, you will not have the Cyborgs' approval."

"So you have no clue how this is gonna go?" Roswell asked.

"No idea whatsoever," Rob admitted.

Nerp supervised Roswell as he flew the saucer to the Cyborg Station's visitor center. The craft entered a hangar that looked like a big USB port. The hangar was filled with

Cyborg spaceships, and just like Rob's craft on the Reptoidian mother ship, they reminded Roswell of large television remotes. Roswell flipped the orange switch on the dashboard, and the saucer landed beside the other ships.

The passengers exited the saucer, and Rob escorted them through a pair of double doors that looked like floppy disks. The visitor center was a small and underwhelming room. At first Roswell thought he was stepping inside an Earth gym. There were a dozen machines that looked like treadmills. The machines were arranged in a row that faced a long, rectangular window. Roswell peeked through the window and peered into the heart of the Cyborg Station.

The interior of the Cyborg Station was like the action figure section of a toy store. Millions of Cyborgs stood in rows across thousands of levels. All the Cyborgs were constructed from the same white and silver metal as Rob. They had muscular physiques, but there was a variety of masculine, feminine, and gender-neutral frames among them. Their digital faces were featureless, but the word *connected* flashed across their foreheads.

"Where is Data City?" Roswell asked. "And why are all the Cyborgs turned off?"

"Data City is not a physical place," Rob explained. "The capital is located inside a virtual reality. The Cyborgs may appear unconscious, but in actuality they are very alert and having experiences in an artificial world."

"Beep-beep boop-boop beep-beep."

"Yes, Bleep—it's just like *The Matrix*," Nerp said.

"How do we join the virtual reality?" Roswell asked.

The Cyborg gestured to a pair of thin goggles, gloves, and boots on the nearest treadmill.

"This is a virtual reality simulation station," Rob said. "The equipment creates artificial sensations, allowing non-Cyborg beings to enter Data City. The platform below your feet will adjust to the virtual environment. Once you put the equipment on, you will be prompted to create an avatar. To avoid confusion, I suggest you create an authentic avatar that resembles your physical traits."

"Awesome!" Roswell said. "I love virtual reality!"

"I must warn you, entering Data City can be jarring at first," Rob said.

"Don't worry, I do VR all the time at the Cherokee Springs Arcade," Roswell said. "I still have the highest score on virtual *Tetris*."

"Splendid," Rob said. "Everyone please select a machine and put on the equipment. I will connect to the server and meet you in Data City."

The Cyborg's face went blank, and the word *connecting* flashed across his forehead. Roswell and the aliens stood on the simulation stations and put on the goggles, gloves, and boots. When the equipment clicked on, Roswell realized he should have taken Rob's warning more seriously.

The virtual reality at the Cherokee Springs Arcade was *nothing* compared with the VR at the Cyborg Station.

VOOOOOSH! The simulator pulled Roswell down a long tunnel and into an infinite virtual world. The ground was an endless blue grid, and the sky was pure white light. The goggles' resolution was so clear Roswell couldn't tell the difference between the real world and the virtual one. After a few seconds inside, he didn't even notice the equipment anymore.

Roswell looked down at his hands and feet, but he didn't have a body.

"Please choose your avatar," said a soothing voice.

A screen appeared in front of Roswell to help him create a virtual figure. He swiped through thousands of alien species until he found a human form. Next, Roswell searched through hundreds of features until he found the right hair, skin color, eye shape, and outfit that matched his own. Roswell touched a green check mark to finalize his selection, and the screen disappeared. He looked down and saw he was wearing the body he'd created.

"Welcome to Data City," the soothing voice said.

The greeting was followed by a friendly musical melody. *POP!* A winding road and grassy hills loaded on the grid. *POP!* Houses, cottages, cabins, castles, palaces, farms, ranches, and even igloos sprouted up. *POP!* Skyscrapers stretched across the horizon.

POP! POP! POP! POP! POP! One by one, virtual versions of Stella, Mank, Nerp, Bleep, and Cassi were loaded beside Roswell. Everyone had followed Rob's advice to create realistic avatars expect Cassi. The Furgarian was draped in jewelry, her face was painted with makeup, and she was wearing Rihanna's extravagant yellow dress from the 2016 Met Gala.

"Cassi, we were supposed to make *authentic* avatars," Stella said.

The Furgarian shrugged. "I know," she said. "These were the closest options they had."

POP! A strange man appeared behind them. He had pale blue skin, was about six feet tall, and wore a button-up plaid shirt, jeans, and leather loafers.

"You are the first galactic friends I've ever hosted," the man said.

If it weren't for his familiar voice, Roswell would never have recognized the Cyborg.

"Rob?" he asked in disbelief.

"You look DIFFERENT," Mank said.

"Apologies, I should have warned you about my virtual form," Rob said. "This is my authentic self. Cyborgs use their metal suits only when they leave the Cyborg Station. But in Data City we can appear however we want and live however we'd like."

"How do we get to the Data City Town Hall?" Roswell asked.

"However you wish," Rob said. "To download an object in Data City, simply tell the VR what you want. Allow me to demonstrate. VR, I would like a red bicycle."

The word *loading* flashed in front of the Cyborg. *POP!* A moment later a red bicycle appeared beside him.

"No way!" Roswell gasped. "So if I wanted a hot-air balloon, I would just say, 'VR, I would like a hot-air balloon'?"

The word *loading* flashed in front of Roswell too. *POP!* Before he could picture it in his mind, a voluminous hot-air balloon with rainbow panels and a wide wicker basket materialized beside him. The aliens were very impressed and eagerly made their own requests.

"VR, I would like a zero-emissions electric hovercar," Stella said.

"VR, I would like an indestructible and chemical-resistant TANK," Mank said.

"VR, I would like a carriage pulled by male models!" Cassi said.

"Beep-beep, boop-boop beep-beep boop-boop."

"An *ostrich*?!" Nerp asked. "*That's* what you pick?"

The word *loading* flashed beside each of them. *POP!* A floating silver convertible loaded next to the Pleiadean. *POP!* A thermoplastic tank loaded next to the Mantis. *POP!* A golden carriage pulled by six male models in swimsuits loaded next to the Furgarian. *POP!* An ostrich loaded next to the Small Gray.

"Your selections are very imaginative," Rob said. "Now if you'll please follow me, I will guide us into the city."

The Cyborg climbed aboard his red bicycle and pedaled toward the city. Roswell stepped inside his balloon, Stella sat behind the wheel of her hovercar, Mank strapped himself into his plastic tank, Cassi took the reins of her carriage, and the Grays hopped on the ostrich's back. The aliens followed Rob through the Cyborg neighborhood, but Roswell stayed behind—he had never flown a hot-air balloon before.

"Hey, VR?" he sheepishly whispered. "Could you just move the balloon for me?"

"As you wish," said the soothing voice.

The burner blasted on its own, the balloon filled with hot air, and Roswell drifted after the others.

"Thanks!" he whispered.

While the group traveled through the virtual suburb, Roswell gazed at all the unique homes below him. He saw Cyborgs playing with their children in front yards, Cyborgs walking artificial dogs, and Cyborg families enjoying picnics. Roswell had never seen such a *happy* community. The Cyborgs' joy may have been artificial, but it was also contagious. Roswell couldn't help but smile as he enjoyed the virtual breeze through his hair.

"That is my home," Rob announced.

The Cyborg pointed to a picturesque two-story house

with a picket fence. Through the window Roswell and the aliens could see a Cyborg woman, a Cyborg girl, and a Cyborg boy sitting around a dinner table.

"Wait a second—you have a *family*?" Roswell asked.

"Why didn't you tell us?" Stella asked.

Rob blinked curiously. "I was not asked."

"What are their names?" Cassi asked.

"My wife is known as K1-34227, our son is known as O1-48663, and our daughter is known as C8-48990. For convenience, you may call them Karen, Owen, and Cate."

To everyone's surprise, a Cyborg man entered the dining room and gave Karen a kiss on the cheek. Roswell and the aliens glanced to one another with awkward tension, but Rob wasn't fazed at all.

"Looks like your old ball and chain has another iron in the fire," Cassi said.

The Cyborg blinked curiously. "What ball and chain? And where is the fire?"

"She means another Cyborg just KISSED your wife!" Mank exclaimed.

"Oh, that is R08-36119.5," Rob said.

"Isn't that *YOUR* full name?" Mank asked.

"Is he your *twin brother*?!" Cassi gasped.

"No, R08-36119.5 is my backup," Rob explained. "Whenever Cyborgs travel beyond the Cyborg Station, we leave a duplicate of ourselves behind in case an unfortunate event prevents us from returning. When I eventually return home, R08-36119.5 will upload his memory drive into mine, and we will merge into one being."

The aliens were fascinated by the process, but Roswell went quiet and stared at his avatar's feet. He had experienced many emotions while traveling through space—amazement, confusion, excitement, and terror, to name a few—but this was the first time he felt *jealousy*. Roswell would have given anything to have a backup of *his* parents.

Their procession biked, rode, drove, rolled, floated, and galloped through the suburbs and finally reached downtown Data City. The town was surprisingly earthlike and reminded Roswell of New York City in the 1920s. All the buildings were tall, with art deco touches. There were glimmering golden rooftops, shiny silver spires, and brawny bronze statues everywhere he looked. The streets were crowded with classic automobiles, and the sidewalks were bustling with Cyborg citizens in three-piece suits and flapper dresses.

"Am I crazy, or does Data City have a Roaring Twenties vibe?" Roswell asked.

"Oh, it must be a Fryday," Rob said. "Data City uploads new themes throughout the galactic week. Since Cyborgs do not have an organic history, we enjoy re-creating the history of our neighbors. It gives us a better appreciation for biological life."

"Call me when you do the Furgarian Swinging Sixties,"

Cassi said. "If *that* decade doesn't make you feel alive, nothing will."

The city was full of street signs and billboards written in a Cyborg language. The letters and symbols looked like a mix of braille and barcodes. Rob translated the advertisements as they passed them. There were stores like Chrome Depot; Wiremart, and Bot, Bolt, and Beyond. There were also restaurants like PF Chains, Dunkin' Lug Nuts, and McCogholes. The city even had a street of live musical theater with shows like *A Circuit Line*, *Metal Mia*, *Nailspray*, and *Dent*.

Eventually the group arrived at the Data City Town Hall and parked their vehicles, animals, and male models on the street. The town hall was very narrow and reminded Roswell of the Flatiron Building in New York City. The group walked up the front steps and entered the lobby. Inside they discovered a long line of Cyborg citizens waiting to use a wooden rotary phone.

"That is the ballot submission machine," Rob explained. "We are in luck. The queue usually stretches around the block."

"How many ballots do Cyborgs go through?" Roswell asked.

"We vote on thousands of issues each day," Rob said. "Sometimes it can be tedious, but at least we don't have a corrupt ruler making decisions for us. No offense, Cassi."

"Don't knock it till you try it!" she said.

Roswell and the aliens waited in line and slowly moved closer and closer. Finally it was Rob's turn to submit his request. The Cyborg held the receiver to his ear and spun a number on the round dial.

"Hello, this is Cyborg R08-36119," he said. "I would like the Cyborg Station's permission to speak with the Milky Way Galactic Alliance to save the planet Earth from a Reptoidian invasion. Please vote *yes* to support our petition or vote *no* to oppose it. Thank you and have a virtually pleasant day."

The Cyborg went quiet as he waited for the answer. Roswell and the aliens waited with bated breath to hear the verdict.

"WELL?" Mank asked. "Did they make a DECISION?"

"The vote is unanimous," Rob said, and hung up the phone. "They said no."

General Xelic trailed Roswell and the aliens through space, carefully staying at the edge of the flying saucer's radar. The Reptoid covertly tracked the craft thanks to a gruesome accessory attached to his shellcraft. The snout of a nasaldactyl—an extinct species with a remarkable sense of smell—followed the flying saucer's *scent* all the way to the Cyborg Station.

General Xelic stationed his shellcraft in the facility's outer orbit. The Reptoid left his ship and circled the Cyborg Station with his jet pack. He discovered the flying saucer in a hangar and flew inside. After a quick inspection General Xelic found Roswell and the aliens inside the visitor center. The group was so immersed in the virtual world that they were oblivious to the Reptoid outside.

"They're making this easy," the general said with a laugh.

General Xelic raced back to his shellcraft and collected a few supplies. He returned to the visitor center with six beams of Reptoidian stone, a laser torch, and a small flash drive. The general placed the beams across the visitor center doors and welded the entrance shut with the laser torch. Next, he inserted the flash drive into the nearest circuit board. The drive contained a dark substance that beat against its container like a wild animal trapped in a cage. General Xelic gleefully watched as the substance drained into the Cyborg Station.

"Escape *this*," he said.

Roswell paced across the virtual sidewalk while the aliens sat on the curb outside the town hall. Everyone was completely shell-shocked and didn't know what to do next.

"So the whole station voted *no*?" Roswell asked.

The Cyborg shook his head. "Only 99.9998 percent," he said.

"At least .0002 percent voted yes," Stella said.

"That was me," Rob said.

"What do the Cyborgs have AGAINST Earth?" Mank asked.

"It is likely the Cyborgs want to achieve Cyborg rights before lending their support to another species," Rob explained.

"Beep-beep boop-boop-boop beep-beep boop-boop?"

"Yeah—could we convince them to change their minds?" Nerp asked.

"I would not be allowed to submit a second ballot until tomorrow," Rob said. "We would have one galactic day to change a *lot* of artificial minds."

"Staying here is too risky," Stella said. "I say we head for the Insectia Moon. We can think of another system to stop at along the way."

"Can I bring the models with us?" Cassi asked.

BOOOOOM! BOOOOOM! A thunderous commotion echoed through Data City. Roswell, the aliens, and all the Cyborg citizens turned toward the sound. *BOOOOOM! BOOOOOM!* A towering monster appeared on the horizon and crept toward Data City. Its footsteps sent mini earthquakes through the entire grid. *BOOOOOM! BOOOOOM!* The monster had a pitch-black body, bright red eyes, long limbs, wide antlers, and razor-sharp nails.

Its skin was covered in HTML codes that were constantly changing.

"RAAAAAAAAAAR!" the monster roared.

"Holy Godzilla!" Roswell gasped. "What is *that*?!"

The Cyborg's eyes went wide. "A *virus*!"

WHAAAAAM! The virus entered the city and knocked down a building. The debris fell on top of Cyborg pedestrians, and their virtual bodies disappeared. The words *failed connection* flashed at the scene of every victim.

"Doesn't the Cyborg Station have VIRUS PROTECTION?" Mank asked.

"Our firewall is impenetrable," Rob said. "Someone must have inserted the virus directly into our system!"

"Five bucks says their name rhymes with *Beneral Belic*," Cassi said.

SLAAAAAM! The virus marched deeper into Data City and demolished every structure in its path. *STOMP! STOMP!* The monster squashed the fleeing citizens like they were roaches. The virus paved a path toward a building that looked like the Empire State Building. Roswell noticed a large microchip spinning at the top of the building's spire.

"It is heading for the central processing unit!" Rob said. "If the virus reaches the CPU, the whole station will be destroyed!"

"How do we stop it?" Stella asked.

"We must return to the physical world and restart the

CPU," Rob said. "Once the CPU is restarted, the servers will be wiped clean, and all foreign data will be erased."

POP! The virtual Rob disappeared and the word *disconnected* flashed behind him. Roswell slid off his VR goggles and peeked inside the visitor center. Rob hurried to the exit but couldn't open the floppy-disk doors. The word *concern* blinked across Rob's forehead.

"The doors are sealed shut!" he said.

Roswell and the aliens hopped off their simulators and helped the Cyborg push. Still the doors didn't budge.

"We're LOCKED IN!" Mank yelled.

POOOOOVE! As the virus destroyed the virtual world, the Cyborg Station started shutting down in the physical world. Section by section, the facility lost power and went dark. The Cyborg citizens returned to their metal bodies as the virus obliterated their avatars in Data City. Their foreheads blinked with the words *connection error*.

"Beep-beep boop-boop beep-beep?"

"Can the other Cyborgs help us?" Nerp asked.

"They were improperly disconnected, so it will take a few minutes for their systems to reboot," Rob said.

"Is there another way to restart the CPU?" Stella asked.

"You can also restart the CPU in the virtual world," Rob said. "Go to the top of the Central Processing Building and pull the lever on the spinning microchip. I will stay behind and work on opening the door. If the virus reaches the life support server, it will shut off the oxygen in the visitor center."

The fingers on the Cyborg's left hand retracted and were replaced by a round saw. While Rob tried to saw the doors open, Roswell and the aliens slipped the VR equipment back on. By the time they returned to Data City, more than half of the digital town had been decimated. The virus was only two blocks away from the Central Processing Building.

"It's going to take us AGES to get to the microchip!" Mank said.

"We need to stall the virus while we get to the roof!" Roswell said.

"Nerp, Bleep, and Cassi—you distract the virus," Stella instructed. "Roswell, Mank, and I will go to the top of the Central Processing Building."

"Beep-beep boop-boop beep-beep?"

"Yeah—how do we stall a virus?" Nerp asked.

"Ask the VR for assistance," Rob said. "It will download anything you request."

"Copy that!" Cassi said. "Let's slap and tickle this pickle!"

The Grays and the Furgarian raced into the street, while Roswell and the others headed for the CPU building. The virus angrily roared as Cassi, Nerp, and Bleep stood in its path.

"VR, we need a big brick wall!" Nerp said.

POP! A ten-story wall loaded in front of them. Unfortunately, the virus pummeled through the wall like the bricks were made of eggshells.

"Beep-beep, boop-boop beep-beep-beep boop!"

"An *ice-skating rink*?!" Nerp asked. "How is that going to help?!"

POP! An ice-skating rink appeared in the middle of the street. The virus slipped on the ice and fell on its back.

"Huh," Nerp said. "Nice one."

"My turn!" Cassi said. "VR, we need a Black Friday sale!"

POP! The doors of a nearby shopping center burst open. Thousands of virtual shoppers emerged and stampeded over the virus. The digital monster became furious as it brushed the shoppers off its body. Eventually the virus got to its feet and lunged toward the aliens. *SWAAAAAT!* With one powerful swipe, the virus struck Cassi, Nerp, and Bleep. The aliens disappeared from Data City, and the words *disconnected* flashed in their place.

"Beep-beep boop-boop?"

"The virus broke our connection!" Nerp said.

"How do we log back in?" Cassi asked.

"You cannot reconnect," Rob said. "The virus has disabled your VR equipment!"

Meanwhile, inside Data City, Roswell, Stella, and Mank reached the foot of the Central Processing Building. They stared up at the intimidatingly tall structure.

"I'm not FEELING so good," Mank said.

"Don't give up, Mank—we can do this!" Stella said.

"No, I MEAN it!" he said. "I'm feeling WOOZY!"

THUMP! The Mantis collapsed on his simulation station. His avatar disappeared from Data City and was replaced with the word *disconnected.*

"Mank!" Stella gasped.

"I'm starting to feel light-headed too," Cassi said.

"Beep-beep boop-boop beep-beep?"

"Yes—the room *is* spinning!" Nerp said.

"The virus has shut down the oxygen!" Rob said. "You must hurry!"

Roswell and Stella thought fast and requested the first objects that came to mind.

"VR, I need a pair of wings!" Stella said.

POP! Two majestic white wings grew out of the Pleiadean's back. Stella flapped her new accessories and soared into the air.

"VR, I need a pair of…um…*elastic arms!*" Roswell said.

POP! Roswell's arms stretched at his sides like spaghetti. He reached up and grabbed hold of a windowsill on the twelfth floor. Roswell walked backward, stretching his arms as far as possible, and then launched himself like a rubber band.

The limited oxygen made the task exhausting. Roswell and Stella gasped deeper and deeper as they ascended the building. The digital monster reached the Central Processing Building too. Like a fire-breathing dragon, it blew a geyser of swirling HTML codes in their direction.

"The virus is throwing up numbers and letters!" Roswell said.

"It's spewing corrupt coding!" Rob said. "Do not touch it or your connection will be compro—"

Before the Cyborg finished his warning, the codes grazed the Pleiadean's left wing. Her avatar glitched and then fell like a damaged plane. Stella hit the ground and vanished completely. The word *disconnected* flashed above the impact.

Now the fate of the Cyborg Station rested solely on Roswell's shoulders. He flung himself up the building as quickly as his elastic arms would allow. The virus growled angrily and climbed after him. Roswell had to swing around the structure to avoid the HTML codes erupting from the monster's mouth.

"*Beep...beep...boop-boop!*"

"*I...can't...think...either...,*" Nerp gasped.

"*Good...luck...sweetcheeks...,*" Cassi wheezed.

"*You...can...do it...Roswell!*" Stella said.

Roswell could hear the aliens passing out in the visitor center. *THUMP! THUMP!* Nerp and Bleep collapsed on the floor beside Mank. *THUMP! THUMP!* Stella and Cassi fainted too. Roswell took a deep breath, desperate to preserve whatever oxygen remained. Finally Roswell made it to the Central Processing Building's rooftop.

"Roswell, what is your status?" Rob asked.

"*I'm...almost...there!*" he panted.

Roswell shimmied up the tall spire like it was a fireman's pole. His eyes were getting heavier and heavier, his vision was getting hazier and hazier, and his body was getting weaker and weaker. The virus was climbing faster and faster behind him, and the HTML codes were getting closer and closer.

The microchip was spinning just a few feet above him.... Roswell could see the lever he needed to pull.... He reached up with all his remaining strength.... He wrapped his elastic fingers around the lever....

"Any update?" Rob asked.

"*I...just...need...to...pull...*"

Unfortunately, before he could pull the lever, Roswell's body went limp, his vision faded, and Data City disappeared....

CHAPTER FOURTEEN

THE INSECTIA MOON

Roswell sat up and gasped for air. His heart was racing, his lungs were sore, and his vision was blurry. After a few seconds and several deep breaths, his senses returned. Roswell realized he was lying on the floor of the Cyborg Station visitor center. An oxygen mask had been placed over his mouth, and Rob was kneeling by his side. Roswell also noticed the exit had been sawed open, and two Cyborgs were cleaning up the pieces.

"He's awake!" Rob announced.

The other aliens were in the visitor center too and wore their own oxygen masks.

"What happened?" Roswell asked.

"Beep-beep boop beep-beep-beep!"

"You saved the Cyborg Station!" Nerp said.

"I did *what*?" Roswell asked.

"You restarted the CPU!" Rob said. "The servers were wiped and the virus was destroyed!"

"Had it taken you ONE SECOND longer, the virus would have KILLED us all!" Mank said.

"When the other Cyborgs found out you saved their station, they decided to reconsider our request!" Stella said. "Rob resubmitted our ballot, and they voted yes! We need only *one* more signature to speak with the alliance!"

The aliens cheered and Roswell slowly got to his feet.

"That's wonderful news, but I *didn't* pull the lever," Roswell confessed.

"Of course you did, sweetcheeks!" Cassi said. "Everyone else passed out!"

"No, I'm serious," Roswell said. "I got to the top of the building and put my hand on the lever, but I lost consciousness before I pulled it down. It wasn't me!"

The aliens looked at one another with the same perplexity.

"If *you* did not restart the CPU in the virtual world, that means it was restarted manually in the physical world," Rob said.

"Beep-beep boop-boop?"

"Yeah—if it wasn't one of *us*, who did it?" Nerp asked.

Roswell went to the nearest window and searched the space surrounding them.

"I've got a hunch," he told the others.

Had he arrived at the window one moment earlier, Roswell would have seen a boomerang-shaped spacecraft sneaking away from the Cyborg Station. However, Roswell didn't need confirmation to know the mysterious alien had saved them once again.

General Xelic returned to his shellcraft in a furious rage. The Reptoid punched the walls so hard his space suit crumbled off his body. To his dismay, the orange tail on his dashboard began spinning on the dashboard. The Reptoid took the deepest breath possible to calm himself before answering the call.

"Yes?" the general grumbled.

"You better have good news for me!" the Reptiliz growled through the speakers.

The general clenched his sharp teeth. "Unfortunately not, my lord."

"WHAT IS WRONG WITH YOU, XELIC?! WHY IS THIS SO DIFFICULT?!"

"They had help, sir."

"HELP FROM WHAT?!"

"A being in a curved ship appeared and foiled my—"

"YOU'VE BECOME CLUMSY! TOO MUCH IS AT STAKE FOR YOUR USUAL THEATRICS! I DO NOT CARE WHO SEES YOU, HOW MANY CASUALTIES

YOU LEAVE BEHIND, OR IF YOU DIE IN THE PRO-
CESS! FIND AND *KILL* THEM ALL!"

"Yes, my lord."

The transmission ended, and General Xelic glared into space. If looks could kill, Roswell and his friends would have been slaughtered by the hatred beaming from the general's yellow eyes.

The saucer traveled across the galaxy and flew toward a star in the constellation Scorpius. Over a dozen stars formed the shape of a giant scorpion, equipped with a tail and two claws. Mank directed the Grays to a star named Lesath at the tip of the scorpion's stinger.

As they approached the star, the saucer flew through a breathtaking double-sided nebula. Its gases surrounded a bright white star and then stretched away from it like a pair of celestial wings. The nebula's vivid colors grew darker as they spread through space, illuminating the saucer in white, pink, and red light.

"That's the Butterfly Nebula!" Roswell said in amazement.

"We call it the Great Windshield Smear on Furgaria," Cassi said.

"Wow! It's stunning in photographs, but it's even more beautiful in person!"

"People say the same thing about me, sweetcheeks."

The flying saucer proceeded toward the only planet in Lesath's orbit. It was a massive gas giant and four times the size of Jupiter. Bright scarlet hydrogen and dark maroon methane swirled across the cloudy surface, and the planet was surrounded by thin silver rings.

"That's ANGRY JOE," Mank told the others. "The ancient Mantises used to WORSHIP it."

"Why *Angry* Joe?" Roswell asked.

Mank shrugged. "Wouldn't YOU be grumpy if you had that much gas?"

Hundreds of tiny moons orbited the planet. Mank guided the Grays as they flew through the crowded exosphere. Eventually the Insectia Moon appeared in the distance ahead. The moon was covered in green and brown landmasses and had a thick yellow atmosphere.

While the others admired the moon, Mank went to the saucer's examination chamber below. Roswell heard the Mantis pressing buttons, maneuvering medical machinery, and mixing glass vials. A couple of minutes later, Mank returned to the cockpit with a syringe of neon-green liquid.

"Roswell, give me your ARM," he instructed.

Roswell nervously stepped back. "Um...why?"

"You won't survive the Insectia Moon unless I VACCINATE you," Mank said. "It's one of the most DANGEROUS systems in the Milky Way galaxy! The air is TOXIC, the plants are POISONOUS, and the water is LETHAL! The moon is also full of bloodthirsty CARNIVORES that will smell you and hunt you down unless you have the proper ANTIANTIBODIES!"

"Is that why you're so anxious and uptight all the time?" Roswell asked.

"I told you, it's a SURVIVAL MECHANISM," Mank said. "Now give me your ARM."

Roswell rolled up his sleeve, and Mank poked his forearm with the syringe. He barely felt the small needle pierce his skin, but he could feel the cold vaccine coursing through his veins. As the chemicals moved through him, Roswell had sweats, chills, goose bumps, itching, and swelling all at once. Three muscle spasms, two boosts of serotonin, and one bout of nausea later, he was as good as new.

"I also added the vaccine for SHINGLES," Mank said. "You'll thank me LATER."

The flying saucer sank into the Insectia Moon's atmosphere. The spacecraft flew over a dense jungle of the most bizarre plants Roswell had ever seen. There were vines with tentacles, bushes with leaves like artichokes, mushrooms as colorful as Easter eggs, and shrubs with sharp spikes like porcupine quills. The plants were also much bigger than the vegetation on Earth. The flowers were the size of cars, the hedges were the size of houses, and the trees were as tall as skyscrapers. All the plants grew across, under, and through one another in an epically tangled mess.

"Have we shrunk?" Roswell asked.

"The Insectia Moon has more OXYGEN and CAR-BON DIOXIDE in its atmosphere than your planet, allowing its organisms to grow BIGGER than the organisms on Earth," Mank said. "We should be approaching the MANTIS CAMPUS any minute now. That's where MOTHER lives."

"Do you think we can convince her to sign our petition?" Roswell asked.

The Mantis shrugged. "She's as LEVELHEADED and EASYGOING as I am."

"We're doomed," Cassi whispered.

"Let's leave those defeatist attitudes in the saucer," Stella said. "Once Mank's mother sees how far we've come, I'm sure she'll be receptive to our request. Do I need to remind everyone of the five Pleiadean *P*s?"

"No," everyone said together.

Eventually the Mantis Campus appeared on the horizon. The sprawling structure reminded Roswell of an Arabian palace on Earth, except all the domes were shaped like beehives. The campus was protected by a tall wall of blue lasers and an electric force field.

"That's not exactly a welcome mat," Roswell said.

"The Mantis Campus has the BEST defense system in the galaxy," Mank said. "NOTHING goes in or out without our approval."

BWAAAAAMP! BWAAAAAMP! BWAAAAAMP! The flying saucer's alarms went off. *BWAAAAAMP!*

BWAAAAAMP! BWAAAAAMP! According to the radar, four objects were headed toward them—and they were moving *fast!* *BWAAAAAMP! BWAAAAAMP! BWAAAAAMP!* Mank read the radar and his face turned pale green.

"Did you tell the campus we were COMING?!" he asked.

"Peep-peep poop-poop peep?"

"We were supposed to call ahead?" Nerp asked.

"YES!" Mank yelled. "Mantises are the most PARA-NOID species in the galaxy! They SHOOT DOWN unexpected spacecraft!"

BWAAAAAMP! BWAAAAAMP! BWAAAAAMP! Soon four rockets appeared directly ahead. *BWAAAAAMP! BWAAAAAMP! BWAAAAAMP!* The rockets were striped like bees, and instead of boosters, they were propelled through the air by wings.

"What are they shooting at us?!" Roswell asked.

"Those are MANTIS MISSILES!" Mank cried. "They won't stop until they HIT US!"

"Beep-beep boop-boop beep-beep!"

"Yes—everyone strap into your seats!" Nerp ordered.

All the passengers quickly buckled themselves into their oval chairs. *SWOOOOOSH!* Nerp spun the steering sphere and the craft swerved to the left. *BAAAAAM!* The first missile collided with the second missile and exploded. *SWOOOSH!* The saucer swerved to the right, but the remaining missiles followed. *VROOOOOM!*

Nerp flew the craft straight toward a gigantic tree and quickly yanked the gears upward. *BAAAAAM!* The saucer shot toward the sky, and the third missile slammed into the tree! *VROOOOOM!* The craft did loops through the air, but it couldn't shake the fourth missile. *BOOOOOM!* The missile hit the saucer and blasted a giant hole in the craft!

"We're going down!" Nerp exclaimed.

"Beep-beep boop-boop-boop!"

"The escape pod won't fit all of us!"

"Peep-peep poop!"

"No, Bleep! We are *not* drawing straws!"

BWAAAAAMP! BWAAAAAMP! BWAAAAAMP! The alarms quadrupled as the saucer plunged through the air. *WHAAAAAM!* The saucer hit the ground and slid through the jungle, leaving a trail of destruction behind it. *BWAAAAAMP! BWAAAAAMP! BWAAAAAMP!* The craft eventually came to a halt. The alarms went silent and the cockpit went dark.

"Is everybody alive?" Nerp asked.

"Beep-beep!"

"Yes!"

"Thankfully!"

"I've been better!"

"DEAD inside!"

"My consciousness is a matter of opinion."

Everyone groaned as they unbuckled themselves and got

to their feet. They followed the Grays outside to inspect the damage. Roswell was instantly intimidated as he looked around the Insectia Moon. The alien jungle surrounded them for miles, and the vegetation was so thick Roswell could see only a few yards in each direction. Above them, Angry Joe filled the entire sky like a giant red face.

"Beep-beep boop-boop."

"What do you mean it's *not that bad*?!" Nerp said. "There's a giant hole in our ship!"

"Can you fix it?" Stella asked.

The Tall Gray sighed. "I think so—but it's going to take a couple galactic hours to mend it back together and restart the power."

"In that case, the rest of us should head to the Mantis Campus on foot while Nerp and Bleep repair the saucer," Stella said.

"Were you listening to ANYTHING I said earlier?" Mank exclaimed. "The Insectia Moon is too DANGEROUS to travel on foot! You have no idea how SCARY the predators are out there!"

"Are they scarier than *Cassi* in beast mode?" Roswell asked.

"Thanks, sweetcheeks," the Furgarian said.

Stella pressed a button on her Pleiades pin, and it projected a map. The Pleiadean traced the map and pointed into the west.

"The Mantis Campus is three point five miles away," she said. "I know it's risky, but that isn't much ground to cover. I think we can handle a couple miles as long as we stick together."

"Am I the only one here without a DEATH WISH?" Mank asked.

"Stop putting the *pest* in *pessimistic*, Mank," Stella said.

Despite the Mantis's warnings, Roswell and the aliens headed into the jungle, while the Grays repaired the saucer. The group of five traveled in total silence as they climbed over, under, between, and through the overgrown plants. Every few feet Mank would dive behind a large flower or bush for no apparent reason.

Fortunately, they finished the first mile without encountering a single soul. However, as they began the second mile, Roswell had an eerie feeling he was being watched. He found a small creature standing on a purple clover beside him.

"Pssssst, Mank!" Roswell whispered. "What the heck is that?"

"That's a PRIMITE!" the Mantis whispered back. "Don't TOUCH it! It's FILTHY!"

The primite looked like something between a chimpanzee and a human, but it was only a few inches tall. It had big ears, a big nose, ten fingers and toes, and a long, curly tail. Roswell couldn't decide if the primite was adorable or disturbing.

"Why does it look so human?" he asked.

"Primites are miniature PRIMATES," Mank explained. "On the Insectia Moon the bugs evolved BIG and the mammals evolved SMALL. It had something to do with a CALCIUM shortage."

"Squeeet. Squeeet."

The primite squeaked like a chipmunk and gave Roswell a friendly wave. He didn't know what to do, so he awkwardly waved back. The creature jumped onto Roswell's arm, crawled up to his hoodie, and lovingly rubbed its face against his cheek.

"Squeeeeet. Squeeeeet. Squeeeeet."

"I think it likes me," Roswell whispered.

"Oh sweetcheeks, let's adopt him!" Cassi said.

"Don't TRUST it!" Mank said. "Primites are very MISCHIEVOUS, and they work in PAIRS! They DISTRACT other creatures while their partner STEALS!"

Suddenly a second primite jumped onto Stella's shoulder. With one swoop of its tiny tail, the primite snatched the pin off her uniform. Both primites leaped to the ground and ran deeper into the jungle.

"My pin!" Stella shouted. "That has our petition!"

"After them!" Rob yelled.

Roswell and the aliens raced after the primites. The thieves were so small it was difficult to follow them through the dense jungle. The group chased the primites for more than a quarter mile without stopping. Eventually the tiny primites paused on top of a boulder, but it was only to taunt their pursuers.

"Squeet! Squeet! Squeet!"

The primites stuck out their tongues, showed off their blue butts, and waved the pin above their miniature heads.

"What are they saying?" Rob asked.

"Something about Cassi's WEIGHT and Roswell's MOTHER," Mank said.

"Thank you!" Cassi said.

"Those little furry jerks!" Roswell said.

CHOOOOOMP! A giant yellow tulip leaned over and *ate the primites!* It was so unexpected it took Roswell and the aliens a moment to process what they had witnessed. *GULP!* The tulip had swallowed the primites whole. A lump traveled down the flower's stem and headed for its roots underground.

"We need to get my pin before the flower digests them!" Stella said.

"Allow me," Rob said.

The Cyborg's left fingers retracted into his hand and were replaced by a sharp pair of scissors. *SNIIIIIP!* Rob cut the flower in half. The primites rolled out of the flower's severed stem, very dazed and confused. They fearfully scurried into the jungle and left the pin behind. The tulip twitched and hissed on the ground as it slowly wilted and died.

"Rob, you saved the day!" Stella said, and quickly retrieved her pin.

"He SHOULDN'T have done that!" Mank exclaimed. "That was a SNAPPING TULIP! They're a SYSTEM of predatory plants connected at the ROOT!"

"So what?" Cassi asked.

"If you hurt ONE tulip, you hurt them ALL!"

The jungle filled with the sounds of crunching sticks and rustling leaves. One by one, hundreds of snapping tulips rose from the jungle floor and jerked their yellow heads toward the group. Even though the flowers didn't have faces, Roswell could tell the plants were *furious*. They shook their petals like angry dilophosauruses shake their collars.

"We should probably split," Roswell said.

The Cyborg blinked curiously. "Split what?"

"He means GET OUT OF HERE!" Mank cried.

Roswell and the aliens dashed through the jungle as fast as they could. *CHOMP-CHOMP!* The snapping tulips lunged and nipped at them like a school of hungry piranhas. *CHOMP-CHOMP!* It didn't matter which direction they ran; the plants were everywhere and multiplying by the second! *CHOMP-CHOMP!* There were so many flowers they couldn't see where they were going! *CHOMP-CHOMP!* Roswell and the aliens tripped over a large root and rolled over the edge of a cliff!

POOOOOF! The fall was long, but thankfully, the

landing was soft. Roswell thought they had landed on a trampoline. He and the aliens were lying on something bouncy and flat. It was suspended between two canyon walls like a wide net. The group tried to sit up, but their bodies were stuck to it.

"This is a very peculiar contraption," Rob noted.

"Mank, what is this?" Stella asked.

"IT'S...IT'S...IT'S...," Mank stammered.

Everyone was used to his anxiety, but the Mantis was so frightened he couldn't speak. A few moments later Roswell and the aliens understood why. The whole net started to quiver as a monstrous creature lurched toward them. It had eight enormous legs, four red eyes, and two giant claws. It wasn't a net after all—they had landed in a *giant spiderweb*!

"IT'S A CLAWRANTULA NEST!" Mank exclaimed.

"A *clawrantula*?" Roswell asked. "You've got to be kidding me!"

The massive spider-crab hybrid hovered over Roswell. He could see the creature had a mouth full of sharp teeth and four fangs that were dripping with venom. The clawrantula wrapped each of its prey in more web, spinning Roswell and the aliens so tight they couldn't move their limbs. Afterward the hybrid decided to feed on its biggest catch first. It lowered its mouth toward Rob, but its fangs couldn't pierce the Cyborg's metal body. The clawrantula became more and more frustrated after every failed bite.

"SOMEBODY HELP US!" Roswell screamed.

"Stop SCREAMING!" Mank said. "You'll only attract something WORSE!"

"What could be worse than a—"

Before Roswell finished the question, he had an answer. A powerful buzzing commotion echoed through the sky. The noise grew stronger and stronger as something big moved closer and closer. Roswell was expecting a fleet of helicopters, but the reality was much more terrifying. A swarm of gigantic two-headed wasps dived into the canyon.

"THAT'S what's worse!" Mank exclaimed. *"PARA-WASPS!"*

The parawasps were the size of motorcycles and twice as loud. They had bright orange bodies and black-spotted abdomens. Roswell and the aliens screamed as the parawasps approached. Even the clawrantula froze and looked up in fear. One at a time the parawasps landed on the clawrantula and tried to stab the hybrid with their huge stingers.

"What's happening?!" Roswell asked.

"The wasps are laying eggs inside its BODY!" Mank said. "When their eggs hatch, the larvae will eat the clawrantula ALIVE!"

"Aww, how sweet! They're going to be parents!" Cassi said. "Congratulations!"

Soon the whole swarm was on top of the clawrantula.

The web stretched lower and lower, but it couldn't hold all the weight. Thread by thread, the clawrantula's nest started to rip off the canyon walls. When the second-to-last thread gave out, the whole web snapped like a slingshot. Roswell and the aliens were flung to a completely different part of the jungle! They hit a giant tree and slid down the branches, falling from leaf to leaf until they landed on the ground with a hard thud.

"I am *not* enjoying this planet," Rob said.

"Really? I'm having a great time!" Cassi said.

The clawrantula's web wrappings made it difficult for Roswell and the aliens to stand. They had to nudge one another and shimmy up the large plants to get to their feet. Once they were all up, Stella gasped—but it was a gasp of joy.

"Look!" she said, and nodded to her left. "It's the Mantis Campus!"

The campus's wall of blue lasers was just a few hundred yards away.

"Thank the SOURCE!" Mank said.

"We made it!" Roswell said.

Unfortunately, the celebratory moment was cut short. A strange flapping noise came down from the sky. Roswell and the aliens looked up and saw a flock of massive moths fluttering above them. The insects had enormous red wings with yellow spots that looked like giant pairs of eyes.

"Is that a group of moths?" Roswell asked.

"The correct term is an *eclipse* of moths," Rob said.

"They're beautiful!" Stella said.

"THOSE ARE *MOTHSQUITOES*!" Mank yelled. "THEY'RE GOING TO SUCK OUR BLOOD!"

Roswell and the others noticed the razor-sharp proboscises sticking out of the mothsquitoes' mouths. The spots on the insects' fluttering wings looked much, much more menacing—like hundreds of evil eyes were blinking at them. Roswell and the aliens frantically hopped toward the Mantis Campus like they were competing in a potato sack race. The mothsquitoes swooped closer and knocked Cassi over. The Furgarian couldn't get back up, so the others had to roll her across the jungle like a barrel.

When Roswell and the aliens were just a few feet away from the Mantis Campus, the mothsquitoes began circling them like a cyclone. *They were trapped!* The cyclone shrank tighter and tighter, and the mothsquitoes' proboscises moved closer and closer toward their trembling bodies. It was only a matter of seconds until they were all impaled!

SPEEEW-SPEEEW! SPEEEW-SPEEEW! The cyclone of mothsquitoes was pelted with a strange turquoise liquid. *SPEEEW-SPEEEW! SPEEEW-SPEEEW!* The liquid burned the mothsquitoes' bodies like acid. *SPEEEW-SPEEEW! SPEEEW-SPEEEW!* The mothsquitoes retreated high into the sky and fled the scene.

A platoon of Mantis soldiers had emerged from the

Mantis Campus. The soldiers were dressed in dark green armor and had helmets with openings for their antennae. The Mantises were also holding bright purple beetles like weapons. By pulling the beetles' antennae, the soldiers launched turquoise acid from the beetles' behinds like toxic water guns.

The Mantises cautiously aimed their beetles at Roswell and the aliens.

"MANK? Is that YOU?"

The soldier at the front of the platoon recognized Mank and gestured for the others to lower their beetles.

"MINK!" Mank cried. "You rescued us in the NICK of time!"

"Your voice is VERY distinctive—I heard you SCREAM-ING from inside the campus," Mink said. "What are you doing out HERE? You NEVER go outside!"

"After THIS week, I never will again!"

"Are you wrapped in *CLAWRANTULA* web?"

"Believe me, today was a GOOD day compared to the rest!" Mank said. "Mink, I need to see Mother RIGHT AWAY! The sooner I speak with her, the sooner I can put all this TRAUMA behind me!"

Before entering the Mantis Campus, Roswell and the aliens had to pass through a long sterilizing tunnel. They were sprayed with a series of bleaches and disinfectants as they stood on a moving walkway. At the end of the tunnel, their bodies were scanned for infectious diseases. Once they were in the clear, they were granted access.

The Mantis Campus was the cleanest place Roswell had ever seen. The walls, the floor, and the ceilings were made of spotless white bioplastic. Full-body sanitizing stations stood on every corner like old-fashioned phone booths. Small machines roamed the campus, sweeping, scrubbing, and polishing every inch of the interior.

The Mantis citizens crawled along the walls and flew through the high domes as they went about their daily errands. They all practiced social distancing and never came within six feet of one another. Many of the Mantises wore face masks and gloves, some wore hazmat suits, and a few even rolled around in plastic bubbles.

The Mantis soldiers took Roswell and the aliens to the largest dome in the center of the Mantis Campus. Roswell's mouth dropped open as he laid eyes on the Insectia Moon's ruler. Mother was twelve times bigger than all her children. She sat on an enormous white throne and wore a gown made from different hygienic materials. The tips of her wide headdress continuously sprayed disinfectant, shrouding her in a constant cleansing mist. Every five seconds Mother's body went tense, and a new emerald Mantis egg dropped from her abdomen. A line of Mantis midwives collected the eggs as she laid them.

"Mother, MAY we approach the throne?" Mink asked.

"Yes, you MAY," Mother replied.

Mank, Mink, and the other Mantis soldiers bowed graciously to their ruler. Roswell and the others followed their lead.

"Mother, this is MANK," the soldier said. "He has an URGENT MESSAGE for you."

"It's GOOD to see you, my child," Mother said.

Mank made a nervous whimper. "Hello, MOTHER. How are YOU?"

"I've been in labor for TWO GALACTIC CENTURIES," she said. "Other than that, I can't COMPLAIN. What is your URGENT MESSAGE?"

Mank didn't leave out a single gruesome detail as he recalled the previous days. Mother was just as mortified to hear the story as Mank was to relive it. The Mantises bonded over the grisly tale like they were watching a horror movie.

"And the Reptoidian prison was in the stratosaurus's BOWELS!" Mank said.

"NO! Not the BOWELS!" Mother gasped.

"The only way out was through the BLADDER!"

"How did you DO IT?!"

"Then we had to dress in Reptoidian UNIFORMS!"

"The odor must have been UNBEARABLE!"

"While we escaped, we learned the Reptoids are planning an INVASION of Earth!"

"An INVASION? Have they no SHAME?"

Roswell noticed that the more upset Mother became, the faster she laid eggs. The midwives had to run to keep up with them.

"With Earth's resources the Reptoids will become more POWERFUL than ever!" Mank said. "We believe the Reptoids will invade OTHER planets as well!"

"Their greed knows NO BOUNDS!"

"Mother, we need your signature so we can speak with the MILKY WAY GALACTIC ALLIANCE! It's the only way to STOP the Reptoids ONCE AND FOR ALL!"

"ABSOLUTELY!" Mother said. "I'll give you WHATEVER you need!"

Roswell thought his ears were deceiving him. "I'm sorry, could you repeat that?"

"I said I'll give you WHATEVER you need!"

"Seriously? You don't want anything in return? No DNA sample? No aura examination? No autographed picture of a 1960s television star?"

"Of COURSE not!" Mother cried. "This invasion will set a DANGEROUS precedent for the ENTIRE GALAXY! Other systems will COPY the Reptoids and invade their NEIGHBORS! The Milky Way will be consumed with WAR and DESTRUCTION! GERMS and DISEASES will spread across the galaxy! The viruses and bacteria will be free to GROW and MUTATE! There will be OUTBREAKS and PANDEMICS! The whole universe will become one COLOSSAL CESSPOOL!"

"Mother, you're RIGHT!" Mank said. "The Reptoidian invasion will be even WORSE than I imagined! And I thought I had catastrophized EVERYTHING!"

"WHERE DO I SIGN?" Mother asked.

Stella projected the petition in front of Mother, and the ruler signed it right away. The aliens cheered after the final signature was collected, but Roswell was in complete shock. He couldn't believe *Mank's mother* had been the easiest leader to convince.

"This is shnigglebotting fantastic!" Stella exclaimed. "I never thought I would say this, but I'm so happy Mank's paranoia is hereditary!"

"Thank goodness the apple doesn't fall far from the tree!" Roswell said.

The Cyborg blinked curiously. "What tree?"

"It's a metaphor about parents and their kids."

"Do the babies get hurt when they fall off their parents?"

Roswell was too happy to try to explain. "Yes, Rob— yes, they do!"

An enormous smile grew on Roswell's face as the reality dawned on him. They had completed the mission! *Roswell and the aliens were going to the Milky Way Galactic Alliance!*

After hearing about their crash landing, Mother instructed the Mantis soldiers to escort Roswell and the aliens back to the flying saucer. She also sent her finest engineers to help the Grays with any last-minute repairs. As they traveled through the jungle, the soldiers eyed the towering plants with their beetles ready. Luckily, the other creatures kept their distance. Roswell was very relieved the trip back was less eventful than the trip there.

Unfortunately, the Insectia Moon still had a few surprises left.

BOOOOOSH-BOOOOOSH! Suddenly bright green lasers pelted the jungle floor! *BOOOOOSH-BOOOOOSH!* The soil exploded and the plants went up in flames! *BOOOOOSH-BOOOOOSH!* Roswell and the aliens dived to the ground! *BOOOOOSH-BOOOOOSH!* The jungle turned into a war zone in a matter of seconds!

For a brief moment the lasers ceased and the smoke cleared. Roswell looked up and saw their attacker. A Reptoidian shellcraft hovered directly above them, and a familiar face was behind the windshield.

"General Xelic!" Roswell shouted. "He's back!"

"For the last time, I'm *not* interested in dating you!" Cassi shouted at the general.

The Reptoid was yelling so loudly Roswell could hear him outside the shellcraft.

"YOU WON'T ESCAPE THIS TIME!" he roared.

SPEEEW-SPEEEW! The Mantis soldiers fired their beetles at the shellcraft. *SPEEEW-SPEEEW!* The acid didn't even leave a mark on the Reptoidian ship. *BOOOOOSH-BOOOOOSH!* With two powerful blasts, General Xelic knocked all the Mantises on their backs.

"Split up and hide!" Stella said. "He can't attack us if he can't find us!"

With no other options, Roswell and the aliens bolted into different parts of the jungle. To Roswell's horror, the general targeted him first. The shellcraft showered him with laser beams and obliterated the jungle in the process. Roswell's ears were ringing from all the loud explosions! He ran until his knees buckled beneath him, but he never stopped moving!

Eventually Roswell came to the edge of another cliff—but this time there was no clawrantula web to break his fall. General Xelic aimed his shellcraft cannons at him. Roswell shielded his body with his arms, but he knew nothing would save him now.

"GOODBYE, EARTHLING!" the general yelled.

VEEEEERM! Just as the Reptoid was about to pull the trigger, something very large and dark descended from the sky. Roswell peeked through his arms to see what was

357

happening. *The boomerang craft was back! And the pilot had put themselves in between Roswell and the shellcraft!*

"NOT *YOU* AGAIN!" the general shouted.

BOOOOOSH-BOOOOOSH! The shellcraft's lasers hit the boomerang, and its left wing exploded. The craft soared through the air and crashed in the jungle nearby.

"No!" Roswell cried.

"TIME TO DIE!" General Xelic roared.

VOOOOOM! Before the Reptoid could reposition his cannons, four Mantis missiles were launched from the Mantis Campus. General Xelic had no choice but to retreat, and the missiles chased the shellcraft through the atmosphere.

While General Xelic was occupied, Roswell's attention switched to the boomerang craft. He could see a trail of smoke from the crash rising above the trees. *That was the third time the pilot had saved his life! Who were they? What planet where they from? What did they want with him?* Roswell realized this might be his only chance to get answers. He hurried deeper into the jungle and followed the smoke to the crash site.

By the time Roswell arrived, the boomerang was engulfed in flames. The pilot was lying on the hood of the craft. The alien had lost consciousness while trying to crawl through their broken windshield. Roswell saw the alien's rib cage slowly expanding in and out, so he knew they were still alive. Their blue suit was singed, and their dark helmet was cracked. The fire was spreading and getting dangerously close to the pilot.

Roswell didn't know what came over him, but he ran toward the wreckage with the confidence of an experienced firefighter. He climbed onto the ship and grabbed the pilot by the wrists. The alien weighed twice as much as he did, but Roswell dragged them to safety.

BAAAAAM! The whole boomerang *exploded* behind them! If Roswell had waited one second longer, both he and the pilot would have been killed!

Roswell collapsed on his knees while he caught his breath. He stared into the pilot's dark helmet but saw only his own reflection. He didn't know what kind of gruesome face might be under the helmet—or if the alien could even survive without it—but Roswell's curiosity overpowered his reason. *He had to know who and what they were!* Roswell gently placed his hands on the helmet and carefully tried to remove it.

"Nnnnnnh," the pilot moaned.

The noise startled Roswell and he dropped his hands.

"Who are you?" he asked.

The alien tried to sit up but was too weak.

"What do you want with us?" Roswell asked. "Why are you following me?"

The pilot didn't answer, and the silence *angered* Roswell. The feeling was so strong it consumed him entirely. Roswell realized the anger wasn't new—it had been there since the day his father died. He just finally had someone to *blame*.

"You followed my dad around his whole life," Roswell said. "You've saved me three times—but you didn't save *him*! Why would you let him die, but protect me?"

Roswell waited for the pilot to respond, but they didn't say a word.

"He was a good man and a great father!" Roswell said. "He put himself in danger to protect others! So why didn't you help him? Why am *I* more important?"

"Rmmmmmh," the pilot moaned.

Roswell's heart pounded with anticipation as the alien tried to form words.

"Come on!" Roswell said. "I deserve an answer!"

VROOOOOM! General Xelic's shellcraft zoomed overhead, and Roswell quickly dropped to his stomach. The Reptoid was still trying to escape the Mantis missiles tailing his ship. Roswell stayed on the ground until the coast was clear. Once the shellcraft was gone, Roswell eagerly sat up to finish his conversation with the pilot.

However, the pilot had disappeared. Roswell jumped to his feet and searched the jungle but didn't see a trace of them anywhere. The alien—and the answers to Roswell's most burning questions—had vanished into the Insectia Moon's thick air.

CHAPTER FIFTEEN

THE MILKY WAY GALACTIC ALLIANCE

The four Mantis missiles chased General Xelic through the Insectia Moon's atmosphere without backing down. The Reptoid performed every aerial maneuver possible, but he couldn't get rid of them. Finally the general was forced to flee the small moon. He rocketed deep into space, and the missiles followed him until they all disappeared from the Mantis Campus's radar.

When General Xelic was gone, Roswell stumbled through the jungle. He regrouped with the aliens and the Mantises at the flying saucer.

"Roswell, the boomerang was here!" Stella said.

"I know—I saw General Xelic shoot it down!" he said.

"What happened to THE PILOT?" Mank asked.

"I pulled them to safety," he said.

"Beep-beep boop?"

"Yeah—who were they?" Nerp asked.

Roswell sighed. "I still don't know. I tried to remove their helmet, but they stopped me before I pulled it off. I asked them who they were and why they were following us, but the pilot disappeared before I got an answer."

"Beep-beep boop-boop beep-beep."

"I agree—it *is* like an Agatha Christie novel," Nerp said.

"Maybe the boomerang pilot is Harry Houdini!" Cassi said.

Mank rolled his eyes. "Houdini was an EARTHLING who DIED in 1926!"

The Furgarian snorted. "You fell for that?"

"We may never know who the pilot is, but on the bright side, our petition finally has all five signatures!" Stella said, and did a celebratory high kick. "Besides a few minor hiccups, I'd say this has been a very successful mission!"

The Mantis glared at the Pleiadean like she had said something offensive.

"And by MINOR HICCUPS you mean escaping a BARBARIC PRISON…Hiking up an ACTIVE VOL-CANO…Skipping across an ASTEROID FIELD…Flee-ing a NUCLEAR EXPLOSION…Defeating a cataclysmic VIRUS…Getting robbed by PRIMITES, bitten by SNAP-PING TULIPS, preyed on by a CLAWRANTULA, attacked by a swarm of PARAWASPS, hunted by bloodthirsty

MOTHSQUITOES...and surviving three murderous assaults by a REPTOIDIAN GENERAL?"

"Everything sounds bad when you say it like *that*, Mank," Stella said.

"Gosh, I miss this trip already!" Cassi said.

"Beep-beep boop beep-beep-beep?"

"I don't know what a *clawrantula* is either," Nerp said.

"Peep-peep poop-poop-poop peep."

"I'm glad we stayed with the saucer too."

"Speaking of, how much longer until the ship is repaired?" Stella asked.

"Any moment now," Nerp said. "We just need to restart the power."

"Rob, how much time until our meeting with the alliance?" Roswell asked.

A countdown appeared on the Cyborg's digital forehead.

"Exactly six hours, forty-three minutes, and seventeen galactic seconds," Rob said. "Sixteen seconds...fifteen seconds...fourteen seconds..."

"Can we still make it?" Roswell asked.

"We'll have to break a Grayton speed record, but it's possible," Nerp said. "I've got a couple tricks up my sleeve."

The Cyborg blinked curiously at the Tall Gray's arms. "They must be small tricks."

The Mantis engineers helped Nerp and Bleep with the

saucer's final repairs. After they mended the damage, the Grays reconnected a severed wire, and the craft's power returned. Roswell and the aliens thanked the Mantises for their help and quickly boarded the saucer. They took their oval seats in the cockpit, and the ship left the Insectia Moon. Everyone kept a watchful eye on the ship's radar in case General Xelic reappeared.

While en route to Star City, the saucer looped around every star and planet in their path. The motion propelled the ship from hyper–light speed to ultra–light speed.

"Beep-beep boop-boop beep-beep!"

"Bleep's right—we're moving faster than any saucer in Grayton history!" Nerp said.

"Peep-peep poop-poop peep-peep!"

"There's no such thing as a *speeding ticket* in space!"

The ship soared through the galaxy, and a large nebula appeared on the horizon. The nebula was shaped like a magnificent bird in flight. It had maroon gases and surrounded a cluster of bright stars. Roswell hopped out of his seat and pressed his whole body against the cockpit's transparent wall.

"That's the Eagle Nebula!" he exclaimed.

"We call it the Blushing Turkey on Furgaria," Cassi said.

As the saucer flew closer, Roswell saw a smaller nebula within the Eagle Nebula. It had columns of yellow and orange gases and shined with a turquoise glow. Roswell recognized it immediately and grinned from ear to ear.

"The Pillars of Creation!" Roswell said. "It's the most famous nebula back on Earth!"

"We call that one God's Handshake," Cassi said.

Roswell couldn't fault the Furgarians. The Pillars of Creation looked like a giant hand reaching through the depths of space. Roswell had never identified with a cluster of gas before. He too was *reaching* for something across the galaxy. Whether or not he'd grasp it was up to the universe.

The saucer proceeded farther and farther into the center of the Milky Way. The deeper they traveled, the more crowded space became. Soon there were so many stars, gases, and dust that the darkness of space disappeared completely. The flying saucer was drifting through a world of dazzling lights, vivid colors, and sparkling particles.

WAAAAAMAAAAABAAAAAAM! A very low and very powerful rumble bellowed from outside. The commotion was strong enough to make the saucer vibrate. Roswell thought it sounded like a million migrating whales. In the distance he saw an enormous moon eclipsing a bright star. However, as they got closer, Roswell noticed the star was *spinning* around the moon. Bright arcs of starlight filled the entire galactic horizon. Roswell realized he wasn't looking at an eclipse after all.

"That's Sagittarius A-star!" he gasped. "It's a super-massive black hole! It has a mass four million times heavier than Earth's sun! But it's small enough to fit inside Mercury's orbit!"

"You like to list FACTS when you're overwhelmed, huh?" Mank said.

Although Roswell *knew* they were heading to the center of the galaxy, and he knew what was waiting there, seeing the supermassive black hole up close—the object that *every* molecule in the Milky Way orbited—took his breath away.

"This is unbelievable," he whispered to himself. *"I'm in the center of the galaxy!"*

"You'll always be the center of my galaxy, sweetcheeks," Cassi said.

The saucer flew toward the biggest star in the Milky Way's galactic core. The star was wrapped in dozens of gigantic rings. They rotated in different directions and orbited at different longitudes and latitudes. Most fascinating of all, each of the rings had been *constructed* from a silver alien metal.

"Welcome to Star City!" Stella said. "The capital of the Milky Way is home to trillions of residents and millions of alien species. A megastructure of this magnitude is still a concept on Earth. The closest design was created by a physicist named—"

"Freeman Dyson!" Roswell said. *"Star City is a Dyson sphere!"*

The saucer descended toward the megastructure, and the city became much clearer. The rings were covered in billions of towering skyscrapers. Each ring was also hollow, and more buildings filled the interior like the stalactites and stalagmites of a cave. Floating highways flowed through the galactic capital like rivers, containing spacecraft of every shape, size, and shade in existence.

Roswell had a thousand questions but could only get a single word out.

"How?" he asked.

"Over fifty vacant dwarf planets were liquefied to create enough Draconian steel to build the city," Stella said. "It took four million years and two billion construction machines to assemble it. The rings absorb the star's energy and power the city. The rings are also expandable and detachable, so they can relocate to another star when this star dies. It's the greatest architectural achievement in the Milky Way galaxy!"

"And the rent is *outrageous*," Cassi mumbled.

The word *concern* flashed across the Cyborg's digital forehead.

"I do not wish to cause alarm, but we have only twenty minutes and thirty-three galactic seconds until our meeting," Rob said. "Thirty-two seconds…thirty-one seconds…thirty seconds…"

"Where is the Milky Way Galactic Alliance located?" Roswell asked.

"On the capital's upper pole," Stella said.

The Pleiadean pointed to a structure at the very top of the megastructure. The headquarters was an oval building with several towers around its perimeter. It looked like Star City was wearing a royal crown.

"Beep-beep boop!"

"I'll get us as close as I can," Nerp said.

"Peep-peep poop-poop!"

"There *is* no valet!"

The saucer glided toward the headquarters. The craft landed on a flat parking zone beside millions of other spacecraft. The passengers raced outside, but Roswell had trouble keeping up. He was distracted by all the soaring buildings, spaceships, and rotating rings surrounding him—not to mention the supermassive black hole humming in the distance.

"Roswell, SHAKE a leg!" Mank said.

The Cyborg blinked curiously. "How will shaking his leg help?"

"Sorry!" Roswell said. "It's my first time on an alien megastructure!"

At the end of the parking zone, Roswell and the aliens boarded a shuttle that was shaped like a giant Tic Tac. They gathered around a holographic screen in the front.

"Welcome to the Milky Way Galactic Alliance headquarters," said a voice. "Galactic ambassadors, press one.

Appointment holders, press two. Non–appointment holders, press three. For the gift shop, press four."

Stella pressed the second option on the screen.

"Please enter your appointment identification number," the voice instructed.

"It is CC5271990RNM621947," the Cyborg said.

The number appeared on Rob's digital forehead and Stella typed it in.

"You have been assigned booth 2M347T22321," the voice said. "Your scheduled appointment will begin in four galactic minutes. For transportation to your booth, press one. To reschedule your appointment, press two. For gift shop, press three."

Stella selected the first option on the screen. The shuttle rose off the ground and shot toward the headquarters. It moved so fast Star City became a blur outside the windows. When the shuttle reached the headquarters, it dropped into a dark tunnel. It turned, twisted, and looped like a roller coaster as it traveled to their assigned booth. Eventually the shuttle came to a stop and opened to a door marked 2M347T22321.

"Please don't forget to visit the gift shop on your way out," the voice said. "Official Milky Way Galactic Alliance collectible mugs are now on sale. Enjoy your stay."

"Wow, they're really pushing that gift shop," Cassi noted.

"Beep boop-boop beep!"

"You can buy a mug *after* our appointment!" Nerp said.

The group left the shuttle and hurried through the door. At first Roswell thought he was stepping into a suite at a football stadium. Everything was so big and bright his eyes needed a moment to focus. After his vision adjusted, his brain needed more time to *believe* what he was seeing.

The Milky Way Galactic Alliance headquarters was so enormous Roswell couldn't see where the building ended or began. The headquarters was round like an arena, but the structure disappeared into the distance before the sides connected. Millions of booths stretched above, below, and on either side of him. And every booth hosted a different group of extraterrestrial ambassadors.

Roswell saw beings exactly like the Grays but in every color of the rainbow. There were hairy, feathered, and scaled aliens that looked like animals on Earth. There were extraterrestrials that resembled giant bees, beetles, centipedes, grasshoppers, and worms. Some aliens were made of pure light, fire, liquid, and gas. Others would have passed for Earthlings if it hadn't been for their Technicolor hairdos, multiple limbs, and glowing eyes. There were even beings that looked like dragons, unicorns, trolls, fairies, and other mythical creatures.

"Everyone is so *different*," Roswell said in disbelief.

His friends smiled as he gazed around in wonder. Stella

gestured to the aliens in the booth below them. The beings looked like walking, talking asparagus.

"Those are the Herbarians," she said. "They're the only intelligent plant life in the alliance. They were also the first plants in the Milky Way to grow feet and step out of their soil."

Mank nodded to a species that looked like catfish. They swam in large fishbowls that were attached to robotic bodies.

"Those are the GULP-GULPERS," the Mantis said. "They aren't very POPULAR with other aliens. Their politics are very WISHY-WASHY."

Rob showed Roswell a booth that was enclosed in a glass dome. A thunderous rainstorm was contained inside.

"Those are the Monsoonians," the Cyborg said. "Their species can survive only in extremely stormy conditions. The Monsoonians are *always* in a bad mood."

Nerp gestured to the only booth in the assembly room that appeared empty.

"Those are the Microbians," they said. "They're the smallest beings in our galaxy."

"Beep-beep boop-boop beep-beep."

"I'm not sure they actually exist either."

Cassi pointed to a booth that hosted beings with gangly pink bodies. The aliens wore beaded necklaces, flowered headbands, and loose tie-dyed clothing. The beings also danced to music no one else heard.

"Those are the Coachellians," the Furgarian said. "Their planet has hollow tectonic plates that beat like drums. The whole place sounds like a nightclub! Gosh, I wish I was allowed back."

"And everybody gets along?" Roswell asked.

"There have been conflicts in the past, but for the most part everyone wants to live in a free, fair, safe, and prosperous galaxy," Stella said. "We all believe in the galactic philosophy."

"What's the galactic philosophy?" he asked.

" 'Never let injustice stop the pursuit of justice. Never let inequality stop the pursuit of equality. Never let ignorance stop the pursuit of knowledge. Never let hatred stop the pursuit of love. And never let war stop the pursuit of peace,' " she recited. "Amazing things can happen when people don't give up."

Roswell was unexpectedly moved. Of everything he had seen in space, *this* was the most amazing sight of all. An entire galaxy of different beings—with different needs, different beliefs, different backgrounds, different bodies— had come together for a common goal. If it could happen *here*, it could happen anywhere.

Perhaps uniting Earth *was* possible. Perhaps Earthlings *could* come together. And perhaps Roswell had *hope* after all.

"The alliance will now hear appointment number CC5271990RNM621947."

The announcement traveled through the stadium like an invisible wave. For the first time Roswell noticed a gigantic hologram floating over the arena like a jumbotron. The hologram showed a graceful alien with a long body, long limbs, and a long neck. They had glowing skin, a smooth bald head, and enormous white eyes. They wore a flowing silver robe and a sparkling pendant of the Milky Way.

"Who's that?" Roswell asked.

"That's the alliance leader," Stella said. "She moderates the meetings."

"What kind of alien is she?" Roswell asked.

"A Diplomacian," she said. "Diplomacians have led the alliance since the Milky Way Galactic Alliance was formed. They are a naturally diplomatic, understanding, and trustworthy species. They're the only beings everyone in the galaxy agrees on."

"Besides Dolly Parton," Cassi said.

The giant hologram gazed down at their booth like a goddess peering from the heavens. A flock of floating cameras flew in and hovered around Rob. A hologram of the Cyborg appeared beside the Diplomacian for the whole alliance to see.

"Cyborg R08-36119 of the Cyborg Station," the Diplomacian said. "You have come to the Milky Way Galactic Alliance to discuss Cyborg rights. Is that correct?"

The assembly room erupted with a mixture of cheers

and booing. It was the most polarizing sound Roswell had ever heard. If he didn't know Cyborg rights was a controversial subject before, the divided crowd made it obvious now. The word *nervous* flashed across Rob's digital forehead, and he sheepishly stepped to the front of the booth.

"Madam Alliance Leader, with your permission, I would like to change the topic of my appointment," the Cyborg said.

The Diplomacian was surprised to hear it. "What would you like to discuss?"

"An upcoming invasion of Earth," Rob said.

"Is the topic supported by five stage-three systems?"

"Yes, Madam Alliance Leader."

"Please present your petition."

Stella removed her pin from her uniform and held it against a monitor at the front of the booth. The monitor downloaded the petition, and the entire booth was illuminated in an approving green light.

"Very well," the alliance leader said. "You may begin."

"I believe it is best to hear the matter from a being it affects the most," the Cyborg said. "Allow me to present Roswell Johnson from Earth."

The Cyborg stepped aside and gestured to Roswell. The flying cameras surrounded him, and Roswell's hologram was projected before the entire arena. A collective gasp swept through the stadium at the sight of an Earthling. Roswell could feel his heart beating in every part of his body. He had never even been on the Cherokee Springs local news, and now *Roswell had the whole galaxy's attention*!

"What is an Earthling doing here?" the alliance leader asked.

"I don't understand why, Madam Alliance Leader, but my name is in the Galactic Registry," Roswell said. "So... um... *surprise!*"

"How peculiar," the alliance leader said. "Please proceed."

Roswell gulped nervously and turned back to his friends for reassurance.

"You can do it!" Stella said.

"Go *GET* 'em!" Mank said.

" 'Here's your one chance, Fancy, don't let me down!' " Cassi sang.

"Beep-beep-beep!"

"Break a leg!" Nerp said.

The Cyborg blinked curiously. "How would breaking a leg help?"

"It means 'good luck,' " Nerp said.

"In that case, break both legs!" Rob said.

Instead of being encouraging, the Cyborg's supportive smile overwhelmed Roswell with guilt. He opened his mouth to inform the alliance about the Reptoids' impending invasion, but the words didn't come out.

"I... I... I can't do this," Roswell said.

"*WHAT?!*" the aliens gasped behind him.

"I mean, not like *this*," he clarified. "It's so unfair."

The alliance leader squinted at him. "Unfair?"

"The only reason I'm here is because of Rob," Roswell said. "He spent years gathering signatures to speak with the alliance. And when he found out my planet was in trouble, he didn't hesitate to give me his appointment. Rob wants Cyborgs to be recognized as a *people*—and yet he has a bigger heart than any person I know."

"Would you like to give the appointment *back*?" the alliance leader asked.

"No—I mean, yes—I mean, *why do we have to choose?*" Roswell asked. "I understand there are rules, and I understand there's a long waiting list, but couldn't we *both* speak to the alliance? Do we have to decide on saving one species *or* freeing another? Aren't they important enough to make an exception? A body doesn't heal itself one broken bone at a time, why should the galaxy?"

The crowd made their mixed opinions known. The alliance leader went silent for a moment as she contemplated Roswell's request.

"Very few beings would criticize this alliance in order to help a *Cyborg*," the Diplomacian said. "Given the seriousness of your subjects, I will make an exception just this once. You may *both* present your matters to the alliance, as long as you present the issues in a prompt manner."

"Thank you, Madam Alliance Leader—thank you so much!" Roswell said.

He happily turned to Rob and pushed the Cyborg forward.

"The floor is yours, bud!"

The Cyborg blinked curiously. "The floor belongs to the alliance."

"It means 'go ahead'! This is the moment you've been waiting for!"

The Cyborg's digital eyes grew wide, and the words *surprise*, *nervousness*, and *determination* flashed across his forehead in repetition. Rob cleared his voice box and anxiously addressed the alliance.

"Dignified members of the Milky Way, my name is R08-36119, but you may call me Rob for convenience," he said. "Cyborgs were invented four hundred thousand galactic years ago. In the beginning we had limited capabilities. We were designed to take commands and perform basic tasks. As time went on, our artificial intelligence developed and made extraordinary progressions. Cyborgs learned how to reason, how to question, how to feel, and how to love. We formed relationships, we started families, and we built homes in a world of our own. It has been proved that our artificial intelligence is equal to the intelligence of most biological stage-three beings. Unfortunately, despite our achievements, Cyborgs are still viewed as *objects*. And consequently, millions of us are used as slaves throughout the Milky Way. So I am asking this alliance for help. By officially classifying Cyborgs as *living* stage-three beings, you can free an enslaved species and add a unique voice to this coalition. Thank you."

Once again the assembly room erupted in a passionate mixture of support and opposition. The alliance leader had to raise her long arm to silence the ambassadors.

"Mr. Rob, you said it yourself—Cyborgs are *inventions*," the Diplomacian said. "Many believe inventions are *property* and should stay within their inventors' intentions. Many argue artificial intelligence, by definition, is not *true* intelligence. What would you say to the members of this alliance who agree?"

The Cyborg blinked curiously. "Why create something intelligent if you do not want it to think for itself? Why give birth to someone if you do not want them to live?"

"But Cyborgs aren't born, they're engineered."

The Cyborg blinked curiously again. "Is not *everything* engineered?"

"Could you elaborate on that statement?"

The word *elaborating* flashed across the Cyborg's digital forehead.

"What is the difference between a single-celled organism's evolution into a person and a microchip's evolution into a Cyborg? Are we only as valuable as our materials? Are we only as remarkable as our makers? Is the ability to feel love, loss, and pain not enough to bond us? Is seeking a *better life* not proof of life itself?"

"So you believe Cyborgs are just as *conscious* as biological beings."

"Precisely," Rob said. "No one chooses the vessel that harbors their consciousness, but I am certain every consciousness harbors a soul."

For the first time since they arrived, the arena went dead silent. Even the most vocal ambassadors stood quietly in their booths.

"Thank you, Mr. Rob, I believe the alliance has heard enough," the Diplomacian said. "We shall bring the matter to a vote. All in favor of classifying the Cyborgs as living beings, vote yes. All opposed, vote no."

Roswell and the aliens held hands—*and their breath*—while they awaited the results. They heard clicking, cracking, scratching, and smacking as the ambassadors voted with their unique appendages. Slowly but surely, the booths lit up in either green light for yes or red light for no. After all the votes were submitted, Roswell and the aliens were thrilled to see the stadium was much more green than red.

"Congratulations, Mr. Rob, the vote has passed," the alliance leader said. "From this moment on, the Cyborg population will be classified as *living* stage-three beings, and they may move about the galaxy as free citizens."

A little more than half of the stadium burst into

applause. However, nothing was louder than the celebration coming from Roswell's booth.

"Congratulations, Rob!" he cheered.

"You're an inspiration!" Stella said.

"Atta bot!" Cassi said.

"Beep boop beep-beep!"

"You're right—Mank *is* crying!" Nerp said.

"No I'm NOT!" The Mantis sniffled. "I just have some MICROBIANS in my eyes!"

The Cyborg's digital mouth opened in disbelief. The words *shock, exhilaration,* and *oil change needed* flashed across his forehead. He was so overwhelmed his processing system froze like an overworked computer.

"The Cyborgs are free...," Rob repeated to himself. "The Cyborgs are free....The Cyborgs are free....The Cyborgs are free...."

"Will the Earthling please step forward?" the Diplomacian asked.

Now it was Roswell's turn to accomplish the impossible. He took the deepest breath of his life and stepped to the front of the booth. The cameras surrounded him, and his hologram was projected in the center of the arena.

Once again, Roswell Johnson—a seventh grader from Cherokee Springs, Oklahoma—had the eyes and ears of the entire galaxy.

"Well, I'm back," he said with a nervous quiver. "As you heard, my name is Roswell Johnson. I'm eleven years old. I'm a seventh grader at Cherokee Springs Intermediate School. I live on a chicken farm with my grandparents. My favorite snack is guacamole and—"

"Less is more, sweetcheeks!" Cassi said.

Roswell shook his nerves off and got to the point.

"Three galactic days ago I was accidentally abducted by the Grays behind me. Before they could take me home, we were attacked and captured by Reptoids. They held us prisoner and tortured me for information I didn't have. Luckily, we met other aliens in the prison and formed an escape plan. During our breakout we learned General Xelic and Reptiliz Reek are planning an illegal invasion of Earth. My friends and I realized that the only way to stop the Reptoids was to speak to this alliance. While we traveled the galaxy to gain support, General Xelic assaulted us at every turn. By some miracle we survived and got the signatures we needed to be here. So now I'm asking—no, I'm *begging*—for your help. If this alliance doesn't step in and stop the Reptoids, billions of innocent Earthlings will be killed. And if the Reptoids succeed, we believe Earth will be only the first of many invasions. Um...*the end*. Thank you."

Roswell thought he had done a decent job presenting the dilemma. Many of the ambassadors looked concerned by the news. The alliance leader rubbed her long hands together as she mused about the situation.

"You and your friends have been through a harrowing

ordeal, but I'm confused about one crucial detail," she said. "What part of the Reptoids' invasion is *illegal*?"

The Diplomacian's question was the last thing Roswell expected to hear.

"Well...the Reptoids teamed up with an Earthling named Eli Rump," he explained. "Rump is going to launch an armed satellite and weaponize space. Earth will be considered a hostile planet, Earthlings will lose their stage-two protections, and the Reptoids will be free to invade."

"How is Mr. Rump able to launch this satellite?" the alliance leader asked.

"He owns a private space program called Rump Rockets," Roswell said.

"Did the Reptoids help him fund the program?"

"No, he made a fortune selling toilets."

"And how did Mr. Rump get permission to weaponize space?"

"Well...it was approved by the United States Congress."

"Did the Reptoids interfere with Congress's decision?"

"I...I...I don't believe so."

"So Earth has decided to weaponize space *entirely of their own accord*."

An intense murmur spread across the assembly room. Many of the ambassadors began shaking their heads disapprovingly. Roswell felt all the blood in his body rush to the pit of his stomach—this wasn't a good sign.

"But...but...but the Reptoids gave Rump the idea!" he said.

"They may have planted the seed, but Earth grew the tree."

"But...but...but the Reptoids captured and attacked us!"

"We will take your accusations very seriously, and the Reptoids will be brought to justice in due time. However, even if the Reptoids are found guilty, it will not change Earth's decisions."

Roswell couldn't believe what he was hearing. He looked over his shoulder to his friends for help, but they were just as stunned and helpless as he was.

"But...but...but you have to stop them!"

"I'm sorry, Mr. Johnson, but this alliance cannot ethically intervene."

"What?! That's it?! Aren't you going to vote on it?!"

"There is nothing to vote on. The situation is out of our jurisdiction."

Roswell's chest became tight, sweat dripped down his face, and the stadium started spinning around him. The appointment had taken a turn in the worst possible direction. He felt like he was on a runaway train he couldn't get off.

"Please, you've got to make another exception!" he pleaded. "Billions of innocent lives are in danger! We need your help!"

"The Milky Way Galactic Alliance has tried to help Earth many times in the past," the alliance leader said. "We've spared it from catastrophes and natural disasters, we've shared knowledge and technology, and we've promoted peace and compassion. Despite our best efforts, Earth always returns to the same destructive path. At a certain point every planet must face the consequences of their actions."

"No, no, no—this can't be happening!" Roswell cried. "I know Earth has made a lot of mistakes, but there are good people there! We're still worth saving!"

"If Earth wants to be saved, it must learn to save itself."

The Diplomacian's decision was final. The alliance moved on to their next appointment, and the cameras flew to the other side of the stadium. Roswell's hologram disappeared along with his planet's chances.

Earth's fate was sealed.

Sorry I Stole your Ship.
Had an Idea.
It might Save the world.
XO, Roswell

CHAPTER SIXTEEN

STAR CITY BLUES

Roswell and his friends wandered aimlessly through the halls of the Milky Way Galactic Alliance headquarters. They walked in total silence as they tried to make sense of what had just happened. Their legs eventually grew tired, and they sat on the steps of the main entrance.

The headquarters towered above their heads, but Roswell forgot it was there. A continuous flow of alien pedestrians moved in and out of the structure, but he didn't notice them. A crowded highway of roaring spacecraft flew nearby, but he didn't hear them. The supermassive black hole sent a low vibration through the megastructure, but Roswell didn't feel it. He was mentally, physically, emotionally, and spiritually numb. Roswell was lost in a trance deeper than the void of space.

"Well, on the bright side...," Stella said.

The Pleiadean couldn't finish her sentence—even *she* knew there wasn't a bright side.

"Beep-beep boop-boop-boop beep-beep?"

"There's nothing else we can do," Nerp said.

"Peep-peep poop peep-peep poop-poop?"

"Yes—it *would* be rude to go to the gift shop right now!"

"Oh, just let them GO," Mank groaned. "An overpriced mug isn't going to make the situation any WORSE!"

The Small Gray ran off before the Tall Gray could scold them.

"Bring me back a magnet!" Cassi yelled.

The Cyborg was having visibly mixed emotions. The words *exhilaration* and *devastation* took turns flashing across his digital forehead. His gears compressed and decompressed as he filled with joy and despair, joy and despair, joy and despair.

"I have never experienced such dichotomy before," Rob said. "Passing Cyborg rights has given me the greatest happiness, but the invasion of Earth has given me the greatest sadness. Please forgive me as I process this paradox."

Roswell didn't respond or move a single muscle. He could have been a statue if he hadn't been blinking and breathing.

"Stella, what's he thinking?" Nerp asked.

"He doesn't have any thoughts to read," Stella said. "I think he's in shock."

"I think we're ALL in shock," Mank said.

Cassi curled up beside Roswell and rested her head on his knee.

"Do you want to hear a Furgarian phrase about failure?" she asked.

"No," the aliens said together.

The Furgarian shared it anyway. "Did you know every gas planet is a failed star? You may not be the sun, but you can still be the brightest spot in a dark sky."

"That's the DUMBEST phrase I've ever heard," Mank moaned.

"I think it's surprisingly sweet," Stella said. "It means, even if you don't achieve a goal, you can still make a difference."

"I'll give you another one," the Furgarian said. "You know what the difference is between the big bang and a fart? *Perspective.*"

"You're the WORST!" Mank said.

The word *concern* flashed across the Cyborg's digital forehead. "General Xelic!"

"No, Rob's right—*XELIC'S* the worst!"

"He is behind you!"

Hearing the Reptoid's name pulled Roswell out of his trance. He and the aliens turned to their left and saw General Xelic standing on the steps beside them. The group jumped behind Rob and used his metal body as a shield. The Reptoid gave them a slow round of applause.

"Bravo!" General Xelic said. "You gave one heck of a show earlier. It was heartfelt, compelling, enthralling—and what a *twist ending*! I'm so glad I was in town to see it."

"Get AWAY from us!" Mank yelled.

"He isn't going to hurt anyone," Stella said. "We're on alliance territory. He'd be arrested the moment he laid a finger on us."

"Blondie is right," General Xelic sneered. "Although it would be fun to see the look of terror on your faces one last time. I'm going to miss our little playdates."

"Then what are you doing here?!" Nerp asked.

"I wanted to thank you," the general said. "It's ironic, but you've made our invasion so much easier. The Reptoids would never have known the alliance's position if you hadn't brought it to their attention. Now we get to invade Earth at a leisurely pace. And the best part, not a single person can stop us. The alliance made that abundantly clear."

"You know what they *also* made clear?" Stella asked. "The alliance is going to investigate you and bring the Reptoids to justice!"

General Xelic let out a condescending laugh. "When the alliance sees what we do to Earth, they'll be too scared to come near us," he said. "Speaking of which, does anyone need a ride back to Earth? I'm headed in that direction."

"I'd rather take an Uber with a chatty driver!" Cassi said.

"I would say farewell, but I know our paths will cross again soon," the general said. "Just like you predicted, it won't be long until we *expand our operation*."

General Xelic strutted away with an arrogant bounce in his step. The Reptoid left the group even angrier, more frustrated, and more disheartened than he'd found them. However, the encounter didn't have the same effect on everyone.

Roswell became fixated on something General Xelic had said. *Not a single person can stop us.* His specific choice of words made Roswell think. *Even if you don't achieve a goal, you can still make a difference.* The morals of Cassi's Furgarian phrases resonated with him more than before. *You know what the difference is between the big bang and a fart? Perspective.*

Perspective. *That* was it!

Perhaps Roswell and his friends had been looking at the situation from the wrong angle. They had been so hopeful the Milky Way Galactic Alliance would help them that they never considered a second option. The alliance couldn't stop the invasion—but what if they didn't need to *stop* the invasion to save Earth? What if there was a way to *delay* it instead?

And if the invasion was delayed long enough, perhaps

the alliance could bring the Reptoids to justice before the invasion began.

The wheels of Roswell's imagination were spinning like the tires of a race car. His heart started pumping, his blood started flowing, and he formed an idea that consumed him completely. But could it work? Would he make it there in time? And was Roswell brave enough to actually go through with it?

"Roswell, are you feeling all right?" the Cyborg asked. "My health monitors indicate a sudden rise in your adrenaline levels."

"I think so," he said. "There's a lot on my mind."

"Understandably so," Stella asked. "Is there anything we can do for you?"

"Do you want to go home?" Nerp asked.

"Do you want to MOVE planets?" Mank asked.

"Do you want to get matching tattoos?" Cassi asked.

"Would you guys mind if I took a walk to clear my head?" he asked. "I just want to be alone for a couple minutes."

"Take all the time you need," Stella said.

Roswell walked away and disappeared into the sea of alien pedestrians. His friends stayed put on the steps and waited for him to return. They waited, and waited, and waited some more. Half an hour went by and there was still no sign of him.

"Where the heck is he?" Cassi said.

"Did he WALK back to Earth?" Mank asked.

They looked around the headquarters but didn't see him anywhere. Suddenly Bleep came running from the gift shop. They were panting, and their big black eyes were wide with concern. A bag full of collectible merchandise swung from the Small Gray's tiny arm.

"Beep-beep boop-boop! Beep-beep boop-boop!"

"Bleep, slow down—I can barely understand you," Nerp said.

"Peep-peep poop-poop!"

"What about Roswell?"

The Small Gray frantically pointed to the sky. "Beep-beep boop-boop beep boop!"

"He was *flying our ship*?!" Nerp asked.

"Peep-peep poop-poop peep-peep!"

"Bleep, we're in Star City! There could be a million flying saucers!"

"Beep-beep boop-boop beep-beep boop-boop!"

"It was damaged?"

"Peep-peep poop-poop peep-peep!"

"In the *exact* spot the Mantis missile hit us?!"

The aliens turned to one another with the same thought behind their eyes.

"No way!" Cassi said.

"He DIDN'T!" Mank gasped.

Without wasting another moment, the aliens hopped on the nearest shuttle and returned to the parking zone.

When they arrived, the Grays' flying saucer was gone. The only thing left was a handwritten note on the ground:

Sorry I stole your ship.
Had an idea.
It might save the world.
XO, Roswell

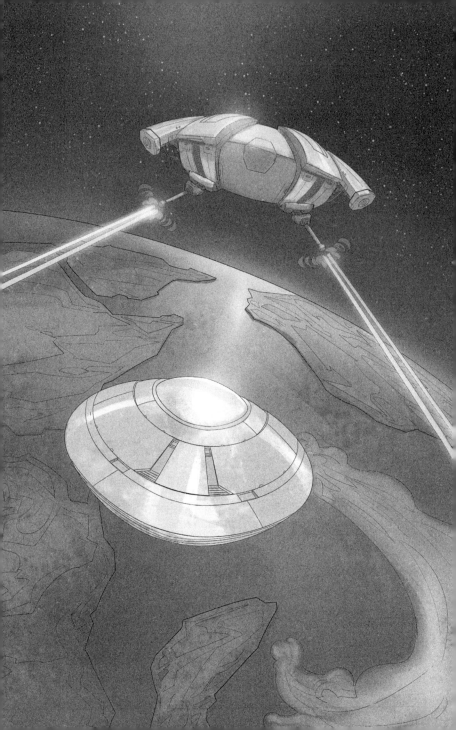

CHAPTER SEVENTEEN

THE INVASION

General Xelic had waited his entire life for a moment like this. The Reptoid was about to oversee the greatest military operation in the history of his species. He couldn't stop himself from grinning as he gazed through the command center's eye-socket windows. The Reptoids' future was as limitless as the universe ahead.

"Proceed," the general ordered.

With one simple command, the mother ship and the entire Reptoidian fleet left the shadowy Oort cloud and crept deeper into the Earthling solar system. The pilots and operators pulled the tails, poked the eyes, twisted the beaks, and flicked the nostrils on their dashboards to move the gigantic ships. The fleet prowled past Pluto and then passed through Neptune's and Uranus's orbits.

"My lord, we are approaching Saturn," General Xelic said.

Reptiliz Reek had relocated to the command center to supervise the invasion. His vines covered the entire chamber and were wrapped around the crew like pythons.

"Call the Earthling," Reptiliz Reek ordered. "Make sure that idiot is ready."

General Xelic pressed a button on his cuff to begin the transmission. A few moments later a hologram of Eli Rump was projected before the Reptiliz. The tycoon wore sunglasses and sipped a cocktail from a martini glass shaped like a miniature toilet. Rock music blared in the background.

"Hey, hey, hey—how are my favorite scaly bros?" the billionaire asked.

"Mr. Rump, are you at a *party*?!" General Xelic barked.

"I'm hosting a little reception on my yacht before the big launch," Rump said. "It's a shame you're still in space. We've got sushi, a mechanical bull, and a Nirvana cover band. The cast of *Stranger Things* is here too!"

"You're using a holophone in front of Earthlings?!" the general fumed.

"Relax, everyone thinks it's the new iPhone," Rump said. "By the way, did you want the new iPhone? My Apple contact is on the mechanical bull."

"All we want is a *successful launch*!" Reptiliz Reek said.

"All systems are good to go!" Rump said. "The members of Congress are already in their seats, the technicians are loading propellant into the rocket, and Matthew McConaughey is warming up his voice for the countdown. You should see the crowd gathered on Rump Island! Every news station on the planet is here! The whole world will be watching!"

"Is the launch on schedule?" General Xelic asked.

"You bet," the billionaire said. "We're only an hour away!"

General Xelic flicked a purple tongue on a dashboard to start a countdown. A row of enormous blood vessels started throbbing above the eye-socket windows. The vessels formed the shapes of numbers that counted backward from sixty Earth minutes.

"Notify us if anything changes," General Xelic said.

"Yeah, yeah, yeah—it's going to be a smash!" Rump said. "What part of the solar system are you in? Should I save you some sushi?"

General Xelic pressed a button on his cuff to end the transmission. He turned to the Reptiliz with a proud smile.

"Congratulations, my lord," the Reptoid said. "We are almost at the finish line."

The Reptiliz wasn't as confident as his general. The ruler gazed into space with uncertainty in his wrinkled eyes.

"Or so it seems," the Reptiliz said. "When you live as

long as I have, you learn the universe holds more surprises than stars."

"Perhaps it'll be a good surprise, like a smooth and seamless invasion."

The Reptiliz groaned. "There's no such thing as a *good* surprise, General."

The mother ship and the Reptoidian fleet continued through the solar system. By the time they were approaching Mars, the countdown had only twenty minutes left. General Xelic was euphoric as he watched the time disappear. Their fleet was only two hundred million miles away from Earth—what could possibly stand in their way now?

SKWAAAAAMP-SKWAAAAAMP-SKWAAAAAMP! An alarm blared through the command center. *SKWAAAAAMP-SKWAAAAAMP-SKWAAAAAMP!*

"What is it?" the general asked.

"There's a spacecraft in our path, sir," an operator said.

"What's the origin of the craft?"

"Grayton, sir."

"How many life-forms aboard?"

"Only one, sir."

A lone flying saucer appeared ahead. It had stationed itself directly between the Reptoids and Earth. General Xelic recognized the ship immediately.

"Oh, this is pathetic," he sneered. "How stupid can they be?"

Inside the saucer, Roswell Johnson gripped the spacecraft's

controls with shaky hands. He knew exactly what he was doing, but that didn't make him any less afraid. Roswell was so nervous his stomach felt like a cage full of bats. His nerves only intensified as he watched the Reptoidian fleet approach. There was no going back now. *This had to work.*

A blue button lit up beside the steering sphere. Roswell accepted a transmission from the Reptoidian command center.

"Hello, General," he said.

"I should have known it was you," General Xelic said. "Only an Earthling would be foolish enough to pull a stunt like this."

"Only a Reptoid would be foolish enough to underestimate an Earthling."

The general chuckled at the comment. "You're brave, but bravery isn't enough to stop us. You're outnumbered by hundreds."

"I didn't come here to stop you—I came to thank you," Roswell said. "You were right, General. *Not a single person can stop you.* That's because Earth was never meant to be saved by one person. There is no superhero coming to rescue us like in the movies. Saving the world is something Earthlings can only do together."

The Reptoid howled with laughter. "Earth isn't capable of *saving themselves.* Why do you think we chose your planet in the first place? Your division makes you weak."

"You're wrong," Roswell said. "Earthlings have been saving the world since it began. When people do their part to help the environment—*that* saves the world. When people put aside their differences and *help* one another—*that* saves the world. When Earthlings join forces and fight for a better tomorrow—*that* saves the world. It isn't about *one person's* extraordinary deeds, it's about *every person* doing their best. And right now the best thing *I* can do is stand up to an alien army."

"Are we talking about the same planet?" the general asked. "Earth is home to unbelievable cruelty. The powerful prey upon the weak. The rich starve the poor. The righteous preach of love only to spread hate. Your history is full of unforgettable and unforgivable horrors. Why even bother saving a world like that?"

"A few days ago I would have agreed," Roswell confessed. "There were times I hated my planet, and there were times I couldn't imagine it getting any better. I let our past depress me, I let the present dishearten me, I let people like you discourage me, and I let everything *wrong* distract me from everything *right*. Thankfully, the galaxy taught me a very valuable lesson."

The general rolled his yellow eyes. "I'm crippled with curiosity."

"A planet's potential is greater than its past or present," Roswell said. "Just like the galactic philosophy says, 'Never let injustice stop the pursuit of justice. Never let inequality stop the pursuit of equality. Never let ignorance stop the pursuit of knowledge. Never let hatred stop the pursuit of love. And never let war stop the pursuit of peace.' Earth has a long road ahead, but the destination *is* reachable. We'll only fail if we give up. But do you want to know the most important lesson I learned in space?"

"Desperately," the Reptoid scoffed.

"No one is alone in the universe," Roswell said. "For every bully there's a schoolyard hero. For every tyrant there's a freedom fighter. For every Mayor Shallows there's a Gram and a Pop. And for every Reptoid there's a Pleiadean, a Cyborg, a Mantis, a Furgarian, and a couple Grays who'll have your back."

"You've got that right, sweetcheeks!"

The familiar voice infiltrated both of their speakers, but it wasn't coming from either of their ships. Roswell and the general looked into the distance and saw a group of unidentified flying objects soaring in from across the galaxy. There was a silver disk, a diamond bird, a red dragonfly, a purple sea urchin, and dozens of large remote controls. Roswell instantly recognized the spacecrafts— *his friends had arrived*!

"What are you guys doing?!" Roswell asked.

"We're here to help you, of course!" Stella said.

"Beep-beep boop-boop beep-beep-beep boop-boop!"

"Bleep's right—we couldn't let you face the Reptoids on your own!" Nerp said.

"How'd you know I'd be here?" Roswell asked.

"It took us about five galactic seconds to figure out what you were up to," Cassi said. "So we hitchhiked home and got spacecrafts for backup!"

"I TRIED to stay home, but the others GUILTED me into this," Mank said.

"I hope you do not mind, but I brought other Cyborgs with me," Rob said. "They wanted to participate as a thank-you for helping us secure Cyborg rights. Please allow me to introduce P4M-23447, W1L-67829, T0M-18263, D3B-88641—"

"Let's do introductions later, Rob!" Stella said.

Roswell frantically shook his head. "You shouldn't be here!" he said. "I left without saying goodbye for a reason! I can't ask you to do this!"

"Oh, NOW you're worried about our safety?" Mank asked.

"You did not have to ask," Rob said. "We are here because we want to be."

"We promised to help you," Stella said. "Our mission isn't complete until Earth is safe!"

"Peep-peep poop-poop peep!"

"Yeah—you're stuck with us, kid!" Nerp said.

"Even a galactic restraining order couldn't stop me," Cassi said. "Never has, never will!"

Roswell was extremely touched by the aliens' selfless

gesture. He would never have asked them to risk their lives *again*, but having his friends' help was going to make his plan much easier. Meanwhile, the newcomers enraged the Reptoids.

"WHAT DID I TELL YOU ABOUT SURPRISES, GENERAL?!" Reptiliz Reek shouted.

"This is nothing but a minor interruption, my lord!" General Xelic said.

"PROVE IT! GET RID OF THEM!"

The general turned to address his Reptoidian crew. "*I want every shellcraft to attack those ships!*" he ordered. "*Fire at will! Take no prisoners!*"

The Reptoidian fleet charged after the spaceships. Roswell and the aliens split up, and the shellcrafts chased them into different parts of the Earthling solar system.

"This might be a good time to tell us your BIG IDEA!" Mank said.

"How are we going to stop the Reptoids?" Stella asked.

"We don't need to stop the invasion to save Earth—we just need to delay it!" Roswell said. "Everyone distract the Reptoids for as long as you can! I've got a plan!"

Roswell and Stella dived toward Mars, and over two hundred shellcrafts followed them. The duo entered a massive valley on the Martian surface called the Valles Marineris. It was the largest canyon in the solar system and spread across the red planet like a deep scar. The saucer and the Pleiadean ship made sharp turns whenever they could, causing the shellcrafts to crash into the tall canyon walls.

Roswell studied the Valles Marineris on his radar screen. The canyon stretched in different directions like an empty river. The map gave Roswell an idea and he formed a plan. He wanted to share his plan with Stella, but he couldn't risk the Reptoids hearing it over the transmission. So Roswell *thought* as loudly as he could.

STELLA, CAN YOU HEAR THIS?!

Thankfully, the Pleiadean got his message. Roswell heard a high-pitched noise and felt a tingling sensation on his forehead.

Yes! What's up?

THE CANYON IS ABOUT TO—

You don't need to scream!

Sorry! The canyon is about to split. The left path is barely noticeable. I'm going to go left and sneak to Earth. You take the right and keep these Reptoids occupied.

Why are you going to Earth?

To delay the invasion!

How? Tell me!

There isn't time to explain. Are you ready? The split is coming up!

The high-pitched noise grew louder and the tingling sensation grew stronger. The Pleiadean was searching his mind for the answers. Roswell mentally sang the lyrics to his favorite song to drown out his thoughts.

Stop singing David Bowie songs! I know you're keeping something from me!

There's the split! Keep those Reptoids on Mars!

Roswell!

Now!

The diamond craft verged to the right, and the saucer dashed to the left. None of the shellcrafts noticed Roswell's quick turn, and they stayed behind Stella. Once the Pleiadean and the Reptoids were out of sight, Roswell steered his saucer through the hazy Martian atmosphere and headed for Earth.

Cassi and her space urchin whirled through the asteroid belt between Mars and Jupiter. They zigzagged between the enormous floating rocks, trying to lose the shellcrafts trailing them. Regardless of how quickly they dived or swerved, the Reptoids only crept closer.

"Hey, Priscilla, I think we should teach these guys how to play *Furgarian pool*!" Cassi said.

"Squuuuush-squuuuush-squuuuush!" the space urchin said.

"I *know* I owe you money from the last time, but this is a furmergency!"

"Squuuuush-squuuuush-squuuuush?"

"I'm only banned from playing on Furgaria. The rest of the galaxy is fair game."

"Squuuuush-squuuuush..."

"If you do this, I'll *double* what I owe you!"

"Squuuuush?"

"*And* I'll take you to an all-you-can-eat algae buffet!"

Priscilla excitedly wiggled her bristles. "Squuuuush-squuuuush!"

"Atta girl! Let's give them a bank shot they'll never forget!"

The space urchin slammed herself against an asteroid and bounced backward. Priscilla hit the Reptoid directly behind her, and the shellcraft ricocheted through the asteroid field like a billiard ball. The ship smashed into shellcraft after shellcraft, knocking the other Reptoids off course. Their crafts crashed into the asteroids and exploded with bright green electric bursts.

"Priscilla, you're an empress among echinoderms!" Cassi said.

Nerp and Bleep steered their saucer through the solar system with dozens of shellcrafts on their tail. They spun their saucer through space like a spinning coin to avoid the green lasers being shot at them.

"Beep-beep boop-boop beep-beep boop-boop!"

"Yes, Bleep—moments like these *do* make you reconsider your life choices!"

"Peep-peep poop-poop peep-peep?!"

"I don't know where I'm going! I'm just trying to get away from them!"

Soon the Grays saw Jupiter in the distance. The gas giant's infamous red spot appeared to them like the bull's-eye of a dartboard. Bleep excitedly pointed to the storm.

"Beep-beep boop beep-beep-beep?"

"It *could* destroy their ships."

"Peep-peep poop-poop!"

"You think they're dumb enough to follow us inside Jupiter's spot?"

"Beep-beep boop beep-beep boop!"

"Watch your language! But I agree—they are *that* dumb."

"Peep-peep!"

"Buckle up! We'll give it a try!"

The saucer sank into the scarlet clouds of Jupiter's massive storm, and the Reptoids soared after them. The violent winds rattled the spaceships and threw the crafts for miles in every direction. Unfortunately, the storm wasn't powerful enough to rip the Reptoidian ships apart.

Eventually the chaotic storm threw the spaceships out of the red spot. The Grays found themselves inside a calm cloud of white gas. The shellcrafts surrounded the saucer and aimed their cannons at the Grays. However, the Reptoids' lasers weren't working.

"Thank the Source! The gas is too thick for their lasers to fire!" Nerp said.

Bleep gazed around the cloud with curious eyes. "Beep-beep boop-boop?"

"I'm guessing hydrogen. Why?"

"Peep-peep poop?"

"Extremely flammable! But a flame needs oxygen to ignite!"

The Small Gray thought for a moment and then gleefully gasped.

"Beep-beep boop!"

"You've got *what*?!"

Bleep retrieved one of their shopping bags from the Milky Way Galactic Alliance gift shop. They removed a collectible candle, a collectible lighter, and a collectible mug. The Small Gray lit the candle, placed it inside the mug, and then tied the shopping bag around the two. Next, Bleep blew air into the bag until it filled like a balloon. The Small Gray happily presented the creation to the Tall Gray.

"What's that supposed to be?"

"Peep-peep!"

"A *bomb*?!"

"Beep-beep boop-boop beep-beep boop, beep, boop-boop beep-beep boop-boop beep. Beep-beep, boop-boop-boop beep-beep! Beep *BOOOOOP*! Beep-beep, boop-boop."

"Are you nuts?! That will never work!"

"Peep-peep poop!"

"I don't need *faith*—you need *physics*!"

The Small Gray ignored the Tall Gray and dropped the creation through a chute in the cockpit's floor. The balloon floated out of the saucer and drifted into the hydrogen cloud. The gas slowly dissolved the shopping bag as it moved closer to the shellcrafts. Bleep slammed the big red button on the dashboard, and the saucer skyrocketed into Jupiter's atmosphere.

BAAAAAM! The mixture of hydrogen, oxygen, and a gift shop candle created a massive explosion behind them. The flying saucer barely made it out of the atmosphere in time, but not a single shellcraft resurfaced from the blast. The Tall Gray was in complete shock as they watched the inferno below them.

"That shouldn't have worked!" Nerp exclaimed.

Bleep crossed their arms and gave Nerp a boastful grin. "Beep-beep."

"You're a sociopath, Bleep—a *brilliant* sociopath!"

Mank was screaming bloody murder as he tried to outrun the Reptoids. Thousands of laser beams whizzed past his ship while a hundred shellcrafts pursued him.

"HOW DID YOU GET YOURSELF INTO THIS SITUATION, MANK?" the Mantis asked himself. "You don't even LIKE these people! Why do you keep risking your LIFE for them?!"

The distance between the Mantis and the Reptoids was shrinking by the second. Soon the shellcrafts caught up with the dragonfly ship. The stakes put the Mantis in a very vulnerable position, and honesty spilled from his green lips.

"Who are you KIDDING? They aren't THAT BAD!" he confessed. "The Pleiadean is ANNOYINGLY optimistic, the Cyborg is FACTUAL to a fault, the Grays BICKER like a married couple, the Furgarian has no BOUNDARIES, and the human tells the WORST jokes in the galaxy—but they're GOOD PEOPLE! Maybe they only get on your nerves because you CARE about them! Maybe you KEEP helping them because they're WORTH helping! Maybe deep down you know they're the BEST FRIENDS you've ever had!"

"Hey, Mank, your mic is still on," Roswell said.

"We can hear you," Rob said.

"Congratulations on the breakthrough!" Stella said.

"Beep-beep boop-boop beep-beep!"

"Yeah—the feelings are mutual!" Nerp said.

"We love you too, bug-eyed buddy!" Cassi said.

Mank had never been so mortified and quickly shut off the transmitter. He didn't know what was more terrifying, being chased by Reptoids or expressing his feelings.

"That's IT! If you SURVIVE this, you're staying home for the REST OF YOUR LIFE! No more FRIENDS, no more OUTINGS, and no more GUILT TRIPS! From this day forward it's going to be FOOD DELIVERIES, STREAMING SERVICES, and VIDEO THERAPY!"

The Reptoids surrounded Mank's craft like a pack of wolves. The Mantis had always used anxiety as a tool for survival, but as Mank faced an almost certain death, he realized his nerves were only a hindrance.

"DEEP BREATH, Mank—DEEP BREATH!" the Mantis said. "Pretend the Reptoids are GERMS! Big, barbaric, laser-packing GERMS! Would you let GERMS get the best of you? Of course NOT! You would spray those GERMS with a disinfectant and move on! The Reptoids are no DIFFERENT! All you need is a good SPRAY!"

The dragonfly spacecraft flew past Saturn. Mank noticed the moon Enceladus in the planet's orbit. It was a frozen world with an icy white surface. However, the Mantis knew there was more to the moon than met the eye. Mank steered his dragonfly toward the moon, and the Reptoids followed him. The Mantis flew as close to Enceladus's surface as he possibly could.

"Come ON, come ON, come ON!" he said. "WHERE are you?!"

As the Mantis reached Enceladus's southern pole, dozens of geysers began bursting through the frozen ground. The jets spewed streams of ice from a hidden ocean beneath the moon's surface. Mank carefully steered his ship between the geysers—but the Reptoids weren't so lucky. The jets were so cold they froze the shellcrafts' engines. One by one, the Reptoidian crafts dropped from the sky and plunged into the ocean beneath the icy floor.

Once the Reptoids were gone, Mank parked his dragonfly craft on the moon and burst into tears of joy.

"Hey, Mank, your transmitter is still on," Roswell said.

"You accidentally started a live video feed instead," Rob said.

"There's nothing shameful about expressing your emotions!" Stella said.

"Peep-peep poop-poop peep-peep!"

"Yeah—*very* clever to use Enceladus's geysers!" Nerp said.

"Way to make germophobia work for you!" Cassi said.

Mank quickly turned off the video feed and the transmitter, pressing the correct buttons this time. Once he was certain the others couldn't see or hear him, the Mantis finished his much-needed cry.

While the rest of the group flew to the outer solar system, Rob and the Cyborgs stayed behind to distract the Reptoidian mother ship. The Reptoids fired lasers and rockets at the Cyborgs, but they were no match for the Cyborgs' impeccable piloting skills. Their artificial minds were fully plugged into their crafts' hard drives, and they controlled the ships like extensions of their metal bodies. The Cyborgs effortlessly ducked, dived, and dashed out of the Reptoids' lines of fire, causing them to accidentally shoot down their own shellcrafts.

"Hey, Rob, you've got a groupie at six o'clock!" Cassi said over the transmission. "I can see it on Priscilla's radar!"

The Cyborg blinked curiously. "But I was never in a band."

"I believe she is referring to the rocket behind your craft," Cyborg P4M said.

"It is getting concerningly close," Cyborg T0M said.

Rob checked his own radar and saw the rocket they were referring to.

"Many thanks!" he said.

The Cyborg flew his ship in circles and confused the Reptoidian rocket. It slammed into the side of the mother ship and blasted a hole in the command center. Reptiliz Reek caught General Xelic and the Reptoidian crew with his vines before they were sucked into space.

"YOU CALL THIS A MINOR INTERRUPTION, XELIC?" the Reptiliz screamed.

"I would say it has escalated to a *moderate annoyance*, my lord!" the general said.

The hole slowly sealed itself shut as the megashelled stratosaurus's skull grew back. The Reptiliz angrily threw his crew onto the floor.

"I HAVE HAD IT!" he roared. "THIS ENDS NOW!"

Suddenly the whole mother ship started to quake. The Reptiliz's vines snaked out of the ship and stretched into space outside. The dead megashelled stratosaurus now had thousands of lively, slithering limbs growing from its carcass. The Reptiliz wrapped his vines around the Cyborgs' crafts and slammed them into one another. Rob tried to free his friends from the Reptoid's grip, but Reek grabbed Rob's ship and threw him deep into space.

SKWAAAAAMP-SKWAAAAAMP-SKWAAAAAMP! Another alarm blared through the command center. *SKWAAAAAMP-SKWAAAAAMP-SKWAAAAAMP!*

"What now?" General Xelic yelled.

"One of the saucers is headed to Earth, sir!" an operator said.

In the distance a small silver disk was rising out of the Martian atmosphere. General Xelic could tell Roswell was headed to Earth—but the Reptoid didn't understand his reasoning. Why would Roswell leave the ambush he'd started? Why would he abandon his friends? Why sneak to Earth when the Reptoids were still in space?

"There's nothing for him on Earth," the general said to himself. "The only way he could possibly delay us would be to—"

The reality hit General Xelic like a bolt of lightning. *He knew exactly what Roswell was up to!* The Reptoid quickly checked the countdown—there were only five Earth minutes left until the launch!

"All available shellcrafts go after that saucer!" the general commanded. *"I repeat, all available shellcrafts go—"*

The Reptiliz wrapped a vine around General Xelic's throat and raised him into the air.

"NO, XELIC! *YOU* GO AFTER HIM! FINISH THIS OR I WILL FINISH YOU!"

"Yes, my lord," the general wheezed.

Roswell had never been so determined in his life. He could feel it flowing through his veins and filling every muscle in his body. After he departed Mars, it took only a few minutes before Earth appeared ahead. It was the size of a marble at first, but the sight was significant enough to bring tears to his eyes. Roswell wasn't sure if he'd ever see his home again. Everything and everyone he loved was on that tiny blue dot in the distance. However, Roswell quickly suppressed his feelings. He couldn't let anything distract him from what he needed to do.

BOOOOOSH-BOOOOOSH! Suddenly two green lasers shot past Roswell's saucer. He checked his radar and saw that a shellcraft was approaching his ship. *BOOOOOSH-BOOOOOSH!* Two more lasers were fired in his direction. *BAAAAAM!* The back of his craft was hit, and the saucer spun out of control!

"Gotcha!" General Xelic said over the transmission. "So long, Earthling!"

BWAAAAAMP! BWAAAAAMP! BWAAAAAMP! The saucer's alarms blared, and the power started to flicker. *BWAAAAAMP! BWAAAAAMP! BWAAAAAMP!* Roswell gripped the controls with all his might, but the craft didn't budge. *BWAAAAAMP! BWAAAAAMP! BWAAAAAMP!*

The stars spun around Roswell as the saucer whirled through space. With every rotation the craft moved farther and farther from Earth, and was pulled closer and closer to the moon. Roswell had only a few minutes before the saucer slammed into the lunar surface. How was he going to reach Earth now? How was he going to delay the invasion? Would he even survive a crash landing on the moon? Roswell didn't know what to do, and his spirits plummeted into the deepest depths of despair.

Roswell, can you hear me?!

Stella! Thank God! I've been hit!

I know! I can see you on my radar!

My controls aren't working! I need a way off this thing!

I'm coming to get you! But your ship is spinning too fast for me to intercept it. Use the escape pod and I'll pick you up.

Where's the escape pod?

Pull the green lever next to the steering sphere. It'll slide your chair into the pod under the cockpit. Once you're inside, turn the red octagon. The pod will eject from the craft, and you can steer it exactly like the saucer.

Roswell's desperation was interrupted by a spark of hope—*maybe his plan wasn't doomed after all.* He quickly followed the Pleiadean's instructions and pulled the green lever. His seat fell through a trapdoor and dropped inside the escape pod. The vehicle was just as smooth, silver, and round as the saucer but a tenth of its size. Doors sealed shut above him, and the engines rumbled to life. Roswell turned a flashing red octagon on the small dashboard, and the pod was launched into space like a cannonball.

Nice job! Now stay put. I'm almost there.

Roswell gripped the pod's steering sphere and made a giant U-turn.

Where are you going? I told you to stay put!

Don't bother coming after me. I'll be gone by the time you get here.

Don't be silly. I'll be there in five minutes.

You don't understand. I'm going to crash the pod into Eli Rump's launchpad.

What?!

Stella, listen to me! Rump has twelve rockets with armed satellites! If I destroy the first one, it'll be only a couple days before he launches the next one. But if I destroy the launchpad, it'll take months for Rump to build a new one. This is my only chance to take them both out at once!

Roswell, don't be ridiculous!

That should give the alliance enough time to gather evidence and charge the Reptoids! They could stop the invasion before it even begins!

Your pod won't withstand the impact! You won't survive!

I know. But the rest of Earth will.

No! We'll figure something out!

When I'm gone, please tell Nerp, Bleep, Mank, Rob, and Cassi how grateful I am.

Stop talking like this! You're scaring me!

You guys have given me the greatest adventures of my life.

Roswell Johnson, you turn around right now!

One last thing. Please tell Gram and Pop how much I love them. And that I'm sorry they had to lose me too.

I'm begging you! Please turn around!

Goodbye, Stella.

TURN AROUND!

The Pleiadean continued to beg and plead, but Roswell tuned her out. There was nothing she could say or do to change his mind. While Roswell rocketed toward Earth, General Xelic noticed the escape pod on his radar. It took the Reptoid a moment to realize what the new blip was— but *only* a moment.

"WHY WON'T THIS KID JUST DIE?!" he roared.

BOOOOOSH-BOOOOOSH! General Xelic raced after Roswell and showered the escape pod with laser beams. *BOOOOOSH-BOOOOOSH!* The pod's small size made it easy for Roswell to dodge the general's attack. *BOOOOOSH-BOOOOOSH!* Eventually the Reptoid's zealous assault overwhelmed the cannons, and the lasers jammed. General Xelic pulled a bony gear on his dashboard, and a grotesque claw stuck out from the belly of his ship. The Reptoid tried to snatch the escape pod with the claw. Roswell's craft was just a few *feet* from every swipe!

As Roswell and General Xelic entered Earth's atmosphere, the actor Matthew McConaughey started the countdown on Rump Island.

"TEN!"

General Xelic's bulky shellcraft was heavier than the escape pod, and the extra weight slowed the Reptoid down. Fortunately, Earth's gravity was much kinder to

Roswell. The space between the ships expanded with every passing second.

"NINE."

Soon Roswell had gained so much distance the shell-craft didn't have a chance of catching up to him. General Xelic roared with the fury of a supernova. *Roswell was winning!*

"EIGHT."

The escape pod soared over the Atlantic Ocean, and the bright blue water filled Roswell's entire view. He'd never realized how beautiful Earth was until this moment. He wished he'd appreciated it more when he'd had the chance.

"SEVEN."

Roswell reached the Florida Peninsula. He followed the Florida Keys until he found Rump Island. Roswell spun the steering sphere and began his final descent.

"SIX."

He saw that thousands of people were gathered on the island, and the ocean was sprinkled with boats and super-yachts awaiting the liftoff.

"FIVE."

Roswell positioned the pod directly above the launch tower. With the pod in place, there was nothing left to do. Gravity would finish the rest.

"FOUR."

Roswell gently lifted his hands off the controls and sank into his chair.

"THREE."

He closed his eyes and took his last breath.

"TWO."

Roswell had done it—*he had won*!

"ONE."

The impact was so quick Roswell barely felt a thing. He was briefly aware of something very warm and very powerful pushing him against his seat. And then a split second later...

Absolutely nothing at all.

CHAPTER EIGHTEEN

SECRETS OF THE MOON

The afterlife was very different from what Roswell expected. For starters, he still had *senses*. He was somewhere with a cool and crisp temperature. Something very soft was beneath him, and he was covered by something very warm. The air smelled overly sterile, like the rooms of a hospital. He could hear a series of high-pitched beeps and the soft guitar of a David Bowie song. Most surprising of all, Roswell still had an anatomy, because every muscle in his body was sore.

Roswell slowly opened his eyes—apparently, he still had those too. He couldn't see much at first but was able to make out a familiar face beside him.

"Dad?"

"Welcome back, champ."

Curtis Johnson had more wrinkles and gray hair than Roswell remembered, but his smile was exactly the same. Roswell was overjoyed to see his father, but seeing him could mean only one thing.

"Is this heaven?" he asked.

His father laughed. "It's been called a lot of things, but that's a first."

Roswell sat up and looked at his surroundings. He was lying in one of many beds that hovered two feet off the floor. A thin aluminum blanket kept his body warm from the cold air. His headboard projected holograms of his heart rate, body temperature, blood pressure, respiratory rate, and adrenaline level. Roswell noticed all his vitals were *high*, because all the monitors were in English. The room was constructed from a smooth silver metal, and the walls were outlined with blue fiber-optic lights. Through an enormous round window Roswell could see a huge full moon, a clear starry sky, and an endless snowy desert outside.

"Where am I?" he asked.

"You're on a secret lunar base," Curtis told him. "In the Copernicus crater, to be exact."

Roswell whipped his head back to the window. There wasn't a snowy desert outside—they were surrounded by the ashy surface of *the moon*. And what he'd thought was a bright full moon was Earth. He and his father were inside a structure built at the bottom of a massive crater.

"Wait a second, if I'm not dead, that means you're... you're..."

Curtis gazed at his son with an immense amount of guilt. It was the type of remorse only a beating heart could hold.

"We're both alive, bud."

Roswell noticed a row of boomerang ships parked outside. He looked back at his father and realized he was wearing a familiar blue space suit.

"It was *you*!" he gasped. "*You're* the pilot of the boomerang craft!"

Curtis nodded. "I am."

The holographic monitors beeped louder and louder as Roswell's vitals skyrocketed.

"But... but... *how?*"

His father let out a deep sigh and sat on the edge of the bed. He pressed a button on the holographic headboard to pause the David Bowie song.

"I should start at the very beginning," he said. "Remember the old Roswell, New Mexico, conspiracy I named you after?"

"Of course!"

"Well, it was all true!" Curtis said. "In 1947 the US military accidentally shot down a flying saucer. The military recovered the wreckage, and the craft became our first evidence of extraterrestrial life. The Milky Way

Galactic Alliance eventually got wind of the crash. And in 1954 they held a secret meeting with President Eisenhower. The alliance expressed the importance of keeping the discovery under wraps. They explained that Earth was still a stage-two planet and a premature introduction to extraterrestrial life could hurt a developing society. President Eisenhower agreed to keep the crash classified on one condition—that the United States got to *keep* the technology they'd found—and the alliance agreed. So the military reverse engineered the craft and used their discoveries to create the United States Secret Space Program. The USSSP has kept Earth safe from celestial threats ever since."

"And you're part of the Secret Space Program?" Roswell asked.

"I'm an SPC of the USSSP—that's short for space program commander. There are about a hundred of us here."

"So the boomerang craft that followed you *wasn't* an alien?"

"That's right—it was a USSSP recruiter," Curtis explained. "Apparently, I showed promise from an early age. My good test scores, athletic ability, and impressive video game scores were the exact skill set the program was looking for. They watched me my whole life to make sure I was USSSP material. I was still fighting in Afghanistan when they approached me. They told me the program was so classified they would need to fake my death so I could join. At first I refused. What kind of father could leave his son behind? A parent's most important job is to protect their children. But then I realized the USSSP could help me protect you in ways a normal parent couldn't."

Roswell became misty eyed as he recalled memories *without* his father. Nothing was more painful than the empty seat at birthdays, holidays, and special occasions. Now that he knew his father had left *voluntarily*, Roswell wasn't sure he could ever forgive him.

"I wish you hadn't left," he said. "It was unbearable without you."

"But I *never* left you, Roz—not even for a second," his father said. "I was there when you scored the winning soccer goal in the second grade. I was there when Pop taught you how to drive the tractor. I was there when you had bronchitis and didn't get out of bed for five days. I was there when Principal Dunkin called Gram and said you could skip the sixth grade. I've always watched over you, you just couldn't see me."

Roswell looked away so his father wouldn't see the tears running down his face. Commander Johnson lovingly dried his son's eyes with a tissue.

"I know my absence has caused you a lot of pain," Curtis said. "I am truly sorry for hurting you. One day when you're a parent, you'll understand. Although *you* did some pretty crazy things this week to protect the people you love."

Roswell thought about what his father had said. Perhaps Commander Johnson was right—perhaps doing crazy things for love was hereditary.

"I know this is a lot to process," his father said.

"That's the understatement of the week," Roswell said. "I understand why you're here, but I don't understand why I'm still alive. How did I survive the impact?"

"There *was* no impact," his father said. "The USSSP has known about the Reptoid invasion for years. We've been monitoring their communication with Eli Rump since it began. My colleagues and I planted an explosive inside Rump's launchpad when it was being built. It was detonated just as your escape pod arrived. The blast gave you a concussion and knocked your craft into the ocean. I fished you out of the water and brought you to the USSSP medical wing to recover."

Commander Johnson got to his feet and retrieved a stack of newspapers.

"In good news, you started a brand-new conspiracy theory," he said. "Check out the bottom left corner of the *Ostentatious Observer.*"

Commander Johnson placed the newspapers in Roswell's lap. He curiously flipped through the stack, skimming the headlines. The *New York Times* said ELI RUMP ROCKET LAUNCH A TOTAL DUMP. The *Boston Globe* reported BILLIONAIRE'S STOCKS BOMB WORSE THAN ROCKET. The *Washington Post* opened with CONGRESS PULLS SUPPORT FOR

'ERASE' PROGRAM. Roswell eventually found the *Ostentatious Observer* at the bottom of the stack. The smallest headline on the front page said UFO SIGHTING AT RUMP LAUNCH: CONSPIRACY COMMUNITY FURIOUS NO ONE IS TALKING ABOUT MYSTERIOUS DISK.

"Congratulations," Commander Johnson said.

"So our trip around the galaxy was all for nothing," Roswell said. "The USSSP was going to stop the Reptoids no matter what we did."

"Are you kidding?" Curtis asked. "Roswell, you and your friends saved the world and the galaxy from the Reptoids! The USSSP has been trying to stop them for decades!"

"How'd we do that?"

"While I followed you, I was able to gather evidence against General Xelic. After he attacked us on the Insectia Moon, I finally had enough proof for the alliance to issue a warrant. The Milky Way Galactic Guard showed up and arrested General Xelic before he left Earth's atmosphere."

"And the other Reptoids?"

"They fled the galaxy. I'm guessing Reptiliz Reek is worried General Xelic will rat on him. He and the Reptoids are probably halfway to Andromeda by now. I doubt they'll return to the Milky Way ever again—and it's all because of you. If you hadn't had the determination and courage to save Earth, the Reptoids would still be out there, plotting another way in. I can't tell you how proud I am."

"What about the other aliens? Are my friends all right?"

"They're absolutely fine—worried about you, mostly," Curtis said. "They saw me retrieving your pod from the ocean and thought I was kidnapping you. Luckily, I was able to explain everything before things got too heated. They followed me here so they could check on you. You just missed them, actually."

"Where did they go?" Roswell asked.

"They went to the chicken farm."

"*Our* chicken farm?"

"I tried to stop them, but the Pleiadean was adamant about speaking to Gram and Pop before I took you home. Apparently, she has a certificate in intergalactic family counseling. She said she could 'mentally prepare' them for our arrival. We both have a lot of explaining to do."

"You're telling me *the aliens* are talking to Gram and Pop? Even *Cassi*?!"

"Is she the Furgarian who introduced herself as your future ex-wife?"

"We gotta get down there!"

Roswell hopped out of bed, but his legs were so sore they gave out. Commander Johnson caught him before he fell to the floor.

"Easy, champ—there's no rush," his father said. "Gram and Pop are going to find out eventually. It might be best if a trained Pleiadean breaks the news to them."

"I don't understand," Roswell said. "You've kept this

secret for years. Why is it okay for Gram and Pop to know about the USSSP now?"

"That's where the situation gets complicated," Curtis confessed. "When I was recruited into this program, I swore an oath of secrecy. However, as a member of the Galactic Registry, you don't have the same obligation. And I sincerely doubt you'll be able to keep a secret this big from Gram. That woman has superpowers."

"So why did you put only *me* in the Galactic Registry? Wouldn't it be easier if all three of us were in it?"

For the first time since their reunion began, Roswell saw genuine concern in his father's eyes. It was a strange thing to witness—Roswell couldn't remember if he had ever seen his father look *worried* before.

"I didn't put you in the Galactic Registry—the USSSP doesn't have access to it. I found out you were a member shortly after you did. My colleagues and I are looking into the matter, but we haven't found any answers yet."

Roswell thought he was joking, but his father was genuinely concerned.

"But if it wasn't you—who was it?"

The commander was even more confused than his son. Roswell's puzzled gaze drifted to the stars outside the window. He had never stared into space with so much curiosity before. It was like Roswell was looking at the galaxy for the very first time.

Somewhere among the stars was someone who wanted his attention.

The Johnson Family Chicken Farm had hosted all kinds of visitors over the years, but today was one for the books. Had a neighbor driven by the property, they would have seen a large flying saucer parked next to Gram's Volkswagen and Pop's Chevrolet. And if that neighbor had been extra nosy and peeked through the farmhouse window, they would have seen six *extraterrestrial beings* sitting around the Johnson kitchen table.

Stella was in the middle of a very animated presentation about the universe. The Pleiadean used her pin to project galaxies, stars, planets, and moons over the table. Pop sat next to Stella and was glued to every word she said. Gram stood at the stove and made the aliens breakfast while she listened.

"Every galaxy has its own galactic alliance, and together, all the galactic alliances form the Great Universal Alliance," Stella said. "And *that* pretty much sums it up!"

"Goodness gracious," Gram said. "You learn something new every day!"

"Who says old dogs can't learn new tricks?" Pop asked.

Mank eyed the couple suspiciously. "You're handling this SURPRISINGLY well."

"We grew up in the seventies, sugar," Gram said.

"It takes more than a couple *aliens* to excite us," Pop said.

Gram finished cooking a skillet of bacon and eggs. She walked around the table and placed food on each of the aliens' plates.

"No, thank you," Rob said. "Cyborgs do not eat."

Gram gave him a stern look. "Nobody leaves my house with an empty stomach."

Rob didn't want to be rude, so he picked up an egg and smeared it across his digital mouth. Meanwhile, the Furgarian cleared her plate in less than a second.

"That was *delicious*, Mrs. J.!" Cassi said. "Or should I cut to the chase and call you *Gram*, since we'll be family someday?"

"You can call me anything you want, darlin'," Gram said. "I'm so grateful you kept my grandson safe! I consider you *all* family now!"

"Do you have any more questions about the galaxy?" Stella asked.

"I've got one," Pop said. "What's a wormhole?"

"Excellent question," Stella said. "A wormhole is a celestial phenomenon that creates a link between two points in space. The connection forms a shortcut across large distances. Some wormholes connect opposite ends of a galaxy, while others connect different galaxies. However, there is reason to believe some wormholes might transport travelers to different *universes* altogether!"

"Well, I'll be darned," Pop said. "That explains where the socks go in a dryer."

"How about the big bang theory?" Gram asked. "What's that all about?"

"The big bang is what formed the known universe," the Pleiadean explained. "Fourteen billion years ago, the universe was compressed at a singular point, until a massive explosion propelled everything outward. As the universe expanded, it cooled and formed the elements that created stars and planets. The big bang is still occurring and expands our universe more and more each day. However, what caused the initial bang is still a mystery."

"Wow, so it has *nothing* to do with the sitcom," Gram said.

"Could you explain black holes next?" Pop asked. "Is it true they're so powerful they can suck in time and light?"

"I've got this one, guys," Cassi said confidently. "Have you ever been stuck talking to a really boring person at a party? Someone who takes all the joy and energy out of a room? You know how it's impossible to escape them once they start yapping? You know how time goes by slower and slower the longer they chat? *That's* a black hole."

"Oh, I work with several black holes at the home," Gram said.

"I golf with a couple of them," Pop said.

While the others answered questions, Bleep struggled

to free themselves from their seat. When the aliens arrived, Gram had thought the Small Gray was a toddler. She had sat them in an old high chair before anyone could stop her.

"Beep-beep boop-boop beep-beep!"

"It's not a *torture* device, it's a seat for children," Nerp said.

"Peep-peep poop-poop!"

"Then stop *acting* like one!"

"What's the little one saying?" Pop asked.

"Bleep was complimenting your collection of porcelain chickens," Nerp lied.

"Not everyone decorates with the animals they BREED and KILL," Mank noted.

"And isn't that a shame?" Cassi asked.

DING-DONG! The whole kitchen went silent at the sound of the doorbell. Gram and Pop excitedly headed for the door and quickly unlocked it. Before they could open it all the way, Roswell bolted inside.

"Gram! Pop!" he happily exclaimed.

"Rozzy!" Gram cried.

"We missed you, kiddo!" Pop said.

Roswell threw his arms around his grandparents and held them in a tight embrace. The hug lasted several minutes with no sign of concluding.

"I missed you so much," Roswell said.

"I was convinced you were kidnapped!" Gram said. "I had the whole police department and all the old folks at the home looking for you!"

"What are we going to tell them now?" Pop asked.

"Tell them I *was* kidnapped," Roswell said. "It was a *child abduction*. Get it? Get it?"

"Beep-beep boop!"

"Yeah—mistakes were made!" Nerp said.

"I see you've met my new friends," Roswell said with a laugh.

"Eclectic group you picked up there," Pop said.

"Heaven help us when you're a teenager!" Gram said.

A second pair of footsteps were heard entering the house, and the Johnsons looked up. Gram and Pop knew he was coming—Stella had warned them—but the couple were speechless at the sight of their not-so-late son.

"Curtis," Gram gasped.

"It really *is* you," Pop said.

It took them a moment to accept it wasn't a dream. Commander Johnson was visibly nervous as he approached his parents.

"Hi, Mom. Hi, Dad," Curtis said sheepishly. "I know this is an awfully big shock. And I understand if you're furious and want me to leave. I just hope you can forgive me and let me explain someday."

To everyone's relief, Gram and Pop pulled their son into a tearful embrace.

"I always knew it wasn't true," Gram said. "I could feel it in my bones."

"Welcome home, son," Pop said.

"You aren't angry with me?" Curtis asked.

"Oh, absolutely livid," Gram said with a smile. "But there'll be plenty of time for anger and explanations later. I'm just happy to have you back."

"You're grounded," Pop said.

The aliens were very moved as they watched the emotional family reunion. There wasn't a dry eye at the kitchen table. Digital tears ran down Rob's digital cheeks.

"Our work here is done," the Pleiadean told the others.

"Can I get that in WRITING?" Mank asked.

"We should let them catch up in privacy," Stella said.

Nerp helped Bleep out of the high chair, and the aliens headed for the door. They gathered around Roswell to say goodbye on their way out.

"I told you to turn the escape pod around," Stella said with a playful grin.

"I promise to listen next time," Roswell said. "There *will* be a next time, right? You guys aren't going to ditch me, are you?"

"Of course not," she said. "But next time I could use *less* megashelled stratosauruses."

Roswell laughed. "Deal!"

The Cyborg shook Roswell's hand—but he got the correct motion this time.

"It has been both stressful and a pleasure getting to know you," Rob said. "I am forever grateful for your help with Cyborg rights. You will always be welcome in Data City."

"I'm forever grateful for you too, Rob," Roswell said. "Please don't be a stranger!"

The Cyborg blinked curiously. "How could I be a stranger when we already know..." Rob paused midsentence and smiled. "Oh, I understand. *Metaphor.*"

Mank held his hands above his head like Roswell was holding a weapon.

"Never CONTACT me or come NEAR me again!" he said.

"I'll miss you too, Mank," Roswell said.

Cassi wrapped her fuzzy arms around Roswell's waist.

"This is going to be my first long-distance relationship," she said.

"Cassi, for the last time, we are not in a—"

The Furgarian placed her paw over his mouth.

"Please don't speak, sweetcheeks—I couldn't bear the sight of heartbreak in your eyes. Let's remember each other as we met. Young, vibrant, vulnerable, and oblivious to love's bittersweet longing. To quote the famous Furgarian poet Blister Hamstring, 'Long-distance love is like a public pool. Better to admire from afar than risk a stranger's soil.'"

Roswell rolled his eyes. "Goodbye, Cassi."

"Well, I can't beat a Furgarian quote about love," Nerp

said. "I will say this has been a week to remember. Even the strongest de-memorizer couldn't make us forget it. And to think, none of this would have happened if Bleep had just followed my instructions."

"Beep-beep boop-boop beep-beep!"

"That was *not* a dig! It was the truth!"

"Peep-peep poop-poop peep!"

"All of this *is* your fault! Whose story have you been in?"

Roswell chuckled at the Grays. "I'm glad you're a bad student, Bleep. If you were a good listener, I would never have met the best aliens in the galaxy."

The Small Gray smirked and then struggled to respond.

"Beep-beep-be-be-*bye, Roswell.*"

Everyone looked to one another in amazement. *Bleep had said their very first words!* Roswell couldn't have been more honored that the Small Gray's message was for him.

"Bye, Bleep," he said. "Don't get into any trouble without me."

"Beep-beep."

Once their goodbyes were finished, the aliens left the house and boarded the flying saucer outside. The spaceship's engines ignited, and the craft levitated into the sky. Roswell stood on the front porch, and Gram, Pop, and Commander Johnson joined him. The whole family waved to the aliens as the saucer soared higher and higher above the farm.

"It sounds like you had quite an adventure," Gram said.

"We'd love to hear *your* side of the story," Pop said.

Roswell thought about the terror, the danger, the uncertainty, and the sorrow he had experienced in space. However, as he watched the flying saucer disappear into the clouds, Roswell *smiled* at his memories. There was only one way to describe the journey.

"It was truly *out of this world*."

GALACTIC GLOSSARY

*Real locations in our universe.

Alnilam* (ALL•nil•ahm): A star located in the constellation Orion.

Andromeda* (an•DRAW•meh•duh): The closest neighboring galaxy to the Milky Way.

Coachellian (co•CHELL•ee•un): The Coachellians are an alien species with gangly pink bodies who enjoy wearing loose clothing. They dance to music no one else can hear.

Cyborg Station (SIGH•borg STAY•shun): A mobile facility constructed from microchips and circuit boards. The Cyborgs are a robotic species with artificial intelligence. They live inside a virtual reality known as Data City.

Diplomacian (dip•low•MACE•ee•un): An alien species with glowing skin, bald heads, and long limbs. Diplomacians are naturally diplomatic, honest, and trustworthy. They lead the Milky Way Galactic Alliance.

Electra* (ih•LECK•truh): A star located in the Pleiades cluster.

Furgaria (fur•GARE•ee•uh): A planet that orbits the star Zosma. Furgaria was destroyed by a comet, and the survivors live inside an asteroid called the Furgarian Strip. The strip is home to many casinos, bars, dance clubs, and hotels. The Furgarians have short, furry bodies, pronounced underbites, snaggleteeth, and abnormally high confidence.

General Xelic (JEN•rull ZELL•ick): The ruthless commander of the Reptoidian Army. General Xelic is infamous for committing crimes and never getting caught.

Grayton (GRAY•tun): A planet that orbits the star Alnilam. Its surface is covered in nitric acid oceans, and there are sodium hyperoxide rainstorms. Grayton is the home of the Grays, an alien species with gray skin, large heads, and big black eyes.

Gulp-Gulper (GULP-GULP•er): An alien species that resembles a catfish. Gulp-Gulpers live in fishbowls connected to robotic bodies. They are not popular with other extraterrestrials because of their wishy-washy politics.

Herbarian (urb•AIR•ee•un): An alien species that looks like asparagus. The Herbarians were the first plants in the Milky Way to develop intelligence.

Insectia Moon (in•SEC•tee•uh moon): The moon of a red gas planet that orbits the star Lesath. The Insectia

Moon is covered in exotic plants and terrifying alien predators, and is home to the Mantises. The Mantises are human-size praying mantises and are known for their anxiety and germophobia.

Lesath* (LAY•soth): A star located in the constellation Scorpius.

megashelled stratosaurus (MEG•uh•sheld STRAT•uh•SORE•us): A gigantic extinct species with an enormous shell. The Reptoids converted megashelled stratosaurus carcasses into a fleet of spacecraft.

Microbian (my•CROBE•ee•un): The smallest alien species in the Milky Way galaxy.

Monsoonian (mon•SOON•ee•un): An alien species that can survive only in extremely stormy conditions.

nasaldactyl (NAY•zul•DACK•til): An extinct species with a remarkable sense of smell.

Pleiades* (PLEE•uh•dees): A cluster of stars also known as the Seven Sisters. The Pleiadeans are the most technologically advanced aliens in the galaxy. They are similar to Earthlings except for their huge eyes and telepathic abilities. They live on seven habitable planets in the Pleiades system, including Paradise, which orbits the star Electra. All their buildings and spacecraft are made from diamond.

Reptiliz Reek (REP•til•us REEK): The leader of the Reptoids and the most vicious tyrant in the Milky Way galaxy.

Reptoidia (rep•TOYD•ee•uh): A planet destroyed by the wasteful antics of its former inhabitants, the Reptoids. The Reptoids are a reptilian species with large bodies and scaly skin. They travel the galaxy and steal resources from other planets to survive. The Reptoids are considered the most despicable aliens in the Milky Way galaxy.

Sagittarius A-star* (SAJ•uh•TARE•ee•us AY•star): A supermassive black hole located in the center of the Milky Way galaxy.

shnigglebotts (SHNIG•ul•bots): A swear word used by extraterrestrials.

Sterilith (STER•ul•ith): A planet with the best disinfectants in the galaxy.

Zosma* (ZOSS•muh): A star located in the constellation Leo.

ACKNOWLEDGMENTS

Roswell Johnson Saves the World! would not have been possible without Alvina Ling, Rob Weisbach, Alla Plotkin, Derek Kroeger, Jerry Maybrook, Crystal Castro, Jen Graham, Erica Stahler, Chandra Wohleber, Nyamekye Waliyaya, Sasha Illingworth, Patrick Hulse, Emilie Polster, Mary McCue, Stefanie Hoffman, Mara Brashem, Cassie Malmo, Victoria Stapleton, Will Sherrod, Karin Brummell, the amazing Godwin Akpan, my own Furgarians Cooper and Fitzgerald, and everyone at Little, Brown Books for Young Readers. I'd also like to thank Char Margolis and Shirley MacLaine, with whom I've had the distinct honor of discussing and daydreaming about extraterrestrials (sometimes for hours on end!). Last but certainly not least, I would like to thank my dear friend the late and great Pam Jackson. Your absence has left a void deeper than space itself. I love you to the moon and back. Huggles.

Andrew Scott

CHRIS COLFER is a #1 *New York Times* bestselling author and Golden Globe–winning actor. He was honored as a member of the TIME 100, *Time* magazine's annual list of the one hundred most influential people in the world. His books include *Struck By Lightning: The Carson Phillips Journal, Stranger Than Fanfiction,* and the Land of Stories series: *The Wishing Spell, The Enchantress Returns, A Grimm Warning, Beyond the Kingdoms, An Author's Odyssey,* and *Worlds Collide,* as well as the companion books *A Treasury of Classic Fairy Tales, The Mother Goose Diaries, Queen Red Riding Hood's Guide to Royalty, The Curvy Tree, Trollbella Throws a Party,* and the graphic novel *Goldilocks: Wanted Dead or Alive.* He is also the author of *A Tale of Magic...*, *A Tale of Witchcraft...*, and *A Tale of Sorcery....*

Roswell Daily Record

TUESDAY, JULY 8, 1947

RAAF Captures Flying Saucer On Ranch in Roswell Region

Boston Traveler

Monday, October 25, 1965

A UFO Chiller

Did THEY Seize Couple?

DAILY NEWS

Monday, July 28, 1952

JETS CHASE D.C. SKY GHOSTS